"I WANT YOU TO WEAR THIS," ADAM SAID.

He opened the box's lid. Inside lay a brooch of diamonds set in platinum and gold, with emerald eyes and an emerald bow on one of its back legs.

Sabrina was stunned. . . . Only royalty could afford priceless gems like this.

She lifted her gaze to his and said, "I couldn't accept—"

"You can and you will." Adam lifted the brooch out of the box and fastened it to her bodice.

His touch assaulted her senses. She felt him with every tingling fiber of her body and feared he could hear the frantic beating of her heart.

Adam lowered his lips to hers. His arms encircled her body and drew her against his chest.

Instinctively, Sabrina surrendered to his warm, insistent lips. Being held in his embrace felt so comforting, so natural, so exciting.

Still reeling from his kiss, Sabrina felt flushed all over. *How could a simple kiss have this effect on her?*

Dell books by Patricia Grasso

VIOLETS IN THE SNOW
MY HEART'S DESIRE
COURTING AN ANGEL
LOVE IN A MIST
DESERT EDEN
HIGHLAND BELLE
EMERALD ENCHANTMENT

No Decent Gentleman

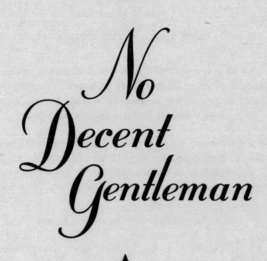

Patricia Grasso

A Dell Book

Published by
Dell Publishing
a division of
Random House, Inc.
1540 Broadway
New York, New York 10036

The trademark Dell® is registered in the
U.S. Patent and Trademark Office.

ISBN: 0-440-22434-9

Printed in the United States of America

Published simultaneously in Canada

February 1999

10 9 8 7 6 5 4 3 2 1

OPM

*For Sharon Winn, my "best-only" friend.
Keep chanting.*

Chapter 1

England, 1815

"Holy hemlock," eighteen-year-old Sabrina Savage muttered in a barely audible voice.

She brushed a few recalcitrant wisps of copper hair away from her face and lowered herself wearily onto the Grecian chaise in the corridor outside Abingdon Manor's second-floor drawing room. After folding her hands in her lap, she lifted her green-eyed gaze from the hallway's blue and gold carpet runner to stare at the closed drawing room door. Anger and sorrow warred within her at the thought of what Vicar Dingle and his six cohorts were doing over her late father's body as they chanted prayers to drive the devil from his soul.

"This is unnecessary," Sabrina complained, turning to her companion. "Burying my father in the dark at a crossroads defies logical reason."

The twenty-five-year-old baron, Edgar Briggs, shifted his gaze to her. "Vicar Dingle is merely performing one of his duties," he said, sitting down beside her. "The law demands a night burial for suicides."

"My father did *not* commit suicide," Sabrina insisted, her emerald gaze glittering with her anger. "The law is as stupid as Vicar Dingle."

"The law is the law," Edgar replied, but softened his words by taking her hand in an obvious attempt to offer solace.

"The law is an arse," Sabrina snapped, yanking her hand from his. Giving him a look filled with accusation, she added, "If you really cared about our friendship, you wouldn't allow the vicar to insult my father like this. Apparently, my father's judgment in refusing your marriage proposal was correct. I would never wish to marry a man who wasn't loyal to me."

"Sabrina, I cannot prevent the vicar from obeying the law," the baron said in a weary voice. "Besides, your father would have agreed to my suit if you had told him you loved me instead of harboring a fondness for me."

"Love has nothing to do with offers of marriage or dowries," Sabrina told him. With a badly shaking hand, she smoothed the skirt of her black bombazine mourning gown and added, "Or meaningless declarations of one's feelings."

"I do love you, but even I cannot change the law to suit you," Edgar said, a frustrated edge creeping into his voice.

Ignoring his profession of love, Sabrina stared at the closed door again, but tried to keep her mind a blank. Her father's untimely passing was difficult to endure, and she needed to remain strong for the sake of her

sister and her aunt. Trying to retain control of her rioting emotions, she concentrated on the various portraits
lining the walls of the hallway.

"As an earl, my father enjoyed friendships with
great peers of the realm," Sabrina said, her gaze fixed
on the portrait of Prince Adolphus, the seventh son of
King George III. "Vicar Dingle will rue the day he
insulted the Savage family with such barbaric actions."

"None of those illustrious peers have ridden to Abingdon to champion your father's cause," the baron
reminded her.

Surprised by his harshness, Sabrina rounded on him,
but the drawing room door opened unexpectedly and
drew her attention. Vicar Dingle stood there; behind
him six parishoners were preparing to act as pallbearers.

"We are ready," Vicar Dingle said.

Sabrina stared at him for a long moment and tried to
find a small sign of sympathy in his solemn expression.
There was none. Finally, she nodded and turned to
walk down the stairs to the reception foyer, where her
younger sister and aunt were waiting. The baron followed behind her.

"The vicar is ready," Sabrina told them, reaching
for her black cloak.

Seventeen-year-old Courtney Savage burst into
tears. Aunt Tess put her arm around her younger niece
and drew her close in an effort to console her.

Sabrina turned her gaze away from her weeping sister lest she, too, begin weeping. She watched the vicar
descending the stairs, followed by the six pallbearers
carrying her father's coffin.

"Please, don't hurt him," Sabrina said in an aching voice.

"Don't hurt him?" Vicar Dingle echoed in an indignant tone of voice. "For his suicide, the Earl of Abingdon's soul faces eternal damnation."

"May consumption catch you," Sabrina cursed the clergyman.

"Sabrina is grief-stricken," Edgar intervened, stepping between her and the vicar. "She doesn't know what she's saying."

Vicar Dingle nodded, then said, "I understand her sorrow, but breeding does tell."

Sabrina stepped back a pace as if she'd been struck. Would she and her sister never be able to escape the fact that they were the illegitimate issue of— Of whom, she had no idea.

"Sabrina is a well-bred young lady and does not deserve your insults," Sabrina heard her aunt Tess saying. "Apologize at once, Vicar Dingle."

"Lady Burke, lest you forget, I was here when—"

"My father legally adopted Sabrina and me," Courtney Savage interrupted with uncharacteristic assertiveness. "Now, get on with the funeral."

Turning to her younger sister, Sabrina smiled for the first time since their father's death the preceding day. "Are we going to bury my father tonight?" she asked the vicar. "Or shall we stand here and debate the possibilities of who my natural parents were?"

"Extreme grief rules your tongue," Vicar Dingle stated disapprovingly and then marched out of the mansion. Lifting the casket again, the six pallbearers followed him outside.

"Your rudeness to a man of the cloth surprises me," the baron said in a loud whisper. "And you, Courtney. I never would have—"

"Oh, Edgar, do be quiet," Sabrina cut his words off. At times, her lifelong neighbor and friend annoyed her more than a toothache.

Pulling the hood of her black cloak up to cover her head, Sabrina followed the pallbearers outside. Behind her walked Courtney, Aunt Tess, and Edgar Briggs.

Sabrina stepped into an unusually warm mid-December night and breathed deeply. The air was hushed as if nature itself mourned the loss of her father. No moon shone overhead. The sky was a black velvet blanket dotted with tiny stars.

In silence, the pallbearers set the late earl's coffin on a cart pulled by one horse. Each of them held a lantern to light his way.

The funeral procession walked down the estate's private lane, which led to the public road, and then turned right. The nearest crossroads lay a half-mile away where the road branched into two, one road leading to the village of Abingdon and the other to the neighboring Briggs estate.

Their small entourage had just reached this traditional burial site for suicides when the unmistakable sound of galloping horses drew their attention. Everyone whirled toward the village road to see four men on horseback advancing on them. The riders reined their mounts to an abrupt halt when they reached the funeral party.

"Who are you?" Edgar Briggs demanded. "State your business."

"We are friends of the late Earl of Abingdon," one of the strangers answered as he dismounted.

Sabrina stared at the tall, dark-haired man who appeared to be in his mid-twenties. She'd never seen him before, but then she and her sister hadn't traveled to London since they were children. She hoped these men were the illustrious peers of the realm who would champion her father's cause.

"Charles, thank God you're here," Aunt Tess cried suddenly. "Vicar Dingle is giving poor Henry a suicide's burial."

Much to everyone's surprise, an older gentleman stepped forward. First he lifted her aunt's hand to his lips, and then he placed a comforting arm around her shoulder. Turning to the others, he introduced himself, saying, "I am Charles St. Aubyn, the Duke of Kingston. This is my nephew, Adam St. Aubyn, the Marquess of Stonehurst, and the others are my nephew's retainers."

Sabrina looked at each of the newcomers in turn. The Duke of Kingston seemed a kindly gentleman, but his nephew appeared darkly dangerous. The marquess's retainers were two of the biggest men she'd ever seen.

"Though the circumstances are sad," Sabrina said, stepping forward to greet the duke, "I am pleased to make your acquaintance, Your Grace. How did you learn of my father's death?"

"Several days ago I received a message from your father, asking me to come to Abingdon," the duke told her. "Then, last night, Tess's message that your father had died arrived. We left London this morning and rode as fast as we could. You are which daughter?"

"I am Sabrina, the elder," she said with a wan smile. "This is my sister, Courtney."

"May we complete the burial?" Vicar Dingle asked in an irritated voice. "The law requires we bury suicides between nine and midnight. At this rate—"

"My father did *not* commit suicide," Sabrina interrupted, rounding on the vicar.

"No one hangs himself by accident," one of the pallbearers muttered.

Sabrina gave the man a murderous glare but refrained from speaking. Nobody would ever convince her that her wonderful father had taken his own life, and she intended to prove he hadn't. She'd make the lot of them eat their words, especially the vicar.

"Lower the casket," Vicar Dingle instructed the pallbearers.

"What about the prayers?" Sabrina cried.

"Praying for suicides is forbidden," the vicar told her.

"A plague take you," Sabrina said, cursing him for the second time that night.

Everyone stared at her in shock. She heard her aunt gasp, and one of the newcomers chuckled.

"Sabrina, how dare you speak disrespectfully to the vicar," Edgar exclaimed, placing his hand on her shoulder. "Apologize at once."

Ignoring him, Sabrina shrugged his hand off and asked the vicar, "Where is the death knell I purchased?"

"Tolling a death knell for suicides is forbidden," Vicar Dingle told her.

"My father will have a death knell even if I must

ring it myself," Sabrina insisted. She turned away
abruptly and bumped into the marquess, who grabbed
her upper arms to keep her from falling. Looking up at
him in surprise, she had the sudden wish that she could
see his eyes in the darkness.

"Mistress Savage, I will escort you into the village
lest someone try to stop you," the marquess said.

Sabrina nodded and gave him a grateful smile.

"Stop them," she heard the vicar order the pallbearers.

With a flick of his hand, the marquess gestured to
his gigantic retainers, who blocked the path. The vicar
and his pallbearers remained rooted where they stood
while the marquess lifted her onto one of the horses.

The Marquess of Stonehurst scooped up one of the
lanterns and then mounted his own horse. "Uncle, escort the other ladies to Abingdon Manor," he said.
"Mistress Savage and I will meet you there later."

"Very good," the duke said.

"Sabrina, think of what you are doing," the baron
called after her.

"Edgar, think of what you are *not* doing," she replied.

Sabrina turned her horse and started down the village road. Beside her galloped the marquess's horse.
They rode in silence into Abingdon and halted their
horses in front of the church.

Still holding the lantern in one hand, the marquess
opened the church's door. Sabrina stepped inside and
the door clicked shut behind them.

"This way, my lord," she said.

Turning to the right, Sabrina crossed the nave and

climbed the narrow spiral staircase until she reached the top, the bell cote. She grabbed the bell clapper and tugged on it nine times, the customary way of signaling the passing of a man. Summoning her strength, she reached for the bell clapper again.

The Marquess of Stonehurst touched her arm and asked, "How old was the earl?"

"Forty-one."

"Take this," he said, passing her the lantern.

Sabrina knew what he was offering to do. "Thank you, my lord," she said, lifting the lantern out of his hand.

With both hands, the Marquess of Stonehurst rang the death knell forty-one times, once for each year of her father's life as was the custom. Sabrina closed her eyes and prayed for her father's departed soul.

Finished with his task, the marquess took the lantern from her and led the way down the narrow staircase again. Outside, he set the lantern down and helped Sabrina onto her horse.

Sabrina watched him retrieve the lantern and mount his own horse. Apparently, her father did have great friends who were willing to champion his cause. How would she ever be able to thank this man for what he'd done for her this night? What he had given her could never be repaid.

Turning their horses in unison, they retraced their path down the village road toward Abingdon Manor. Without saying a word to each other, they stopped when they reached the crossroads. The two burly body-guards still kept the vicar and his pallbearers at bay.

"Let them leave," the marquess called to his men, who stepped aside instantly.

"I forgive you," the vicar said, his gaze fixed on Sabrina. "In a few days you will regret your actions tonight."

"No, Vicar Dingle, you will regret *your* actions," Sabrina replied. "Your church will never again receive one shilling from the Savage family."

Vicar Dingle shook his head sadly as if he couldn't credit what he was hearing. "Because of your father's suicide, the Savage estates are forfeit to the Crown." With those parting words, the vicar and his six pall-bearers started walking down the road to the village.

"Is that true, my lord?" Sabrina asked, beginning to panic, turning to the marquess. How would Courtney and she live if they lost everything? How could she prove that her father's death had been an accident?

"Please, call me Adam," the marquess said.

"Then you must call me Sabrina."

"Very well, Sabrina."

"You haven't answered my question," she said.

"By law a suicide's assets are forfeit to the Crown, but we may be able to get around that," the marquess told her. "My uncle has friends at court who have the power to certify your father's death an accident."

"My father's death was no suicide," Sabrina said. "How should I go about proving that?"

For a moment Adam was silent. Then he replied, "Do you believe your father was murdered?"

"My father had no enemies."

"Every man has enemies," the marquess said grimly. "We will discover who your father's are."

Then he called to his men, "Sagi and Abdul, remain here on guard until the dawn."

"Why should they guard my father's grave?" Sabrina asked, surprised by his command.

Now it was the marquess's turn to look surprised. "Sabrina, have you never heard of Resurrection men?" he asked.

"You don't think someone would steal my father's body?" she asked, shocked. "He was an earl."

"Most Resurrection men prefer to work near London where there are more donors," he replied. "We'll be certain that no one disturbs your father's grave if my men stand guard for a week."

"I'll send my servants with blankets, food, and a lantern," Sabrina called to the two men.

Both men nodded, acknowledging her words, but said nothing.

"What strange names your servants have," Sabrina remarked as they started down the road toward Abingdon Manor. "Are they foreigners?"

The marquess nodded.

Sabrina glanced sidelong at him but couldn't see his face very clearly in the darkness in spite of the lantern he carried. "Where do they come from?"

"The East," he said simply.

"I see."

The Marquess of Stonehurst turned his head to look at her. "No, Princess, you do not see, but you will understand one day soon."

Sabrina remained silent. She had no idea what he meant and wasn't certain she wanted to know.

Sabrina and Adam passed through the open gate

onto the Savage estate and rode at a more leisurely pace toward Abingdon Manor. In the distance, beeswax candles and paraffin lamps glowed like fireflies from the mansion's windows and grew brighter as they neared the house.

Sabrina halted her horse in the circular drive in front of the mansion and dismounted without waiting for assistance. Two stableboys appeared to take charge of their horses.

The front door opened just as they reached it. The Savage majordomo stepped aside to allow them entrance.

"The others are waiting in the drawing room." He reached to help Sabrina remove her cloak.

"Don't bother with me, Forbes," she said. "Send a footman with food, blankets, and lanterns to the crossroads. Then prepare the dining room for our guests."

The majordomo looked surprised. "You want to send a footman to the crossroads with—?"

"The Marquess of Stonehurst was kind enough to leave his men guarding Papa's grave," Sabrina explained.

"Very good, my lady," Forbes replied. He started to turn away to do his mistress's bidding, but paused and said, "Lady Sabrina, I heard the death knell. My compliments on a job well done."

"Thank you."

"I never did like Vicar Dingle," Forbes muttered as he walked away. "Self-righteous men are the devil's spawn."

The majordomo's sentiment matched hers. Sabrina laughed, a sweetly melodious sound, so at odds with her behavior that night. Flicking the hood of her cloak off her head, she turned to properly greet the man who'd saved her father from a final indignity.

Surprised by his dark handsomeness, Sabrina could only stare at him. She suffered the absurd notion that seeing him by lantern light did him no justice.

A couple of inches over six feet, Adam St. Aubyn stood a good foot taller than herself, and Sabrina had to tilt her head back to look up at his face. Marring his handsome features, a thin scar ran from the corner of his mouth to his right cheekbone. He wore his midnight-black hair long on his neck as if he hadn't the time to cut it properly. Its ebony color contrasted sharply with blue eyes so distinctively piercing that Sabrina felt he could see to the very depths of her soul. His smile on her was warm and—

Sabrina realized the marquess was watching her study his appearance. Embarrassment flushed her cheeks a rosy hue, which made his smile widen into a grin.

"Let me help you with that," he said in a husky voice, reaching for her cloak.

God shield me, Sabrina thought. Even the man's tone of voice suggested intimacy. She hadn't noticed it earlier.

Sabrina wanted to say something wonderfully witty, but her mind went blank. Thinking of something witty to say would take her an hour, and *wonderfully* witty would waste several days.

Instead of speaking, Sabrina smiled shyly and offered him her hand. "Your arrival tonight was a mira-

cle,'' she said when he accepted it. ''I don't know what
I would have done without your assistance.''

''I commend your loyalty to your father,'' Adam
replied.

''Sabrina!''

Both Adam and Sabrina turned toward the voice and
saw Edgar Briggs walking across the foyer. As if by
mutual consent, they released each other's hands.

The baron nodded once at the marquess and then
rounded on Sabrina, beginning his lecture with ''Your
behavior tonight was unpardonable.''

''Oh, Edgar,'' she said in a weary voice. ''Please,
let's not go into it now and certainly not in front of the
marquess.''

''I cannot hold my tongue until the morning,'' he
said, and then turned to the marquess. ''If you will
excuse us, my lord, I wish to speak privately—''

''I have no intention of being rude to my guests,''
Sabrina interrupted him. ''Whatever you want to say
will wait until tomorrow.'' She grasped Adam's forearm and escorted him toward the stairs, saying, ''The
drawing room is this way, my lord.''

Though the whole chamber had been draped in
dreary black, ease and comfort had replaced formality
in the drawing room. Sofas and chairs had been positioned closer to the warmth of the fire, and a variety of
tables had been scattered about for convenience and
utility. In the far corner of the chamber stood a pianoforte and a harp, both instruments also draped in black.

At their entrance, the Duke of Kingston rose from
the sofa and crossed the chamber to greet Sabrina prop-

erly. "Henry and I were great friends," he said, taking her hands in his. "I grieve for your father's passing."

"Thank you, Your Grace."

"Let's not stand on formality, my dear child," the duke said, escorting her to the sofa near the hearth. "Please call me Uncle Charles."

"Oh, but I couldn't," she protested.

"Yes, you can," he disagreed in a gentle voice. "Courtney has already agreed to do so.

Sabrina smiled. "Very well, Uncle Charles."

"That's better."

"I don't know what we would have done if Adam and you hadn't arrived when you did," Sabrina told him.

"Adam, is it?"

Sabrina blushed and flicked a glance at the marquess, who stood beside the hearth. "Adam has given me permission to use his given name."

"Sabrina, I really must speak with you," Lord Briggs said.

"Your lecture can wait until morning," Sabrina replied, irritation lacing her voice.

"Lecture?" the duke echoed.

"Apparently, Edgar feels the need to lecture me about my treatment of the vicar," Sabrina explained.

"Vicar Dingle has more hair than wit," Aunt Tess said. "I never liked him."

"Neither did I," Courtney agreed.

Sabrina said nothing. Though Adam St. Aubyn remained silent, she was acutely aware of him. His dark, commanding presence attracted her, and she had a difficult time keeping herself from staring at him.

"As I told you earlier, I received a message from your father to come to Abingdon as soon as possible. He said it was an important matter," the duke was saying. "And then Tess's message arrived."

"I wonder what the problem was," Sabrina interjected, speaking her thoughts aloud. She looked at the duke, saying, "Vicar Dingle told me the Savage estates are now forfeit to the Crown."

"The land will be auctioned," Edgar informed her. "You need not fear losing Abingdon Manor, for I plan to purchase the estate for you."

"The Savage lands will not be auctioned," Adam disagreed, speaking up for the first time since entering the drawing room.

"Adam is wealthy, and I enjoy friendships in the most exclusive circles," the duke explained, looking at the baron. "A few words spoken into a royal ear and a healthy bribe will give my nephew the right to oversee the Savage assets until we can straighten out this whole sorry affair. I can almost guarantee that your father's death will be ruled accidental."

Sabrina felt the fear rush out of her. For the moment she need not worry about how to care for her sister and her aunt. Nor would she need to feel obligated to Edgar in any way.

And then the Duke of Kingston surprised her by saying, "As you may know, I am the executor of your father's will."

"I didn't know that," Sabrina said, surprised. "How long had you known my father?"

"We shared chambers at school," the duke answered. He smiled, adding, "Our accommodations became rather cramped when Adolphus and his dog moved in with us.''

''Adolphus?'' Courtney exclaimed. ''King George's son?''

''The son of a king is always given the title of *prince*,'' Aunt Tess corrected her younger niece.

Sabrina smiled at her aunt's ridiculous statement. ''How did you manage to keep up your friendship?'' she asked the duke.

''I'll answer all of your questions tomorrow,'' the duke said, patting her hand. ''Recently, your father sent me a codicil to the will.''

''A codicil?'' the baron echoed. ''Concerning what?''

''Are you a member of the Savage family to be privy to the late earl's business affairs?'' Adam asked, a challenging tone in his voice.

Recognizing the angry glint in Edgar's hazel eyes, Sabrina prevented an argument by saying, ''Uncle Charles, I hope that you and Adam will consent to be our guests at Abingdon Manor.''

''We would love to accept your invitation,'' the duke answered. ''Tonight, however, we must return to the inn. We left my sister at High Wycombe for the night. She will arrive in Abingdon tomorrow morning.''

''Adam's mother?'' Sabrina asked.

''No, Adam's mother is another sister of mine,'' the duke told her. ''This one is Lady Belladonna DeFaye.''

''Well, I'll be,'' Aunt Tess exclaimed. ''I haven't seen Belladonna in years.'' She looked at her niece, adding, ''Belladonna and I were great friends during our first season out. We lost touch with each other after

we met our husbands. I suppose marriage has a way of
separating friends."

"Lady DeFaye will also be a welcome addition to
our household," Sabrina said, rising from her chair.
"For now, come to the dining room and refresh yourselves with a light supper."

Adam stepped forward before Sabrina could offer to
escort the duke. "Allow me to walk with you downstairs," he said, taking her hand.

His words and his touch surprised Sabrina, but she
didn't draw back. Instead, she dropped her gaze to their
hands. His touch was firm yet gentle, and he stood so
close that his clean, spicy bay scent assailed her senses.

Sabrina suddenly wondered what it would feel like
to kiss this handsome man. Lifting her gaze, she
blushed with embarrassment. His piercing blue eyes
seemed to say that he was aware of his effect on her.

Recovering her composure, Sabrina acquiesced with
a silent nod. The Duke of Kingston escorted Aunt Tess,
leaving Edgar to walk with Courtney.

Entering the dining room on the first floor, Sabrina
was pleased to see the table set with their finest Wedg-
wood china. Covered dishes had been placed on the
table, and their Worcester tea and coffee service sat on
the sideboard.

"Uncle Charles, please do us the honor of sitting at
the head of the table," Sabrina said.

The duke obliged her. Aunt Tess, Courtney, and Edgar sat on his left side while Sabrina and Adam sat on
his right side.

Forbes lifted the covers off the platters to reveal dev-
iled eggs, potted mushrooms on toast, and pork balls in

tomato sauce. They served themselves in the family style.

"Simply delicious," the duke said after tasting the potted mushrooms. "My compliments to the cook."

"The cook is sitting on your right," Courtney told him.

The duke turned to Sabrina, asking, "You prepared the mushrooms?"

She nodded. "I prepared everything."

"Sabrina cooks herself into a frenzy when she's upset," Courtney said. A mischievous gleam entered her eyes when she added, "There have been times when I purposely drew her into an argument."

"You are exaggerating," Sabrina said with a smile.

"Do you remember becoming aggravated with me a few months ago because I'd borrowed your blue shawl without asking your permission first?" Courtney asked her.

"Yes."

"I never wore it," her sister admitted. "I took it from your chamber and folded it across my bed so that you would *believe* I'd worn it. As I recall, supper was heavenly that night."

Everyone laughed.

"Why didn't you simply ask me to prepare supper for you?"

"What makes your cooking special is the secret ingredient of anger," Courtney informed her. The seventeen-year-old dropped her gaze to the potted mushrooms and added forlornly, "Or sadness."

A glum silence descended over the table. Sabrina felt a lump of raw emotion forming in her throat. Fear-ing she would embarrass herself by weeping at the table, she shifted her gaze to the duke and said, "Uncle Charles, tell me about your friendship with my father."

"Prince Adolphus, your father, and I became close friends while at Eton," the duke began. "Prince Adolphus disliked having his own chamber so he moved his belongings into ours. The prince once brought his dog to school with him after holiday and was ordered to send the dog home. Dogs were strictly forbidden in the dormitory." Here the duke chuckled at the memory.

"What is so funny?" Sabrina asked.

"Adolphus brought his dog home, but returned with his pet bear," the duke told her, making them smile. "So the school administrators gave him permission to keep his dog instead of the bear. I swear, that dog weighed more than the Regent and absolutely adored your father. Tiny—that was the dog's name—insisted on sleeping with your father every night."

"I never heard that story," Sabrina said with a smile.

"Papa never mentioned that he and the prince were friends," Courtney added.

"Tell us another," Sabrina said.

"I'll think about it tonight and come up with a story suitable for young maidens' ears," the duke told her.

"Sabrina, I must leave," the baron said, rising from his chair. "Will you walk with me to the foyer?"

"Excuse me," Sabrina said to the duke. "I'll return in a moment."

They walked in silence until they reached the foyer. It was then that Edgar Briggs grasped her forearm and warned, "Do not place your faith in the duke. You never met the man until today, and I fear he does not have your best interests at heart."

"And you do?" Sabrina asked.

"Do you doubt it?" he asked.

"The proof lies in a man's actions not in his words," Sabrina answered. "Tonight you sided with the vicar."

The baron tightened his lips in anger, but said nothing. When he moved to plant a kiss on her cheek, Sabrina stepped back and said, "I buried my father just a few hours ago. Please leave now."

"Grief rules your actions and words," Edgar said, walking out the door. "I'll see you tomorrow."

Sabrina watched him leave and then turned to retrace her steps to the dining room. She stopped short when she spied the marquess standing in the shadow of the stairs, watching her.

"How long have you been there?" Sabrina asked. "Were you eavesdropping on me?" In the next instant she realized how rude she sounded and amended herself. "I'm sorry. Today has been terribly difficult, and Edgar has been no help."

"Are you and the baron betrothed?" Adam asked.

"Edgar and I have been friends forever," Sabrina told him.

"But there is something more than friendship between you," the marquess said.

"Edgar did offer for me," she said. "I am thankful my father refused his suit."

"Your father's disapproval did not disappoint you?" Adam asked.

Sabrina shook her head. "I would have felt as though I'd married a brother or a cousin, but I hadn't the heart to refuse Edgar's offer. My father saved me the trouble by refusing for me. I suppose that makes me a coward."

The marquess's blue eyes gleamed with amusement. "And what if your father had approved the match?"

"I knew there was no chance of that," Sabrina admitted. "In spite of the fact that my sister and I are adopted, my father planned to give us a season in London so that all of the realm's most important men could fall in love with us. That way we'd have our choice of whom we wished to marry."

"Important men?" Adam echoed, giving her a boyish, thoroughly devastating grin. "You mean, a prince?"

Sabrina nodded. "Or a duke."

"How about a marquess?" Adam suggested, the intimate tone of his voice caressing her senses.

Precluding further conversation, the Duke of Kingston walked into the foyer with Aunt Tess and Courtney. "My nephew and I must also leave," he said, taking her hands in his, "but we will return with my sister tomorrow."

"There is a question I must ask you," Sabrina said, lowering her voice.

The duke gave her an expectant smile.

"My father adopted Courtney and me," she said. "Do you know where we came from?"

"Child, let us save this conversation for tomorrow," the duke replied.

Sabrina nodded. She'd waited eighteen years to

learn the truth surrounding her birth. Waiting a few more hours certainly wouldn't kill her.

Aunt Tess and Courtney went directly upstairs after the duke and the marquess had taken their leave, but Sabrina knew sleep would elude her for some time that night. She stepped outside the front door and gazed up at the stars in the moonless sky. They appeared as lonely as she felt. She'd always longed to know who her natural parents were, but now there was something in her life more important than that knowledge.

"Papa, I will prove you innocent of suicide and see you buried in hallowed ground," Sabrina whispered. "Even if I must dance with the devil to do it."

Chapter 2

🌱 "Your frown could frighten the sin out of Satan."

Adam shifted his gaze from the passing scenery outside the coach's window to his aunt. "I beg your pardon?" he said, realizing he'd been caught daydreaming.

Lady Belladonna DeFaye smiled at him. A shade above forty, his aunt had broken many hearts in her day and was still a charming temptress to most older gentlemen who crossed her path. Auburn-haired, brown-eyed, and dimpled, Belladonna DeFaye retained the essence of youth.

Adam wondered briefly if his own mother still retained the essence of youth. He hadn't seen her in fifteen years, but she and Belladonna carried the St. Aubyn blood in their veins. In his mind Adam could only picture his mother as he'd last seen her; no amount of passing years could put wrinkles on her face or thicken her waist. She would always be the beautiful young woman who'd sent him away.

"Have you heard from your mother lately?" the duke asked, as if he'd read Adam's thoughts.

"Yes, both she and my brother are well."

"I cannot understand why your mother chose to remain in Istanbul when she could have returned to England," Belladonna said. "After all, your father is dead."

Adam sighed. He had explained his family's situation to her at least a hundred times, but his aunt refused to understand.

"At my brother's court in Istanbul, my mother is Sultana Valide, the most powerful woman in the empire," Adam told his aunt in a patient tone of voice, as if this was the first time he'd related the story.

"But she sent you, a prince in your own land, to live—"

"My mother sent me to England secretly," Adam interrupted, knowing full well what his aunt's next words would be. "My countrymen believe I died, otherwise my brother would have been forced to lock me up as the custom in my land demands. In olden days, he would have been required to execute me when my father died. There can be only one sultan. Eliminating all potential political rivals has kept the empire from crumbling beneath civil war."

Lady DeFaye shivered delicately and then smiled. "I understand now," she said.

Until the next time, Adam thought.

"I will never understand why your mother chose to

stay with your father after the promise of her release had been secured," Belladonna remarked.

"Perhaps she loved her husband," the duke interjected. "Contrary to your own experience, some women actually love their husbands."

"Oh, really, Charles," Belladonna drawled, clearly unamused. "I valued Francis until the day he died." Her smile was feline when she added, "Fortunately, his death was sooner rather than later. What I can't understand is how a woman could love her abductor."

"My father did not abduct my mother," Adam corrected his aunt.

"His minions did abduct her from the ship bound for France," Belladonna reminded him.

Adam shrugged. "Apparently, love can be found in the most unlikely places. Being abducted and given as a gift to the sultan was my mother's fate, as was falling in love with him."

At that, Adam turned his head to stare out the window. Where would he find his own love? he wondered. Was she waiting for him at Abingdon Manor?

"You are frowning again," Belladonna said. "How will you secure a wife if you walk through life frowning?"

"Most women are attracted more by a man's finances than by his smile," Adam replied. "Besides, I was thinking, not frowning."

"About what?"

"A business matter."

"Have I told you how delightful Henry Savage's daughters are, especially Sabrina?" the duke asked, turning to his sister.

"Several times," Belladonna drawled.

Adam gazed out the coach window and contemplated Sabrina Savage. She was a rare and marvelous creature. In his mind's eye, he conjured up her sweet expression, her delicate features emboldened by emerald eyes and hair the color of molten fire.

The lady's temperament was as fiery as the color of her hair. Adam recalled the way she had defied the vicar and dismissed the baron. He admired her loyalty to her father and felt like applauding her plucky spirit. As long as she never directed it at him, they would get along harmoniously.

How fortunate for the late Earl of Abingdon to possess a daughter who demonstrated her love and loyalty even to the brink of his grave. Adam only wished that someday he would possess a wife and children who would honor and love him so much that they would defy the world for him.

If wishes were horses, then beggars would ride, Adam thought sardonically. Sabrina Savage was an aberration in a world filled with untrustworthy women.

"Well, Adam, what do you think?" his uncle asked, intruding on his thoughts. "Shall I destroy those documents?"

"Sabrina Savage suits me," he answered simply without taking his gaze from the passing scenery. "I only hope that I suit her. Unlike my father, I would never coerce a lady into my bed."

"Take an old man's advice," his uncle said. "Proceed slowly and with caution."

"Of course you'll suit her. You're rich, aren't you?"

Belladonna chuckled throatily and added, "A fiery temperament runs in that bloodline."

"Sabrina is adopted," Adam said, flicking a quick glance at her.

"Yes, I know," she replied with a feline smile.

"She knows?" Adam asked, turning to his uncle.

The Duke of Kingston shrugged. "Belladonna has known for years."

"You've known for years and haven't circulated that delicious bit of gossip?" Adam said, smiling. "Why, Aunt, I'm proud of you."

"It hasn't been easy," Belladonna complained. "That knowledge and my enforced silence have tormented me."

"I can well imagine the horror of it," Adam said, as he feigned a shiver of fear.

Belladonna burst out laughing. "Oh, Adam, what a tease you are. I wonder what the Countess of Rothbury will do when her marriage plans go awry."

"What marriage plans?" Adam asked.

"Do not play coy, darling," his aunt said. "I know that Alexis Carstairs is your mistress and hopes to be the Marchioness of Stonehurst."

"Dearest Aunt, if you should run out of money, *The Times* could use you as a reporter," Adam said.

Belladonna smiled at him and then glanced out the window. "Is that where they buried poor Henry?" she asked.

"I'm afraid so," the duke answered.

Adam shifted his gaze to the crossroads as their coach passed by. Sagi and Abdul had left at dawn to get a few hours sleep. At twilight they would return to guard the late earl's grave until his decomposed body would be of no use to any Resurrection men in the area.

Soon their coach turned off the main road and began its journey to the mansion. Woodsmoke from the manor scented the air, and Adam smiled to himself. He couldn't help but wonder what Sabrina was cooking up.

And then Adam caught his first glimpse of Abingdon Manor in daylight. The mansion was an incongruous yet pleasing blend of architectural styles. The main house had obviously been built during Elizabethan times, but the mellow-red brick addition was definitely Jacobean.

Their arrival had been noted. Dressed in mourning black, the Savage sisters and their aunt stood beside the majordomo to greet them.

When his gaze fell on Sabrina, Adam suddenly wished to see her garbed in the most fashionable gowns and materials and colors that money could buy. Her luxuriant copper mane would be striking if set off by celestial blue or primrose or gold lamé on gauze, velvet, or satin.

"Welcome to Abingdon Manor," Sabrina said in a soft voice, stepping forward to greet them.

With a smile lighting his expression, Adam reached out with one finger and wiped the spot of flour from the tip of her upturned nose. "Pardon my boldness," he said. "You've been baking."

"Lemon cookies," she said, returning his smile, a rosy blush staining her cheeks.

Adam stared into the most disarming green eyes he'd ever seen. If a man wasn't careful, he could drown in their fathomless depths. And then the exclamations from the two older women broke the spell Sabrina Savage had cast upon him.

"Belladonna," Aunt Tess was saying.

"Tess, darling," Belladonna replied, hugging the other woman.

"How many years has it been?" Tess asked. "Ten or twenty?"

"Not that many, darling," Belladonna told her. "Do not forget how young we are."

"Why it seems like only yesterday that we were making our coming-outs and being squired around London by all those dashing young men," Tess said.

"Too bad we cannot turn back the hands of time," Belladonna said, a wistful tone to her voice. "At my age, though, I'm uncertain if I have the energy for the social whirl."

"You haven't aged a day," Tess said.

"God bless you, darling," Belladonna replied.

Sabrina glanced at Courtney, who rolled her eyes heavenward. Uncle Charles and Adam smiled politely.

"Belladonna, these are my nieces, Sabrina and Courtney," Aunt Tess introduced them.

The Savage sisters curtsied respectfully.

"Why don't you go off by yourselves and catch up on your news?" Uncle Charles suggested to the two women.

"I'll escort you to your bedchamber," Tess said, taking the other woman's arm and guiding her toward the staircase. "It's so nice to have company. Since Henry's wife died ten years ago, I've been too busy helping with the girls to keep in touch with my old friends. I want to hear a decade's worth of gossip."

Belladonna paused, flicked a glance at Adam, and called, "Courtney, darling. Come with us and hear about the old days."

"I can tell what you are thinking by your expression of consternation," Uncle Charles said gently to Sabrina, after the three women had disappeared up the stairs. "My sister meant no offense by not including you. She knew we had business to discuss, and you are the official head of the Savage family."

"Would you care to have our discussion in my father's study?" Sabrina asked.

"Adam will take care of that for me," Uncle Charles said. "I would like to rest awhile. My heart is weak, and all of this excitement has tired me."

Sabrina nodded. "Forbes, please escort His Grace to his bedchamber."

The majordomo stepped forward. "This way, Your Grace."

Watching her, Adam knew she was feeling awkward. Her gaze was downcast and a high blush colored her cheeks. How long had it been since he'd seen a sincere blush color a woman's cheeks?

"Shall we go to your father's study?" he asked.

She raised her gaze to his and nodded. Adam fell into step beside her as they walked down the long corridor to the earl's study. He stopped short when he heard her say, "This is where we found him hanging from one of the overhead beams."

"You found your father?" Adam asked, staring at her pale face.

"Lord Briggs and Forbes broke into the study

through the window. Edgar warned me not to enter until they could cut him down, but I—''

"Would you prefer going to another chamber instead?'' Gazing down at her, Adam knew what she was going to say before she said it.

Sabrina squared her shoulders, lifted her chin a notch, and shook her head. "I must go into that room again someday. It may as well be now.''

"You're certain?''

She gave him a wobbly smile and nodded. Then she led him through the mahogany door into the chamber.

Located in the Tudor section of the mansion with heavy-beamed rafters overhead, the study emphasized a sense of comfort and could very well have been used as a smoking room. Bookshelves, filled to capacity, lined three-quarters of the walls. Portraits of earlier earls and countesses adorned the walls above the bookcases. Chairs and a sofa had been drawn close to a black marble fireplace, but the portrait above its mantel caught Adam's attention. It was Sabrina and Courtney. Opposite the fireplace was the earl's mahogany desk. On it sat a table globe, quill pen, and Sheffield-plate wax jack for melting sealing wax. On the wall to the left of the desk were two floor-to-ceiling windows.

"Your sister and you make a fetching picture in your blue gowns,'' Adam remarked, his gaze fixed on the portrait over the fireplace.

"Father had that commissioned last year,'' Sabrina told him. "He said he wanted our images in here so that he could look at us after we were gone.''

"Gone where?''

Sabrina blushed. "Married.''

"That doesn't sound like a man contemplating suicide," Adam remarked.

"My father would never have taken his own life," Sabrina said vehemently, then added in a more subdued voice, "Would you care to sit in front of the hearth?"

Adam watched her sit down on the sofa and arrange the skirt of her black gown. In spite of her fiery copper hair and emerald eyes, the somber color made her skin appear pale. He sensed her weariness at having to be strong for the sake of her sister and her aunt, and his heart went out to her.

Adam knew etiquette demanded he sit on the chair facing the sofa. He knew she was expecting him to sit there. And he also knew he was about to startle her, but he couldn't help himself. She attracted him as no woman ever had.

Adam sat down on the sofa beside her, so close, the side of his breeches brushed the skirt of her gown. He smiled when she quickly turned toward him with a horrified expression on her face.

In an instant, Sabrina bolted to her feet and announced in an insulted tone of voice, "Though customs may have changed in London, we in the countryside still adhere to rules of propriety. Sitting so close beside me is improper, especially in view of the fact that we are practically strangers." With those words, she sat down on the chair facing the sofa.

"I apologize for my boldness," Adam said, with an unrepentant smile. He knew from her expression that she realized his apology was insincere. "As you may know, I own many businesses." He spoke up quickly before she could scold him again. "My major holding is in shipping. I can never completely escape my responsibilities. Too many men depend upon me for their living. Would you mind if I used this room to conduct my business while I am in residence?''

"You are very welcome to use this chamber,'' Sabrina said, appearing to relax.

"As my uncle intimated, he and I have no secrets from each other,'' Adam went on, reaching into his coat pocket to produce a paper. He passed it to her, saying, ''This is the message your father sent my uncle.''

Sabrina perused it and then looked up, saying, ''Yes, its tone is urgent, but I have no idea what it concerns. The date it was written—''

"What about the date?'' Adam prodded her.

"I believe the date is the same day my father rejected Edgar's offer to marry me,'' she said, ''but I'm positive this note has nothing to do with that.''

"How did the baron react to the bad news?'' Adam asked.

Sabrina shrugged. ''Edgar believed my father would change his mind.''

"And he wasn't upset about it?''

She turned and looked at him. His question had obviously surprised her. ''You can't really believe that Edgar—?''

"If I am going to help clear your father's name, I must know something about the day he died,'' Adam explained, and smiled at her reassuringly ''Are you up to this conversation or should we delay it?''

Sabrina nodded. ''What do you need to know?''

"Your father died by—''

"Hanging," Sabrina told him. "He was hanging from that rafter over there."

Adam felt like applauding her courage. "Was there a chair nearby?" he asked.

She made a sweeping gesture to the chamber, saying, "The room is filled with chairs."

"I meant, near his body."

"The desk chair lay on its side near him," Sabrina answered.

"Was there anything else unusual about the way you found your father?" he asked.

"He'd locked himself inside this room," she admitted. "As I said earlier, Edgar and Forbes needed to break the window. We're still waiting to have it repaired," she said, indicating the boarded-up section of the window.

"But there was no suicide note?"

Sabrina shook her head.

"Uncle Charles and I will do whatever we can," Adam assured her. "However, the chair and the locked door indicate suicide."

"My father did *not* commit suicide," Sabrina insisted, her emerald eyes flashing.

"Uncle Charles sent a message to Prince Adolphus asking for his help," Adam said, ignoring her outburst. "We'll know the status of the Savage estates in a few days."

"I am very grateful," Sabrina said more calmly. Then, in a voice tinged with doubt, she asked, "You don't actually believe my father would commit suicide, do you?"

Adam decided to be honest. "Everything you say

points to one thing; your father's death was no accident."

"What do you mean by that?"

"Only time will tell us the answers we seek, Princess."

She gave him a wobbly smile. "I am no princess."

"You are lovely enough to be one," Adam said in a husky voice.

Sabrina lost her smile. She bolted off the chair and said, "I do not appreciate your boldness. Your previous apology doesn't give you the right to do it again."

Adam inclined his head.

Without another word, Sabrina turned and walked across the chamber to the door. She used every ounce of inner strength she possessed to keep from slamming it behind her.

Though he was undoubtedly one of the handsomest men she'd ever seen, the marquess was impossible, Sabrina decided as she marched down the length of corridor toward the foyer. He didn't behave as a marquess should. His sitting beside her on the sofa had been a shocking breach of etiquette, especially since they'd been alone in the study. No decent gentleman would place a lady in such a precarious position.

Sabrina slowed her pace, and smiled grudgingly as her anger melted. No man except Edgar had ever complimented her so boldly. Yes, the marquess had no right to speak intimately, but her father would have had no death knell if it hadn't been for him. She should be grateful. Adam St. Aubyn had defended her against the vicar's wrath. Edgar Briggs had not.

As if her thoughts had conjured the baron, Sabrina

saw him stepping into the mansion just as she reached the foyer. Suddenly, Edgar Briggs with his blond hair and hazel eyes didn't seem attractive to her any longer. Was that because of his failure to defend her against the vicar the preceding evening? Or was she comparing him to the Marquess of Stonehurst and his dark good looks?

Instead of greeting him, Sabrina turned first to the majordomo, saying, "Forbes, please brew a cup of my special hawthorne tea and bring it to me here. Don't forget to put a few of my lemon cookies on the tray too."

"Yes, my lady." The majordomo disappeared down the corridor.

"Good afternoon, Edgar," Sabrina said, turning to the baron.

"Sweetheart, I want to apologize for failing you last night," Edgar said, lifting her hand to his lips. "I realize now that I should have taken your side against the vicar."

"Why didn't you?"

He seemed at a momentary loss for words. "Well, I suppose because I've been taught from birth to respect and obey the clergy."

"I forgive you," Sabrina said, managing a faint smile for him.

"Have your guests arrived?" he asked.

"Yes, they are settling in." Then, for some unknown reason, she lied to him. "I'm going to spend the remainder of the afternoon in my chamber."

"Has your father's will been read?" Edgar asked.

"His Grace wasn't feeling well so we are going to do that tomorrow," Sabrina answered.

Edgar gave her a reassuring smile. "Even if the Crown auctions your lands, I will purchase them back for you."

"Only if you can meet the price," Sabrina said, unable to keep the worry out of her voice.

"You should trust in me, sweetheart," Edgar said, raising her hands to his lips. "No one will bid as high as I will for your lands."

"How do you know?"

Edgar grinned. "The land is not as valuable to anyone else as it is to me because I own the adjacent property."

Sabrina nodded in understanding. "With Uncle Charles's connections, the Savage lands may not be auctioned, but I am grateful for your concern. Why don't you return here for dinner the day after tomorrow?"

"The day *after* tomorrow?" Edgar echoed, clearly surprised by her halfhearted invitation. "Are you still angry with me?"

"His Grace will probably pass the remainder of the day resting," Sabrina explained, feeling a bit guilty about putting him off. "Tomorrow he will read my father's will and the codicil. So—"

"So I should be present for that," he interrupted.

"That is for the family only," she told him.

"I am practically family," he argued.

Sabrina suddenly felt irritated at her longtime friend. He was making this difficult time even more difficult for her.

"Practically family is not family," Sabrina told him. "Besides, my father refused your suit."

"Why are you pushing me out of your life?" Edgar asked, his voice filled with hurt and disappointment.

"Please, let me grieve for my father in my own way and in my own time," Sabrina said, a catch of raw emotion in her voice.

The baron remained silent, but then inclined his head.

"Return to Abingdon Manor the day after tomorrow," Sabrina said, touching his arm. "If I need you before then, I'll send for you."

Clearly unhappy, Edgar Briggs walked out of the mansion. Watching him, Sabrina felt unexpectedly relieved at the thought of not seeing him for a while.

"My lady?"

Sabrina turned around at the sound of the major-domo's voice. "I'll take that," she said, lifting the tray out of his hands and crossing the foyer to the stairs. She knew Edgar's curiosity about her father's will stemmed from his concern for her welfare, but his possessiveness was annoying her.

When she reached the third floor, Sabrina walked the length of the corridor and stopped at the duke's bedchamber. She cocked her head to one side against the door, trying to gauge whether he was asleep or not, and then knocked. She couldn't bear to wait another moment to ask him her questions.

"Yes?" she heard the duke call.

"It's Sabrina."

"Come in, child."

Balancing the tray on one arm, Sabrina opened the

door and stepped inside. She smiled when she spied him sitting in one of the upholstered chairs in front of the hearth. After placing the tray on the table next to him, she sat in the chair opposite his.

"How are you feeling?" she asked.

"Much better. Come the morning, I'll be fine."

"I've brought you my special hawthorne tea, which strengthens the heart," Sabrina told him. "You should drink one cup of hawthorne tea each day."

"It will strengthen my heart?" he asked skeptically.

Sabrina nodded. "Hawthorne also helps mend broken hearts."

"Will it *prevent* a broken heart?" the duke asked.

"You are teasing me," she said with a smile.

"Do you love Lord Briggs?"

The smile left Sabrina's face. "Adam asked me the same question, and I snapped at him."

"Oh, dear. You aren't going to snap at me, are you?" the duke asked, feigning fright. "I'll swoon dead away if you do."

"Then I shall try to control myself," Sabrina replied, unable to suppress a smile. "I wonder why Adam and you are so interested in my relationship with Edgar."

"I cannot speak for my nephew," the duke told her, "but I am merely curious and apologize for intruding in your personal life."

"Uncle Charles, you've done nothing that requires an apology," Sabrina assured him, shifting her emerald gaze to the hearth. She longed to question him about her origins, but feared the answer she might receive.

Summoning her courage, Sabrina looked the Duke

of Kingston in the eye and asked, "Do you have any knowledge of who my natural parents were?"

"What did your father tell you about your origins?" the duke asked.

"After our adoptive mother died, he told Courtney and me that we are half sisters," Sabrina answered. "The same nobleman sired us. He also told me that a mutual friend of that nobleman and his delivered my sister and me to Abingdon Manor. Do you know the identity of either man?"

The duke shifted his gaze to the hearth and shook his head. "For your sake, child, I wish I did."

"After last night, I was so certain you knew something," Sabrina said, unable to keep the disappointment off her face.

"I'm sorry, child," he replied. "Prince Adolphus was also a good friend of your father's. When I return to London, I will ask him if he knows anything."

"Thank you, Uncle Charles," Sabrina said, managing a smile for him. "Father never mentioned that you and Prince Adolphus were his friends."

The duke shrugged. "I suppose he had his reasons, none of which are important. We corresponded, of course, and saw each other on his infrequent visits to London." Changing the subject abruptly, the duke asked, "What do you think of my nephew?"

Sabrina gave him a confused smile. How was she to answer that? She didn't really understand what he was asking.

"I don't know what you mean," she said after pausing for a long moment. "He behaves rather oddly for a marquess."

"In what way, child?"

"He tried to sit close beside me on the sofa," Sabrina told him.

The duke smiled. "Child, if I were Adam's age, I'd wish to sit close beside you on the sofa too."

Sabrina blushed and dropped her gaze to her hands, which were folded in her lap.

"Do you find him attractive?"

Startled by the question, Sabrina quickly looked up at the duke. "Yes, Adam is a handsome man."

"Except for that scar, of course."

"His scar gives his face more character," Sabrina replied. "How did he get it?"

"I'll let him tell you that story," the duke said. "I must admit, though, that my nephew is an oddity among the men of the ton. He's taken his inheritance and tripled it with his shipping business."

"He must be exceedingly intelligent," she remarked.

The duke cocked his head to one side and stared at her. "Do you like intelligent men?" he asked.

"I suppose they make better companions than stupid men," Sabrina answered, making him smile.

"I see that my questions are unwelcome and make you uncomfortable," the duke remarked.

"Oh, no . . ."

"And you are kind enough to lie about it."

Sabrina smiled. "You have my permission to ask as many unwelcome questions as you want."

"Thank you, child," the duke said. "Run along now, and I'll see you later."

"Have a good rest, Uncle Charles," Sabrina said, rising from her chair.

Intending to steal a few moments for herself, Sabrina started down the corridor to her own chamber. She hadn't slept very much the previous night. In fact, she'd spent most of the night in the kitchen. Cooking and baking always made her feel better. She wondered briefly if great artists felt the same sense of accomplishment when their masterpieces were finished that she felt when she took a dish out of the oven.

"Lady Sabrina?"

She turned at the sound of the majordomo's voice. "Yes, Forbes?"

"The cart is waiting in the front drive. Would you like a couple of footmen to accompany you?"

Sabrina shook her head. Instead of entering her chamber, she walked down the corridor with him to the main staircase. "This task should be done with loving hands."

"I loved him too," Forbes said.

"I know you did," Sabrina said, "but I'd rather do this myself."

"What about Lady Courtney?" Forbes asked.

"If Courtney breaks down," Sabrina said, "then I will too."

Reaching the foyer, Forbes wrapped her black woolen cloak around her shoulders. Sabrina gave him a grateful smile and stepped outside. First she checked the contents of the pony cart and then allowed a groomsman to help her up.

"Lady Sabrina, I would like to accompany you," the groomsman said, passing her the reins.

"No, but thank you for offering," she replied. "My father would have appreciated your loyalty."

Sabrina pulled the hood of her cloak up to cover her head and then started the pony cart down the private lane that led to the main road. She drove half a mile down the main road until she reached the crossroads and then tugged on the reins to halt the pony. Climbing down, she looked inside the cart at the items she'd ordered—a spade, a white wooden cross to be used as a gravemarker, and a seasonal wreath made from holly and pine clippings.

Sabrina lifted the spade out of the cart and walked to her father's grave. Adam's servants were nowhere in sight. She supposed there was no need for them to guard her father's grave during daylight hours when there was no danger that Resurrection men would disturb it. She stood there for a long moment and stared down at the grave.

Within the year you will rest in hallowed ground, Sabrina promised her father. Then she grasped the spade tightly and placed her booted foot on it in preparation for digging the shallow hole needed to secure the cross.

"I'll do that," said a voice behind her.

Sabrina whirled around. The Marquess of Stonehurst stood there towering over her. Her breath caught in her throat at the sight of his dark, imposing figure.

Dressed completely in black except for his stark white shirt, the marquess appeared more attractive than original sin. And infinitely more dangerous.

His midnight-black hair conspired with his piercing blue eyes to tempt any female who happened to cross his path. The thin facial scar that ran from the corner of his mouth to his right cheekbone lent him an aura of danger. The marquess was more handsome than Lucifer before the fall.

God shield me, Sabrina thought. The devil *is* a gentleman.

"You needn't bother," she said, a high blush staining her cheeks. "I can manage."

He reached for the spade, saying, "I insist."

Sabrina inclined her head and passed him the spade. "How did you know I would be here?" she asked as he started digging.

"I was riding in the parkland and saw you leave," Adam told her. "I knew where you were headed."

"How could you possibly know?"

Adam paused in his digging and smiled at her. "Princess, I'm an excellent judge of character. I knew you wouldn't rest until your father's grave had a marker. I mean that as a compliment."

"Thank you."

Adam returned the spade to the cart and lifted the wooden cross, asking, "Why didn't your sister accompany you?"

"I didn't tell her," Sabrina admitted. "I feared she would break down."

Adam fixed his blue gaze on her. "And then you would break down and be unable to complete the task?"

Sabrina tore her gaze away from his and mumbled, "I suppose so."

Adam set the wooden cross into the hole and pushed

down with all of his strength. "Please hold it steady while I anchor it," he said.

Sabrina stepped forward. With both hands, she kept the cross from wobbling until he'd refilled the hole and packed the dirt in place. Then she walked back to the cart and returned with the wreath.

After placing the wreath over the marker, Sabrina stared at her father's grave for a moment and then knelt to pray. When she'd finished, the marquess's hand was there to help her up.

"Thank you, my lord," Sabrina said in a voice barely louder than a whisper.

"You are welcome."

"How will I ever repay your kindness?" she asked.

"Kindness is its own reward," he answered.

"An honorable sentiment, but hardly expected from a sophisticated aristocrat."

Adam grinned. "Why, Princess, do you doubt my goodwill? Even the irredeemably jaded have honorable moments. No man is wholly good or bad."

At that, Adam lifted her onto the cart and, after tying his horse's reins to the back of the cart, climbed up beside her. Taking control of the reins, he turned the cart around, and they started down the road toward Abingdon Manor.

"You didn't have anything carved on the gravemarker," Adam commented.

"I saw no need," Sabrina replied, flicking a sidelong glance at him. "My father won't be staying there permanently."

Ten minutes later, Adam halted the cart on the circular drive in front of Abingdon Manor. He leaped down first and then lifted Sabrina out. Together, they walked into the foyer.

"Thank you again," Sabrina said.

"You are welcome again."

Intending to rest before dinner, Sabrina crossed the foyer to the staircase. She started up, but then paused and turned around. The marquess still stood there, watching her.

"I forgive you for your boldness and prying into my personal affairs," Sabrina said without preamble.

"I appreciate your generous heart," Adam said, a devastating smile lighting his expression. "Thank you for not slamming the study door this afternoon."

"Which you expected me to do?" Sabrina asked.

"I'll see you at dinner," Adam said, ignoring her question.

Sabrina turned and hurried up the stairs. She never looked back, yet she could feel his piercing gaze upon her until she vanished from sight.

How did he manage to confound her? Sabrina wondered, reaching the refuge of her own chamber. The marquess exasperated and attracted her at the same time. Being that handsome should be forbidden by law.

Chapter 3

Holy hemlock, Sabrina thought in surprised dismay, pausing in the threshold of the drawing room. She'd come downstairs to join the others for dinner, but only the marquess stood in front of the hearth. Where were the others? Was she expected to spend the evening alone with the marquess? What would they talk about? She had no experience in entertaining gentlemen. Edgar didn't count; she'd known him forever.

Unaware of her presence, Adam stood with his back turned to her, and Sabrina let her gaze drift down his body. He wore a black waistcoat with a white shirt and black tight-fitting trousers.

Lord, but the marquess was the perfect image of a well-bred aristocrat. The only things missing from this perfect picture were the requisite snifter of brandy and the monocle, fashionable affectations of those in his social position.

Adam turned around suddenly, as if feeling her interested gaze upon him. "I was beginning to think I would be dining alone," he said, giving her an easy smile.

Sabrina smiled as she walked across the room toward him. "Would you care for a brandy?" she asked, an imp entering her soul. "Or wine? A Madeira, perhaps?"

"Drinks are never served before dinner," Adam told her, amusement lighting his blue eyes. "Wine is served with the food, and gentlemen drink their brandies after leaving the ladies."

"I knew that," Sabrina said, a blush staining her cheeks. "I offered because we seem to be waiting for the others."

"Uncle Charles won't be joining us tonight," he told her.

"What about Lady DeFaye and Aunt Tess?" she asked.

Adam shook his head. "Your aunt pleaded a headache, and my aunt decided to keep her company." He smiled then and added, "Though, I do believe that my aunt is the source of your aunt's headache."

Sabrina felt her confidence waning. "My sister should be along any moment now."

"Lady Courtney sent her regrets," Adam said. "She's also suffering with the headache."

"My sister has never had a headache in her life," Sabrina exclaimed, becoming suspicious. The whole household seemed to be conspiring in an effort to get her alone with the marquess.

"Your sister has never before listened to our aunts

babble on endlessly about the good old days," Adam said with a boyish smile.

"She might need my assistance," Sabrina said, anxious to be away. "Will you excuse me?"

"No."

"I beg your pardon?"

"Forbes has taken care of your sister's headache," Adam informed her. "He mentioned taking her a cup of your chamomile tea."

Hemlock would cure her for good, Sabrina thought, annoyed by her sister's desertion. *Or perhaps a dram of henbane.*

"Shall we go down to dinner?" Adam asked.

Sabrina stared at him in growing panic. What reason could she use to avoid being alone with him?

"Are you ill?" he asked, with concern etched across his features. "You're quite pale."

"Pale complexions are the curse of redheads," Sabrina said, managing a smile.

"For a moment I thought I would be dining alone," Adam said, and then gave her a devastating smile. "Life's pleasures are more enjoyable when shared with another."

Sabrina accepted his offered arm to walk downstairs to the dining room. "What other activities are better done with another?" she asked, seizing on his words as a topic of conversation.

He was smiling again. She noted that as soon as the last word slipped from her lips.

"There's always church service," Sabrina rambled on, "but I do not consider that to be one of life's pleasures."

Adam chuckled. "Spoken like a woman who has just quarreled with the vicar."

"I do not consider church services a pleasure under any circumstances," Sabrina said with a rueful smile. "Dancing is another activity which requires a partner. I can't think of anything else. Can you?"

"I can think of several others," Adam said in a husky voice as they walked into the dining room.

"Such as?" she asked in innocence.

"I'll tell you another day," he answered with laughter lurking in his blue eyes.

"Are these activities disreputable?" Sabrina asked.

"Exceedingly."

Adam sat at the head of the table, and Sabrina sat on his right side. The dining room seemed so large with only the two of them and the majordomo.

Standing near the sideboard, Forbes served them himself. There were baked salmon steaks enlivened with onion relish and vinaigrette, stewed tomatoes, stuffed mushrooms, saffron buns with butter, and Madeira wine.

Catching her eye, Adam raised his wine goblet in salute. Familiar with this dinner custom, Sabrina raised her own goblet to return his salute.

God shield me, Sabrina thought, staring down at her plate. *I forget how to eat.*

She felt awkward to be dining alone with a man. Suddenly, moving a forkful of food from her plate to her mouth became the most difficult task in the world.

"The salmon tastes delicious," Adam remarked. "Did you—?"

"The accolades belong to the cook," Sabrina told him. "However, I did prepare the dessert."

"And what would that be?"

"Cherry syllabub, nougat, and Turkish delight."

"Nougat and Turkish delight?" Adam echoed, a boyish smile lighting his whole expression.

"I see that you adore sweets."

"Nougats taste like French sunshine in summer," Adam said. "Those rose-scented Turkish delights remind me of faraway places and exotic indulgences."

"You sound dreamy, my lord," Sabrina said, charmed by his words.

"I would never describe myself as dreamy," Adam replied, giving her an amused look. "I am a well-traveled owner of shipping lines."

"Tell me about your travels," Sabrina said, glad to have found a suitable topic for conversation.

"I've seen most of Europe," Adam told her. "I've even sailed to New York once."

"You sailed to America?" Sabrina echoed, sweeping him a flirtatious look from beneath the thick fringe of her coppery lashes. "How very impressive. What was New York like?"

Adam shrugged. "People are basically the same all over the world," he answered. "Only the climate and the customs change."

"How did you become involved in the shipping business?" she asked.

"I decided to make use of connections I had in the East," Adam answered. "The business grew, and now my ships sail all over the world."

"What connections?" Sabrina asked.

Adam gave her a boyishly charming smile and then said, "A successful businessman never divulges his connections lest he lose them."

"What about your family?" she asked.

"Uncle Charles and Aunt Belladonna are the only family I have left," Adam told her. "My parents and my brother are dead."

"I'm so sorry," Sabrina gushed, placing her hand over his, her heart wrenching at the thought of his losing everyone he loved. "How did they—?"

"Speaking about my loss is painful," Adam interrupted.

"I understand," Sabrina said sympathetically. Then she changed the subject, asking, "What are the chances that Prince Adolphus will help my sister and me retain control of the Savage estates?"

"I predict Prince Adolphus will be successful in circumventing that ridiculous law," Adam assured her. "That one is as bad as bastards being unable to inherit."

Cringing inwardly at the word *bastard,* Sabrina dropped her gaze to her plate and lost her appetite. She despised that particular word and all that it implied about her less than respectable origins.

"Would you care to walk outside instead of retiring to the drawing room?" Adam asked, as if sensing that she was upset.

Sabrina lifted her gaze to his but saw no pity or superiority in his eyes. "I'd like that," she said.

After retrieving their cloaks in the foyer, Adam and Sabrina stepped out of the front door and began strolling down the lane that led to the public road. Though the unusually warm weather had held, there was a crispness in the air.

Sabrina gazed up at the night sky. Again, no moon shone overhead, only hundreds of tiny, distant stars.

"Tell me about yourself," Sabrina said, trying to make conversation.

"There is nothing to tell."

"I know you are a successful businessman and a peer of the realm," Sabrina said.

Adam nodded. "That much is true. As you know, my mother was the duke's sister, and my father hailed from another country."

"You are only half English," Sabrina said. "Where did your father come from?"

"Near the Mediterranean."

Sabrina suppressed the feeling that he was hedging on the truth. "The south of France?" she persisted.

Adam seemed to hesitate, but then inclined his head.

"Did you always live in England?" she asked.

"I was ten years old when my father died," he answered. "My mother sent me to be educated in England. Then she passed out of my life too."

"So young to be orphaned," Sabrina said. Glancing sidelong at him, she asked, "Why do you carry the St. Aubyn name instead of your father's?"

"My uncle adopted me when he made me his heir," Adam answered. "Uncle Charles's wife died miscarrying his child, and he never remarried."

"How sad for both of you," Sabrina replied. "I'm glad that you have each other. How did you—"

Adam stopped walking and turned to her, saying, "You are very curious, Princess."

"I apologize for prying," Sabrina said, flustered by his intense gaze.

"Ask me anything."

"Where did you get that scar?"

"Eton," he answered, touching the trace of scar that ran from the corner of his mouth to his right cheekbone.

Ask him anything, Sabrina thought, but he won't give me a straight answer. "How did you get it?" she asked.

"I was involved in a fight." Adam stepped closer and gazed down at her. In a husky voice he asked, "Where did you get those disarming green eyes?"

Sabrina blushed furiously. She could feel the heat emanating from her cheeks and hoped the darkness would cover her embarrassment.

Without warning, Adam reached out and gently placed the palm of his hand against her cheek. "Why are you blushing?" he asked. "I hope I'm not making you feel uncomfortable."

If possible, Sabrina felt her blush deepening. Redheads were absolutely the worst blushers in the world.

"I spent an hour in your father's study just staring at your portrait," Adam said in a husky voice. "You have the most arresting face and eyes."

How should she reply to that? Sabrina wondered, feeling awkward. She dropped her gaze to the ground between them. Somehow, his staring at her portrait made her feel vulnerable. No man had ever spoken so intimately to her.

"Look at me," Adam said quietly.

Sabrina raised her gaze to his chest.

"A little higher, please," he added with laughter lurking in his voice.

Sabrina lifted her gaze to his and became mesmerized by his penetrating blue eyes. When he dipped his head closer to her face, his clean, spicy bay scent intoxicated her senses and her heartbeat quickened. His lips were periously close to claiming hers.

"The past few days have been difficult," Sabrina said, stepping back a pace. "I would like to retire now."

Adam inclined his head. "Run along inside. I want to steal a few more minutes before facing my business ledgers."

The short distance to the front door seemed like a million miles away. Forcing herself to walk with slow dignity, Sabrina felt his gaze on her every step of the way and berated herself for retreating from what would have been her first kiss.

When she entered the foyer, Forbes was there to take her cloak. "His lordship will be returning shortly to work on his ledgers," she told the majordomo. "Set a tray of nougats, Turkish delights, and port in the study."

"Yes, my lady."

Taking a night candle in hand, Sabrina climbed the stairs to the third floor where her bedchamber was located. She set the candle on the dresser, but instead of changing into her nightshift, she crossed the room to the window.

Sabrina gently drew the curtain aside and peered into the night. In the drive below her window, she spied the telltale glow of the marquess's cigar. The glow seemed like a lonely firefly trying in vain to brighten the night.

The sight of that solitary pinpoint of light made her feel strangely sad. Sabrina had the feeling that, in spite of his immense wealth and title, the marquess was as lonely as she.

Sabrina smiled at herself. What foolishness was this? The Marquess of Stonehurst was exactly what he appeared to be—a worldly aristocrat who had never known a moment of insecurity in his life.

"Here she comes now," Aunt Tess said.

Walking into the drawing room the next afternoon at teatime, Sabrina sat down beside her sister on the sofa. Across from them sat Aunt Tess and Lady DeFaye. Uncle Charles looked comfortable in the upholstered chair near the sofa, while Adam stood near the hearth.

A platter of cucumber sandwiches and a plum cake sat on the rectangular table perched between the two sofas. Forbes poured tea into porcelain cups from the service's matching teapot.

Sabrina glanced at the marquess. His attention was on Forbes. Without a word, Adam caught the major-domo's eye and gave him a pointed look. Forbes left the drawing room and closed the door behind him.

Sabrina thought that was odd. In her memory, nobody had ever closed the door during teatime.

The Duke of Kingston peered over his shoulder as if verifying that the door was closed. Then he turned his full attention on Sabrina and Courtney.

"Rather than boring you with all of those tedious

legal terms, I decided to tell you in my own words what your father's last will and codicil states,'' the duke began. ''Of course, you are welcome to read it yourselves if you wish. I hope you have no objection to Belladonna and Adam listening since they will be indirectly involved in this matter.''

Adam St. Aubyn involved in her father's last will? Sabrina thought in surprise. Uncle Charles probably meant receivership of the Savage properties.

''Sabrina?''

''I have no objection,'' she said, focusing on him.

''Your father designated Tess and me as guardians until you wed or reach the age of twenty-one,'' the Duke of Kingston informed her, smiling fondly at her aunt. ''In the event that we die before that time, Prince Adolphus will become your guardian.''

''Prince Adolphus will be our guardian?'' Courtney echoed in excited surprise.

''Only if both Aunt Tess and Uncle Charles die,'' Sabrina said, touching her sister's hand. ''We wouldn't want that to happen.''

''Oh, no,'' Courtney said. ''I only meant—''

''We know what you meant,'' Sabrina said. ''Please continue, Uncle Charles.''

''Your father wanted stipends for Courtney and Tess placed in trust with Adam,'' the duke continued. ''I suppose he judged that a successful businessman would be wise enough to make those stipends grow through investments. The remainder of the Savage assets are bequeathed to you, Sabrina, because you are the oldest child. With Prince Adolphus's assistance, your father managed to obtain royal permission to pass his title to you rather than let it die with him. Child, you are now the Countess of Abingdon.''

Sabrina was so surprised by this turn of events she didn't know what to say. Courtney giggled. ''Must we curtsey to you?'' she asked her sister.

Sabrina gave her an unamused look.

''Does this mean you'll never cook for us again?'' Courtney asked.

''I will always cook and bake for you,'' Sabrina answered with a smile. ''How could I not when you are so flatteringly appreciative?''

''Tell them about the codicil.'' Aunt Tess spoke for the first time.

''Your father believed that life must always move forward,'' the duke told them. ''His codicil states that he did not want his death to interfere with the living. In other words, he wanted his daughters' coming-outs, betrothals, and weddings to go on as planned without waiting the usual year of mourning.''

''Meeting the codicil's terms will be easy,'' Sabrina said. ''Courtney and I have no plans to do any of those things.''

''You are wrong, Princess,'' Adam spoke up.

''What do you mean?'' Sabrina asked, meeting his gaze.

''Courtney and you will come out in the spring,'' Belladonna explained, drawing their attention. ''We'll need to leave for London after the first of the year, though. Both of you need a completely new wardrobe.''

''I am not going to London,'' Sabrina stated. ''I am in mourning.''

"So am I," Courtney agreed.

"Would you ignore Henry's last wishes?" Aunt Tess asked.

"No, but—"

"I agree with Tess," Uncle Charles announced. "You honor your father's memory by doing what he wished for you."

"In London you will have the opportunity to meet Prince Adolphus," Belladonna pointed out. "The prince is an influential man with the power to declare your father's death an accident. You do want his body moved to hallowed ground?"

"I want to prove my father did not commit suicide," Sabrina said.

"Discovering the truth may take some time," Aunt Tess reminded her.

"You will help Sabrina, won't you, Adam?" Belladonna asked.

"I've already promised to do what I can," Adam answered, his blue gaze fixed on Sabrina.

"Then everything is settled," Belladonna announced, taking charge. "Tess and the girls will take up residence with me in London. Charles, you can move in with Adam."

"That sounds reasonable if Adam doesn't mind," the duke replied.

Adam smiled at his uncle. "You are welcome to be my guest for as long as you like."

Sabrina stared at her hands folded in her lap. Within the short span of one week, her entire world had gone spinning out of control. And then an unpleasant thought occurred to her.

"Eventually, London society will learn that we are not who they think we are," Sabrina said, beginning to wring her hands in her lap. "Being on the receiving end of a social cut would be too humiliating to endure."

"But you are not imposters," the duke said, apparently confused by her remark.

"She means people will not accept them because they are adopted," Adam explained.

"That is utter nonsense," the duke said.

"Courtney and I are bastards," Sabrina said in a voice raw with anguish. "Papa told us that our natural parents never married."

"Do *not* ever let me hear you describe yourself like that again," Uncle Charles said in a stern voice.

"Darling, I can guarantee that you will be hugely successful in society," Belladonna added.

"You cannot predict the future," Sabrina replied.

"Trust me, darling," Belladonna said. "I know exactly what I am doing. Society will know how much your father valued you. . . . So, what do you say to it?"

Sabrina looked at her sister, who gave her an encouraging smile. "Very well," she relented. "But breaking mourning troubles me."

A knock on the door drew their attention. Forbes stepped inside and in a low voice said, "Lord Briggs is here to see you."

"Don't bother to announce me, Forbes," Edgar said, brushing past the majordomo. "Abingdon Manor is more home to me than my own estate."

Smiling broadly, Edgar Briggs walked across the

drawing room toward Sabrina. He seemed indifferent to the fact that he'd arrived uninvited, and everyone was staring in silence at him.

"What are you doing here?" Sabrina asked, irritated and surprised by his arrival. "My dinner invitation was for tomorrow night."

"Yes, I know," Edgar replied. "I am on my way to visit a friend but decided to stop in to say hello. I miss you."

Sabrina felt a surge of relief that he wasn't staying, but then Courtney blurted out, "Sabrina is now the Countess of Abingdon."

"Your father gave you the title?" Edgar asked in surprise.

"Sabrina and I will make our coming-outs in London society this spring," Courtney continued excitedly in a loud voice, as if eager to spread the news.

The baron looked shocked. "You are in mourning."

Sabrina shrugged.

"Sabrina has no need for a coming-out," Briggs said, turning to the others. "She has an admirer here in Abingdon."

"Darling, a woman can never have too many admirers," Belladonna drawled.

"It is what Henry wanted for them," Aunt Tess added.

"If that is what Henry stipulated, then that is the way it will be," Edgar replied, his smile not quite reaching his eyes. "By the way, what was in that codicil to the will?" he asked.

"Nothing of importance," Sabrina hedged, knowing he would propose marriage again. Edgar believed that only her father had blocked their marriage. Now she wished she had refused his suit without relying on her father.

Edgar nodded his head tentatively and then turned to Adam. "If the weather holds, my lord, would you care to go foxhunting?"

Adam's face remained expressionless, but there was an edge of contempt in his voice when he answered, "I never kill for sport."

"And what do you kill for, my lord?" Edgar asked.

"I kill only in self-defense," Adam answered.

The marquess's answer lightened Sabrina's mood. She despised the barbaric ritual of killing animals for pleasure. Certainly there must be other ways for the male of the species to amuse himself.

"Killing only for self-defense is a noble idea but decidedly out of fashion," Edgar was saying, obviously trying to anger the marquess.

"I have no need to impress others," Adam replied, giving the baron a stiff smile. "I leave that to the social climbers."

Sabrina's lightened mood vanished beneath the enmity between these two men. Lord, why couldn't people get along with each other?

"Social climbers?" Edgar echoed, his irritation obvious in his voice.

"You know, those unworthies who try to get ahead in life by clinging to their betters," Adam answered. This time the marquess's smile was infuriatingly sincere.

"Do you mean, for example, a baron who wishes to marry a countess?" Edgar challenged.

"I never said that."

"You were implying—"

"Edgar, it's time for you to leave," Sabrina interrupted, ending their verbal sparring.

"Will you walk with me to the foyer?"

Sabrina would have agreed to almost anything to get him out of the drawing room. She nodded once and rose from her perch on the sofa.

In silence, Edgar and Sabrina walked the length of the corridor to the main staircase and down one flight to the foyer. Forbes stood near the door, and when he saw them approaching, retrieved the baron's cloak.

Sabrina felt like laughing. It seemed that everyone, including Forbes, was anxious for the baron to be gone.

"Thank you for stopping by," Sabrina said when they reached the foyer.

"How can you agree to a coming-out when you are in mourning?" Edgar asked without preamble.

"My father's codicil stipulated that in the event of his death, he didn't want my and Courtney's coming-outs postponed," Sabrina answered. "I guarantee I won't enjoy myself."

"What about the possibility of forfeiture on the Savage estate?" Edgar continued.

"Prince Adolphus is going to arrange for me to keep the lands," Sabrina told him.

Edgar looked shocked. "Do you mean that a member of our royal family will condone breaking the law of this land?"

Sabrina narrowed her gaze on him. "Do you want me to lose the land?"

"No, of course not. I am merely disappointed that I

will not be rescuing you.'' Edgar lifted her hand to his lips, saying, ''Marry me, Sabrina.''

''How can you ask that when you failed to take my side against the vicar?'' Sabrina asked, yanking her hand back. She knew that evading the marriage issue was cowardly, but she didn't have the strength for another stressful confrontation. In a few days she would tell him that marriage was out of the question.

''I've apologized for that,'' Edgar reminded her in an accusing voice. ''You said you forgave me. I've given you my heart, and now you are trampling upon it. Are you developing an interest in the marquess?''

Sabrina felt the rising tide of irritation surging through her. If he truly cared about her, why was he making life so difficult? Steeling herself against him, she lifted her chin a notch and ordered, ''Leave Abingdon Manor, and do not return until you are thinking clearly.''

The look he gave her was one of barely suppressed anger. Sabrina stepped back a pace.

Without another word, Edgar walked the short distance to the front door. As he passed the majordomo, Forbes said, ''Have a good evening, my lord.''

Sabrina sighed with a mixture of relief and remorse as the door clicked shut behind the baron. She disliked being so harsh with her oldest friend, but with any luck, he wouldn't return until after she'd left for London.

Turning away from the door, Sabrina crossed the foyer to the main staircase. Slowly and wearily she climbed the stairs, but stopped short in surprise when she neared the second-floor landing. The marquess sat in the shadows on the top stair.

"You've been eavesdropping again," she accused him.

"I couldn't help but overhear." Adam grinned unrepentantly and then added, "The baron appears to be in ill humor. Do you think he's having digestive problems?"

"Stop spying on me," Sabrina ordered, her voice raised. She brushed past him, but instead of returning to the drawing room, she raced up another flight of stairs to the third floor.

Sabrina burst into her bedchamber and surrendered to the overpowering urge to slam the door. Good Lord, she felt like baking all night, but didn't think there was enough flour in the cupboard to calm her rioting nerves. A week ago her life had been proceeding steadily and peacefully; now she felt like she'd been trapped on the road to—to where?

Sabrina dropped into the chair in front of the hearth and breathed deeply trying to calm herself as she had done the day of her father's death. She was as unsuccessful now as she had been then.

How dare the marquess meddle in her relationship with Edgar! Yes, he had offered to aid her in clearing her father's good name, but that did not give him the right to—

A knock on the door drew her attention.

"Who is it?" she snapped, certain the marquess was standing in the corridor.

"His Grace requires your immediate presence in the study," Forbes told her.

"Thank you, Forbes. I'll be right along."

A few minutes later Sabrina paused outside the closed study door and wondered what Uncle Charles wanted. Had he forgotten some important detail concerning her father's will? Or did he intend to scold her for yelling at his nephew?

Without bothering to knock, Sabrina opened the door and stepped inside. The first person she saw was the marquess sitting in one of the two chairs in front of her father's desk. The duke was sitting behind the desk. Both men stood when they saw her.

"You wanted to see me, Uncle Charles?" Sabrina asked, ignoring the marquess.

"Yes, child," the duke said. "Please sit down."

Sabrina marched across the chamber to the desk as the two men sat down again. "I'll stand," she said, casting the marquess a sidelong glance.

"I really think you ought to sit," the duke said.

"Just tell her," Adam said.

A bolt of apprehension shot through her. Sabrina looked at him and then at the duke. "Tell me what?" she asked.

The duke glanced at the marquess, who said, "Give her the short version."

"Sabrina, dear child, continuing your intimate friendship with the baron is ill-advised," the duke said, shifting his gaze to her. "You can never become betrothed to Baron Briggs or any other man because you are already betrothed to my nephew."

Sabrina stared back at him in shock.

"Are you ill?" Adam asked, starting to rise.

"Keep your distance," Sabrina cried. She fixed her

gaze on the duke and said, "I don't believe you. My father never told me any such thing."

"Henry died so suddenly," the duke said. "I'm certain he meant to tell you when he deemed the time was right. Here is the contract."

Sabrina stared at the marriage contract. It had been negotiated fifteen years earlier when she'd been a child of three.

"Is that your father's signature at the bottom?" the duke asked.

"It appears to be his, but it could be a good forgery," she replied.

"Trust me, Princess," Adam said. "That is no forgery."

"Trust you?" Sabrina glared at him. "I hardly know you. How can I be sure you aren't a swindler in search of a wealthy wife?"

"I am ten thousand times wealthier than you," he said quietly.

"Adam *is* one of the wealthiest men in England," the duke interjected.

"Why do you wish to marry me?" Sabrina asked.

"I always keep my word," Adam told her. "I intend to honor the contract that I signed fifteen years ago. You come from an excellent family, and—"

"I am an adopted bastard," Sabrina said baldly.

"You have more nobility in your little finger than any woman I've ever met," Adam told her. He lowered his voice, adding, "I admire your fearless loyalty. I admire the warmth and the respect you show others, whether they be servant or titled. . . . And I love the way you blush as you are doing now. You do remind me of a rare and beautiful rose.''

Sabrina dropped into the vacant chair and stared at him in surprise. Caught by the intensity in his blue gaze, she felt the blush heating her cheeks, but at the same time, the husky intimacy in his voice sent shivers racing down her spine. How could this man, a virtual stranger, have such a profound effect on her?

The duke cleared his voice, drawing her attention. ''Adam is willing to keep your betrothal a secret and allow you a London season.''

''*Allow* me a London season?'' His choice of words brought her anger rushing back. Sabrina couldn't credit what she was hearing. ''Where do you get the gall to— How dare you aspire to *allow* me to do anything?''

Instead of responding in anger as she had expected, Adam said in a quiet voice, ''Princess, listen to me for a moment.''

Sabrina glared at him. When he hesitated to speak, she snapped, ''Well, get on with it. I'm listening.''

''Princess, your father chose me for your husband,'' Adam said. ''However, I give you the choice to marry me or not at the end of your season. If there is another gentleman you prefer, I will gladly step aside, providing, of course, the gentleman in question is suitable. In return, you must promise to spend time with me each week so that we can become acquainted. Do we have a bargain?''

Sabrina refused to speak. Apparently the aristocratic scoundrel wasn't above blackmail.

''Either we have a bargain,'' he said in a much more

determined voice, "or I'll drag you to the altar to-night."

He wasn't above threats, either. Sabrina didn't know what to do, but if she consented to his bargain, she would have time to find a way out of this sordid mess. "Yes, we have an agreement," she said finally. "On one condition," she added.

For some strange reason, her words brought a smile to his lips. His incredibly, wonderfully formed lips, she couldn't help noticing.

"And what is the condition?" he asked.

"You must clear my father's tarnished name," she answered.

Adam inclined his head. "I've already promised to help."

"Helping isn't good enough," Sabrina replied, meeting his gaze unwaveringly. "Either you clear my father's name of the taint of suicide, or I will not cooperate with you. Aunt Tess will help me repudiate that betrothal agreement."

"Our aunts have known about our betrothal since the day the contract was signed," Adam said, surprising her.

"My aunt knew about this and never told me?" Sabrina exclaimed, her green eyes flashing.

"I promise to salvage your father's reputation even if it takes ten years."

"That would be a rather long betrothal," Sabrina said, a cutting edge to her voice.

Ignoring her tone, Adam said, "Your sister can remain ignorant of our betrothal if that is your wish. The choice is yours."

Sabrina nodded, acknowledging that he'd spoken.

"Let's send Forbes for a bottle of champagne and toast the future," the duke suggested.

"I have a headache," Sabrina said, rising from her chair. "Please excuse me."

Without sparing the marquess a glance, Sabrina crossed the chamber, but his voice stopped her at the door, "Princess, you have promised not to avoid me."

"That would be rather difficult since you are sleeping beneath my roof," she said without turning around, effectively avoiding his piercing gaze.

Holy hemlock and henbane, she thought as she quit the chamber. The scoundrel gave orders like a prince. Apparently, His Arrogant Majesty had never met a strong-willed female like her and needed to be taught a lesson.

Teaching the marquess a lesson would be like poking a tiger, Sabrina thought, a grudging smile appearing on her face. He was the most commanding man she'd ever met. He positively reeked with masculinity.

Betrothals usually ended in marriage, she thought, a chill of excitement rippling down her spine. What would marriage to the marquess be like? How would she feel climbing the stairs to their bedchamber each night? How would it feel to have his strong hands caressing her naked flesh?

Sabrina felt a hot blush rising on her cheeks. Determined to clear her head of such impure thoughts, she climbed the stairs to the third floor. If only the marquess weren't the handsomest man she'd ever seen. Even scarred, the Marquess of Stonehurst was too damned attractive for her peace of mind.

Chapter 4

Sabrina hid in her bedchamber the next day.

In an effort to avoid the marquess, Sabrina feigned a headache the following morning and resigned herself to a lonely day. After washing and donning a fresh nightgown and robe, she placed a cold compress on the bedside table and then crossed the chamber to peer out the window.

The weather mirrored her mood. Gray clouds drooped sadly in a low overcast sky, and mist as sheer as a bride's veil hung in the air.

Was it only last week that she'd been happy? Her life had changed so rapidly and drastically since then. First had come her father's sudden death. That had been followed almost immediately by Edgar's disloyalty at the first sign of trouble from Vicar Dingle. Now she was betrothed to the marquess, a man she hadn't known until three days ago. How much suffering could she endure? Her problems seemed insurmountable.

With a heavy sigh, Sabrina pressed her forehead against the coolness of the window. A solitary tear trickled down her cheek. And then another.

A knock on the door startled her. Sabrina hurried back to her bed, yanked the coverlet up, and grabbed the damp cloth, placing it on her forehead.

"Who's there?" she called in a weak voice.

"It's Courtney."

"Come in."

The door swung open, and her sister crossed the chamber to sit on the edge of the bed. Courtney gazed at her worriedly.

"Forbes told me you were ill," she said in a voice no louder than a whisper. "How bad is your headache? Is there anything I can do?"

"Marry the marquess," Sabrina answered, tossing the cold compress aside.

Courtney stared at her in surprise. "What are you talking about?"

"My head feels fine. What I have is a royal pain in the arse," Sabrina said. "Last night, Uncle Charles informed me that Adam and I have been betrothed since childhood."

"What wonderful news!" Courtney exclaimed, smiling. "The marquess is so handsome, and you'll become a duch—" The seventeen-year-old realized her sister wasn't smiling and quickly amended, "Oh, what a terrible shock it must have been."

Sabrina burst out laughing. "Sister, with a little practice, you would make an excellent diplomat."

"Do you really think so?"

"No."

"The marquess is wealthy, titled, handsome, and kind," Courtney argued. "Compared to the marquess, Edgar is a dishcloth." She rose from her perch on the edge of the bed. "You'll be down for luncheon?"

Sabrina shook her head. "I'm avoiding the marquess."

"Avoiding him will not alter the situation," Courtney said.

"I commend your practicality," Sabrina told her, "but I am not trying to alter the situation, at least not right now."

Courtney looked puzzled. "Then why are you feigning a headache?"

"The marquess insisted that he would not allow me to avoid him," Sabrina explained. "I've decided to teach him a much needed lesson about the many methods of avoidance."

"He won't be pleased," her sister warned.

"Do I look as if I care?" Sabrina asked, smiling. "If he doesn't like it, he can fiddle the devil."

Courtney shook her head in disapproval. "The point is that you may care someday."

Sabrina lifted her nose into the air, saying, "I doubt that."

"I suppose you know what is best," Courtney said, turning away. "He did ring the death knell for Papa, though."

"You won't tattle on me, will you?" Sabrina called.

Courtney turned around and then gestured as if buttoning her lips together.

"Thank you, Sister."

Sabrina spent the next few hours playing solitaire.

The lunch hour came and went, each passing moment adding to her restlessness.

The marquess had made her a prisoner in her own bedchamber, Sabrina thought in growing irritation. In her mind's eye, she conjured his image—black hair, blue eyes, distinguishing scar, and devastating smile. Yes, she finally admitted to herself, Adam St. Aubyn was a prime catch.

If only he weren't so damned attractive.

If only she didn't feel vulnerably awkward in his presence.

If only she hadn't been born a bastard.

Sabrina sighed. As long as she was wishing for the impossible, she might as well wish her beloved father alive again.

A knock on the door drew her attention. Hastily, she pushed the cards beneath the coverlet and reached for the cold compress.

"Who is it?" she called in the weakest voice she could manage.

"Aunt Tess."

The door opened, and her aunt walked inside. Behind her aunt walked the marquess carrying a tray.

Sabrina dropped her mouth open in surprise. His intrusion into her bedchamber was utterly inappropriate.

Beneath her aunt's supervision, Adam set the tray on the bedside table. Then he perched on the edge of the bed.

"Adam is worried about your health," Aunt Tess explained.

"Chamomile tea and lemon cookies," Adam added, gesturing to the tray.

Sabrina finally found her voice through her surprise. "My lord, kindly remove yourself from my chamber," she said, "or I will be ruined."

"No one but your aunt knows I'm here," Adam said, silently refusing to budge from his perch on the bed.

"Servants see everything and tell their friends, who, in turn, tell their employers," Sabrina countered.

"The marquess is your betrothed," her aunt said, making herself comfortable in the chair in front of the hearth.

"I haven't forgotten," Sabrina said dryly. "However, engaged to be married doesn't mean married. And why didn't you tell me about this betrothal?"

"Oh, dear, I'm so forgetful," Aunt Tess said suddenly, rising from her chair. "I've left my needlepoint in my chamber." She hurried to the door and left before Sabrina could stop her.

"Your face is as red as your hair," Adam said, smiling. He reached out and touched her forehead, adding, "You don't seem to have a fever."

"I really must protest your presence in my chamber," Sabrina said as soon as her aunt had gone. "This is unseemly."

Ignoring her statement, Adam passed her the cup and said, "This will make you feel better."

"I don't want tea."

"What would you like, Princess?"

Sabrina smiled suddenly. "A nap, I think."

"Shall I hold you in my arms until you fall asleep?" he asked in a husky voice.

Sabrina felt the blood rushing to her face. "A tarnished reputation is no joking matter, my lord. Especially—" She broke off, unwilling to add the words *especially for a bastard like me.*

Except for the vicar on the night of her father's burial, no villager had ever insulted her or her sister in any way. However, sometimes she'd catch people looking at them and she felt certain that they knew of their ignoble origins.

Abingdon was one of those small villages where gossip traveled fast. It seemed to her that everyone knew everyone else's secrets.

On the other hand, maybe she'd imagined those pointed looks because she felt unworthy. Her sister seemed unaffected by the secrecy surrounding their births.

"Especially?" Adam prodded, drawing her attention away from her troubling thoughts.

Sabrina focused on him. "Never mind."

Adam reached over and lifted something off the floor. One of the playing cards, she realized. It must have fallen off the bed when she'd yanked the coverlet up.

"I thought you were suffering with a headache," Adam said.

"Courtney visited earlier and tried to amuse me with a game of cards," Sabrina replied by way of an explanation.

"Princess, you are trying to avoid me," he said, fixing his blue gaze on her.

"How can you even think that?" she asked, pasting an innocent expression on her face. "Why, I am in danger from expiring from the pain in my head."

"Where does it hurt?"

"My temple."

Adam cocked a dark brow at her. "Which one?"

"Both."

"Close your eyes," he ordered in a quiet voice. When she'd done that, he placed his hands on either side of her head and began to massage her temples.

Sabrina nearly swooned when he first touched her, but soon yielded to his expert ministrations. His touch on her was firm but gentle; his fingers' rhythmic, circular motion on each of her temples was oh, so relaxing.

God shield her, she felt like purring.

And then his hands were gone.

Sabrina opened her eyes as he rose from the bed.

Adam stared down at her for a long, long moment. "Enjoy your games, Princess," he said in an amused tone of voice. "I will win in the end."

Sabrina met his gaze unflinchingly. "I hate losing."

Adam smiled at her. "Then we do have something in common after all." At that, he left the chamber and quietly closed the door behind him.

Sabrina passed the remainder of the day in her chamber. After supping alone, she leaned back in the bed. Unfortunately, sleep refused to come, and Sabrina fidgeted with the overwhelming need to bake her worries away. And she would do just that—as soon as the others had retired for the evening.

By ten o'clock, Sabrina judged that no one but servants would be about. She leaped out of bed and, without bothering to change into a gown but simply donning a robe, she headed for the door.

Sabrina paused to press her ear to the door. The corridor outside her chamber was quiet.

Ever so slowly, Sabrina opened the door a crack and peered out. The corridor was deserted. She hurried on bare feet down the length of the corridor to the servants' staircase at the rear of the mansion. In the event the marquess was on his way to bed, she would avoid meeting him on the main staircase.

Sabrina raced down the narrow staircase and burst into the kitchen, startling several servants. She quickly donned an apron and ordered, ''Fetch me molasses, butter, brown sugar, flour, ginger, allspice, bicarbonate of soda, milk, and eggs.''

''Lady Sabrina, how is your headache?'' Forbes asked as the scullery maids tripped over each other to do their mistress's bidding.

Sabrina narrowed her gaze on him and cast him a jaundiced look. The majordomo chuckled.

''What are you baking tonight?'' he asked.

''Thick gingerbread.''

''Ah, one of my favorites.''

Forbes verified that all of the items had been placed on the table and then asked, ''Will there be anything else, my lady?''

''I'd like to be alone,'' Sabrina told him.

Forbes inclined his head, saying, ''Very good, my lady.'' At that, the majordomo signaled the maids to leave the kitchen and before following them, called, ''Pleasant baking.''

Sabrina set to work immediately. She stoked the fire

of the oven, sifted the flour into a large basin, and then mixed in the brown sugar, ginger, and allspice. Humming contentedly to herself, she melted the butter and molasses over a low heat and stirred it into the other ingredients along with the bicarbonate of soda dissolved in warm milk.

After lightly whisking the eggs, Sabrina added them to the gingerbread mixture and began beating it.

"Ah, Princess, I see you are feeling better," said a familiar voice.

Sabrina whirled around in surprise and demanded, "What are you doing here?"

"You invited me to be your guest for several days," Adam replied, sauntering across the kitchen toward her.

Sabrina was not amused. "I meant, what are you doing in my kitchen?"

Adam smiled. "I was on my way upstairs when Forbes informed me that you were making the best gingerbread in England," he said. "I do love gingerbread with clotted cream."

Sabrina could have throttled the majordomo. Resigning herself to the marquess's presence, she gave him the sweetest smile she could manage and said, "You'll need to whip the cream."

"I would love to whip your cream," Adam said in a husky voice.

Sabrina looked at him for a long moment. There was something about the way he'd said those words that made her suspicious of his meaning. Was that laughter lurking in his blue eyes? What was so damned humorous about whipping the cream?

Letting his comment pass unanswered, Sabrina set a

bowl down in front of him. She poured chilled cream into it and handed him a whisk.

Without taking his gaze from hers, Adam lifted the whisk and began his task.

"Do not overwhip," Sabrina ordered.

"Heaven forbid," he said with a smile.

Sabrina poured the gingerbread mixture into a pan, put it into the oven, and then sat down at the kitchen table.

"Do not tell a soul that you saw me doing this," Adam said, glancing over at her, "or I'll be the laughingstock of London."

"I'll consider remaining silent," Sabrina said with an impertinent smile.

"What made you want to bake so late in the evening?" he asked.

"I always bake my anxieties away," she answered.

"And what anxieties would those be, Princess?"

"Clearing my father's name and my betrothal to you," she answered honestly.

"Why don't you like me?" Adam asked.

"You are overwhipping the cream," she told him. Do you want to top your gingerbread with butter?"

"You haven't answered my question," he replied.

"Why would one of England's wealthiest aristocrats wish to marry a perfect stranger?" she asked.

"Do you always answer questions with questions?" he asked.

"Not always."

"Well, you've answered your own question," Adam said, gifting her with one of his devastating smiles.

"You are a perfect stranger. Simply perfection, rarer than a rose in winter or a snowdrop in summer."

Sabrina blushed hotly at his outrageous compliment. She shifted her gaze to his and became caught by the intensity of his gaze. How was she to reply to that? No man, including Edgar, had ever spoken so intimately to her.

"What a blusher you are," Adam teased in a husky voice.

Finally, Sabrina managed to tear her gaze from his. "My lord, I believe the cream has been whipped enough." Judging the gingerbread done, she grabbed two potholders and lifted it out of the oven to cool a few minutes before cutting it into squares.

"Do you like yours topped with whipped cream?" Adam asked.

"I love whipped cream," Sabrina admitted.

Without saying a word, Adam dipped a finger into the bowl of whipped cream and then offered it to her. Shocked, Sabrina blushed and stared at him.

"Taste it, Princess," he said in a voice barely louder than a whisper, his finger hovering near her lips.

Scandalized but excited, Sabrina could only stare at the finger coated with whipped cream.

"You don't want it to melt, do you?" Adam coaxed her.

On impulse, Sabrina flicked her tongue out and tasted the whipped cream. "Delicious, my lord. You've done an excellent job."

"And so have you," Adam said in a husky voice. He turned his finger and said, "You missed the cream here."

Sabrina decided that he was trying to embarrass her but refused to give him the satisfaction of blushing. Instead, she stepped close to him and licked the remainder of the cream off his finger.

A devastatingly lazy smile spread across his handsome features. Adam leaned an inch closer, and his blue gaze captured hers. Slowly, his mouth descended to claim hers.

Sabrina closed her eyes before their lips met. His lips on hers felt warm and gently insistent, sending a delicious chill rippling down her spine. Leaning heavily against him, she surrendered to the new and exciting sensations.

Sabrina shivered with their passion when he deepened the kiss. As if from a great distance, she heard her own soft moan of pleasure.

The sound hit her like a bucketful of cold water. In one swift movement, Sabrina pulled out of his embrace and leaped back two paces before he could stop her.

"Never take such liberties with me again," Sabrina ordered, trying to regain her composure.

"You didn't like it?" Adam asked, wearing a knowing smile.

"No," Sabrina lied, and turned away when she felt the blush rising on her cheeks.

Now that she'd let him kiss her, how could she ever face him again and feign nonchalance? The marquess seemed so casual about what was to her one of life's milestones: her first kiss.

Embarrassed by what she'd done, Sabrina busied herself with cutting the gingerbread into thick squares and then placing them on their plates. Finally, she dabbed each with whipped cream.

"This feels very domestic," Adam said, sitting across the table from her.

The word *domestic* made Sabrina blush again. Why had the good Lord made her a redhead, the absolute worst kind of blusher in the whole wide world?

"I like gardening, golfing, and horses," Adam said without preamble, as if he wanted to avoid the subject of their kiss. "I despise men who hunt. What about you?"

"I love children and animals," Sabrina told him.

"Don't forget cooking and baking."

Sabrina nodded. "I also admire the fact that you don't kill for pleasure," she said. "Have you ever killed in self-defense?"

"Killing is not a suitable topic for our conversation," Adam told her. "I own three dozen ships which trade all over the world."

"I've never been on a boat," Sabrina admitted. "In fact, I haven't been to London since I was a child."

"Would you care to accompany me to Oxford tomorrow?" Adam asked. "It's a beautiful city."

Sabrina felt herself falling beneath the spell his gaze cast upon her, but was powerless to resist. Yes, she was in mourning, but what harm could a short excursion do? Especially with the man who'd already promised to help clear her father's name.

"I'd like that," she said. "Shall we invite Courtney and the others?"

"No, I think I'd like to use the time to become better acquainted with you."

Sabrina blushed. "Very well, my lord. We'll go alone."

Holy hemlock! Sabrina thought the next morning. Her fiery red hair prevented her from appearing as drab as a dormouse, which was exactly what Sabrina wished to be at the moment in order to discourage the marquess.

She had risen early and dressed in a black bombazine walking dress and black kidskin boots. After weaving her hair into a thick braid, she'd coiled it into a knot at the nape of her neck.

Grabbing her black woolen cloak, Sabrina sneaked one last peek at herself in the full-length mirror and silently cursed the wanton color of her hair and eyes. Oh, what she wouldn't give to have been blessed with mousy brown hair and dark eyes. Not that she considered herself a beauty. No, the acclaimed beauties usually had blond hair and blue eyes—never a harlot's red hair and emerald-green eyes.

Had her real mother given her the fiery tresses and green eyes? Sabrina wondered. Or had they been her father's legacy to her?

Sabrina left her bedchamber and started down the third-floor corridor. How could she possibly entertain the marquess for the whole day? She wasn't one of his sophisticated London flirts. She hardly knew the man. Whatever would they talk about? Not whipped cream, she hoped, inwardly cringing at her outrageous behavior the previous evening when she'd licked the cream off his finger and then kissed him.

Sabrina spied the marquess waiting in the foyer. He

turned around, as if sensing her arrival, and watched her descend the last few steps.

How did he know exactly what to do to fluster her? When she reached the foyer, Sabrina felt relieved that she hadn't tripped and toppled down the final steps.

"You are late," Adam said, smiling.

"Barely five minutes," Sabrina defended herself.

Taking her arm in his, Adam escorted her toward the door, saying, "Shipping magnates are exceedingly attached to schedules."

"I wonder that you tore yourself away from your business ledgers," Sabrina replied, glancing sidelong at him.

"You'd be surprised at what I'd be willing to do in order to spend a few hours alone with you," Adam told her, his voice husky.

Sabrina blushed. She tried to think of a witty reply, but her wits failed her. Again.

Bearing the ducal insignia on the door, a coach waited in the circular drive. Apparently, the marquess's men were accompanying them, for Sagi held the door open and Abdul sat in the driver's seat.

Sabrina sat on the coach's leather upholstery and watched Adam climb inside. For one awful moment, she feared he would sit beside her, but following proper etiquette, he sat across from her.

The day's unusual warmth hinted that the upcoming holiday was Easter, not Christmas. With the sun shining brightly, it didn't at all seem like late autumn, the wettest and dreariest time of the year.

"Tell me more about yourself," Sabrina said, in an effort to make conversation.

"Tell me more about yourself," Adam replied.

"I asked first," she said with a smile.

"I asked second," he said, returning her smile.

"How did you get that scar?" Sabrina persisted.

Adam reached up and touched the faint scar that ended at his right cheekbone. "When I first arrived at Eton, I found it difficult to make friends," he told her, and then surprised her by smiling, as if the memory was fond instead of painful. "One day I became involved in a disagreement with another boy, who used his riding crop to give me this. I returned the favor by giving him the same treatment, and we've been the best of friends ever since."

Shocked by his story, Sabrina could only stare at him. She never imagined that well-bred boys would resort to violence to settle their differences. On the other hand, she'd never had a brother.

"Yes, Princess, boys *are* different from girls," Adam said, as if reading her thoughts. "Jamie Armstrong, now the Duke of Kinross, and I soon became the terrors of Eton and were nearly sent down a couple of times. Fortunately, boys grow up and learn to control their savage impulses. You'll meet Jamie when you come to London."

Sabrina nodded in acknowledgment, but said nothing.

"Jamie married a girl from your former colonies last year," Adam added.

"An American girl?"

Adam inclined his head.

"Why do you say *your* instead of *our*?" she asked.

"No particular reason," he answered with a shrug.

"I never say things without a reason," Sabrina told him. "I doubt that you do either."

"Do you believe I am lying?" Adam asked, cocking a dark brow at her.

"No, you are evading my question."

"What was your question?"

Sabrina narrowed her gaze on him. "You are still evading my question."

"I've forgotten the original question," Adam replied with a boyish grin.

"Do you feel like an Englishman or a Frenchman?" Sabrina asked. "France is where you were born, isn't it?"

Adam nodded but remained silent.

"Well?"

"Some days I feel English," he answered finally. "Other days I feel French."

His words did nothing to relieve Sabrina's growing frustration. Was the man incapable of giving an honest answer? She didn't want a betrothed or a husband who refused to confide in her.

"What do you feel like today?" Sabrina asked, giving him one last chance to offer information about himself.

Adam leaned close and gave her a devastatingly wicked grin. "I feel like the luckiest man in England to be riding alone in this coach with you."

"Keep your secrets to yourself," Sabrina snapped, masking her embarrassment with anger.

"You are blushing again," Adam teased.

"Be quiet, or I'll order your men to return to Abingdon,'' she threatened, and then turned her head to gaze out of the window.

''Your every wish is my command,'' Sabrina heard the marquess say. And then she realized that he'd effectively stopped her from asking more questions. She would let him think he'd won this time, but he wouldn't always be so lucky.

Oxford lay seven miles north of Abingdon. Their journey ended a little more than an hour later when their coach turned down High Street.

''That's St. Mary's Church,'' Sabrina said, assuming the role of tour guide. ''Oxford is known as the 'city of spires' because of its skyline of towers and spires. The Bodleian Library lies north of High Street, and the parks are located in the northeast sector of the city. Would you care to take a ride around the university?''

''Not particularly.''

His refusal surprised her. ''I beg your pardon?''

''I wasted a year of my life here as a university student,'' he told her.

''You attended Oxford?'' Sabrina exclaimed, unable to keep the surprise out of her voice.

''Now, why do I have the suspicion that surprises you?'' Adam asked.

''Because it does surprise me,'' Sabrina replied, exasperated. ''You invited me to drive seven miles to show you a city you didn't wish to see?''

''Abdul, pull the carriage over,'' Adam called. He looked at her and said, ''I wanted to shop and needed your advice.''

Sabrina narrowed her gaze on him.

Adam chuckled at her suspicious expression. "I
have no experience with little girls and need to purchase a doll for a friend's daughter. I thought you
might be willing to help me choose one."

Sabrina's expression cleared. Of all the things he
could have said, purchasing a doll for a little girl was
what she'd least expected. "I can help you do that,"
she said.

By this time, their carriage had halted, and Sagi was
opening the door for them. Adam stepped down first
and then helped Sabrina.

"We'll be shopping and then dining at the Turtle
Dove," Adam told his men. "Meet us at the end of
High Street."

Sabrina accepted his arm and let him escort her
down the street. "Let's go in here," she said as they
were about to pass a toy shop.

Once inside, the shopkeeper led them to a display of
exquisitely beautiful dolls. One doll had a wax head
and human hair. Another doll had been created with a
fine Dresden china head, a body of pink kid, and a
muslin dress. Still another was wooden with jointed
limbs.

"What do you think?" Adam asked her.

"Do you think she wants to play with it or merely
look at it?" Sabrina asked.

Adam shrugged. "I would guess she'd want to play
with it."

"Then none of these will do," Sabrina told him.
Turning to the shopkeeper, she asked, "Do you have
any cloth dolls?"

"Why, yes," the shopkeeper answered, "but I hardly think a cloth doll worthy of—"

"Show us the cloth dolls," Adam said. "I'll also take the doll with the muslin dress." He winked at Sabrina, saying, "She'll look at one and play with the other."

With Sabrina's guidance, Adam purchased an enormous, stuffed cloth doll wearing a brightly colored, crocheted outfit. The shopkeeper boxed both dolls together and tied the whole thing with a bright ribbon.

"I never would have imagined you purchasing a dolly for a girl," Sabrina remarked as they left the shop.

"I like children and hope to have a house filled with my own someday," Adam replied, glancing sidelong at her. "What about you?"

Sabrina blushed and shifted her gaze away from his. "Ah, here is your man," she said, ignoring his question.

"Take this," Adam ordered, passing the box to Sagi. "We're going to dine now and will meet you later."

Sagi nodded and then walked down the street to where Abdul waited with the coach.

"Your servants are men of few words," Sabrina said.

"True, but when they do speak, I listen," Adam told her.

An enormous, incredibly dirty dog sat near the entrance of the Turtle Dove Inn and whined as they started to pass it. When Sabrina stopped and turned to it, the dog raised one of its paws.

"Hello," she greeted it, accepting the offered paw. "Are you waiting for your master?"

"Never get too close to a dog you don't know," Adam said, drawing her into the inn.

"Nonsense, the dog would have growled if it wasn't friendly," Sabrina replied.

Adam insisted on sitting in one of the small private rooms. They dined on roasted beef served with Yorkshire pudding and horseradish sauce, and a variety of cheeses.

While Adam's attention was on pouring the wine, Sabrina sneaked a few pieces of roasted beef into her handkerchief, which she then hid inside her reticule. She realized the reticule would probably be ruined, but the poor creature whining outside the inn looked hungry. She would never be able to pass him again unless she had a bite to offer him.

"Now, how will we clear my father's name?" she asked.

"I'm still pondering that problem," Adam answered. "We may never be able to prove his death wasn't suicide, but I'm certain I can get permission to bury his remains in hallowed ground. Will that do?"

"No, I will never stop trying to clear his reputation," Sabrina insisted. "I certainly will not marry until I do."

"Is that a threat?" Adam asked, cocking a dark brow at her.

"I am merely stating a fact," she answered.

"When are you planning to tell Lord Briggs about us?" he asked.

His question surprised her. "You told me I needn't

decide about going forward with the betrothal until after the season," she reminded him.

"True, but the baron is an unsuitable choice for a husband," Adam said.

"Holy hemlock!" Sabrina exclaimed. "Who gave you the right to decide who is suitable for me and who is not?"

"Uncle Charles."

"I beg your pardon?"

"Uncle Charles relies heavily on my judgment," Adam said with a smile.

Uncertain of how to reply to that, Sabrina narrowed her gaze on him. How did he dare walk into her life one day and begin to order her about? She damned well would consider anyone she pleased for a possible husband.

"Be careful," Adam teased her. "Your face might freeze like that, and then what would you do?"

"Marry you," she snapped.

Adam threw back his head and laughed. "Princess, you are incorrigible and, although a bit tempestuous, a worthy mate for me."

The filthy dog was still sitting outside the inn when they left. He stared up at them through sad brown eyes that seemed to beg for help.

"Wait a minute," Sabrina said, and then turned to the dog. She removed the handkerchief from her reticule and placed the pieces of beef on the ground in front of the dog, who gobbled them up and then looked at her for more.

"We'll never get rid of him now," Adam said.

"He'll probably follow the coach until we're well away from town."

"What breed is he?" Sabrina asked, reaching out to pat the dog's enormous head.

Adam studied the dog for a long moment. "Well, I'll be damned," he said. "Beneath the grime, he appears to be a wolfhound."

"A wolfhound in Oxford?"

Adam shrugged. "Obviously, one of the students brought him to school and then abandoned him."

"Abandoned? Oh, can't we—?"

"Absolutely not."

Feeling his hand on her arm, Sabrina walked down the street beside Adam. When they reached the end of the block, she peeked over her shoulder to see the dog following them.

Sabrina stopped walking and turned around. The dog stopped walking and sat down, his doleful gaze never wavering from hers. She glanced sidelong at Adam. The moment her gaze met his, Adam gave her a defeated smile and then called, "Come, dog."

The dog leaped up and loped down the street. When he'd closed the distance between them, the wolfhound sat down and waited.

"Princess, he's all yours," Adam announced with an amused grin.

The coach was waiting. This time Abdul opened the door for them and Sagi sat in the driver's seat. Sabrina climbed inside first and sat down on the leather-upholstered seat. Adam sat down beside her, committing a terrible breach of etiquette, and then called the dog, who sat in the seat opposite them.

"You do realize he's only half grown," Adam said.

"He's the biggest dog I've ever seen," Sabrina said. "He's built like a pony."

"Beneath that filth, the dog is pure Irish wolfhound," Adam said.

"Let's name him," Sabrina said. "Is it a boy or a girl?"

Adam leaned closer to the dog to check its genitals, and then announced, "It's a boy."

"I do wish animals wore clothing," Sabrina muttered, a rosy blush staining her cheeks.

"How about Rover?" Adam suggested for a name.

"No, he looks dignified, like a Winston," Sabrina said, and turned to Adam in excitement. "We'll need to bathe him as soon as we get home."

"We?" Adam echoed.

Sabrina looked at him through her disarming green eyes and said, "You will help me, won't you?"

Adam grinned. "Princess, you are the only woman I've ever known who invited me to bathe her dog. How could I possibly refuse your invitation?"

Excited by the prospect of having a pet, Sabrina forgot to question Adam about his background until they reached Abingdon Manor in midafternoon. By then it was too late, but there would be other times in the days ahead.

Forbes opened the door, but leaped back in fright when Winston bounded inside. "What's this?" the majordomo exclaimed.

"Forbes, meet Winston," Sabrina said. "Winston needs a large bowl of food, preferably meat, and a tub of warm water set up in the study." She looked at

Adam and explained. "The kitchen will be too busy at this hour of the day; besides, I would like a happy memory associated with that particular chamber."

"You expect me to bathe that creature?" Forbes asked.

Sabrina cast Adam a flirtatious look and answered, "No, his lordship is going to bathe Winston. With my help, of course. Come, Winston."

At that, Sabrina started down the corridor that led to the study. Adam and Winston followed behind her.

"My lady?" Forbes called. When she turned around, he told her, "Lord Briggs came by this morning. He said he would return tonight."

"If Edgar returns tonight, tell him I retired early and will receive him in the morning," Sabrina instructed the majordomo.

"With pleasure, my lady," Forbes said, unable to keep the smile off his face. "With immense pleasure."

Chapter 5

Sabrina shifted the food-laden tray to her left arm and opened the study door. She stepped inside and, with one foot, closed it again. Adam stood near the floor-to-ceiling windows, and beside him sat Winston, who lifted his nose to sniff the air as the aroma of the food wafted across the room to him.

"I can never walk into this room without thinking of my father," Sabrina said, setting the tray on the desk.

"We could have gone to the kitchen," Adam replied, coming over to meet her.

Sabrina shook her head. "Winston wouldn't care for the activity there at this hour." She turned to the dog, asking, "Are you ready to eat?"

Winston stared up at her with doleful dark eyes. Rivers of drool hung from both sides of his mouth and dropped onto the floor to form two tiny puddles.

"If you keep him waiting much longer, we're in danger of drowning," Adam said.

Sabrina set a large bowl filled with lamb stew on the floor. The dog wolfed it down within mere seconds and then looked up at her for more.

"These are for us," she told Adam, lifting a plate of cucumber sandwiches off the tray and setting it on the desk.

Sabrina then put the tray on the floor. Winston instantly began eating the joint of roasted beef it held. When he finished that, he found the hambone that lay beside it for dessert.

"That dog is eating better than most of London's poor," Adam said.

"I can't do anything about London's poor at the moment," Sabrina replied, "but I can feed one starving dog."

"Would you care for a brandy to fortify yourself for his bath?" Adam asked. His blue eyes gleamed with a smile and his voice held a challenge.

"I'd love a brandy," Sabrina said, accepting his challenge.

Adam poured brandy into two snifters and passed her one of them. Then he lifted his glass in salute and said, "To Winston, the newest addition to our family circle."

"*Our* family?" Sabrina echoed.

"We *are* betrothed."

Sabrina let his reminder pass without comment. Instead, she lifted her glass and sipped the amber liquid. In the next instant, her green eyes widened as the brandy burned a path to her stomach, stealing her breath and making her cough.

"Excellent spirits," Sabrina gasped, catching her breath.

Adam nodded. "Would you care for a cigar?" he asked, amusement lighting his eyes.

Sabrina laughed. "I believed I'll pass on that."

A knock on the door drew their attention. Finished with his meal, Winston sat erect with his ears cocked into alertness.

"Come in," Sabrina called.

Carrying towels and soap, Forbes opened the door and stepped inside, but kept his gaze fixed on the monstrous dog. "The footmen are in the corridor with a tub and warmed water."

"Tell them to set it up in front of the fireplace," Sabrina instructed him.

Forbes hesitated, as if wishing to speak.

"Princess, some of the servants may be frightened by large dogs," Adam said, and then gestured toward the windows. "Why don't I take him outside while they set up?" He crossed the chamber, opened the window, and then stepped outside. The dog followed him.

Sabrina closed the window behind them, noting that the broken pane of glass had been replaced while they'd been in Oxford. The reason for the broken windowpane had been the locked study door on the day they'd found her father hanging from the overhead beam.

Under the majordomo's supervision, two footmen carried the tub into the study and placed it in front of the black marble hearth. A parade of servants followed and filled the tub with buckets of warmed water.

"Will there be anything else?" Forbes asked before leaving.

"No, thank you." Sabrina tapped on the window as Forbes left the chamber. Adam and Winston returned the same way they had left.

Adam led the dog to the tub. Sabrina tested the water's warmth while Adam removed his jacket and rolled his sleeves up.

"Climb into the tub," Adam ordered the dog.

Winston lay down on the floor and rested his head on his forelegs. When Sabrina giggled, the enormous dog swished his tail as if he understood.

"Please, Winston," she said, tapping the side of the tub.

The dog whined.

Adam cleared his throat and ordered in a stern voice, "Get into the tub now." The dog stood, leaped into the wooden tub, and plopped down into the water, splashing them.

"Good boy," Adam said, patting him. He picked up the soap and began lathering him. "Apparently, someone trained him."

"Why do you think his former owner abandoned him?" Sabrina asked.

"I don't know that he did," Adam replied. "The dog could have been lost somehow. Fetch me that bucket of water to rinse him."

Sabrina passed him the bucket and took one for herself. Both dumped the contents onto the dog, who lifted his head and howled his displeasure like a wolf.

"Holy hemlock!" Sabrina exclaimed.

"Winston is pure white," Adam said, sounding as surprised as she felt.

"I thought he'd be beige," she said, placing a towel on the floor.

"That grime hid his true color," Adam agreed. "Winston, out of the tub."

The wolfhound didn't need a second invitation. He leaped out of the wooden tub and shook himself, sending a shower of water droplets in all directions.

Working together, kneeling on opposite sides of the dog, Adam and Sabrina toweled it dry in less than a half hour. Sabrina flashed a warning look at Adam when their fingertips touched by accident. His blue gaze was fixed on her, and the hint of a smile softened his expression.

"Princess, we work well together," he said in a husky voice.

"We need a ribbon for Winston," she said, pointedly ignoring his remark, tearing her eyes from his. "I want him to look pretty when he meets my family."

"No ribbons for boys," Adam protested. "I'll take him outside for a walk while you change for tea. We'll go out that way. The rear gardens are more private than the front drive."

Sabrina glanced toward the floor-to-ceiling windows and then asked, "How will you get back inside?"

"We'll walk through the front door like most people do," he told her.

Sabrina blushed at her own stupidity. After they'd disappeared out the window, she locked it behind them. Again she thought of the day her father died. Alarmed by her father's failure to answer her call, Sabrina had ordered Forbes to fetch the key, but the majordomo hadn't been able to find it. Edgar and he had walked outside and broken the window in order to get inside.

Leaving the study, Sabrina walked upstairs to her own chamber and gazed out the window that over-looked the front drive. Through the early evening's darkness, she spied the telltale glow of the marquess's cheroot. She recalled the feel of his warm mouth pressed against hers and reached up to glide her finger-tips across her lips.

Handsome and wealthy and titled, Adam St. Aubyn was an amazing man with enough compassion to adopt a stray dog. Somehow, she couldn't envision Edgar Briggs doing the same.

Sabrina gave herself a mental shake and turned away from the window. She removed her damp gown and donned another black bombazine dress. She was in mourning and refused to set black aside until the London season required her to.

Sabrina sat down at her dressing table and stared at herself in the framed mirror. Taming her unruly copper locks would require a miracle tonight.

A knock on the door drew her attention. Her sister, no doubt.

"Come in, Courtney," she called.

The door opened slowly. Surprising her, Winston ran into her bedchamber, his tail wagging back and forth like a conductor's baton.

"How did you—" Sabrina glanced toward the door-way, where the marquess stood. A smile lit his expression.

"What are you doing here?" she demanded.

"I was hoping to catch you in a state of undress," he said wickedly. "I see I've arrived too late."

"I must protest your presence," Sabrina said, feeling the heated blush rising upon her cheeks. Without bothering to brush her hair, Sabrina crossed the chamber to the door and stepped into the corridor. As they started down the corridor, she said, "Our agreement does not give you the liberty to—"

Sabrina stopped talking and rounded on him when she felt his fingers on her back. "What are you doing?" she cried.

"You missed a button," Adam told her, his expression of innocence not fooling her for a moment.

"No decent gentleman would touch a woman without her permission," Sabrina said. "Kindly refrain from doing so."

"Surely you haven't mistaken me for a decent gentleman," Adam countered, reaching out to capture a wisp of her wanton red hair and secure it behind her ear. "Besides, there's no harm in an engaged couple's touching each other."

Sabrina quickly stepped back a pace, making him smile. Not only was the marquess no decent gentleman, she decided, he seemed to revel in defying the conventions of proper behavior.

"You assume too much," Sabrina warned, meeting his gaze unwaveringly. "I'm positive that London is filled with potential husbands, most of whom are decent gentlemen."

"Decency can be excruciatingly boring," Adam replied, giving her a wicked grin.

"I'll be the judge of that," Sabrina announced, and continued walking down the corridor to the stairway.

"I love it when you blush, Princess," Adam said in a husky voice, walking beside her. "The rosy color accentuates your green eyes."

"Don't say things like that," Sabrina said, and flicked a sidelong glance at him.

"Why?"

"You make me feel uncomfortable."

Sabrina heard him chuckle but refused to look at him again. She knew that would only encourage his bad behavior.

"A beast," Sabrina heard Aunt Tess cry when Winston bounded into the drawing room ahead of them. She and Adam walked into the room just in time to stop Winston before he reached the platter of cucumber sandwiches and lemon cookies.

"Sit, Winston," Adam ordered. Hearing the voice of authority, the dog halted instantly and sat down beside the platter of food.

"Good boy," Adam praised the dog, patting his head.

"That's a dog?" Belladonna drawled.

"He looks more like a pony," Aunt Tess said.

"That is pure Irish wolfhound," Uncle Charles told them. "I do believe he's almost as big as Tiny, Prince Adolphus's dog at Eton."

"Winston, is it?" Courtney asked. "Don't you think a ribbon would make him look prettier?"

Sabrina glanced at Adam and sent him an I-told-you-so look.

"No ribbons," he said.

"Oh, my Lord, look at that disgusting drool," Belladonna said.

Two rivers of saliva hung from the corners of Winston's muzzle as he stared at the tempting platter.

Sabrina took a handkerchief from her pocket to wipe the drool and then gave him a cucumber sandwich. Winston swallowed it without chewing.

"A growing pup has a healthy appetite," Adam said with a smile. Then he ordered, "Winston, lie down." The dog lay on the rug and rested his head on top of his forelegs.

"Where did you get him?" Uncle Charles asked.

"The Countess of Abingdon possesses a big heart, and apparently wishes to adopt any stray that crosses her path," Adam replied.

"There are worse things in life," Sabrina said. Sitting on the edge of the couch, she leaned close to the dog and patted his head. "Winston is such a pretty boy."

The dog lifted his head and offered her his paw.

"Boys are handsome, not pretty," Adam corrected her.

"A courier arrived from London," Uncle Charles said.

That got Sabrina's attention. "And?"

"Prince Adolphus received permission from Prinny—"

"The Prince Regent?" Courtney exclaimed.

Uncle Charles smiled and nodded. He looked at Adam, saying, "Prinny will give you receivership of the Savage assets."

"For a price, of course."

Uncle Charles shrugged. "You know that Prinny has holes in his pockets."

"I don't understand," Sabrina said, looking from the duke to the marquess.

"For a fee, the Prince Regent will give me the authority to oversee your assets until a final determination is made about your father's death," Adam explained.

"I will reimburse you when this matter is settled," Sabrina promised.

"Don't bother yourself about the money," Adam told her. "It's all in the family."

"We are not family yet," she reminded him.

"Sabrina!" a voice called from the doorway before the marquess could reply.

Everyone turned to see Lord Briggs crossing the drawing room toward them. Winston lifted his head, sat up, and growled at the baron. Edgar stopped short and stared in surprise at the dog.

"What is that?" Edgar asked.

"My dog," Sabrina answered.

"Winston, lie down," Adam ordered.

Instantly, the dog lay down again and rested his head on his forelegs. However, his small ears remained pricked as if alert to a dangerous presence in the chamber.

"A lady requires a lapdog, not a monster," Edgar said to Adam.

Adam raised his dark brows at the baron. "I didn't give her the dog."

"We found him in Oxford today," Sabrina said.

"Will you never learn?" Edgar said in a stern voice, shaking his head.

Winston growled but remained where he lay.

"I don't think Winston likes your tone," Adam said with a smile lurking in his voice.

Lord Briggs ignored the marquess. "Sabrina, I must speak privately with you."

"That can wait until tomorrow," Sabrina said, refusing to listen to another of his lectures. "Why don't you join us for tea?"

"I am leaving for my sister's in the morning," Edgar said. "I told you I was spending the holiday with her this year."

Sabrina felt unaccountably relieved that he'd be going away. Then, guilt for feeling that way replaced the relief.

"Oh, I'd forgotten." Sabrina rose from her perch on the couch, saying, "Let's walk downstairs."

Sabrina crossed the chamber, but before leaving, glanced over her shoulder and told the others, "I'll return shortly."

Sabrina and Edgar walked in silence down the corridor to the main staircase. Descending the stairs, Sabrina nearly burst out laughing when she spied Forbes reaching for the baron's cloak in preparation for his departure.

Poor Edgar, she thought. Apparently, no one at Abingdon Manor wanted him there.

When the majordomo handed him the cloak, Edgar looked pointedly at the man until he left the foyer. Then he turned to stare unhappily at her.

"I feel like an unwanted outsider," Edgar said.

"Forgive me," Sabrina apologized, reaching out to touch his arm. "I never intended to make you feel that way. My father's sudden death has sent my world spinning out of control, and I'm still trying to find my balance."

His expression softened. He reached into his pocket and produced a small box. "I have a gift for you."

"You shouldn't have bought me a present," Sabrina said, shaking her head. How could she accept a gift from a man when she was betrothed to another?

Edgar opened the box. Lying on a bed of black velvet was a diamond heart-shaped pendant attached to a gold chain. "This necklace belonged to my mother," he told her.

"I cannot accept such an expensive gift, especially one with sentimental value," Sabrina said.

"Please, Sabrina."

She shook her head. "That necklace is for your future wife, whoever that may be."

"I was hoping that would be you," Edgar said, his love for her apparent in his gaze. "Besides, the necklace is for whomever I wish to wear it." He placed the box in her hand, adding, "Keep it as a token of our long friendship."

Sabrina felt like the lowest creature on earth. "I'll keep it safe for your future betrothed," she agreed reluctantly. "Whenever you want it back, I will be happy to return it to you."

Edgar smiled. "Thank you."

"I have nothing for you," she said.

"I've always longed to kiss you," Edgar said, slowly inching his face toward hers.

Just as their lips would have met, Sabrina heard a low, menacing growl. She leaped back a pace and turned to see Adam and Winston standing at the base of the staircase. Anger swelled within her like a sudden gust of wind. How could he have intruded on such a private moment? Where did he get the gall?

"That dog is dangerous and should be destroyed," Edgar said in an annoyed tone of voice. "If I ever come across him alone, I'll do just that."

Sabrina didn't know whom she wished to throttle first. Adam should never have intruded on this moment, but Edgar shouldn't have threatened the life of her dog.

"If you do that, I'll never speak to you again," Sabrina returned his threat, rounding on him. "Get off my property." She showed him her back and took one step away.

"You were sweet and biddable until *he* arrived," Edgar said, his voice filled with bitterness.

"Sweet and biddable?" Sabrina echoed, turning around slowly. "Keep your damned necklace." At that, she tossed the box at him.

Briggs caught the box before it hit him. Giving her an angry look, he stalked out the door.

"You, my lord, are an aristocratic arse," Sabrina announced, rounding on Adam. "Stay out of my private affairs. . . . Come, Winston." With the dog in tow, she brushed past him and started up the stairs.

"I can't," Adam said in a quiet voice.

Sabrina stopped and turned around, asking, "What did you say?"

"As your betrothed, your private affairs are my business," Adam told her.

"My private affairs are *my* business," Sabrina insisted. "Your constant intrusion into my life is annoying me. I certainly will never marry a man who is so . . . so . . . *intrusive.*"

Adam smiled unrepentently. "All men are instrusive when the matter at hand concerns their women."

"I am not your woman," she snapped.

"You will be if I choose to spread the word of our betrothal in London," he countered.

"Keep out of my way," Sabrina threatened, "or you'll be sorry."

"What will you do?" Adam asked, wearing an infuriating smile. "Challenge me to a duel?"

"Nothing so obvious as that," Sabrina replied, gazing down at him like a haughty young queen. "I'll spike your clotted cream."

His smile grew into a grin. "With hemlock or henbane?"

She cocked a brow at him. "That death would be much too quick. Not enough suffering, you know. A purgative, perhaps."

Sabrina started up the stairs again. She refused to spare him a glance when she heard his shout of laughter.

Gaining her chamber, Sabrina sat in the chair in front of the hearth to pat the dog and fume. Why couldn't Edgar accept the fact that they would never marry? Her father had refused his offer of marriage. Why would he believe she'd accept him now? And that meddling marquess! Adam St. Aubyn had better keep his distance from her and cease intruding on her private business. A fifteen-year-old betrothal contract did not give him exclusive ownership of her.

Soon the movement of her hands on the dog soothed

her as much as the animal himself, and she felt able to get some sleep. With Winston curled into a gigantic ball on her bed, Sabrina slept more peacefully than she had since her father's death. The sound of the door opening awakened her early the next morning. Sabrina opened her eyes to see Winston lifting his head, and then she heard a low whistling. The dog bounded off the bed, and a moment later the door clicked shut again.

Was the marquess now invading her bedchamber? Sabrina wondered drowsily. His behavior was entirely too familiar and totally inappropriate, even for a fiancé. She would give him the lecture of his life when she went down to breakfast.

Two hours later, Sabrina stood outside the dining room. She squared her shoulders, preparing to do battle with the marquess, and marched into the room. Uncle Charles, sitting alone at the head of the long table, was just passing Winston a piece of Oxford sausage.

"Good morning," Sabrina called, relieved that she need not confront the marquess just yet.

"A good morning to you, child," the duke greeted her.

"I see that you've made a new friend," she said, taking the seat on his right side.

Uncle Charles chuckled. He lifted another piece of sausage off his plate and passed it to Winston. "Adam is waiting to speak privately with you in the study."

Sabrina gave him the sweetest smile she could muster and said, "Let him wait."

"He'll be leaving shortly and did wish to—"

"You're leaving?" Sabrina interrupted in surprise. "I thought you were staying through the holiday."

"I'm not going anywhere," he assured her, reaching out to pat her hand, "but business demands that my nephew return to London. By the way, I'm glad you're sorry to see him go."

"I never said that."

"You didn't need to." The duke winked at her and said, "I can see the regret in your pretty green eyes."

"What you see is the gleam of anger, not the glistening tears of regret," Sabrina corrected him, rising from her chair. At that, she marched the length of the dining table to the door, but paused when the duke called to her.

"Child, I do believe Winston cares more for you than sausage," he said.

Sabrina shifted her gaze from the duke to the dog, who stood right behind her. "How comforting to be held in such high esteem," she replied. "Come, Winston."

Followed by her dog, Sabrina walked the length of the long corridor to her father's study. The door was closed, just as it had been on that tragic day. She reached out to knock but then thought better of it; Abingdon Manor was her home, not his. Instead of knocking, Sabrina turned the knob and walked inside.

In the act of packing his papers into a satchel, Adam looked up and then stood as she crossed the chamber. "Come and sit by the hearth," he said. "I want to speak to you."

"I prefer to stand," Sabrina said coolly, crossing the study to the black marble fireplace.

Adam inclined his head and joined her in front of the hearth. Winston lay down on the rug.

"In the future, refrain from barging into my chamber," Sabrina said, folding her arms across her chest as if to ward off his nearness, staring him straight in the eye.

"I never did that," Adam said, staring back at her.

"You opened my door this morning and whistled to Winston."

"Yes, I did," Adam admitted with a smile. "A world of difference lies between whistling at the threshold and entering the room. Knowing you were sleeping behind that door was an enticement. Princess, you are simply irresistible."

Sabrina dropped her arms to her sides and stared at him in surprise. She couldn't credit that this sophisticated man of the world found her irresistible. She didn't know if she should feel flattered or insulted.

"Stop spying on me," Sabrina managed to say finally. "How can I find a potential husband if you stand guard constantly?"

"I said a *suitable* gentleman," Adam corrected her. "I do not consider Lord Briggs suitable."

"Why not?"

Adam merely smiled at her.

"Whom do you consider suitable?" Sabrina asked.

"Me."

Sabrina gave him a jaundiced, unamused look.

"I'm sorry, Princess. I must leave for London this morning," Adam said, lifting an ornately carved box off the table. "I've been saving this gift for you since we become betrothed fifteen years ago."

Sabrina could only stare at him. She'd lived her whole life receiving gifts only from her father, and now two men in two days wanted to give her a gift.

"My mother once told my father the story of a princess who kissed a frog and turned it into a charming prince," Adam continued. "Afterward, my father gave my mother this gift."

He opened the box's lid. Inside lay a frog brooch of diamonds set in platinum and gold, with emerald eyes and an emerald bow on one of its back legs.

Sabrina was stunned. Never had she seen a more exquisite brooch. Nobody she knew could purchase such expensive jewels. Who had his father been? Only royalty could afford priceless gems like this.

"I want you to wear this," Adam said.

Sabrina lifted her gaze to his and said, "I couldn't accept—"

"You can and you will." Adam lifted the brooch out of the box and moved to fasten it to her bodice.

"I'll do that," Sabrina said, reaching out to stop his hands before he touched her.

Gently but firmly, Adam pushed her hands down to her sides, saying, "I'll fasten it."

When he inched closer to pin the brooch to her bodice, his touch and his clean masculine scent assaulted her senses. She felt him with every tingling fiber of her body and feared he could hear the frantic beating of her heart.

Finished with his task, Adam slid his fingertips down the side of her breast. Shocked by the intimacy of his touch, Sabrina leaped back from him and, at the same moment, raised her hand to slap him. He caught her wrist before her hand found its target and pulled her against his strong, muscular body.

"You go too far," Sabrina said vehemently.

"Give over, Princess," Adam coaxed in a quiet voice, his blue gaze holding hers captive. "I only want a thank-you kiss."

Sabrina stared at him for a long tension-filled moment. "You may kiss me," she finally relented, offering him her cheek.

"Oh, no, you don't," Adam said, a spark of grudging admiration in his voice. With one finger, he turned her head to face him.

Adam lowered his head to claim her lips in a slow, soul-stealing kiss while his arms encircled her body and drew her against the hard, muscular planes of his chest. His lips on hers were warm and firm and demanding. He flicked his tongue across the crease of her mouth and, when it opened, slipped his tongue inside to taste the sweetness beyond her lips.

Overwhelmed by his intimate touch and the incredible sensation of his tongue caressing her mouth, Sabrina shivered with passion and surrendered to his consuming kiss. She entwined her arms around his neck and returned his kiss in kind. Being held in his embrace felt so comforting, so natural, so exciting.

Winston whined.

And their kiss ended as suddenly and unexpectedly as it had begun.

"That despicable dog has been in residence less than a day, and he's spoiled," Adam said, tracing a finger down the side of her face. "I'll miss you while I'm in London."

Still reeling from his devastating kiss, Sabrina felt flushed all over. Holy hemlock! How could a simple kiss have this effect on her?

"I'm leaving now," he said. "Walk with me."

Uncle Charles was waiting in the foyer, which prevented a repeat of their kiss. Sabrina felt relieved. At least she wouldn't be required to kiss him in front of an audience.

"You'll first call upon Adolphus?" the duke asked Adam.

"Everything will be settled by the time you arrive in London," Adam assured him. He turned to Sabrina, saying, "I'll see you in a few weeks. Admit that you'll miss me."

"I'll miss you"— Sabrina smiled sweetly—"almost as much as my last toothache."

Adam grinned and leaned close to kiss her cheek. Without another word, he walked out the door.

Sabrina watched him climb into the coach. Sagi and Abdul climbed onto the driver's seat, and off they went.

Watching the coach take the marquess away to London, Sabrina didn't feel as relieved as she'd thought she would. In fact, she felt disappointed. Abingdon Manor would seem empty without him.

Sabrina shifted her gaze to the duke and blushed to find his gaze upon her. He looked at the brooch she wore and then smiled.

"I believe this will be my best year ever," he said, and then walked away.

Sabrina touched her frog brooch and smiled to herself. She looked at Winston, who stood beside her wagging his tail.

"Come with me, my friend," Sabrina said, turning away from the door. "I have a pretty blue ribbon I want you to wear."

Chapter 6

The month since his departure from Abingdon
had passed excruciatingly slowly, Adam decided, relaxing against the leather seat in his
coach. Those twenty-six days and nights had seemed
more like twenty-six years.

His shipping business and financial investments had
kept his days filled with activity. The nights had passed
slowly, especially the small hours of the morning when
he was alone with his thoughts.

Avoiding his former mistress, Adam had remained
at home in the evenings or only ventured to White's
Gentlemen's Club to have a drink or a hand of cards
with Jamie Armstrong, his closest friend.

Had his abrupt departure from Abingdon Manor relieved or disappointed Sabrina? Adam wondered.
Though he'd only known her for a few weeks, being
away from her made him feel as if something of value
was missing from his life. Could a man actually be-

come emotionally attached to a woman in such a short period of time, or was this attraction merely physical? Her kiss had been sweetly seductive, so unlike those of the sophisticated London flirts.

Adam smiled to himself. Poor Winston had probably been subjected to wearing ribbons since his departure. And pink ribbons at that.

His coach halted in front of number 10 Berkeley Square, the elegant home of Alexis Carstairs, the Countess of Rothbury, his former mistress. Adam lost his smile when he realized he'd reached his destination.

What was so damned urgent? he wondered. He had several things to do before Sabrina's scheduled arrival in London later that day. He hoped Alexis wouldn't make life difficult for Sabrina.

Adam reached for the knocker and slammed it hard against the door several times. A moment later the Carstairs majordomo opened the door, allowing him entrance.

"Good afternoon, my lord," the man greeted him.

"Where is Lady Carstairs?" Adam asked, marching into the foyer, too hurried to exchange pleasantries with the servant.

"My lady is still closeted in her bedchamber," the majordomo answered.

"Tell her I'm here," Adam ordered, crossing the foyer to the staircase. "I'll wait in the drawing room."

"Lady Carstairs bade me tell you to go directly to her chamber."

Adam nodded, acknowledging the man's words, and started up the stairs. How like Alexis to order him to her bedchamber like a queen granting an interview to a courtier. To make matters worse, the servants obviously knew she was receiving him in her bedchamber. Didn't Alexis have sense enough to realize that the servants from one house gossiped with those from another?

Standing outside the third-floor bedchamber, Adam reached for the doorknob but then hesitated. He lifted his hand and knocked instead.

"Come in," called a sultry voice.

Bloody hell, Adam thought when he stepped inside the room. She was waiting for him in bed.

Blond and blue-eyed and voluptuous, Alexis Carstairs appeared like a goddess of love as she lay languidly beneath the thin coverlet. Her nakedness was apparent.

"I thought you'd never get here," Alexis said in a breathless whisper, obviously meant to entice.

"What is so damned urgent?" Adam asked, staring down at her.

She pouted prettily. "I missed you."

"That is why you summoned me here?" There was no mistaking the irritated disbelief in his voice.

"I want to discuss something with you," she replied.

Adam lifted her black lace nightgown off the foot of the bed and tossed it at her, ordering, "Cover yourself."

Her expression mirrored her surprise. Instead of watching her rise nude from the bed like Venus rising from the sea, Adam crossed the chamber and gazed out the window overlooking the garden.

Alexis stood beside him, slipped her arm through his, and brushed her breast against it. "Remember the night you climbed up the oak tree and into my chamber?'' she asked with sultry amusement. ''I'll never forget how glad I was that you had persuaded me not to cut it down.''

Adam nodded, but refused to spare her a glance.

''You used to be *sooo* romantic,'' Alexis said with a sigh, ''but you haven't touched me since my beloved Rupert passed away. That was—let me think—six months ago.''

''You are in mourning,'' he reminded her.

''I'm wearing black.''

In spite of his irritation, Adam couldn't suppress a smile. The idea of that black lace nightgown being appropriate mourning attire was simply too absurd. The beautiful minx had shed no tears for her husband's passing. Well, he supposed that was the way of the world when a lovely young woman married an old man.

''I've escorted you to the opera and various other activities,'' Adam defended himself. ''Which, I might add, caused a small sensation since mourning precluded you from going about.''

''Yes, but you haven't called upon me since returning from Abingdon,'' Alexis said. ''By the way, I met an acquaintance of yours at Lady Chester's soirée last night.''

Her nonchalant tone of voice alerted him to trouble. He turned his head to look at her, asking, ''Who would that be?''

''Lord Edgar Briggs from Abingdon.''

''Lord Briggs is a social-climbing buffoon,'' Adam said with a sardonic smile. ''The man doesn't know his left elbow from his arse.''

"I think you underestimate the man," Alexis disagreed.

"Why do you say that?" he asked.

Alexis shrugged. "The baron seemed an intelligent, determined man to me." She paused a moment to slide her hand up the length of his arm and then said, "Let's announce our engagement. I'll cut my mourning period short so we can marry in a few months."

"My dear, you have never observed any mourning period," Adam said dryly.

His flippant remark seemed to anger her, but she recovered herself before offending him. "I'm serious, Adam. You need a sophisticated wife who will give you heirs. What better choice than me?"

"I need no one," he replied, disengaging himself from her grasp.

"Who is Sabrina Savage?" Alexis demanded.

Adam inclined his head. "I see Briggs has been a useful source of information."

Staring down at her angry expression, Adam decided the moment for truth had arrived. The best policy would be to get this distasteful scene out of the way before Sabrina arrived in London. On the other hand, Alexis could be particularly vicious, and he didn't want Sabrina to suffer. Perhaps he could sugarcoat the truth.

"Sit down over there," Adam said.

Obediently, Alexis sat down on her dressing table stool. Adam remained standing near the window.

"Sabrina and Courtney Savage recently lost their father, the Earl of—"

"Suicide, I heard," Alexis interrupted.

"What else did Briggs tell you?" Adam asked.

"Both girls are adopted bastards."

That bit of information surprised Adam. He would have sworn that the baron truly cared for Sabrina. What kind of man would denounce the woman he loved as a bastard?

"My Uncle Charles is executor of the late earl's will," Adam told her, ignoring her comment on bastardy. "I will take charge of the Savage assets for the time being. According to the late earl's wishes, they will make their coming-outs this season."

Alexis brightened. "So, you are a guardian of sorts?"

"Not precisely," Adam replied. "As children, Sabrina Savage and I were betrothed."

"What?" Alexis bolted off the stool.

"Sit," he ordered sternly.

Alexis sat down again. Her blue gaze sparkled with anger.

"Lady Sabrina is reluctant to keep the bargain made by her father all of those long years ago," he continued. "I have given her a way out of it. If she meets some other suitable gentleman during the season, she may nullify our betrothal and marry him."

Alexis's smile was feline and calculating. "So, if the girl falls in love with someone else, the betrothal between you is nullified? Both of you will be free to—"

The unexpected sound of excited female voices in the corridor drew Adam's attention. He looked at Alexis, who gave him an innocent smile. In that split instant Adam knew what was happening; Alexis had engineered him into a compromising position to force him to marry her.

"You conniving witch," he said, leveling a deadly look on her. At that, he flung the window open and climbed outside onto the giant oak to descend the two stories to the garden below.

Lucky for her that the tree aided his escape, Adam thought. If not, Alexis Carstairs would be ruined, for he had no intention of marrying her.

Reaching the street, Adam was surprised to see Abdul and Sagi waiting there with the coach. He'd left them parked near the front door. Sagi sat in the driver's seat while Abdul held the coach door open for him.

Adam smiled at them. "How did you know?"

"The best servants anticipate their masters' needs, my prince," Abdul informed him.

Sagi called from where he sat, "We noted the ladies' arrival and assumed you would require a fast escape."

"Thank Allah for that," Adam said, "but you must remember always to call me *my lord.*"

Abdul nodded. "As you wish, my prince."

Adam ducked into his coach, and his bodyguard closed the door. He relaxed back on the leather seat for the ten minute trip to his town house on Park Lane, the most fashionable street in London.

Without waiting for Abdul to open the door, Adam climbed out of the coach and started up the front stairs of his house. He heard someone calling his name and turned to see James Armstrong, the Duke of Kinross, stepping out of his coach.

"Come inside, Jamie," Adam said, smiling at his

friend from Eton schooldays. "Let's toast the great escape I've just made."

Jamie grinned. "Escape from what?"

"Why, I've neatly escaped the trap Alexis set for me," he answered.

Jamie laughed. Together, the two friends walked into the town house.

Inside the foyer stood two men. Short, dark, and rotund, Razi had come from the East and acted as his valet. Higgins, his majordomo, was tall and dignified-looking.

"Welcome home, my lord," Razi greeted him as if he'd been gone for two days instead of an hour.

"Has my uncle arrived yet?" Adam asked.

"No, my lord," answered Higgins in a cultured voice. "His chamber is in readiness."

Adam nodded. "Inform me as soon as he sends word of their arrival."

"Without fail, master," Razi promised, obviously eager to please.

"Master?" Jamie echoed as they walked the length of the corridor to the study. "My servants don't give me that much respect. How do you manage such loyalty?"

Adam shrugged. "Razi is a bit old-fashioned."

James Armstrong sat down in the upholstered chair in front of the enormous oak desk while Adam poured two drams of whiskey. "All of the ton prefers mahogany while you cling to sturdy oak," he remarked.

"I set my own standards," Adam said, passing him the whiskey. He sat in his chair behind the desk and raised his glass in salute, saying, "To my latest escape from the clutches of Alexis."

Jamie sipped his whiskey and then asked, "What did Alexis do this time?"

"She lured me into her bedchamber in order to place me in a compromising position," Adam told him. With a smile, he added, "I escaped out the window, and thank God for that oak tree."

Jamie burst out laughing. "I stopped into White's last night," he said. "You are officially the hottest wager in that infamous betting book."

"I am?"

Jamie nodded. "They're wagering on whether or not Alexis Carstairs will trap you into marriage."

Adam smiled. "And?"

Jamie grinned. "Popular opinion is running against you."

"What did you wager?" Adam asked, arching a brow at his friend.

"I didn't," Jamie answered. "That would be the tip about which way the wind was blowing."

"I suppose you're correct," Adam replied, inclining his head. "Listen, you don't mind if I cut short our visit? I'm expecting Prince Adolphus any minute now."

Jamie nodded and set his glass down on the desk. He rose from his chair, saying, "I expect to meet the Savage girl as soon as possible."

"I want you and your wife to meet her tomorrow," Adam said, standing to walk him to the door. "I'll send a message around to your house."

"I do hope that Lily and she will become fast friends," Jamie said.

"I'm certain they will." Adam shut the door behind his friend and sat down at his desk to do some paperwork before the prince arrived.

Focusing on his ledgers that day proved impossible. One particular image, parading across his mind's eye, broke his concentration—fiery tresses framing a hauntingly lovely face, disarming green eyes sparkling with anger or gleaming with mirth or blurred by unshed tears . . .

Bloody hell, Adam thought, and threw his quill down in disgust when he caught himself doodling her image on the damned ledger. To make matters worse, he'd added her saying the words *I love you.*

How could he explain this to his army of accountants? He'd be the laughingstock of London. He could hear the gossipmongers now. The fabulously wealthy, aristocratic rogue who'd broken more than a few hearts had been shot by Cupid's arrow and become smitten by an unsophisticated country girl, albeit a titled aristocrat. *The Times* would profit handsomely by that juicy piece of gossip.

And then Adam smiled. There really was no need to lose face with his employees. He lifted the container of ink and poured it over the page, effectively blotting out his weakness. Ah, well, accidents did sometimes happen, and there was nothing to be done for it.

"Come in," Adam called when he heard the knock on the door.

Razi and Higgins hurried inside. The little valet and

the dignified majordomo shot daggers at each other with their gazes.

"I'll introduce him," Razi said.

"No, I will," Higgins replied. "I am the marquess's majordomo."

"But I am his most trusted valet."

Instead of arguing, Higgins announced, "His Royal Highness, Prince Adolphus, the Duke of Cambridge, has arrived."

"You forgot the Earl of Tipperary and Baron Culloden," Razi added angrily. "Prince Adolphus is those things too."

"Please escort the prince here," Adam said, rising from his chair.

Razi turned around and called, "Come on inside."

"You idiot," Higgins said, cuffing the back of the little man's head.

"I wanted no fanfare," Prince Adolphus said, walking into the study, "but they insisted."

"Your Royal Highness, I am honored by your presence in my home," Adam greeted him with a smile as his retainers left the room. "Please sit down."

At forty-two, Prince Adolphus was a big man who covered his growing baldness with a blond wig. He was affable by nature and well respected by the general public. Unlike his brothers, he had never had scandal attached to his name.

Adam sat when the prince sat. "Have you brought those documents?" he asked.

"I have them right here," Adolphus answered, reaching into his jacket. "Yes, I do . . . I do . . . I do."

Adam smiled to himself as he lifted them out of the prince's hand. So, it was true. He'd heard that Adolphus was becoming a bit eccentric in his midlife and had even picked up his mad father's habit of sometimes saying the same words three times.

Adam quickly perused the document granting him receivership of the Savage assets. Then he reached for his quill to affix his name to it.

"My God, what happened to your ledger book?" Adolphus asked.

"Nothing really," Adam replied, signing the document. "I spilled ink on the page."

"Accidents will happen," Adolphus said, nodding. "Yes, they will."

"Now, Sir, the Savage assets are safe," Adam said, sitting back in his chair. "Is there anything else?"

"There is a great deal else," Adolphus replied. "Do you believe poor Henry committed suicide?"

Adam shrugged. "I know for a fact that his death was no accident, and Sabrina insists her father would never have taken his own life."

Adolphus appeared shocked. "Are you suggesting murder?"

"Sabrina says her father had no enemies," Adam answered.

"What do you believe?" the prince asked.

"I trust Sabrina's judgment about her father's state of mind," Adam answered, choosing his words carefully. "However, I believe she's much too innocent to recognize an enemy when she meets one. Now, what about the burial in hallowed ground?"

"I'm still working on that," the prince answered.

"Prinny is not a favorite of the clergy." He raised his eyebrows, adding, "You know his lifestyle. Very immoral . . . immoral . . . immoral. Tell me about the daughters."

"Courtney, the youngest, is brown-haired and brown-eyed," Adam told him. "She's also sweet and biddable. I think Dudley Egremont, Viscount Dorchester, would suit her very well, and I intend to bring about a match between them."

Adolphus nodded in agreement. "Dorchester is a good man. What about the other sister?"

"Sabrina is the opposite of her sister," Adam said with a smile. "She possesses fiery red hair and enormous green eyes and a temperament to match her beauty."

"She sounds as tempestuous as her mother," Adolphus said, and then chuckled. "Now there was a plucky woman. Plucky . . . plucky . . . plucky."

Adam grinned.

"By the way, thank you for allowing me to invest in your businesses," the prince rambled on. "They have proven quite lucrative."

Adam inclined his head and then changed the subject. "You will attend the girls' coming-out? Your presence would assure them social success."

"I owe Henry Savage a great debt for his selfless friendship and wouldn't miss his daughters' coming-out for all of the gold in the world," Adolphus replied. "No, no, no. Missing their debut wouldn't do at all."

Adolphus rose from his chair. Adam stood when the prince stood.

"For the moment our business is concluded," Adolphus said, shaking his hand.

"Let me escort you to the door," Adam said.

The two men walked down the corridor to the foyer. Higgins and Razi, obviously bickering, saw them approaching and snapped to attention.

"I appreciate all that you are doing, son," Adolphus said, shaking his hand again.

Adam inclined his head. "Being of service is my pleasure, Sir."

"Remarkable servants, those two," the prince said, turning to leave. "If ever they leave your employ, I would be glad to invite them into mine. Yes, I would . . . I would . . . I would." And then he was gone.

Adam looked at his majordomo and his valet. Both men stood proudly erect, preening beneath the prince's compliment. "Any messages?" he asked.

Higgins spoke first, saying, "The Duke of Kingston and his entourage—"

"—have arrived at Grosvenor Square," Razi interrupted, earning himself a glare from the majordomo.

"Have Abdul and Sagi bring my carriage around front again," Adam instructed.

"Immediately, my lord," Higgins said.

"I'll do it," Razi said, and hurried down the corridor.

Like a rival schoolboy reluctant to give his adversary the advantage, Higgins rushed after the little valet and called, "His Lordship told me to do it, you tiny toad."

While Adam was riding in his coach the short distance to his aunt and uncle's Grosvenor Square town house, Sabrina walked down the main staircase to the foyer and sat on an upholstered bench. Ten minutes earlier, Forbes had taken Winston out to the garden area and would be returning soon.

Sabrina fingered the frog brooch the marquess had given her. Would he notice it? she wondered. As if her thoughts had somehow conjured the man, the marquess stepped into the foyer at that moment.

The first sight of the marquess in almost a month made Sabrina's heartbeat quicken with anticipation. In spite of his unacceptable boldness toward her, Abingdon Manor had seemed so empty without him. She never felt so alive as when they were together, even if they were arguing.

"Thank you, Baxter," Adam said, passing his cloak to the majordomo.

The man inclined his head. "You are welcome, my lord."

Adam turned and saw her, and then crossed the foyer to where she sat near the staircase. He bowed in courtly manner over her hand and gave her a devastating smile that made her feel as if she'd swallowed a butterfly.

"You're wearing the frog brooch," Adam said.

Sabrina smiled, pleased that he'd noticed right away.

"I missed you," he added. "Did you miss me?"

"I told you a month ago that I would miss you as much as my last toothache," she answered with a smile.

"You are still wearing black," Adam observed.

Sabrina lost her smile. "I am still in mourning."

Adam let that remark pass without comment and asked, "Why are you sitting alone in the foyer?"

"I am waiting for Forbes to return with Winston," she told him.

"You brought Forbes and Winston to London?" Adam asked, looking surprised.

"If I left Winston behind, he would surely pine for me," Sabrina said. "Forbes came along, too, so he could visit his cousin, Baxter."

Adam turned around slowly to stare in surprise at his uncle and aunt's majordomo. In response, the man rolled his eyes heavenward in a long-suffering gesture.

"Forbes hails from the unfortunate side of the family," Baxter said. "In the thirty minutes that he has been here, I have recalled why I limited our communication to one letter per year."

Adam gave the man a lopsided smile, but Sabrina was not so amused.

"That isn't very kind of you," she scolded. "He spoke highly of you along our journey."

"I apologize, my lady, and will assuredly make my cousin welcome here," Baxter replied.

"Where is everyone?" Adam asked her.

"Our aunts and my sister went upstairs to rest before tea," Sabrina told him. "Uncle Charles has retreated to his study."

"Shall we go see him?" Adam asked, offering her his hand. "Prince Adolphus visited me today, and I can share the particulars with both of you."

Eager for news, Sabrina needed no second invitation. She rose from her perch on the bench and slipped her arm through his as if it were the most natural thing in the world to do.

When they walked into the study, Uncle Charles

rose from his chair in front of the hearth. The two men shook hands, and Sabrina sat in the vacant chair beside the duke's.

Adam gestured to his uncle to sit down again and then reached into his jacket to produce the document, saying, "Prince Adolphus delivered this to me today." He passed the document of receivership to his uncle, who perused its contents. Sabrina leaned close and read it too.

"Good, Henry's assets are safe now," Uncle Charles said, nodding. "With your business acumen, those assets will surely grow, and you won't need to bother Tess or me for our signatures any time you make investments or expenditures."

"What about my father's burial in hallowed ground?" Sabrina asked.

"The prince is still working on that," Adam answered. "The request goes through Prinny, who, as you may know, is not held in the highest regard by the Church."

"Fiddle the Church," Sabrina exclaimed, making both men smile. "My father did not commit suicide. His body lying at that infernal crossroads is a travesty."

"Princess, I agree with you," Adam replied. "Unless Prince Adolphus can finagle a special dispensation, we must investigate the circumstances surrounding your father's death."

"How will we do that?" she asked.

"In a few days we will sit down and discuss the events of that day," Adam told her. "Until then, I want you to begin writing down everything you can remember. Start with a week or so before his death and stop when Uncle Charles and I arrived in Abingdon. Consider no detail too small. The more you write, the more you will remember.''

''I understand.''

''Shall we go in search of Forbes and Winston?'' he asked. ''I assume they went outside to the garden.''

Sabrina nodded. She turned to the duke and said, ''We'll meet in the drawing room for tea shortly.''

Adam and Sabrina left the study and walked down the corridor to the rear of the town house. He led her down one flight to the lowest level and out the door that opened onto the foggy garden area.

''When January dies, the fog dies with it,'' Adam told her. ''November is the worst month of the year for it.''

''Where does it come from?'' Sabrina asked, unable to see more than a few feet in front of her.

''Coal fires.''

''And what is that horrid smell?'' she asked.

''Horse manure,'' he answered with a smile. ''And don't ask where that comes from.''

''I prefer the pristine countryside where January's sunsets are reflected on the glazed surface of snow,'' Sabrina said, giving him an unamused look. ''In Abingdon, we mark the passing of the seasons through nature, not the density of the fog. Now, where is the dog?''

Adam whistled. Forbes and Winston materialized out of the fog from the far side of the garden. Obviously happy to see the marquess, the wolfhound leaped up, placed his forelegs against Adam's solid chest, and tried to lick his face.

"Sit down," Adam ordered.

Hearing the voice of authority, the dog obeyed instantly.

"Thank you, Forbes. You may return to your duties," Adam said, pulling the pink ribbon off Winston. He turned to Sabrina, whose emerald gaze was fixed on the ribbon. "Boys do not wear ribbons. How demeaning for a wolfhound to endure the indignity of a pink ribbon."

"Winston likes pink ribbons," Sabrina insisted.

Adam cocked a dark brow at her. "And when did he share this preference with you?"

"Don't be absurd," she snapped in irritation. How dare he treat her like a peabrain.

"You, on the other hand, would look most becoming in a pink ribbon," Adam said. A devastatingly wicked smile kissed his lips when he added, "Especially if you wore nothing else."

"How dare you," Sabrina exclaimed, blushing furiously. "You, my lord, are the boldest man I've ever met. No decent gentleman would speak so provocatively to a lady." At that, she showed him her back.

"I apologize for behaving badly," Adam whispered against her ear. "Shall we return inside?"

His warm breath on her neck sent a delicious shiver dancing down her spine. His clean masculine scent of bay assaulted her senses and made her feel weak all over.

Sabrina shook her head and turned to face him, telling his chest, "I have something I wish to discuss before we join the others."

"What is that, Princess?"

Summoning her courage, Sabrina looked up at him. "I do not like breaking mourning," she said. "I don't feel right, even though my father wished it."

"You are suffering from a mild case of nerves," Adam told her, hooking her arm through his and leading her toward the door. "Meeting new people can be frightening. Trust me, Princess, all will be well in the end."

Sabrina let him escort her inside. What had she expected? That he would free her from their betrothal? Send her home to rusticate in Abingdon Manor until she felt ready? That would be a kindness foreign to his authoritarian nature.

"We'll go riding in Hyde Park in the mornings," Adam said as they walked up the stairs to the drawing room. "All the very best people do. Have you ever been in London?"

Sabrina shook her head. "I visited once as a child."

"I'll take you sightseeing," he said. "What would you like to see first? Westminster Abbey? The shops on Bond Street? One of the palaces?"

"The Tower of London," she told him.

"Ah, what a bloodthirsty wench," he teased, making her smile. "The Tower of London it shall be."

They walked into the drawing room in time to see Winston make a mad dash for the food tray. "Winston, sit," Adam called.

Unlike his first night at Abingdon Manor, the wolfhound ignored the command and began gobbling up the cucumber sandwiches. Adam grabbed him by the scruff of the neck and yanked him back, ordering, "Lie down." This time the dog obeyed him.

"Winston has developed a fondness for cucumber sandwiches," Belladonna drawled.

"He even drinks tea," Tess added, making everyone but the marquess smile.

Adam turned to Sabrina and leveled an accusing look on her, saying, "You've spoiled him."

Sabrina didn't know what to say to that. She hadn't really spoiled him, merely lost a bit of control, though she would never admit it to him.

Adam dropped his gaze to her gown. "This is the last time I want to see you in black." He rounded on his aunt and said, "Throw all of their black gowns out."

"That won't be necessary," Sabrina spoke up.

"It is if I say so," he said quietly, raising an eyebrow.

"You do not own Courtney and me," Sabrina told him, ready to do battle. "We will wear whatever—"

"Oh, but I do own you," Adam interrupted her intended tirade. "I hold the receivership rights to the Savage assets."

Sabrina clamped her lips shut.

"That's better."

"Sabrina, dear, look across the drawing room," Aunt Tess said in a poor attempt to change the subject. "What a lovely lacquered screen, don't you think? Charles said it came from the Orient."

Sabrina glanced across the room at the full-length lacquered, handpainted screen. "Yes, quite a lovely piece," she agreed, her irritation apparent in her voice and expression.

Baxter and Forbes chose that moment to walk into the drawing room with trays of more sandwiches and cookies. "See, cousin," Forbes was saying as they crossed the chamber. "I told you the first setting was for the dog."

Baxter looked at the dog with a mixture of fear and disgust. When he started to pour the tea, Adam stopped him.

"We'll serve ourselves," he said.

"As you wish, my lord."

"I've already informed your staff that the coming-out ball will be held here," Adam told his uncle. "My staff is prepared to help."

Uncle Charles nodded. "I knew you'd take care of the arrangements."

"Tess and I did so wish to plan this party," Belladonna said.

"Time was of the essence," Adam told her, softening his voice. "Lady Burke and you have authority over the girls. Nothing is more important than our little debutantes."

"And when is this gala to take place?" Sabrina asked coldly, still smarting over being rebuked.

"The first day of February."

"That's Saturday," Courtney exclaimed.

Sabrina felt a rising tide of panic swelling within her breast. Managing to maintain a calm exterior, she said, "We can't possibly be ready—"

"You can, and you will," Adam cut her words off. "Being introduced into society will be easier during the little season. After Easter, every aristocrat in England will be in residence. This way, by the time the majority of them arrive, you will already possess the experience to handle the great bejeweled horde. I have sent the invitations, and Prince Adolphus is definitely attending.''

''There's your opportunity to ask the prince if he knew your natural parents,'' Uncle Charles said.

''Well, I suppose so.''

''Thank heavens you had the foresight to send London's finest dressmakers to Abingdon,'' Belladonna said to Adam.

''Their wardrobes will be delivered in the morning,'' Tess added.

''Excellent. Now, I regret I am late for an appointment,'' Adam said. He turned unexpectedly to Sabrina and asked, ''Will you walk with me to the foyer?''

''I don't think so,'' Sabrina replied tightly.

''Yes, my lady, you will walk with me to the foyer,'' Adam countered, then added more softly, ''Or would you prefer to argue in front of our relatives? I'm certain a few of the servants are lurking about. They'll tell their friends, who, in turn, will tell their masters. And then—''

''And then the sky will fall or the oceans will swell or the earth will swallow us up,'' Sabrina snapped, surrendering to the inevitable. She rose from the chair and, without waiting for him, crossed the drawing room to the door. Fuming over his highhandedness, she refused to look at him or speak as they descended one flight to the foyer.

Baxter handed the marquess his cloak. With a flick

of his wrist, Adam gestured Baxter and Forbes to withdraw a bit down the corridor.

"Look at me," Adam said to her.

Sabrina stared at his chin.

"A little higher, please," he said, laughter lurking in his voice.

Sabrina lifted her gaze to his and saw him smiling at her.

"Princess, have I ever mentioned that anger becomes you?" he asked.

"From this moment on, I shall endeavor to be pleasant," she replied, and then forced a stiff smile onto her face.

Adam chuckled. "Countess, you are more entertaining than a troupe of Drury Lane players."

"And you are more arrogant than Napoleon," she shot back.

Adam inclined his head, acknowledging her wit. "I'll be bringing my friend, the Duke of Kinross, and his American wife to visit tomorrow," he told her. "I hope that you and Lily will become friends. She's had a difficult time making friends among the ton, though no one has been particularly rude to her."

Sabrina arched a perfectly shaped copper brow at him. "Two outcasts united in their misery?"

"That's not what I meant," Adam said. "I simply believe that you and she will be good companions, as long as you don't hold it against her that I introduced you."

"I would never do that," Sabrina defended herself. "I prefer to judge people on their own merits."

"Unlike your neighbor Lord Briggs."

"What do you mean by that?"

"I must warn you," Adam said, lowering his voice. "A friend told me that the baron is in London and telling people that you and your sister are adopted bastards."

"I don't believe you," Sabrina cried, too angry to wince at the word she'd come to despise. "Edgar would never hurt me in any way."

"Then how would this friend know you are adopted?"

"Perhaps your friend has the Sight," Sabrina suggested. "Please leave me. Your words have given me a headache."

"Countess, you are made of sterner stuff than that," Adam said.

Without warning, he leaned close and drew her against his body. Before she could react, his mouth swooped down and captured hers in an ardent, lingering kiss that stole her breath away.

"I've wanted to do that for a month," Adam whispered against her lips. Then he released her and walked out the door.

Dazed by his ardor, Sabrina raised her fingers to her kiss-bruised lips and stared after him. What would it be like to be kissed that way every night for the next fifty years?

When she regained her composure, Sabrina turned away from the door and crossed the foyer to the staircase. "Forbes! Baxter!" she shouted.

The two men came running.

"Baxter, hurry to the kitchen," Sabrina ordered. "Tell the cook I'll need flour, eggs, baking soda—"

"Flour, eggs, baking soda?" Baxter echoed in shock.

"That's what I said. Is your hearing impaired?" she snapped. "Forbes, tell him what I'll need directly after supper is finished."

"Cousin, my lady feels the need to cook," Forbes said, already turning away to do her bidding.

"The countess is cooking?" Baxter sounded even more shocked.

"No, I'm baking tonight."

"Baking?" Baxter echoed.

"I'm baking something special for the marquess."

"Thick gingerbread, my lady?" Forbes asked, a knowing smile appearing on his face.

"No," Sabrina answered, turning to march up the stairs. "Hemlock pie."

Chapter 7

Winston growled.

Alone in the drawing room, Sabrina shifted her gaze from her needlework to the wolfhound. The growling dog, alert to danger, had lifted his head and was staring toward the doorway.

Sabrina whirled around to see no one, but a second later Baxter walked into the room. "Hush, Winston," she ordered as he continued growling low in his throat. "You know Baxter."

"My lady, Lord Briggs has arrived for a visit," Baxter announced. "I tried to tell him you weren't—" Before he could finish, Edgar brushed past him and walked across the drawing room toward her.

"Edgar, what are you doing here?" Sabrina asked, rising from the couch.

"I've come to visit my dearest friend," the baron answered, giving her an easy smile.

Winston growled again and Lord Briggs stopped short ten paces from her.

"Winston, lie down," Sabrina ordered, imitating the marquess's stern tone of voice.

The wolfhound obeyed, but he kept his dark eyes fixed on the baron. His small ears cocked into alertness.

"I've missed you," Edgar said, closing the distance between them and taking her hands in his. He smiled warmly at her and let his gaze drift downward to her outfit.

Sabrina thought she looked pretty, in spite of her misgivings about breaking mourning. Her short-sleeved gown had been fashioned in white silk with forest-green polka dots. Its bodice and overskirt were solid forest-green velvet. A bow and long streamers of forest green adorned her right shoulder, and she wore matching velvet slippers on her feet.

"You're not wearing black," Edgar said, his hazel gaze returning to hers.

His remark surprised her. "What excellent eyesight you have," she teased him.

"But you are in mourning," he reminded her.

Sabrina shrugged. "The marquess has forbidden Courtney and me to wear black during the season."

"By what right does he—?"

"The marquess holds the receivership rights to the Savage assets," she interrupted. "Please, sit down and enjoy a pleasant visit with me."

Sabrina sat down on the couch again. Instead of sitting in the adjacent chair as propriety demanded, Edgar sat beside her, which earned him a warning growl from Winston.

"That dog is a menace," Edgar said.

"Winston is only being protective of me," Sabrina replied. "Why, he's as gentle as a lamb. A growling dog never bites, you know."

"No, sweetheart, a barking dog never bites," Edgar corrected her. He glanced around the drawing room at the richly appointed chamber and then asked, "Where is everyone?"

"Uncle Charles moved in with Adam for propriety's sake," Sabrina told him. "Lady Belladonna has taken Aunt Tess and Courtney to visit friends."

"I see," he said. "What kept you at home today?"

Sabrina felt reluctant to tell him that Adam and his friends were planning to visit. Instead, she pointed to the table and said, "I was trying my hand at needlework and writing."

"Writing?" Edgar echoed, a surprised smile appearing on his face. "What are you writing?"

"Adam—I mean, the marquess—has promised to help me clear my father's reputation," Sabrina answered. "He suggested that I write down everything I can remember about the day my father died and leave no detail out."

Edgar lost his smile. "Am I mentioned in your writing?"

Sabrina shook her head. "I haven't reached that part yet."

"Sweetheart, your father committed suicide," Edgar said in a gentle voice, taking her hand in his. "No amount of writing will change that fact."

"My father did *not* commit suicide." Sabrina yanked her hand out of his and rose from the couch.

She stood in front of the hearth and stared for several long moments at the hypnotic flames.

"I am sorry for upsetting you," Edgar said. "That was never my intention."

Sabrina turned around and looked at him. Suddenly, Edgar Briggs didn't seem so attractive anymore. No longer was he the older boy whom she had idolized as a child. He had become . . . She didn't know what he had become. She only knew that, when compared with the marquess, Edgar lacked some indefinable quality.

"Sabrina?"

"I accept your apology," she answered, managing a smile for him.

Edgar stood then and lifted her hand to his lips, saying, "Thank you, sweetheart."

His lips on her hand irritated her. The moment for a gallant gesture had occurred the night of her father's funeral.

"I forgive you your unfounded belief," Sabrina said, disengaging her hand from his grasp. "I shan't forget it, though."

"Please, let me try to make it up to you," Edgar said, his smile ingratiating.

Sabrina arched a copper brow at him. "How?"

"I want to take you to Hyde Park where all of the Quality rides," Edgar told her. "Then we'll attend the opera, the ballet, and—"

"That isn't possible," Sabrina said, once again wishing that she'd refused his offer of marriage instead of relying on her father. If she had, she wouldn't be in such an uncomfortable position now.

A confused expression appeared on his face. "But why?" he asked.

"The reason Courtney and I are making our coming-outs is to meet suitable matrimonial prospects," Sabrina told him.

"I love you, Sabrina," Edgar said passionately, reaching for her hand again. "I have always loved you. Say that you'll marry me."

"I cannot marry you," Sabrina said, disengaging her hand again. "Before his death, my father refused your suit. Since then, I have learned his reason; I am already betrothed to the marquess."

"What?" Edgar exclaimed, clutching her forearm.

Winston's growling drew their attention. The wolfhound was on his feet, his fangs bared and his hackles raised in preparation to attack.

"Winston, sit," Sabrina ordered.

The wolfhound remained statue-still and continued growling.

"Slowly release my arm and step back a couple of paces," Sabrina ordered Edgar. When he'd done so, she commanded, "Winston, sit."

This time the wolfhound obeyed, but he remained at alert attention, his dark gaze fixed on the baron.

A feeling of guilt swept through Sabrina. She'd never harbored a grudge against anyone in her life, and keeping one against her oldest friend was a terrible thing. She supposed that his believing her father had committed suicide was logical, but his lack of faith in her father disappointed her.

"My father and the duke had been friends since their days at Eton," Sabrina explained, deciding that her oldest friend deserved to know the truth. "When I was an infant, my father betrothed me to the marquess. To his credit, Adam has offered me a way out of the marriage."

"What is that?" Edgar asked coldly.

"If I meet a suitable gentleman during the season, I will be free to marry him," Sabrina said.

Edgar brightened visibly.

"However, Adam does not consider you a suitable prospect," Sabrina added, effectively wiping the smile off his face. "I'm sorry, but I agree with him on that point."

"I see that a countess is too good for a mere baron," Edgar said curtly, his face mottling with anger.

"Your thinking is wrong," Sabrina replied, his insinuation angering her as well. "I could never marry a man who made the rounds of London and spread the word that Courtney and I are adopted bastards."

"I never did such a thing," Edgar insisted. "Who told you that lie, the marquess?"

Sabrina refused to reply.

"Did you know that your precious marquess is practically wed to another woman?" Edgar continued. "Alexis Carstairs, the Countess of Rothbury, has been his mistress for more than a year. Even as we speak, wagers are being made in White's Betting Book as to when they'll announce their wedding plans."

Sabrina felt as if she'd been kicked in the stomach. She paled, his hurtful words and the virulence of his dislike for the marquess making her weak. One of her hands flew to her chest as if to protect herself. She stepped back several paces and then turned to sit on the couch.

"How dare you turn away from me," Edgar said, his voice raised. He reached out to seize her wrist, but the wolfhound leaped to her defense.

Snarling, Winston lunged at the baron. He caught one of his trouser legs and pulled.

When the baron raised his fist to strike the dog, Sabrina sprang into action. She deflected the blow with her arm and tried to leap between them.

"Winston, sit," the marquess ordered from the doorway.

Releasing the baron's trousers from his powerful grip, the wolfhound sat but continued growling low in his throat. Dropping to her knees, Sabrina wrapped her arms around the dog's neck as much to protect him as to hold him back.

"Sweetheart, I'm sorry," Edgar apologized, but refrained from helping her off the carpet. "I didn't mean to strike you, only to protect myself."

Sabrina nodded in understanding but remained silent. She didn't trust herself to speak lest she tell her oldest friend in no uncertain terms what she thought of him at that moment.

"What is going on here?" Adam demanded, marching across the drawing room toward them.

"That dog attacked me and should be put down," Edgar said.

"Put down for protecting me?" Sabrina cried. "I think not."

"Winston was protecting you?" Adam echoed. He

turned a deadly gaze on the baron and stepped closer, asking, "What were you doing to her?"

"Sabrina and I were arguing when she paled as if faint," Edgar explained. "When I reached out to help her, this monster attacked me."

Sabrina snapped her gaze to the baron. He was lying, albeit to protect himself from the marquess's wrath, but that lie had slipped from his lips as if they'd been greased.

A man who lies once will lie many times, Sabrina thought. How many of his past lies had she believed without question? How could she trust a friend who lied with such ease?

Adam looked from the baron to Sabrina. Unwilling to cause anymore trouble, she dropped her gaze to the dog.

"Well, Lord Briggs, I'm certain Sabrina appreciates an old friend stopping by for a visit," Adam said in a not so subtle hint for the man to leave. "Will we be seeing you on Saturday?"

Instead of replying, Edgar turned to Sabrina and said, "I apologize for the misunderstanding and will, of course, be attending your coming-out. If you need me, I am staying at my sister's in Bedford Square." At that, he walked across the drawing room and disappeared out the door.

"Shame on you," Adam scolded the dog, reaching out to pat his head. "What kind of hound mistakes a weasel for a wolf?"

Winston whined as if he understood.

Sabrina felt confused. She could have sworn that the marquess disliked Edgar.

"Why did you invite him to my coming-out?" she asked.

"I thought you and Courtney would be glad that an old friend from Abingdon was there," Adam told her. He glanced toward the empty doorway and added, "I like Edgar Briggs as much as I trust him, which is not at all."

"Edgar has been behaving badly since the day of my father's death," Sabrina said. "Your appearance in Abingdon only made matters worse. I don't much like him anymore either."

"Shall I univite him?" Adam interrupted.

Sabrina shook her head.

"You make a fetching picture in your new gown," Adam said, reaching out to help her off the floor. "Isn't this better than draping yourself in dreary black?"

Baxter walked into the drawing room before she could reply. Keeping a wary gaze fixed on the wolfhound, the majordomo announced, "The Duke and Duchess of Kinross have arrived."

"Show them in," Adam said.

When the majordomo left, Sabrina took a moment to smooth her gown. She peeked at the marquess, who was watching her.

"Don't trouble yourself about your appearance," Adam said. "Improving upon perfection is an impossible task."

Sabrina blushed at his outrageous compliment. She dropped her gaze to Winston and asked, "Are they afraid of dogs?"

"We love dogs and various other creatures," a man's voice said, drawing her attention.

James Armstrong, the Duke of Kinross, appeared as tall and well built as the marquess. His dark hair matched Adam's, but his eyes were blacker than a moonless midnight.

The Duchess of Kinross was petite and sported thick ebony hair, but her blue eyes rivaled the marquess's for brilliance. Exquisitely lovely, she'd been blessed with a warm, infectious smile.

"James and Lily, may I present Sabrina Savage, the Countess of Abingdon," Adam made the introductions. "Sabrina, these are my friends the Duke and Duchess of Kinross."

"Your Graces, I am honored to make your acquaintance," Sabrina said, and then curtsied.

"Call me Lily," the duchess said. "I only married the title."

"Call me Jamie," the duke said. "Please, no curtseying to me. It makes me feel older than my twenty-five years. Besides"—he glanced at his wife and winked—"I didn't earn the title, merely inherited it."

"I wouldn't wish to make you feel old," Sabrina said with a smile, and relaxed.

"Is this the wolfhound you found in Oxford?" Lily asked, her gaze on the dog.

"Yes, this is Winston." Sabrina blushed to realize the marquess had spoken of her to his friends.

Lily promptly removed her gloves and offered the wolfhound her hand. Winston sniffed her palm and then licked it.

"You adorable puppy," Lily said, patting him.

"My wife loves all sorts of creatures," Jamie told Sabrina.

Lily smiled at her husband as if his remark held a secret meaning for her. "A ribbon would dress Winston up prettily, don't you think?" she asked.

Sabrina rounded on Adam and gave him a look that said *I told you so*.

"Let's sit down in front of the hearth," Adam suggested.

Sabrina and Lily sat on the couch. Adam and James occupied the chairs opposite them. Sabrina had the sudden feeling that the duke and duchess knew the secret of her betrothal. Or perhaps sitting there together made her feel that Adam and she were the two halves of one couple.

"When we left the house, Sarah was playing with the doll you gave her," Lily said to Adam. "Chewing on it, as I recall."

"Sabrina deserves the credit for choosing the cloth doll," Adam replied.

"On behalf of my daughter, I thank you," Lily said, turning to her.

"How old is she?" Sabrina asked.

The topic of her daughter brought a smile to the duchess's lips. "Sarah is just a year old."

"Walk with me to the study," Adam said to Jamie. "I promised to retrieve some papers for my uncle."

Jamie immediately rose from his chair, saying, "If you ladies will excuse us, we'll return shortly."

Without another word, the two friends left them alone in the drawing room. Sabrina and Lily looked at each other uncomfortably before their gazes skittered away.

Sabrina worried about what topic would be appropriate to discuss with the beautiful American duchess. And then it struck her. The weather was always suitable. No danger there.

"We've been enjoying good weather, don't you think?" Sabrina said stiffly.

"Yes, the weather has held marvelously well," Lily replied, glancing sidelong at her. Then she drawled, "If a person likes yellow fog, that is."

Sabrina smiled. "Actually, I prefer the country to city life."

"No fog?"

"None whatsoever."

The two women smiled at each other.

"You do realize the gentlemen left us alone on purpose," Lily said. "My husband wants us to become friends."

"We needn't be friends if you'd rather not," Sabrina said.

"London society hasn't exactly welcomed me with open arms," Lily admitted. "Although no one has dared to be rude, I'm certain they consider me an American upstart. I thought you might disapprove of me too."

"I'm sorry for your bad experience," Sabrina replied.

"Don't be sorry," Lily said, reaching for the needlework on the table. "The fault doesn't lie with you."

Sabrina felt an embarrassed blush slowly heating her cheeks when the duchess opened the cloth to examine the crooked stitches. Embroidery was one feminine pastime she had never mastered. In fact, she hadn't cared a fig about sewing until this very moment when the duchess was inspecting her stitches.

"What remarkable needlework," Lily commented, glancing at her.

"Remarkably horrible."

"You sew much better than I do."

"Do I?" Sabrina just knew the American was patronizing her.

Lily opened her reticule and pulled out a handkerchief. "Look at this," she said, offering it to her. "Don't worry; it's clean."

That remark brought a smile to Sabrina's face. She opened the handkerchief and laid it flat on her lap. In the next instant, Sabrina burst out laughing. The duchess had spoken truthfully; her stitches were even more crooked than her own.

"Why, Winston could do a better job," Sabrina said, relief loosening her tongue.

Lily laughed. "I have no doubt of that."

"I meant no insult," Sabrina said.

"None taken," Lily told her. "Your embroidery is horrid too until compared with mine."

Forbes and Baxter walked into the drawing room. Each carried a silver tray; one held a Worcester tea and coffee service and the other a platter of almond cake slices.

"Down, Winston," Sabrina ordered when the dog stood to gobble the cake.

The wolfhound lay down again but kept his gaze

fixed on the food. Streams of drool began to slide from the corners of his mouth.

Sabrina lifted two pieces of cake off the platter, broke them up onto a serving dish, and set it down in front of the dog. Winston leaned his head over the dish and began eating.

"Surrendering to the inevitable is sometimes easier," Sabrina said. "I baked last night, and Winston simply adores my—"

"You bake?" Lily asked in obvious surprise. "Did you bake this?"

Sabrina nodded.

"Delicious," Lily exclaimed after tasting the almond cake. "I didn't realize that the English aristocracy cooked and baked."

"Cooking and baking relax me," Sabrina told her. "I do it whenever I'm upset or nervous."

Lily grinned. "Oh, I do believe we'll be great friends after all," she said.

"Do you bake when you're upset?" Sabrina asked.

"No, I eat."

Sabrina burst out laughing.

"I'm so glad you're not snobby like those other ladies I've met," the duchess said, reaching out to touch her arm.

"I'm relieved to have found you," Sabrina agreed. "Do you have any hobbies? I mean, in addition to embroidery."

"I'm learning the pianoforte," Lily told her. "Baby Sarah shrieks with displeasure whenever I practice, so I don't think I'm ready for a recital."

Sabrina smiled at the other woman's honesty.

"I love animals, read voraciously, and am acquiring a taste for shopping." Lily paused for a moment and, with a smile, added, "You could say that my love for reading brought James and me together."

"His Grace has an interest in reading, too?"

"His Grace had a profound interest in my choice of reading material," Lily answered.

"What was it?" Sabrina asked.

"Secret codes, maps, and messages."

Sabrina felt confused. "I don't understand."

"I have been blessed with the ability to look only once at a page of writing and repeat what it says without changing a word," Lily told her. "During the recent conflict between our countries, I aided the American cause by memorizing British codes or giving detailed descriptions of supposed spies. James felt certain that this gift of mine had secured his brother's capture and death as a spy. He abducted me and dragged me to England to sit out the rest of the war. We fell in love and married."

"How wildly romantic and adventurous," Sabrina exclaimed. "Weren't you frightened?"

"I was angry," Lily answered. "And, as I recall, I wasn't feeling particularly romantic at the time. Adventures aren't as exciting as you might think."

"May I ask you a question?" Sabrina said, uncertain if she was doing the right thing by speaking up.

Lily nodded.

"This morning an old friend from Abingdon stopped by and told me that Adam has a mistress named Alexis Carstairs. Do you know her?"

"That doesn't sound like a friend to me," Lily said.

"You haven't answered my question," Sabrina said.

"Alexis Carstairs is the very beautiful and very wealthy widow of the late Earl of Rothbury, a man old enough to be her grandfather," Lily said, lowering her voice. "Shallow, arrogant, and conniving are the words I'd use to describe her. She's been angling after Adam since I've known him, even before her husband died."

"Is she . . ." Sabrina hesitated for a moment but then continued, asking, "Is she really his mistress?"

The other woman's cheeks turned pink. "I don't know, but I could ask my husband if you wish."

"That won't be necessary," Sabrina said, shaking her head. "I apologize for making you uncomfortable."

Lily patted her hand. "Adam has as much integrity as my husband. I'm certain he's never succumbed to that woman's wiles."

Speaking so intimately about the marquess made Sabrina feel uncomfortable, but she thought the duchess might know something about Adam's background.

"The marquess has told me that he hails from the south of France," Sabrina said. "I know his father died when Adam was ten. It was then he came to England for his education. While he was here, his mother and his brother died."

"Yes, that's true," Lily said with a nod.

"Do you know anything else about him?" Sabrina asked.

Lily gave her a puzzled look and answered, "Why don't you ask Adam?"

"He evades almost all of my questions," Sabrina

replied. "I've had the feeling that he's hiding something from me and thought that you—"

Lily burst out laughing. "I'm sorry, but you make him seem so nefarious. I'm positive the man is merely being perverse to annoy you. However, my husband knows absolutely everything about the marquess. I could ask him some questions for you, if you'd like."

Sabrina shook her head. "I'm afraid he'd tell Adam that I'd been prying. I'll probably learn more in time." Changing the subject, she said, "Tell me about America."

"America is almost paradise," Lily said.

Sabrina smiled. "You remain loyal to your native country."

"I hope you aren't overly patriotic," Lily said, "for I don't want my pet to offend you in any way when you come to visit."

"What kind of pet do you have?"

"An albino pig," Lily answered. "When he was a mere piglet, I saved him and his mother from becoming dinner on board my husband's ship."

"What does a pig have to do with patriotism?" Sabrina asked, puzzled.

"I named him Prinny in honor of the Prince Regent."

Sabrina burst out laughing, and Lily joined her. When Winston sat up and stole a piece of the almond cake off the table, they only laughed harder. Adam and Jamie found them like that when they walked into the drawing room a moment later.

"You know the dog cannot be trusted near food," Adam said to Sabrina.

"Let it go," Jamie said, obviously pleased that his wife had apparently found a friend. "Lily and I must be leaving."

Lily rose from the couch. "You will come to tea one afternoon?" she asked.

"I'd like that very much," Sabrina answered, rising from the couch when the other woman did. "Give Prinny my best regards."

As soon as the duke and duchess disappeared out the door, Adam turned to her and gave her a devastating smile. "I'm pleased that you and Lily like each other."

"She's not what I expected," Sabrina said.

His expression on her was warm. "And what did you expect?"

Sabrina thought of Alexis Carstairs. "I expected shallow, arrogant, and conniving."

"You will meet plenty of those types among the ton," Adam told her, and then changed the subject. "Have you begun your journal writing?"

"Yes, I was writing when Edgar arrived," Sabrina replied.

"Let's sit down and discuss what you've written," he suggested.

Sabrina followed Adam to the hearth. When Adam sat down on the couch, she sat in the chair opposite him. Lifting the journal off the table, she flipped through its pages to refresh her memory.

"I haven't progressed to the actual day," Sabrina said, looking up at him. *Oh, Lord,* she thought, realizing just how perfectly blue his eyes were.

Adam smiled as if he could read her thoughts. "Tell

me what you've written," he said in a husky and intimate tone of voice.

"I began a week before my father's death," Sabrina began, tearing her gaze away from his. "That was the day Edgar asked for my father's permission to marry me if I'd have him."

Adam leaned back on the couch and stretched his left arm out across the top of it. His casual gesture caught her attention, and she wondered what life would be like married to the marquess and sitting together in front of the hearth each night.

"So, tell me what happened."

Sabrina gave herself a mental shake and focused on him. "As I said, Edgar asked for my hand in marriage, but my father refused."

"Were you there?" he asked.

Sabrina nodded.

"What was the baron's reaction to that?" Adam asked.

"He seemed surprised," Sabrina answered, gazing off into space, conjuring the scene in her mind's eye. "Edgar tried to reason with him by saying that our lands would be joined after his death, which would be a great inheritance to any son we produced. My father told him that I was never meant for him, which definitely made Edgar angry. He glanced in my direction and calmed down enough to apologize to my father for behaving badly."

"Did the baron visit you anytime after your father refused his suit?" Adam asked.

"Edgar visited me several times and insisted that my father would change his mind," Sabrina answered.

"He would wait a week or two and then ask my father again."

"To your knowledge, did the baron ever threaten your father?"

"You cannot mean that Edgar had anything to do with my father's death."

"I am not implying any such thing," Adam assured her with a smile. "I merely want to know all of the facts."

Forbes and Higgins chose that moment to walk into the drawing room. Higgins served them a fresh pot of tea. Forbes carried a silver tray bearing cucumber sandwiches and slices of fruit pie.

Winston lifted his head in the air and sniffed. Aware that food had arrived, he sat up and stared at the contents of the tray.

"Lemon pie for my lady," Forbes said, passing her a dish. "And for my lord, hemlock pie."

Sabrina burst out laughing. Forbes winked at her.

"What is the joke?" Adam asked.

"It's a private matter," Sabrina said, setting her plate on the table.

"Very well, Princess. Keep your secrets," Adam said as the two majordomos left the room. "Winston, lie down."

The wolfhound refused to budge except to inch closer to the platter.

"The food is tormenting him," Sabrina said.

"Winston must learn not to touch food meant for people," Adam replied, and rose from the couch. Gently but firmly, he forced the wolfhound to lie down.

Then he looked at Sabrina and asked, "My lady, may I have this dance?"

"What?"

"Dance with me while we train him," Adam said.

"I know how to waltz, but there's no music," Sabrina protested.

"Come, Princess," Adam said, holding out his hand to her. "Trust me."

Sabrina was unable to resist his devastating smile. Rising from the couch, she walked into his waiting arms as if she belonged there.

"Each time we dance past the table, I'll order Winston to lie down if he is standing," Adam told her. "That way he'll learn not to touch food even if no one is watching him."

Sabrina smiled as Adam began humming a waltz and leading her in a sweeping circle around the drawing room. He danced with the grace and ease of a man who had waltzed a thousand times.

"You waltz divinely," Sabrina complimented him.

"And so do you," Adam returned the compliment. "Who taught you how to dance?"

"Who taught you?" Sabrina countered.

"I asked first," he said.

"I asked second," she replied, echoing the coversation they'd had on their coach ride to Oxford.

"Eton required their students to learn social graces like dancing," Adam said with a smile. "Jamie Armstrong was my dancing partner."

Sabrina burst out laughing. "When Aunt Tess came to live with us after Mother died, she taught Courtney and me several dances," she told him. "Later on my father hired a dancing master to complete our dancing education.''

"Were you and Courtney dancing partners?" he asked.

"No, Edgar partnered both of us," she answered.

Adam lost his smile. "I don't approve of your choice of partners."

"And I don't approve of yours," Sabrina countered with a jaunty smile.

Adam chuckled. "You needn't be jealous of my feelings for Jamie Armstrong."

"And you needn't be jealous of my feelings for Edgar Briggs," Sabrina said without thinking.

"My lady, you've set my mind at ease." Adam tightened his hold on her and whirled her to the far end of the drawing room.

The constant swirling motion combined with the man to intoxicate her senses. His piercing blue gaze mesmerized Sabrina. She was unable to resist when he stopped dancing and gently drew her into his embrace.

Adam inched his handsome face closer to capture her lips with his own. Enchanted with the man, Sabrina made no move to pull away. She closed her eyes at the very last moment.

Their lips touched, sending a jolt of delicious sensation coursing through her. His mouth felt warm and gently insistent.

Surrendering to his kiss, Sabrina sagged against his hard, unyielding body. His strong arms kept her imprisoned within his embrace, and she reveled in these new and exciting sensations.

And then the kiss was over as unexpectedly as it had

begun. Sabrina opened her eyes and stared in a dreamy daze at him.

"I didn't mean to force you into a kiss," Adam apologized, wearing an unrepentent smile.

"You didn't force me," Sabrina said, a rosy blush staining her cheeks. Embarrassed now, she flicked a quick glance toward the other side of the drawing room and said, "Look."

Adam turned around. Winston sat beside the table and licked his lips. An empty platter lay on the table in front of the wolfhound.

"Winston may be beyond redemption," Adam said.

"You should be leaving," Sabrina said. "Staying here while the others are out could be misconstrued."

Adam nodded. "Be ready at ten tomorrow morning. I'm taking you on the tour of the Tower. Afterward, we'll promenade down Bond Street and window shop. Courtney and our aunts, of course, are invited to accompany us."

Adam leaned close to plant a chaste kiss on her cheek. And then he was gone.

Adam St. Aubyn was too dangerously handsome, Sabrina thought, staring at the empty doorway. She especially liked his smile. His attitude was poor, though. His authoritarian nature was a gigantic flaw. She hoped his overcoming it wouldn't prove insurmountable.

Sabrina thought of Alexis Carstairs, for the moment a name without a face. Lily had insisted that Adam possessed an abundance of integrity. No decent gentleman would ever consider sharing a physical intimacy with a woman who wasn't his wife. No, that simply wasn't done.

Chapter 8

"Make love to me."

Sitting alone in his private box at the opera, Adam recognized the sultry voice. He had to give his former mistress credit; she was persistent, if nothing else. She'd known he always attended the opera alone to think. What she didn't know was that most operas had a theme he could easily relate to: namely, the loss of a loved one.

Adam turned his head to stare through the semidarkness at her perfect profile. And then he felt her hand caress his thigh.

"You want to make love here?" Adam asked, leaning close to whisper in her ear.

"Actually, I'd prefer the satin sheets on my bed," Alexis replied, giving him a feline smile.

Adam dropped his gaze to her daring display of cleavage. He remembered how silken those perfect globes of flesh were.

"You know I always attend the opera alone," Adam said, leaning close again. "I dislike being bothered here."

"You left in such a hurry the other day," Alexis said, her hand on his thigh moving upward slowly. "I never said a proper goodbye."

Adam removed her hand from his thigh and placed it on her own lap. "I don't appreciate being trapped into marriage."

"I had no idea those ladies would be calling on me," Alexis defended herself, giving him an innocent look. "Don't you trust me, darling?"

"I'll trust you on the day there's a snowball fight in hell."

"You can't really be interested in that little country mouse from Abingdon?" Alexis asked.

"That little country mouse is the Countess of Abingdon," Adam replied without answering her question.

"She's also an adopted bastard."

"If you make trouble for Sabrina or her sister, I will ruin you financially," Adam threatened in a harsh whisper.

"I have no intention of making trouble for her," Alexis replied. "In fact, I hope she's a huge success and pursued by every gentleman who sees her."

"That's unusually kind of you," Adam said. "Now, return to your own seat before intermission."

"Promise me you'll stop by my house later," Alexis said.

At that point Adam would have agreed to almost anything to get her out of his box before intermission.

He didn't want anyone from *The Times* reporting on his public appearance with Alexis Carstairs.

Adam inclined his head. "Very well, I'll stop by later."

Alexis smiled with satisfaction. "What time, darling?"

"I don't know," Adam answered. "If you press me, I won't come at all."

Alexis planted a kiss on his cheek and whispered, "I'll see you later." She slipped out of his opera box as silently as she had entered.

Alone again, Adam relaxed back in his chair, but the soothing calmness of the opera had disappeared with Alexis's intrusion on his privacy. He fixed his gaze on the world-renowned diva, so famous she needed only one name. A shade above forty, Madame Esmeralda still sang with the strength and vigor of her youth and carried the audience to wherever she wanted them to go.

Adam stared hard at the soprano. There was something vaguely familiar about her. And then he knew. The diva reminded him of Sabrina. He shrugged that absurd notion away. The woman resembled Sabrina because both of them had hair the color of molten fire. Any similarity ended there. The curtain closed to thunderous applause as intermission began.

Adam decided he'd had enough of the opera for one night. He stood to leave but noticed the crowd of admirers in Alexis's opera box across the theatre. Among the small crowd stood Lord Edgar Briggs. Mulling that over, Adam left the theatre.

"St. James's Street," he called to his drivers.

Adam climbed into his coach and leaned back against the leather seat. An uneasy feeling settled in the pit of his stomach. Troubling possibilities had surfaced this night. What was Edgar Briggs's motive in paying court to Alexis? Did he intend to whisper more gossip about Sabrina into her ear? Or was it the other way around? Was Alexis supplying Briggs with information on him?

Adam knew one thing for certain. He was not going to visit Alexis Carstairs that night or any other night.

Dressed almost completely in black like Lucifer himself, Adam walked into White's Gentlemen's Club. He waved at Jamie Armstrong and gestured that he'd join him in a moment.

Aware that most gazes were fixed on him, Adam marched across the room toward the infamous betting book. Slowly, he turned each page and read the wagers concerning his forthcoming offer of marriage to Alexis Carstairs. His gender's lack of faith in one of their own appalled him.

Finally, Adam lifted the quill and wrote his own wager. The gentlemen who had betted against him were destined to lose. He set the quill down and crossed the chamber to sit with Jamie Armstrong.

"You certainly know how to draw a crowd," Jamie said, inclining his head toward the betting book.

Adam followed his friend's gaze and smiled. Several men had descended on the book and were inspecting what he'd written. Their numbers grew with each passing second.

"I thought you were going to the opera tonight," Jamie said.

"I did go," Adam told him. "Alexis decided to slip into my box."

"Are you certain you don't want to change that bet you just made?" Jamie asked.

Adam grinned.

"Good evening, Your Grace," a voice beside their table said to Jamie. Then, "Lord Stonehurst, may I speak with you?"

Adam looked up at Dudley Egremont, Viscount Dorchester. He suspected the evening was about to take a turn for the better.

"Sit down, Dorchester," Adam invited him.

Twenty-year-old Dudley Egremont sat down and immediately apologized, saying, "I'm sorry to intrude upon your evening, but I happened to see you and did not want to miss this opportunity."

"What's on your mind, Dorchester?"

Dudley smiled nervously. "I met Mistress Courtney Savage at my aunt's house this afternoon and would like your permission to call upon her."

Adam stared at the younger man, making him squirm. "Why are you asking for my permission?" he asked finally.

"I understand that you hold the receivership rights to the Savage assets," Dudley replied. "I assumed you were Courtney's guardian."

"Courtney hasn't made her coming-out yet," Adam said curtly, without bothering to correct the younger man's mistaken assumption.

"I am willing to wait until her coming-out," Dudley said.

Adam cocked a dark brow at him. "Do you think the lady will welcome your attentions?"

"She seemed to like me very well," Dudley answered. "Though, I cannot guess what will happen once the other bachelors meet her."

Adam lifted his brandy snifter to toast the younger man, saying, "Here's to your success with my ward."

"Thank you, my lord," Dudley said, rising from his chair. "You won't regret giving me your approval."

"I haven't given you my permission to marry the girl, merely to call upon her."

"I understand, my lord," Dudley said, and backed away from the table. "Good evening to both of you."

"You wanted Egremont and Courtney to meet," Jamie said, watching the viscount walk away. "How fortuitous that she was visiting his aunt."

"Fortuitous, my arse," Adam said with a smile. "Aunt Belladonna loves matchmaking intrigues and was only too eager to bring them together."

"Why were you being so difficult with him?" Jamie asked.

"A man values most what is difficult to win," Adam answered.

Jamie smiled and then rose from his chair. "I'm going home to my wife."

Adam stood when Jamie did. "I'm going home too," he said. "I promised Sabrina a tour of the Tower in the morning."

The two friends headed for the door, located on one side of the bay windows. When they stepped outside the club, thick yellow fog greeted them like an old friend. The street seemed eerie with only the glow from the gaslights.

Suddenly, a lone horseman galloped down St. James's Street. When the dark figure came abreast of them and halted his horse, he raised a pistol and fired at them. In an instant, he'd reined his horse away and galloped down the street.

Adam and Jamie dove behind one of the carriages. They heard the alarmed shouts of their coachmen as they gave chase and the sounds of the retreating horse. Several men from inside White's came running out.

Adam stood first and offered his hand to his friend. Jamie accepted it.

"Who wants you dead?" Adam asked him.

Jamie grinned. "I was about to ask you the same question."

"Are you injured?" Dudley Egremont asked, obviously worried.

Adam shook his head. "Both of us are well."

"Who do you think it was?" one of the spectators asked.

"I didn't see his face," Adam answered.

"The man was wearing a mask," Jamie spoke up. When Adam turned to him in surprise, he shrugged his shoulders and smiled, saying, "I've learned never to take my eyes off an enemy, no matter what. While we were diving behind the coach, my gaze was on him."

"Is there anything we can do?" a second spectator asked.

Adam shook his head. "Please, gentlemen, go inside and continue your evening. We'll be fine. I see our coachmen returning, unfortunately without the culprit.''

Still talking excitedly with one another, the wealthy patrons of White's Gentlemen's Club returned to their evening's pursuits. Only Dudley Egremont lingered there.

"Are you certain you're not injured?" the young viscount asked, using his handkerchief to brush the dirt from Adam's cloak.

"Dorchester, unless you are applying for the position of valet, go inside with the others," Adam ordered.

Egremont instantly dropped his hands to his sides. "You're certain—?"

"You are beginning to annoy me," Adam warned. "I would hate to revoke my permission for you to call upon Courtney."

"I bid both of you a good night," the viscount said, and then hurried inside the club.

"Someone wants you dead," Jamie said when they were alone.

"You're the man who snatched an American girl and forced her to England," Adam shot back.

"Her father forgave me for that," Jamie replied. "On the other hand, you have paupered more than a few businessmen, and then there's the possibility of—"

"Do not even speak the words," Adam interrupted.

Jamie nodded in understanding.

"The man disappeared down an alley," Abdul said when he reached Adam and Jamie.

Sagi nodded. "The coach was too big to follow and much too slow to overtake the horse."

"Now that we've been forewarned, we'll keep our eyes open and catch the scoundrel the next time he tries something," added Jamie's coachman.

"Take care of yourself," Jamie said, shaking his friend's hand. "Please, let those two giants do their jobs." He turned to his own coachman and said, "Let's go home, Duncan."

"Forgive us, my prince, for failing to protect you," Abdul said as soon as Jamie walked away.

"We will not fail you again," Sagi promised.

"You could not have foreseen this after all of these years," Adam said, absolving them of any wrongdoing. "Visibility is poor tonight, or you would have reacted sooner." He hesitated and then asked, "Do you think the assassin was sent from the East?"

"Your mother knows all and would have sent a warning," Sagi answered.

"Besides, an Eastern assassin would never have missed his target," Abdul agreed.

"That makes me feel so much better," Adam said dryly.

"Perhaps the bullet was meant for the Duke of Kinross," Sagi said.

"The bullet was meant for me," Adam said resignedly, before climbing into the coach. "Nobody can ever know all. I will send a message to my mother in the morning. Take me home by way of Grosvenor Square."

The ride to Grosvenor Square took less than fifteen minutes. Adam tapped on the roof of the carriage when they came abreast of his uncle's town house, and the coach halted.

"I'm not getting out," Adam said when Abdul opened the door.

Adam stared through the thick fog at his uncle's darkened town house. Sabrina was probably sleeping. What was she dreaming about?

He couldn't seem to get enough of her. In spite of her few eccentricities, Sabrina Savage had more honor and gentility in her little finger than all of the women of the ton put together. She was more than worthy to marry him, a prince in his own land.

Adam closed his eyes and conjured her image in his mind's eye. Her green eyes made him feel as if he was drowning in a fathomless pool, her lips begged to be kissed, her fiery hair shouted her stubborn determination to the world.

A beautiful enigma, Sabrina was a countess who cooked and baked and hugged wolfhounds. She would never properly fit into the ton, and he loved her for that.

He loved her.

That astonishing thought hit him like a wall of bricks.

Bloody hell, Adam cursed himself. He'd done what he'd promised himself never to do, fall in love and surrender his heart to another. That road led to pain.

What would Sabrina say when she learned the truth about their relationship? Would she insist on dissolving it? What would she do when she learned his real identity? Would she be angry that the man she'd married had turned into a prince? He could never live with a woman who refused to tolerate his beliefs. That was out of the question.

"Sagi, take us home," Adam called, tapping on the roof of the carriage.

Sabrina stared out her bechamber window at the dismal morning. Windswept rain poured down from above and slashed against her window. Would they still tour the Tower? She really didn't want to go out in this weather, and it would be improper to do so. Once her sister and the older women had seen the windswept rain, all three of them had begged off and returned to their beds.

Sabrina had been dressed and ready for more than an hour. For the tenth time, she crossed the room and inspected herself in the full-length framed mirror.

Her high-waisted walking dress had been fashioned in forest-green merino over a cambric petticoat. Its skirt was level to the top of her black demi-boots, and her black woolen cloak lay across her bed awaiting the marquess's pleasure. She absolutely refused to wear any of those ridiculous hats that were all the rage among the fashionable.

Sabrina was looking forward to seeing the marquess. Was she developing a fondness for him? No, she merely admired and liked him. After all, the marquess had sided with her against the vicar and promised to clear her father's name from the taint of suicide. Since the day she'd met him, though, she'd done little else but conjure his image in her mind's eye.

With his black hair and piercing blue eyes, Adam St. Aubyn was the handsomest man she'd ever seen, which verified the old saying that the devil had the power to disguise himself in a pleasing form. On the other hand, she could not abide his highhandedness. Why, the man gave orders as if they were already married, which annoyed her in the extreme. Would his authoritarian nature worsen after the wedding? That is, if she agreed to marry him.

And yet, the marquess excited her as no other man ever had. Though his boldness was unnerving, she never felt so alive as when she was with him.

Sabrina had to admit to herself that she loved his drugging kisses. Each time his lips covered hers, she yearned for more.

"Who is it?" Sabrina called, hearing a knock on her door.

"His lordship has arrived," Baxter informed her.

"I'll be down shortly."

Sabrina sat in the chair in front of the hearth and began counting to one thousand. She didn't want to appear too eager. A short wait would make it apparent to the marquess that he wasn't important to her.

Fifteen minutes later Sabrina rose from the chair and retrieved her cloak from the bed. Winston, curled in a gigantic ball, leaped off the bed and followed her out of the chamber.

Reaching the second-floor landing, Sabrina started down the last flight of stairs. She spied the marquess pacing back and forth in the foyer. In this unguarded moment he seemed so intent, as if precoccupied by a problem. She wondered what was bothering him.

"Good morning," Sabrina called, descending the last few steps.

Adam turned toward the staircase and gave her a devastating smile. He seemed happy to see her. What would life be like if he smiled at her each day for the next forty years or so?

"I'm late," Sabrina said, crossing the foyer.

"Princess, your lovely appearance is well worth the wait," Adam said, reaching down to pat Winston.

Sabrina blushed at his compliment. "You seemed preoccupied."

"I was thinking about yesterday's events," he told her.

"Events?"

"You wouldn't understand."

"Try me," Sabrina said, irritated by his superior attitude.

Adam gifted her with a wicked smile. "Someday I will, Princess."

Sabrina blushed in offended embarrassment. How could she possibly reply to that suggestive comment? Or did he believe her so naive that she wouldn't understand what he was referring to?

"I cannot keep our plans to tour the Tower," Adam told her, surprising her by placing the palm of his hand against her burning cheek and then smiling. "An urgent problem has arisen, and I have several appointments regarding this development."

Sabrina was unable to keep the look of disappointment off her face. She banished it almost as quickly as it appeared. "Perhaps we'll go tomorrow if the weather clears, and you solve your business problem."

"Tomorrow is impossible," Adam told her. "I never go about on Fridays."

His remark puzzled her. What a strange quirk the marquess possessed. What was so special about Fridays? If he had said Sundays, the day set aside for church and prayer, she could have understood. But Fridays?

"What is so special about Fridays?" Sabrina asked, expecting him to evade her question as he usually did.

"Abdul and Sagi are Moslems," Adam answered. "Friday is their Sabbath. Choosing other men to guard me on that day would be an insult to my most trusted and loyal retainers."

Sabrina gave him a smile filled with sunshine. For the first time since she'd met the marquess, she sensed that he was speaking honestly.

"I commend your loyalty to your servants," she said.

"Abdul and Sagi are more than servants to me," he replied, handing her a bouquet of flowers wrapped in a linen cloth. "I've brought you a gift."

Sabrina unwrapped the bouquet. There was a medley of white and pink winter roses interspersed with sprigs of evergreen. Accompanying the winter roses were snowdrop blossoms, their white doubled petals accentuated by their blue-green leaves.

"Where did you find flowers in winter?" Sabrina asked with a delighted smile.

"I have my sources," Adam said, returning her smile. "You remind me of the winter rose: lovely, delicate, but hardy in the face of adverse conditions. The snowdrop is a brave little blossom that flowers in winter and, as a harbinger of spring, brings hope to all who see it."

His flowers, his words, and his masculine presence wove an enchanter's spell around her. No man had ever spoken so romantically to her, and Sabrina stared into his blue eyes, mesmerized by the man.

"Where is everyone?" Adam asked, breaking the spell he'd cast over her.

"They're still sleeping," Sabrina told him. "Once they spied the rain, the three of them begged off."

"I have time before my appointments," Adam said.

"Would you like breakfast?" she asked.

"I'd love it." Adam turned to the majordomo, saying, "Baxter, serve us coffee in the drawing room."

"I'll take tea and a vase for the flowers," Sabrina told the man. She lifted a napkin tied with a blue ribbon off the foyer table.

With Winston following behind, Adam and Sabrina walked upstairs to the drawing room. She peeked at him once and caught him peeking at her.

"Winston, lie down," Adam ordered when they entered the drawing room.

The wolfhound curled up into a ball in front of the hearth. Sabrina sat down on the couch, and Adam sat close beside her. Sabrina knew she should tell him to sit in the chair or she should sit in it herself, but his finally giving her an honest answer had made her more tolerant of his boldness.

"What do you have there?" Adam asked, dropping his gaze to the napkin.

"French sunshine and exotic locales," Sabrina said, passing him the napkin.

Adam unfastened the ribbon and peered inside the napkin. He smiled at the sight of Turkish delights and nougats. "Should I assume something upset you last night?"

"I grew tired of writing in my journal but felt restless," she answered. "You know that cooking and baking relax me."

"Tell me where you learned to make Turkish delights," Adam said.

"I got the recipe from Mrs. Eliza Acton's cookbook," Sabrina told him. "Mrs. Acton lived in France for a time and collected exotic recipes from all over the Mediterranean while there."

"Is Mrs. Acton a friend from Abingdon?" Adam asked.

Sabrina laughed. "Mrs. Acton published her recipes in a book. I do love a challenge in the kitchen."

"Princess, you are an original," Adam said, smiling. "I see my uncle's chess set over there. How about an interesting game of chess?"

Baxter chose that moment to walk into the room. He carried the coffee and tea service while Forbes carried a platter of sweet rolls and butter and the vase for the flowers.

"We'll serve ourselves," Adam dismissed the two men, who left the room immediately.

"Tell me, Countess, would you have gone for a tour of the Tower alone with me?" Adam asked, pouring tea and passing the cup to her.

"I didn't know what I was going to do until the moment actually arrived," Sabrina answered.

"I'd wager my last shilling that you would cancel," he said.

"How can you be so certain?" she asked.

Adam grinned. "The only risks you ever take are in the kitchen."

"I have my rebellious moments," Sabrina disagreed. "You know, if you didn't give orders like a prince, I would be more relaxed."

"Perhaps I *am* a prince," Adam countered. "In disguise, of course."

"Men who believe they are princes vacation in Bedlam Hospital," she told him.

Adam burst out laughing. "You'd like to lock me away, wouldn't you?" he said. Leaning back on the sofa, he stretched his arm out and rested it on the sofa behind her.

Smiling, Sabrina leaned toward him and said, "If you insist on being a prince, then I must reveal my true identity."

"And who is that?"

"Lady Godiva."

Again, Adam burst out laughing. "Princess, if you're not careful, you'll find yourself sharing a room with me at Bedlam."

"That would be unendurable," Sabrina said with a jaunty smile. "Imagine a lifetime of being ordered about by a pretend prince. Why it's enough to make one yearn for the gallows."

"What will you do if you awaken one morning to discover that the man you had married really was a prince?" Adam asked, his expression suddenly serious.

Sabrina lost her smile. She looked at him in confusion. What kind of game was this? Was he speaking truthfully? That was too absurd even to consider. What did she really know about his life, especially his origins?

"Shall we play chess?" Adam asked, changing the subject before she could question him.

"How can chess possibly be interesting?" Sabrina asked, banishing troubling thoughts from her mind.

"We'll place a small wager on the outcome," he suggested.

"I'm not a betting woman," she told him.

"The wager needn't be money," Adam said. "The winner receives a favor from the other."

Sabrina became suspicious. "What kind of favor?"

"If I win, I'll give you a kiss," Adam said, maintaining a serious expression. "If you win, you'll give me a kiss."

"Your kissing me is no favor." Sabrina looked away and lied. "Besides, I don't want to kiss you."

"You're afraid," Adam said.

Sabrina bristled. "I am not afraid of anything," she informed him.

"Prove it," Adam challenged her.

The gauntlet had been thrown, and Sabrina could not ignore it. "Close your eyes," she said. When he did, she leaned close and planted a chaste kiss on his cheek.

"You call that a kiss?"

"You didn't like it?"

"Princess, a kiss should be filled with unspoken emotion," Adam said. "Slide closer and put your arms around my neck."

"No, I don't think so," Sabrina refused, shifting her gaze to the far side of the drawing room. If she looked into his eyes, she would weaken in her resolve to resist him.

"You said you weren't afraid," he reminded her.

"The servants might interrupt us," she replied. "Then they would tell their friends, who, in turn, would tell—"

"Tossing my own words back into my face is grossly unfair," Adam said with a smile. "Besides, everyone expects engaged couples to kiss."

"Very few people know about the betrothal," she reminded him.

Adam caught her gaze with his own and said one word that spurred her into action. *"Coward."*

In spite of her uncertainty, Sabrina slid closer and wrapped her arms around his neck. "Now what?" she whispered, excited by his masculine scent.

"Close your eyes and touch my lips with yours," he instructed her.

When she'd done as instructed, she asked, "Is that all?"

"No, Princess, that is not all," Adam said, putting his arms around her.

Adam captured her mouth with his own. His tongue teased the crease of her lips apart, and Sabrina felt hot and cold all at the same time.

"You smell like roses," he murmured against her lips.

Winston's growling brought them back to reality. They broke apart and looked toward the doorway, where Uncle Charles stood with another gentleman.

Sabrina blushed in mortification at being caught kissing the marquess.

"Prince Adolphus," Adam whispered, making her feel even worse.

Sabrina felt like swooning to escape the embarrassment. Of all the ignominious moments for the prince to arrive. No doubt he would consider her a wanton.

Adam and Sabrina rose from the couch. Together, they crossed the room to greet the two gentlemen.

"How lovely you look today," Uncle Charles said, making her blush even more. He turned to his friend and said, "Prince Adolphus, I wish to make known to you Sabrina Savage, the Countess of Abingdon."

Sabrina curtsied. "I am honored to meet you, Your Royal Highness."

"Thank you, child," the prince replied. "The pleasure is mine. Mine . . . mine . . . mine."

Puzzled by his odd behavior, Sabrina flicked a glance at Adam. He was smiling.

"Of course, you already know my nephew," Uncle Charles said.

Adam shook the prince's hand and then suggested, "Why don't we sit over here?"

Adam and Sabrina resumed their seats on the couch. Uncle Charles and Prince Adolphus sat in the chairs opposite them.

"And who is this big fellow?" Prince Adolphus asked, his gaze dropping to the wolfhound.

"My dog, Winston," Sabrina answered.

"He reminds me of Tiny," Adolphus said.

Uncle Charles smiled, saying, "I said the same thing the first time I saw him."

"I felt I must pay you and your sister a condolence

call," Adolphus said to Sabrina. "I am saddened by your father's passing."

"Thank you, Sir," Sabrina said. "Your words bring me comfort."

"Courtney and our aunts are still closeted in their chambers," Adam said. "We can send for her."

"No, don't disturb her," the prince replied. "I will be gone by the time she arrives if she's like most ladies. Ladies . . . ladies . . . ladies. How tardy they can be."

"My sister will be disappointed to have missed you," Sabrina said.

"The prince will meet Courtney at your coming-out party," Uncle Charles said.

"I want to have the first dance with you and the second with your sister," Adolphus said.

"You honor me with your request," Sabrina said. She hesitated a moment and then added, "Your Royal Highness, I must ask you something."

Adolphus gave her an affable smile. "Ask away."

"As you know, Henry Savage adopted me and my sister," Sabrina began. "Do you know where we came from? Do you have any idea who our real parents were?"

"That's two questions you asked, not one," Adolphus corrected her, and then grew serious. His gaze skittered away from hers when he answered, "I don't know who your real parents were."

Sabrina sensed that the prince was being less than truthful. But what could she do? One did not go about calling the prince a liar.

"He does have good news for you," Uncle Charles piped up.

"Madame Esmeralda is an old friend of mine and, as a favor, has agreed to sing at your coming-out," Adolphus informed her. "Esmeralda has never performed at a private party before. I do believe society will be squabbling over invitations to your ball. You and your sister will be a social success."

"I've never heard of her," Sabrina admitted. "Esmeralda is a singer?"

"Why, child, she's the most renowned opera singer in all of Europe," Adolphus said. "Esmeralda is so famous that she needs only one name. Sort of like royalty."

"Thank you for helping to launch my sister and me into society," Sabrina said with a smile.

"You are very welcome," Adolphus said, rising from his chair. "I really must be leaving . . . leaving . . . leaving."

Uncle Charles stood when the prince stood. "Be certain to tell Belladonna about our little visit."

"Thank you for visiting," Sabrina said, starting to rise.

"Don't get up," Adolphus ordered. "Carry on as you were. As you were . . . As you were."

The two older gentlemen crossed the drawing room to leave. Sabrina glanced at Adam, who wore a grim expression on his face.

"What is wrong?" she asked.

"Nothing is wrong," he said, and gave her a reassuring smile. "Now, I must be leaving for my appointments."

Without warning, Adam leaned close and planted a kiss on her lips. Then he turned away and left the drawing room.

The marquess was lying, too, Sabrina decided. Something was definitely wrong, or he wouldn't have been wearing that expression. If mistaken, she'd eat a piece of her own hemlock pie.

Chapter 9

Had it only been two days since she'd waltzed with the marquess in the drawing room? Sabrina wondered as she paced back and forth across her bedchamber. Those two days felt more like two minutes now that the moment had arrived to attend her coming-out ball. Almost as bad, the urge to bake was growing stronger with each passing second.

"Come in," Sabrina called when she heard someone knock on her door.

With a blush of nervous anticipation staining her cheeks, Courtney walked in and closed the door behind her. "Belladonna and Aunt Tess are tormenting me with the rules and regulations of London society," her sister complained, sitting down on the edge of the bed. "I thought I might escape them here."

Sabrina smiled and joined her sister on the edge of the bed. "You look lovely in your white gown," she said, and then fixed her gaze on her sister's neck. "Where did you get those pearls?"

"The marquess purchased them to complement my gown," Courtney told her. "Isn't he the most thoughtful man in the whole world?"

"I have not thought of Adam in those precise terms," Sabrina said dryly. "In fact, I've—"

"Have you begun to love him?" Courtney asked baldly.

"You certainly get straight to the point," Sabrina said with a smile. "To answer your question, I don't know how love feels. I consider Adam a charming and attractive man, but he is also exceedingly arrogant and much too authoritarian."

Courtney placed a hand over her sister's. "I'm certain that you and the marquess will enjoy a long, happy marriage."

Sabrina burst out laughing. She was sorry she hadn't been quieter when her aunt opened the door.

"Here they are," Aunt Tess called, marching into the bedchamber. Behind her walked Lady Belladonna.

"Stand up," Belladonna cried. "You'll wrinkle your gowns before the guests arrive."

In an instant, Sabrina and Courtney rose from their perch on the edge of the bed. The two older women descended on them, smoothing nonexistent wrinkles and fixing perfect coiffures.

"We want to give you a few last-minute instructions," Belladonna announced, standing in front of them like a general addressing his troops.

"Oh, dear!" Aunt Tess exclaimed. "Sabrina's gown is cut too low in the front."

"Nonsense, that neckline is all the rage," Belladonna assured her. She gave the girls her attention again. "We'll stand in the reception line until Prince Adolphus arrives and then escort him upstairs to the ballroom."

"Don't eat too much when we go down to supper," Aunt Tess ordered. "Ladies do not stuff themselves."

"Don't dance with any gentleman more than twice," Belladonna advised. "To do so would cause a scandal because you were favoring one gentleman over the others."

"You need not accept a dance with a gentleman merely because he asks," Aunt Tess added. When Sabrina and Courtney looked at each other and dissolved into giggles, she demanded, "What is so funny?"

"Dear Aunt, I believe that both Courtney and I have been concerned with a lack of requests to dance," Sabrina said.

"Don't be ridiculous," Belladonna admonished them. "Courtney and you will need to fight potential suitors off. In a manner of speaking, that is." She turned to Tess and asked, "Can you think of anything else?"

Aunt Tess nodded and, in a stern tone of voice, ordered, "Don't forget to smile. Let's go downstairs now. Our guests will soon be arriving."

"I'll be along in a moment," Sabrina said. "I need a few minutes to myself." She glanced at her sister's frightened expression and added, "I'll be there before the first guest arrives."

How long would it be before the ton learned that she and her sister were frauds? Sabrina wondered, crossing the chamber to the window to gaze at the night sky. What would they do when the rumor spread that she and Courtney were adopted bastards?

Sabrina knew the humiliation of their social cuts would be unendurable. If only the St. Aubyns had never come to Abingdon, she would be enjoying a peaceful evening at home, where she was accepted. On the other hand, her father would have been buried without a death knell if Adam St. Aubyn hadn't arrived when he did.

Sabrina closed her eyes. Would she meet the man of her dreams tonight? Or had she already met him? The marquess's image floated through her mind.

Sabrina crossed to the full-length framed mirror to inspect herself one last time. Her ice-blue satin gown was high-waisted with a deep V-neck where she'd pinned the marquess's diamond frog brooch. The gown had short melon sleeves and a hemline border of white silk roses. Her elbow-length gloves were white kid, as were her sandals with crossed ribbons.

Winter roses, Sabrina thought, staring at the border of embroidered roses adorning her gown's hemline. The marquess had said that was what she reminded him of.

Sabrina lifted her hand to touch her frog brooch, and the softest of smiles touched her lips. If she kissed the marquess—*really kissed him*—would he turn into a handsome prince?

Sabrina knew the moment to go downstairs had arrived. She didn't want to be put in the embarrassing position of having the marquess come looking for her. Taking a deep breath, Sabrina turned away from her image and crossed the chamber to open the door. Discordant notes wafted up the stairs as the musicians tuned their instruments.

Sabrina walked down the third-floor corridor like a woman going to the gallows. Reaching the top of the stairs, she stopped short in surprise. Leaning against the mahogany banister with his arms folded across his chest, the marquess waited for her.

Adam St. Aubyn reminded her of Lucifer before the fall. He wore formal black trousers, black jacket, and black waistcoat with white shirt and tie. The starkness of the colors accentuated his dark good looks and his penetrating blue eyes. When he smiled, as he did now, his teeth appeared strong and straight and almost as white as his shirt.

Sabrina stared at him in fascination. The marquess was the handsomest man she'd ever seen. He reeked of health and virility. How could any woman not be attracted to him?

"I wondered how long finding your courage would take," Adam said.

"If I really lacked courage, Winston would be standing by my side," Sabrina said.

"Why depend on Winston when you have me?" he replied.

His words flustered her. She didn't think she could handle the ton and his suggestive bantering at the same time.

Adam gave her his devastating smile. His gaze drifted from her face down her body, pausing only for a brief second on the frog brooch. When his eyes met

hers again, they gleamed with appreciation and possessiveness.

"My compliments to whoever your natural parents
were," he said.

Sabrina felt the blood rushing to color her cheeks at
his reminder of her bastardy. She used every ounce of
inner strength to remain rooted where she stood instead
of running back to her chamber.

"My words compliment your beauty," Adam said,
as if he recognized her distress.

Sabrina inclined her head. "Thank you . . . I
think."

"You aren't suffering the urge to bake?" he teased
her.

"I managed to fight it off," she answered with a
smile.

"The others are in the foyer, but I wanted to speak
with you privately before the evening begins," Adam
said, taking her arm in his and escorting her down the
stairs. "Will you accompany me to the drawing
room?"

"I don't think we should," Sabrina said, too nervous to be alone with him when he looked so devastatingly handsome. "I promised Courtney not to leave her
alone to greet the guests."

"Please?" he coaxed. "I promise to deliver you to
the receiving line before any guests arrive."

Sabrina nodded. What other choice did she have
when he was holding her arm?

The orchestra music grew louder as they descended
the stairs to the second floor. Passing the ballroom,
Sabrina heard the distinctive sounds of a cornet, a pi-

ano, a cello, and several violins. She couldn't help thinking that five hundred members of the ton would soon crowd into the ballroom, and the marquess expected her to mingle with them.

God shield her, but she felt like a fraud. Those unsuspecting members of society had no idea that they were welcoming two adopted bastards into their fold.

"Be careful, Princess," Adam murmured. "Your face might freeze into that pinched expression."

"My nerves will calm as soon as the guests arrive," Sabrina said, managing a faint smile for him.

Adam led the way into the drawing room. With one slight flick of his wrist, he sent the servants scurrying out and closed the door behind them.

Sabrina wondered how he managed to order the servants about without ever saying a word. A remarkable talent, to be sure.

"Prince Adolphus wants the first dance with you," Adam said, crossing the chamber to stand in front of the hearth. "Uncle Charles wants the second dance. I want the third, the one before supper, and the last dance of the evening with you."

"Our aunts said not to dance more than twice with any man," Sabrina protested.

"They meant any man except me." Adam gave her a devastatingly wicked smile. "I am your betrothed."

"Very few people know that."

"I am your guardian," he amended himself.

"Uncle Charles and Aunt Tess are my guardians," she corrected him.

"Don't forget, Princess. I hold the purse strings to the Savage assets," Adam pointed out.

"You blackmailing, arrogant—" Sabrina paused, unable to conjure more vile insults to hurl at him.

"Always keep your expression placid, Princess, no matter your inner turmoil," Adam said.

"My lord, I thank you for your sound advice," Sabrina said. She lifted her upturned nose into the air, showed him her back, and walked toward the door.

"I haven't finished, Princess."

Sabrina turned around. Keeping a placid expression on her face, she arched a perfectly shaped copper brow at him and asked, "There's more?"

Adam grinned. "I knew you'd be a quick learner."

His smile and his words conspired against her. In spite of her annoyance, Sabrina returned his smile.

"Come, Princess," Adam said, holding out his hand. "I have a gift for you."

Sabrina closed the distance between them. Adam reached into his jacket pocket and produced a small gift box. He opened it to reveal a magnificent, obviously priceless ring. Before she could protest, he slipped it onto the third finger of her right hand, saying in a husky voice, "I want you to have this for luck."

Sabrina stared down at the exquisite piece of jewelry. Lying on a bed of diamond ice were pearl snowdrop blossoms surrounding an enormous ruby rose.

"As I said before, roses and snowdrops remind me of you," Adam told her.

Sabrina hesitated. "I don't know what to say."

"Say thank you."

"Thank you, my lord." Sabrina looked at the exquisitely lovely ring again. Something about it bothered her. And then she knew.

"This has the look of a betrothal ring," she said in an accusing voice, expecting him to deny it.

"It is a betrothal ring."

"But you promised—"

Adam placed one finger across her lips to silence her. "When you are ready to accept our betrothal, simply move the ring from your right hand to your left hand."

"And if I never accept it?" she asked.

"You will."

His arrogance annoyed her. "How can you be so certain?" she asked.

"I am certain because I have seen the sorry lot of bachelors that English society has to offer," Adam answered, and then winked at her.

Her annoyance left her as quickly as it had come. "You speak as if you don't consider yourself one of them."

"Only my mother was English," he replied. "Remember?"

"Perhaps someday you will tell me who you really are," she teased him.

"What do you mean?"

"I'm beginning to believe that you could be a prince in disguise. You certainly order everyone about as if you were royalty," Sabrina answered. "I sense that you have omitted important details about yourself. Will I ever know the real Adam St. Aubyn?"

"Princess, I will explain everything once we are married," Adam answered.

"Do you actually believe I'd marry a man without

knowing him?'' Sabrina asked, wondering for the thousandth time what he was hiding.

''Trust me, Princess. You will marry me,'' Adam replied with a confident smile. ''Shall we go downstairs?''

In spite of her misgivings about what he'd said, Sabrina accepted his arm. Tonight was not the time for her to delve further into his past life. Together, they left the drawing room.

''The room adjacent to the ballroom has been set aside for refreshments,'' Adam told her. ''Beyond that is the card room and then the ladies' retiring room. Aunt Belladonna's maid will be available for minor repairs to gowns. The study downstairs will be used as the gentlemen's smoking room.''

''You seem to have forgotten nothing,'' Sabrina said.

''I've asked Jamie to come early,'' Adam said as they walked down the stairs to the foyer. ''Lily can offer you and Courtney moral support.''

Sabrina gave him a grateful smile. And then her aunt's voice reached her.

''Oh, how I wish Henry were alive to see how beautiful you and Courtney look tonight,'' Aunt Tess was exclaiming as Sabrina took her place beside her sister.

''Do you think Dudley Egremont will attend?'' Courtney whispered, a high blush of excitement staining her cheeks.

''He'll be here,'' Sabrina assured her.

''Where did you get that ring?'' Courtney exclaimed in a voice loud enough for all to hear.

Sabrina flicked an embarrassed look toward the marquess and then held her hand up for everyone's inspection, saying, "Adam gave it to me." She glanced at Uncle Charles, who was beaming with approval, and suffered the sudden feeling that she was being trapped into an engagement with the marquess.

"It looks like a betrothal ring," Courtney said. "Are you going to announce your betrothal?"

"No," Sabrina said emphatically, and sent the marquess a decidedly unhappy look.

How could she meet and encourage eligible gentlemen if they believed she was betrothed to Adam St. Aubyn? Was this a plan to discourage other gentlemen? If so, why would the marquess bother when he could have any woman he wanted? What was so damned attractive about her?

"The Duke and Duchess of Kinross," Baxter announced, drawing her attention.

James Armstrong winked at the haughty majordomo as he and his wife walked past him. Sabrina wished that all of the ton could be like Adam's friends.

"Both of you come with me," Lily Armstrong ordered.

Sabrina and Courtney followed the Duchess of Kinross to the opposite side of the foyer. In a low voice, she began a lecture obviously meant to bolster their courage.

"No one could have been more nervous than I was the first time Jamie introduced me into society," Lily began. "And I didn't enjoy the luxury of having someone like myself to lend me support."

Both Sabrina and Courtney smiled at that.

"The ladies of the ton are sharks ready to draw

blood at the first oportunity," Lily continued. She glanced at Courtney and warned, "Do not even consider swooning." She looked back at Sabrina and said, "There is a way to confound them, however."

"What would that be?" Sabrina asked.

"Develop an attitude," Lily answered. "Pretend you are doing them a favor by speaking with them."

"I'm not sure I could do that," Sabrina said.

"I wouldn't know how," Courtney agreed.

"Whenever someone intimidates you, picture the offending person with a remarkably ugly appearance," Lily told them. "An annoying gentleman receives buckteeth and crossed eyes. I always imagine an obnoxious lady as suffering from baldness."

Sabrina burst out laughing. "I can do that."

"So can I," Courtney agreed.

"Then it's settled. You will not be nervous," Lily insisted, as if saying made it so, and returned them to the receiving line.

Sabrina overheard Adam saying to Jamie, "The arrow has left the bow."

"When do you think Ambassador Zaganos will receive a reply?" Jamie asked.

"These things take time," Adam answered with a shrug. "Patience is a virtue."

"Patience is reckless when your life is at risk," Jamie disagreed. "Let those two giants of yours do their jobs until then."

"I wouldn't have it any other way," Adam said.

Overhearing their conversation, Sabrina froze in fear. Was Adam's life in danger? Who would want to hurt him?

"Sabrina, we'll see you upstairs," Lily was saying, accepting her husband's arm and letting him lead her toward the stairs. "Prinny sends his best regards," she called over her shoulder.

"The Regent?" Courtney exclaimed.

"No, the pig," the duchess called, and disappeared up the stairs with her husband.

"The Duchess of Kinross has a pet pig named Prinny," Sabrina told her sister.

Turning to the marquess, Sabrina whispered, "Your life is at risk? Did someone threaten your life?"

"Nothing important has happened," Adam lied, his gaze on her warm. "I'm pleased that you fear for my safety."

Sabrina flicked him a sidelong glance and said, "My assets are invested with you, and I don't want to lose them."

Adam smiled at her words and leaned close, saying, "I know you are hiding your true feelings for me behind cruel words."

Unamused by his arrogance, Sabrina could only stare at him. Answering would only encourage him.

"Well, how do I look with buckteeth and crossed eyes?" he asked.

"My lord, you are incorrigible," she said with a smile.

"Thank you for the high praise," he replied.

Their guests began arriving. Adam and Uncle Charles flanked Sabrina and Courtney and made the introductions. Aunt Tess and Lady DeFaye stood on the other side of Uncle Charles.

Dudley Egremont, Viscount Dorchester, arrived in

the company of his mother and his aunt. The viscount bowed low over Courtney's hand and insisted, "I claim all of your dances."

"My lord, you know that isn't possible," Courtney said with a shy smile. "The first dance belongs to Uncle Charles and the second to Prince Adolphus. You may have the third."

"Then I request the third dance, the last dance, and the one just before supper," Dudley said.

Courtney inclined her head. "I would like that very much."

Sabrina watched the viscount move away with his relations and then whispered to the marquess, "I thought only two dances were permitted with the same man."

"Correct, but I approve of Dorchester and believe Courtney and he would make a good pairing," Adam replied.

"A pairing?" Sabrina exclaimed. "Are we a couple of mares to be bred?"

"Lower your voice," Adam whispered. "I mean no insult to Courtney or you, but meeting marriage prospects is the purpose of a coming-out ball."

"Your word choice is poor," she told him.

"I apologize, Princess," he said. "I promise to choose my words more carefully in the future."

With a smile frozen on her face, Sabrina soon realized that Lily Armstrong had been correct. The ladies of the ton were like sharks looking for a weak spot in order to let blood. Looking past their smiles, she saw in their eyes that they considered her a potential rival for the season's prime husband catches. And from the looks the females were giving Adam, Sabrina realized they considered him to be one of the prime catches. For some unknown reason, that made her jealous. Touching her frog brooch or her ring made her feel more confident.

The moment Sabrina had been dreading arrived. Lord Briggs stood before them. With him was a voluptuous blonde wearing a white gown that left almost nothing to the imagination.

So much for undying devotion, Sabrina thought, disgruntled by his defection.

"Good evening, Edgar," Sabrina greeted him with a smile. "I'm pleased to see a familiar face."

"Sabrina, you have never looked lovelier," Edgar said, bowing over her hand. "May I make known to you Alexis Carstairs, the Countess of Rothbury."

Alexis Carstairs possessed the sweet expression of an angel and the body of a goddess. She had blue eyes, a straight nose, and flawless ivory skin.

The two women smiled insincerely at each other, natural enemies at first sight. Each saw in the other the qualities she lacked.

"Lady Rothbury, I am pleased to make your acquaintance," Sabrina greeted her.

"Adam has told me so much about you," Alexis replied, giving her a feline smile.

Sabrina nearly flinched at her words, but caught herself in time and managed to keep her expression placid. And then she recalled Lily's advice and imagined the woman without any hair on her head.

Determined to stand her ground, Sabrina touched

the diamond frog brooch with her right hand. Both the brooch and the ring glittered in the foyer's candlelight.

"Dear Adam has been so helpful," she drawled, casting "dear Adam" a look of adoration. "I don't know how we would have survived without him."

"Yes, Adam can be so helpful. I'll see you upstairs," Alexis said stiffly, and yanked Edgar away.

"She forgot to keep her expression placid," Sabrina said, turning to the marquess, whose shoulders shook with silent laughter.

"How could I ever have thought you needed my protection?" Adam leaned close and whispered, "How does Alexis look as a bald woman?"

"She's not one of the acclaimed beauties, but she would be an original."

Adam burst out laughing, drawing everyone's attention. Sabrina noticed Uncle Charles's smile of approval and the speculative glances of several guests.

"What does the phrase 'The arrow has left the bow' mean?" Sabrina asked.

"It means whatever will be will be," Adam answered. "Fate has been set into motion and cannot be undone."

Sabrina never got the chance to question him further. A big middle-aged man wearing a blond wig stood in front of them.

Sabrina smiled, recognizing Prince Adolphus.

"Lady Abingdon, you are the perfect vision of loveliness," Prince Adolphus greeted her. "So lovely . . . so lovely . . . so lovely."

"Your presence honors me, Your Royal Highness," Sabrina said, dropping him a curtsey.

"This is Courtney, Sabrina's younger sister," Uncle Charles told the prince.

With an affable smile, Prince Adolphus turned to Courtney, who blushed and dropped him a curtsey. "I have wanted to meet you for the longest time," he told her.

"Your Royal Highness, I am honored," Courtney replied.

Adolphus looked from brown-haired Courtney to copper-haired Sabrina and then back at Courtney again. "Two sisters who look so very different," the prince remarked. "No family resemblance there. None . . . none . . . none." He turned next to Adam and said, "I heard about the shooting incident at White's. Glad to see you are as hale and hearty—"

"Thank you, Your Royal Highness," Adam interrupted. "Shall we go upstairs and begin the ball?"

Sabrina turned her head and stared at the marquess. Someone had taken a shot at him? Who would want him dead and then act upon that wish? Edgar Briggs popped into her mind, but she banished that thought as absurd. Edgar was incapable of stepping on an ant. Why, the marquess must have dozens of enemies. Successful businessmen were notoriously ruthless and ruined the hopes and the dreams of others.

"Sabrina?"

Adam's voice drew her out of her thoughts. She smiled and let herself be escorted up the stairs to the ballroom. Prince Adolphus walked beside her while Uncle Charles escorted Courtney. Adam walked behind with their aunts.

The orchestra began playing as soon as they entered

the ballroom. Prince Adolphus escorted Sabrina onto the dance floor, and Uncle Charles did the same with Courtney. The two couples waltzed alone on the dance floor as custom required that the debutante and the most important man in attendance open the ball.

"Esmeralda will arrive later in the evening," Prince Adolphus told her. He chuckled and added, "She loves to make a grand entrance. Loves it . . . loves it . . . loves it."

Sabrina didn't give a fig about the opera singer. "Tell me what happened outside White's the other night," she asked the prince.

"An assassination attempt is no suitable topic for a lady's conversation," Adolphus chided her gently.

The dance ended before she could press him for more information. Courtney and she switched partners.

"Your father would be proud of you tonight," Uncle Charles said as they waltzed around the ballroom.

"Tell me about the incident at White's," Sabrina said without preamble.

"I don't know anything about it," Uncle Charles told her. "Adam doesn't tell me everything."

He was lying, Sabrina decided, but kept her expression placid. Since the night she'd met them, the St. Aubyns had lied to her about most of the important things. What else could they be keeping from her? In spite of their kindnesses to her, she was beginning to doubt their trustworthiness.

Adam claimed her for the third dance. He waltzed with the same ease and grace he'd demonstrated the day they'd danced without music.

"Making idle conversation while one dances is customary," Adam said.

"You never mentioned that rule to me," Sabrina replied. "My, how divinely you waltz."

"And you feel so good in my arms that I might never let you go," Adam said in a husky voice.

Sabrina blushed. Good Lord, why did he always find a way to confound her?

"You failed to tell me about the incident at White's," she said.

"It was nothing."

"You call an assassination attempt nothing?" Sabrina exclaimed, missing a step.

"Smile, Princess. Society is watching," Adam said. "Do not give them anything to gossip about."

Instantly, Sabrina smiled at him.

"That is absolutely the most insincere smile I've ever seen," Adam teased her.

"You didn't say smile sincerely, my lord, only smile."

Adam inclined his head. "*Touché*, Countess. Someone took a wild shot at Jamie and me the other night. We are investigating who the culprit might be."

Sabrina nodded. Her gaze drifted away from him until she spied her sister dancing across the hall. "Courtney seems to like Dudley Egremont," she remarked.

"I was hoping they would like each other," Adam replied. "They might find happiness as a married couple. . . . How was that for word choice?"

"Much better," Sabrina said. "I knew you would be a quick learner."

Adam laughed to hear his own words thrown back at him.

When the music ended, Adam led her toward the refreshment room, but Lord Briggs blocked their way before they reached it.

"Dance with me, Sabrina?" he asked.

Sabrina smiled. "Why, Edgar, I would love to dance with you."

She let him lead her onto the dance floor. The two longtime friends whirled around the ballroom together.

"Who would have guessed that we would end like this, waltzing in London," Sabrina said.

"Do not say *end* but rather *begin*," Edgar said. "Marry me, Sabrina."

"I have already explained my situation," Sabrina said. "Why do you insist on making this difficult?" She looked away, unable to bear the hurt in his hazel eyes, and missed a step when she saw Adam dancing with Alexis.

The baron's gaze followed hers. "They've been lovers since before her husband died."

"I don't believe you," Sabrina said, shocked. "No woman would be unfaithful to her husband."

"Your innocence is a most endearing quality," Edgar said. "May I call upon you?"

Sabrina managed a smile for him. "Visit me whenever you wish, Edgar. I will always have time for an old friend."

Sabrina begged off from his company when the music ended. Although she kept a smile and a pleasant expression on her face, the gossip about the marquess troubled her.

A man who cheated on his betrothed, Sabrina decided, would also cheat on his wife. She refused to marry a man who was destined to become a faithless husband.

Sabrina determined to put a brave face on the situation and ignore the gossip. She flirted and waltzed with Jamie Armstrong, Dudley Egremont, and a different man for each of the waltzes before intermission; but the thought of the marquess and that countess making love never left her.

Finally, when Adam presented himself for the last waltz before supper, Sabrina could scarcely meet his gaze. She was unusually quiet as they swirled around the ballroom.

"Princess, smile and say something," Adam ordered. "Unless you want to create a bit of gossip?"

Of all the unmitigated gall, she thought mutinously. How dare he threaten her with the danger of gossip. How did he even sleep at night? That harlot had a nerve showing up at her coming-out ball.

"You waltz divinely," Sabrina said with the sweetest of smiles.

"You said that during our last dance," Adam reminded her. "Only middle-aged people repeat themselves."

"Wonderful weather we've been having," Sabrina changed the subject. "Don't you think?"

Adam inclined his head.

"A bit dark tonight," she continued. "I dare say, the sky will lighten toward morning."

Adam burst out laughing, drawing the attention of

several couples near them. "Princess, you are an incorrigible imp."

"Do you really think so?" Sabrina drawled. "I suppose one must always follow the rules: no laughing, no bolting food, no picking your nose."

"Enough," Adam said, laughing. "You've drunk too many glasses of champagne without food. I'm taking you to supper."

"I haven't had any champagne," Sabrina told him.

"Then that is exactly what you need."

Adam stopped dancing and, taking her hand in his, led her toward the door. The others followed them down to supper.

In the crowded dining room, Sabrina sipped her champagne and picked at a piece of turkey. "Why aren't you eating?" she asked.

"Custom requires that ladies eat first," Adam told her. "I'll have something later."

"Of all the stupid rules you've told me, that is the stupidest," Sabrina announced in a loud whisper, her green eyes gleaming with mischief. "Do you really care what these people think?"

Adam glanced from her face to the guests and then whispered, "No, of course not."

"Good." Sabrina speared a piece of turkey with her fork and raised it to his lips.

Accepting her challenge, Adam ate the piece of turkey. He glanced around and saw the shocked expressions on the faces of a few of the older women.

"Breeding does tell," Sabrina said, spearing another piece of turkey.

"Don't," Adam ordered in a quiet voice, touching

her wrist. "Your future children will need the approval of these people."

"Quite right, my lord." Sabrina set the fork down and leaned close, asking in a whisper, "Is Alexis Carstairs still your mistress?"

"Princess, you have no tolerance for champagne," Adam said, avoiding her question.

"I suppose that's the way with your family." Sabrina sighed with exaggeration. "The St. Aubyns deal only in lies, half-truths, omissions, and avoidance."

"The truth should only be told in tiny pieces to those who might crumple beneath its full weight," Adam said seriously, his piercing gaze fixed on hers.

"I have never crumpled in my life," Sabrina informed him. "And you still haven't answered my question."

He stared at her for so long that Sabrina thought he wasn't going to answer.

"Alexis Carstairs is not my mistress," Adam said finally.

"Did she ever hold that exalted title?" Sabrina asked.

"Sorry, Princess. The rules permit only one prying question each evening," Adam said.

"Apparently, the rules need to be changed," Sabrina replied. "I am just the woman to do it."

"You will do no such thing," Adam told her.

When supper ended, the guests drifted upstairs to the ballroom once more. Walking beside the marquess, Sabrina could hear the musicians fine-tuning their instruments again. She also noted the surreptitious, longing glances that many of the females cast at the marquess. He appeared oblivious to all of that female adoration.

Once inside the ballroom, Sabrina left him. She danced the next nine waltzes with different men, each one handsomer than the last. Whirling around the ballroom, she kept an eye on Adam, who leaned against a wall and kept an eye on her. Surrounding him were several beautiful ladies, all of whom vied for his attention.

When the ninth waltz ended, Adam presented himself before Sabrina to claim her for the final dance. Before the musicians could begin playing, Baxter stepped into the ballroom and announced in a loud voice, "Madame Esmeralda."

An excited murmur raced through the crowd, and Prince Adolphus stepped forward to greet his old friend. Sabrina watched the prince kiss the diva's hand and then lead her across the room toward her.

"Esmeralda, I present Sabrina Savage, the Countess of Abingdon," Adolphus introduced them.

"Your presence at this gathering brings me honor," Sabrina said.

"The honor belongs to me," Esmeralda said, studying her with obvious interest. "I knew your father many years ago before you were born. I am sorry for his passing."

"Thank you," Sabrina said, and then realized the diva might know something about her origins. "Perhaps we could speak privately at a later time."

"Feel free to call upon me whenever you wish," Esmeralda said, inclining her head like a queen granting a favor to a courtier.

Prince Adolphus led Madame Esmeralda to the top of the room, where the musicians stood. The diva proceeded to sing several songs of lost love, finishing to thunderous applause. Afterward, the prince led her back to Sabrina and the others.

"Thank you for sharing your voice with us," Sabrina said.

"Thank you for allowing me to share it, child," Esmeralda replied. She turned to the prince and said, "Are you ready, Your Royal Highness?"

"You aren't leaving?" Sabrina asked.

"An opera singer's life isn't as glamorous as you may think," Esmeralda told her. "Lack of sleep is a risk to my voice."

"Then I won't keep you," Sabrina said. "We'll meet again?"

"I am looking forward to it." At that, Esmeralda accepted the prince's arm and let him escort her out of the ballroom.

The musicians began playing the last waltz as soon as the prince and the diva disappeared. Adam led Sabrina onto the dance floor. Waltzing in his arms felt so natural, as if they'd done it a thousand times before.

"Do you think Esmeralda knows who my real parents were?" Sabrina asked him.

"If you are wise, Princess, never ask her that question," Adam replied, surprising her. "The knowledge will not enrich your life."

Sabrina refused to let him ruin her good mood. "Spoken like a man who knows where he came from," she teased.

"You are correct," Adam agreed with her. "I cannot know your feelings because I do not share your experience.''

His words surprised her again. Sabrina had always considered members of the aristocratic set to be shallow, but the marquess was proving that assumption wrong.

The guests took their leave when the music ended. Adam stayed by her side until the last one had walked out the door. Only Uncle Charles remained behind, waiting in the drawing room for his nephew.

"Did you enjoy yourself?" Adam asked her when they stood alone in the foyer.

Sabrina smiled. "The evening went better than I'd expected."

"I never believed you'd be anything but a huge success," he told her.

"I thank you for your confidence," she replied.

Holding her hands in his, Adam faced her and said, "What would make this evening perfect for me is a good-night kiss."

"And what will you do if I refuse?" Sabrina asked, gazing into the bluest eyes she'd ever seen.

"I'd throw myself off London Bridge."

Sabrina cocked her head to one side and gave him a look of disbelief.

"I'd steal a kiss anyway," Adam amended himself.

"That sounds more like you," Sabrina said with a smile.

Without giving her a chance to protest, Adam pulled her into his embrace. While she stared up at him, his mouth swooped down and covered hers in a lingering kiss, its passion tempered only by the fact that they stood in the foyer.

"Now then," he said, drawing back. "Tomorrow morning—"

Sabrina reached up and placed one finger across his lips in a gesture for silence. "What would make this evening perfect for me is your refraining from giving me another order."

"Never?"

"I'll settle for tonight."

"Princess, your wish is my command."

Uncle Charles walked into the foyer at that moment and said, "The evening went smashingly well."

"By tomorrow morning you and your sister will be considered the toast of the ton, two of this season's acclaimed beauties," Adam told her.

"Why, Grosvenor Square will probably be congested with traffic because of your visitors," Uncle Charles added.

"God shield me," Sabrina exclaimed, making them laugh. "I doubt there's enough flour in England to calm me if that happens."

"Good night, Princess." Adam lifted her hand to his lips. "May all of your dreams be pleasant."

Sabrina started up the stairs, but her thoughts remained with the marquess. Adam St. Aubyn was entirely too handsome for her peace of mind. At times, he seemed like a prince who'd stepped out of a child's story, yet she couldn't help feeling that he was hiding something from her.

Sabrina banished her doubts as she walked down the

corridor to her bedchamber. She giggled out loud at the absurdity of her impending popularity. Without a doubt, Grosvenor Square would be deserted in the morning.

Chapter 10

"When will you tell Sabrina and Courtney who their natural father is?" Adam asked. Sitting behind the oak desk in his study, he stared at his uncle, who fidgeted beneath his piercing blue gaze.

"That knowledge would serve no purpose," Uncle Charles answered, tearing his gaze away from his nephew's. "Neither girl will ever be acknowledged."

"Sabrina yearns to know where she came from," Adam told his uncle.

"You yearn to return to your homeland," Uncle Charles replied. "I yearn to be twenty years younger. All of us yearn for something, but if we achieved our goals, we'd be yearning for something else."

A knock on the door drew their attention. Higgins and Razi rushed into the room as if they were racing against each other.

"I'll do this," Higgins told the little man. "I am his majordomo."

"Very well, I'll take the next one," Razi said.

"The Earl of Tunbridge requests an interview," Higgins announced in a haughty tone of voice.

"Ask him to come in," Adam instructed. He sent his uncle a puzzled look.

"I'll leave you to your guest," Uncle Charles said, starting to rise from the chair.

"Stay where you are," Adam ordered, gesturing him to remain seated. "We aren't finished yet."

The thirty-year-old Earl of Tunbridge walked into the study. He crossed the chamber, nodded at the duke, and reached out to shake Adam's hand.

"Please sit down," Adam invited him.

"No, thank you. I won't be staying long," the earl refused.

Adam looked at him expectantly.

"I would like your permission to court Sabrina Savage," Tunbridge announced. "I assure you that my intentions are serious and honorable."

Adam glanced at his uncle, who wore an infuriating grin. "The Duke of Kingston is her guardian."

The Earl of Tunbridge turned to the duke, saying, "Your Grace, I would like permission to—"

"Repeating yourself is unnecessary," Uncle Charles said, holding his hand up. "You have my permission as long as the lady welcomes your attentions."

"I thank you, Your Grace," the earl said. "Stonehurst, good day to you." At that, the Earl of Tunbridge left the study.

"I wish you hadn't done that," Adam said.

"You wanted Sabrina to meet other bachelors," Uncle Charles said in a surprised voice.

"I disapprove of Tunbridge," Adam told him.

"What's wrong with him?"

"Tunbridge drinks too much."

"Oh, I didn't know that," Uncle Charles said, and then shrugged. "I'm certain Sabrina will weed him out."

"By any chance, would Madame Esmeralda be Sabrina's mother?" Adam asked, changing the subject abruptly.

"Why would you think that?" Uncle Charles asked, shaking his head. "Because they have the same color hair?"

"You haven't answered my question," Adam said.

"I don't know who Sabrina's mother is," Uncle Charles answered, his gaze drifting to the window that overlooked the garden area.

He's lying, Adam decided, staring hard at his uncle. The old man knew more than he would ever admit. Adam admired his uncle's loyalty in keeping silent, but that same silence frustrated him. He decided to drop the matter for the moment.

"What do you think of Courtney and Dorchester?" Adam asked.

"They would make an excellent match," Uncle Charles answered, visibly relaxing. "I assume Belladonna is furthering that cause."

Adam nodded. Before he could speak, a second knock on the door drew his attention. "This must be Jamie Armstrong," he said. "He's already an hour late for our appointment."

"Lord Huntingdon requests an interview," Razi announced, entering the study.

"Send him in." Adam looked with growing irritation at his uncle. The old man was smiling, obviously enjoying himself.

The twenty-eight-year-old baron marched into the study. He crossed the chamber, nodded at the duke, and shook Adam's hand.

"Please be seated," Adam invited him.

"I won't be staying long," the baron said in refusal.

Adam flicked a glance at his uncle and then asked, "What can I do for you, Huntingdon?"

"I want your permission to court Sabrina Savage."

"Then you must speak with the Duke of Kingston, for he is her guardian," Adam told him.

Baron Huntingdon turned to the duke, saying, "Your Grace—"

"You have my permission providing the lady welcomes your attentions," Uncle Charles interrupted him.

"Thank you, Your Grace." Lord Huntingdon turned to Adam, saying, "Good day to you, Stonehurst." He left the study.

Adam narrowed his gaze on his uncle as soon as the door closed behind the baron.

"What did you expect me to do?" the duke asked.

"You could have refused him."

Uncle Charles sent him an incredulous look. "What is wrong with Huntingdon?"

"He gambles too much."

"Oh, I had no idea." Uncle Charles shrugged and said, "Sabrina has a good head on her shoulders. I'm certain she'll weed him out."

"Sabrina refuses to marry until her father's name is

cleared," Adam said. "Perhaps that will discourage Tunbridge and Huntingdon."

"What are the chances of clearing Henry's name?" his uncle asked him.

"No one hangs by accident."

"Do you believe Henry committed suicide?"

"I didn't say that," Adam answered. "I said his death was no accident."

"Are you implying Henry was murdered?" Uncle Charles exclaimed, his expression mirroring his shock. "Henry Savage was an affable, kindhearted gentleman. I cannot imagine anyone wanting him dead."

"Every man has enemies," Adam replied. A knock on the door drew his attention. "This must be Jamie."

"Viscount Lincoln requests an interview," Higgins announced as he walked into the study, making the duke chuckle.

Adam rolled his eyes and said in a weary voice, "Send him in."

Twenty-two-year-old Viscount Lincoln swaggered into the study. He nodded curtly, acknowledging the duke, and then turned to Adam, who held up his hand in a gesture for silence.

"The Duke of Kingston is Sabrina's guardian."

The viscount turned his back on Adam. "Your Grace, I want permission to marry your ward, Sabrina Savage."

"Marry?" Uncle Charles echoed.

"That is correct, Your Grace."

"My answer is *no*," Uncle Charles replied, "but I give you permission to call upon her."

"That will do for now." The viscount looked at Adam and said, "Good day to you."

Once the door clicked shut behind the suitor, the duke said, "I suppose there is something terribly wrong with Lincoln too?"

"The boy is uncouth."

"Uncouth?" Uncle Charles echoed.

"One night during intermission at the opera, I saw him adjusting his privates," Adam said.

His uncle burst out laughing. "Well, there is always Edgar Briggs."

"I don't like him."

"Mark my words. Sabrina will send them all away," Uncle Charles predicted. "Will you find fault with every gentleman who shows an interest in her?"

"Probably."

"Tell me about the assassination attempt," his uncle said, changing the subject.

"Someone took a shot at Jamie and me," Adam said.

"What are you doing about it?"

"I've hired men to investigate my business competitors," Adam told him. "I've also sent a message to the East through Ambassador Zaganos. Mother will look into the possibility of an Eastern connection."

"Do you think that is possible after all of these years?"

"Someone may have discovered that I survived childhood," Adam said with a shrug. "Being thorough is the best policy."

"I agree," Uncle Charles said, nodding.

The door opened suddenly to admit Higgins. Two

steps behind him ran Razi, complaining, "It's my turn."

"The Duke of Kinross has arrived," Higgins announced, ignoring the little man.

"Praise Allah," Adam muttered. "Send him in."

Wearing a broad grin, Jamie Armstrong walked into the study. He nodded at the duke and then sat in one of the chairs, saying, "Sorry I'm late."

"We've been under siege from all of Sabrina's would-be suitors," Adam told him. "Viscount Lincoln had the audacity to ask for her hand in marriage."

"That explains it," Jamie said. "The whole area around Grosvenor Square is congested with traffic."

Adam rose from his chair as unfamiliar jealousy swelled within his chest. "Make yourself at home," he said, walking toward the door. "I'll return as soon as I can."

"Where are you going?" Jamie called.

"Grosvenor Square," Adam answered over his shoulder. The sound of his uncle's and his friend's laughter transformed his jealousy into anger.

Enough is enough, Adam thought, blaming Sabrina for the number of men who wanted her. Granted, he preferred that Sabrina marry him willingly, but he refused to stand in line for what was his by right.

Adam debated walking to his uncle's town house but decided against it because of the attempt on his life. The carriage ride to Grosvenor Square should have taken no more than ten minutes. Twenty minutes later his carriage was hopelessly caught in the congestion on Upper Brook Street.

Disgusted, Adam opened the door and leaped out of

the carriage. "I'll walk the rest of the way," he called to his men. "Take the carriage home."

"I will guard you, my prince," Abdul said, leaping off the driver's seat.

Adam inclined his head. "As you wish."

Together, Adam and Abdul walked briskly down Upper Brook Street, which led to Grosvenor Square. Several aristocrats waved a greeting to Adam, and when they entered Grosvenor Square, Adam recognized Viscount Lincoln leaving his uncle's town house and climbing into his carriage.

Racing up the stairs, Adam opened the front door without knocking and walked into the foyer. Abdul followed behind him.

"Good afternoon, my lord," Baxter greeted him, snapping to attention.

Adam nodded at his uncle's majordomo and then shifted his gaze to the foyer table against the wall. Two silver trays sat there filled with calling cards. He assumed one tray was for Sabrina and the other for Courtney.

"The ladies are not receiving company today," Baxter informed him. "Except for Viscount Dorchester and his aunt, of course."

Apparently he'd underestimated Dudley Egremont, Adam thought. The pup had enough intelligence to outfox his competition. While other callers were being sent away, Egremont had used his aunt to gain access to Courtney. The boy certainly would be a worthy brother-in-law.

"The drawing room?" Adam asked.

"Yes, my lord."

Leaving Abdul in the foyer, Adam climbed the stairs and then walked down the second-floor corridor. He stopped short when he stepped into the drawing room. Everyone but Sabrina had gathered there.

"Adam, darling, come and visit with us," Belladonna drawled.

Adam greeted them with a curt nod and then turned away to retrace his steps to the foyer. "Where is she?" he growled at the majordomo.

"She, my lord?"

"Sabrina, damn it."

"The countess is in the kitchen," the majordomo informed him.

"Why didn't he tell me in the first place?" Adam muttered loudly, walking down the corridor toward the kitchen.

"I would have told him if he'd asked," Baxter complained in a voice loud enough for Adam to hear.

Like an invading general, Adam marched to the kitchen, but then paused outside the door. Was he angry because other men found Sabrina attractive? If they did, that wasn't her fault. Or was it? She'd danced and flirted with many bachelors at the ball last night.

He was jealous, Adam admitted to himself. And he didn't like the feeling one damned bit.

He burst into the kitchen, startling Sabrina. She whirled around in fright. Winston, sitting beside the table, leaped up and tried to lick his face.

"Sit, Winston," Adam ordered, patting the wolfhound's head. When the dog obeyed, he said, "Good boy."

Adam looked at Sabrina and smiled. He reached out

with one finger and wiped the flour smudge off the tip of her nose. "What are you making?" he asked.

"Coconut cake."

"Should I assume you are upset about something?" he asked.

"I feel hunted," Sabrina said. "Did you see the tray of calling cards in the foyer?"

"I hadn't noticed," Adam lied. "I suppose that is the price one must pay for being an original."

"Thank you for the compliment, but I hardly consider myself an original," Sabrina said with a smile. "Life would be more peaceful as part of the pack."

"If no gentleman interests you," Adam said, his jealousy subsiding, "there will be others at the next social event."

"On the contrary, I found several gentlemen appealing," Sabrina said, surprising him.

"Who?"

"I thought the Earl of Tunbridge was pleasant," Sabrina said.

"He drinks too much."

"Lord Huntingdon was charming."

"He has already lost a small fortune at the gaming tables," Adam informed her.

Sabrina's expression began to register irritation. "Viscount Lincoln was pleasant."

Adam shook his head. "He is uncouth."

"Uncouth? I cannot believe my ears," Sabrina cried. "You wanted me to meet bachelors, and now you disapprove of anyone I mention. All of them cannot be flawed, my lord."

"The men you mentioned are unworthy of you,"

Adam said. "Ride with me tomorrow morning in Hyde Park."

"I already have a date to ride with Edgar Briggs," Sabrina told him.

"Briggs is unsuitable, so riding with him is a waste of time," Adam replied. "I forbid it."

"You forbid it?" Her expression mirrored angry disbelief. "How dare you dictate to me."

"Ride with me the day after tomorrow," Adam said, ignoring her anger.

"I promised the Earl of Tunbridge I'd ride with him that morning," Sabrina said.

Jealousy and anger swelled within Adam. "Our agreement stipulated that you would spend time with me each week," he reminded her.

"And so I will," Sabrina replied. "You need to make an appointment."

"I refuse to stand in line with your admirers," Adam told her, his voice rising in direct proportion to his annoyance.

"As you wish, my lord," Sabrina surrendered to his demands. "I will save every Friday for you."

"Friday?" Adam exploded. "I never go about on Fridays."

Sabrina's smile was positively feline. "Yes, I know."

"You are straining my patience," he warned, narrowing his gaze on her.

"You? Patient?"

"Select a day," Adam ordered, his voice rising with his anger.

"Let me see," Sabrina said, placing one finger to

her right temple as if she needed to concentrate. "I'm riding with Lord Briggs tomorrow. The following day belongs to the Earl of Tunbridge. I'm obliged to Lord Huntingdon after that, and then there's Viscount Lincoln." She smiled sweetly. "Next Saturday would be the best day for me."

"Six days from now?" Adam practically shouted, as if he couldn't believe what he'd heard.

"Very good, my lord," Sabrina teased, savoring the feeling of having the upper hand with him for once. "I see that you know your days of the week."

"Princess, sarcasm does not become you." Without another word, Adam quit the kitchen. Reaching the foyer, he spied his aunt waiting there for him.

"I want to speak to you," Belladonna said.

"What is it?" he growled.

"You forgot to keep your expression placid," Belladonna said with a knowing smile.

In return, Adam gave her a look of total disgust and tried to brush past her.

"I know how to bring Sabrina to you," his aunt said.

Adam stopped, then turned around slowly. "I do not need advice concerning women," he told her.

Belladonna smiled. "Yes, I can see how successful you've been today. At this rate, you and Sabrina will be married in the next century."

Adam stared at her for a long moment. "Go on," he said finally.

"I overheard Sabrina complaining to her sister about Alexis Carstairs," Belladonna told him. "I believe her exact words were 'that brazen harlot.' "

"And?" Adam asked, a grudging smile flirting with
his lips.

"Apparently, Sabrina is susceptible to jealousy,"
Belladonna said. "I will keep you informed about her
schedule, and you contrive to be there with Alexis Carstairs."

Adam inclined his head. "I will consider your
offer."

Who did the marquess think he was? Sabrina fumed,
early the next morning as she dressed for her ride with
Edgar. Adam St. Aubyn was not her keeper and had no
right to forbid her to see anyone. She would make a
point of seeing those men whom he considered unsuitable, and thereby teach him a lesson he would not soon
forget.

Sabrina dressed in a sapphire woolen gown and
matching cloak with a muff. She brushed her copper
hair back off her face and tied it in a knot at the nape of
her neck.

"Come, Winston," she called, heading for the door.
The wolfhound followed her out of the bedchamber and
then ran ahead of her down the stairs to the foyer.

Sabrina smiled to herself when she heard the omi-
nous sound of the dog's growling. Apparently, Edgar
had already arrived and awaited her in the foyer. Walking down the last section of the staircase, she spied
Edgar standing statue-still while Winston stood in front
of him and growled his dislike.

"Sit, Winston," she ordered in a stern voice, imitating the marquess. Instantly, the dog obeyed her.
"Forbes, take Winston to the kitchen for a treat."

"I still say that dog is a menace," Edgar said,

watching the wolfhound walk away with the major-domo.

"Winston is sweeter than walnut pudding with choc-olate sauce," Sabrina replied.

Winter wore a serene expression that morning. The fog seemed sheerer than usual, and Sabrina thought she saw a brightening in the eastern sky where the sun should have been at that time of day.

Within ten minutes, Edgar steered their carriage through Grosvenor Gate into Hyde Park. From there, they drove down the lane toward Rotten Row. Several passing gentlemen whom she'd met at her coming-out tipped their hats in her direction and called a greeting to Edgar.

Sabrina suffered only one bad moment. When Edgar turned their carriage around to retrace their route down Rotten Row, she spied a man and a woman on horse-back riding toward them. Her heart sank to her stomach when she realized who they were: Adam and Alexis Carstairs.

"Good morning, Edgar," Alexis called when her horse came abreast of them. "Nice to see you again, Sabrina."

"Good morning," Edgar returned her greeting.

For his part, Adam tipped his hat at her and gave Edgar a curt nod. Sabrina lifted her nose into the air and refused to acknowledge either one of them.

"I told you Lady Rothbury and the marquess were lovers," Edgar said after they'd passed the couple.

"I have a headache," Sabrina announced, unac-countably troubled by the sight of Adam with that woman. "Please, take me home now."

The following morning the Earl of Tunbridge arrived in the foyer precisely on time for his appointment with Sabrina. His eyes were rimmed in red, and Sabrina thought she smelled spirits on his breath, but she was determined to go riding with him because Adam had discouraged it. Besides, she had no idea how to break an appointment without offending the other person.

Sabrina felt relieved that the earl hadn't drunk enough to impair his carriage-driving skills and place her in jeopardy. As they made their return trip down Rotten Row, Sabrina spied Adam with Alexis Carstairs again. The couple turned their horses and rode in a different direction when they saw her.

Watching them ride away together, Sabrina felt pangs of jealousy shoot through her. Did the marquess really care about Alexis Carstairs? If he did, why had he bothered to maintain his betrothal to her? Was he intent on marrying her out of some misplaced sense of loyalty to their fathers' wishes? She didn't want a husband who loved another woman.

"I toasted Stonehurst's almost-betrothal last night at White's," the Earl of Tunbridge said, yanking her out of her thoughts. "I don't understand why he didn't appreciate it."

Sabrina looked at the earl more closely. Adam had been correct; the earl loved his drink.

"I have a headache," Sabrina announced, her dejection making her want to escape. "Please, take me home now."

On Wednesday morning, Lord Huntingdon escorted Sabrina on a carriage ride through Hyde Park. He followed the same route she'd taken the preceding two mornings.

Again, Sabrina saw Adam and Alexis riding together. Full-bodied jealousy swelled within her breast and made breathing difficult.

"I have a lot of money wagered in favor of their marriage," Baron Huntingdon said, leaning close to whisper in her ear. "Would you care to place a small wager on whether I'll win?"

Sabrina snapped her head around to stare at the baron. Adam had been correct; the baron did love to gamble.

"I have a headache," she told the baron. "Take me home please."

Sabrina had no date to ride in Hyde Park on Thursday morning, but that brought her no peace. Opening *The Times*, she found almost a whole column devoted to Lady Smythe's ball the previous evening and the activities of Adam and Alexis. The reporter even had the audacity to speculate about how much time would pass before the Marquess of Stonehurst and the Countess of Rothbury announced their betrothal.

The anger that had been simmering inside Sabrina became a raging boil. How dare the marquess squire another woman around town when he was her betrothed and had been for the past fifteen years. The fact that he'd given her time to decide if she wanted him did not give him the right to make a spectacle of himself with another woman.

Accompanied by her sister and their aunts, Sabrina attended the opera that evening with Viscount Lincoln. Adam had kindly loaned them his private box.

The opera began. In the dimness of the theatre, a
movement on her right side caught her attention. Sabrina flicked a sidelong glance at the viscount and
caught him with his hand on his own groin. Shocked
and offended, Sabrina wanted to leave but remained
where she was. What reason could she possibly give for
wanting to leave almost as soon as the opera began?
Keeping her attention focused on the stage, she refused
to look at the viscount even when he spoke to her.

And then intermission arrived. Across the theatre
Adam sat with Alexis Carstairs. The sight of them together again was more than she could endure.

"I have a headache," Sabrina announced, rising
from her chair abruptly. "I am going home and will
send the carriage back for you."

"I'll escort you there," Viscount Lincoln said, starting to rise.

"No, you won't," Sabrina snapped. She covered her
lapse in manners with a smile and said, "Stay and enjoy yourself. I'll be fine in the morning."

"You have suffered several headaches this week,"
Belladonna remarked. "I think you should see a physi-
cian."

"We'll discuss that in the morning," Sabrina said,
and escaped from the box.

Twenty minutes later, Sabrina was walking into the
town house in Grosvenor Square. With a heavy heart,
she climbed the stairs to her third-floor bedchamber
and sat down in front of the hearth. Winston licked her
hand as if he sensed her mood.

Adam St. Aubyn certainly behaved as if he had no
betrothed, Sabrina thought in dejection. She should

have seen him for what he was from the very beginning—a scoundrel of the first rank.

Glancing down at the ring he'd given her, Sabrina decided that it meant nothing. She removed the betrothal ring and placed it inside a drawer in the high-boy.

Sabrina suffered the almost overpowering urge to bake but fought it back. Tomorrow morning would be soon enough.

After a restless night, Sabrina rose early and changed into a simple muslin dress. She wished her black gowns hadn't been packed away, for the somberness of black matched her mood.

Leaving her chamber, Sabrina and Winston walked downstairs to the foyer. Baxter was just opening the front door to allow someone entrance. The wolfhound barked and dashed toward the newcomer.

"Sit, Winston," Adam said, patting the dog's head. "Good boy."

Sabrina threw the marquess a quick glance and didn't bother to greet him. Instead, she started down the corridor toward the dining room.

"Sabrina," he called.

She paused and, without bothering to turn around, said, "Yes, my lord?"

"Look at me, please."

Slowly, Sabrina turned around. He would have had to be blind not to recognize the frigid look in her expression.

"Get your cloak," he ordered. "We are riding in Hyde Park this morning."

Sabrina arched a brow at him. "I thought you didn't go about on Fridays."

"I am making an exception for you," he replied.

"I have a previous appointment with Lord Briggs," she lied. "Riding with you is impossible this morning."

"When the baron arrives, send him away," Adam ordered, turning to the majordomo. "Tell him Lady Sabrina is feeling under the eaves today."

At that, Adam started walking toward her. He appeared to be a man with a purpose.

Instinctively, Sabrina stepped back a pace, but he caught her wrist and forced her to walk with him down the corridor to the study. She could either go with him willingly or struggle with him in front of the servants.

Once they'd gained the study, Sabrina whirled around to confront him. She saw him drop his gaze to her right hand and felt satisfied when surprise registered on his face.

"Where is your ring?" Adam demanded.

Sabrina ignored his question.

"I'm waiting for an explanation."

"Where is Alexis Carstairs?" Sabrina asked. "I thought the two of you were joined at the hip. I think the gossip about you is nauseating in the extreme."

"And so do I," Adam said. "However, we aren't here to discuss my lack of morals."

"Are you implying that I lack moral fiber?" she demanded, her green eyes glittering with anger.

"Riding with a different man each morning will cause gossip," he told her. "Your behavior is unbecoming to the future Duchess of Kingston."

"In order for me to become the Duchess of Kingston, I would need to be your wife," Sabrina said.

"The point is you will be my wife one day," Adam said.

"You arrogant, faithless—I wouldn't marry you if you were the last man in England," Sabrina cried, searching her mind for a worse insult to hurl at him.

"Princess, we are married."

Chapter 11

Shock knocked the breath out of Sabrina. She felt as though she'd been kicked in the stomach and couldn't catch a breath. The room spun dizzyingly, and the carpet rushed up to greet her.

Something wet tickled her cheek. Sabrina opened her eyes to see Winston, and she realized she was lying on the couch near the hearth. Sabrina focused on the marquess, who crouched beside the couch and watched her.

"You will feel better in a few minutes," Adam said, lightly caressing her arm. A hint of a smile touched his lips when he added, "I knew you would crumple beneath the truth."

"Do you refer to *the* truth or *your* truth?" Sabrina asked coldly. She tried to sit up, and when Adam reached out to help her, she snapped, "Don't touch me."

Adam withdrew his hand and straightened his body.

"My truth is the truth," he said, looking down at her through piercing blue eyes. "As children, we were wed."

"I don't believe you," Sabrina told him.

"I can produce the marriage certificate," he told her.

Sabrina cocked a copper brow at him. "A forgery, perhaps?"

"If you don't believe me, ask my uncle," Adam replied.

"Your uncle is your accomplice," Sabrina said, rising unsteadily from the couch.

"Then ask your aunt. She's known about our marriage for years."

"Aunt Tess?" Sabrina felt confused and betrayed. Why hadn't her aunt told her? Why had her father done this to her?

"Your father refused Edgar Briggs because you already had a husband," Adam told her.

Sabrina didn't know what to believe. If it was true, she thought, becoming angry, then the marquess had been committing adultery with Alexis Carstairs. God only knew who else had shared his bed. Apparently, his pleasing appearance hid a wicked heart. The marquess was not the kind of man she would choose for a husband. Once an adulterer, always an adulterer.

"Assuming I believe you, you did give me the option of finding a suitable husband," Sabrina said. "What would you have done if I had fallen in love with another gentleman?" Sabrina asked.

"There was no danger of that happening."

"You arrogant, conceited, insufferable—"

"Tread lightly, my lady," Adam interrupted.

"I refuse to let you ruin my life," Sabrina said, her voice rising with her anger. She turned away and showed him her back.

Adam whirled her around. Grasping both of her forearms, he yanked her close to his body.

Surprised, Sabrina stared into his eyes. "You are hurting me," she said.

Instantly, Adam loosened his grip. "Let me recount the ways I have ruined your life," he said. "I rang the death knell for your father and promised to clear his name from the taint of suicide. I have also given you a season in London, a completely new wardrobe, and priceless jewels."

Sabrina felt ashamed of herself. The marquess was correct; he had shown her many kindnesses. That did not give him ownership of her person, though.

"I do appreciate what you have done for me," Sabrina said. "But I prefer—"

"Spare me your preferences," Adam said, his tone of voice colder than ever.

Like a sudden gust of wind, Sabrina's anger returned to vanquish her shame. Holding on to the image of Alexis Carstairs, Sabrina informed him, "I have no wish to marry you."

"Too late, my lady," Adam said. "Come the first day of April we will celebrate our fourteenth wedding anniversary."

God shield me, Sabrina thought, uncertain of what her next move should be. And then an idea popped into her mind.

"I want an annulment," she told him.

A brief expression of pain crossed his face, then vanished as if it had never been there. "Don't be absurd," he said.

"I am not being absurd," Sabrina insisted. "I want you out of this room, out of this house, and out of my life."

Instead of shouting at her as she expected, Adam stared at her for several long moments. Then, without saying another word, he turned and left the study.

Watching him walk away, Sabrina felt an urge to call him back but successfully squelched it. She plopped down on the couch, and, surrendering to her tears, covered her face and wept.

Slurp! Something wet tickled her hand.

Sabrina looked up to see Winston sitting in front of her. She put her arms around the dog's neck and gave him a hug.

What had she done? Sabrina wondered, sitting back on the couch. She'd lost her temper and hurt a man who had been kind to her, kinder than any other man she'd ever met. But how could she accept the fact that they were actually married? She hardly knew him.

And yet, everything the marquess said sounded like truth. Why couldn't he have courted her like any normal man and won her affections?

He tried to court you, an inner voice answered. *Jealousy made you rebuff him.*

And then Sabrina thought of her father. She couldn't believe her wonderful father would marry her off at the age of three to a complete stranger. If it was true, he must have had a good reason, but when had he planned to tell her the shocking news? And then there was the matter of her aunt. If Aunt Tess had known for years, why hadn't she told her? Didn't a woman have the right to know if she was married or not?

Sabrina rose from the couch. Her head was beginning to pound with a *real* headache. She needed time alone to think and didn't want anyone to see her like this.

Followed by the wolfhound, Sabrina left the study. She stopped in the foyer before climbing the stairs to the third floor.

"I am not receiving company today," she told the two majordomos.

"Very good, my lady," Baxter replied.

"Have you been weeping?" Forbes asked. "What did the marquess—?"

Sabrina held her hand up in a gesture for silence. "I have a headache and wish to rest undisturbed for the remainder of the day."

With the wolfhound beside her, Sabrina started up the stairs. She hadn't reached the first landing when the front door swung open. Lady Belladonna, Aunt Tess, and Courtney entered the foyer.

"Sabrina, darling," Belladonna called. "We've just seen Adam driving away as if the hounds of hell were after him."

"You haven't annoyed the marquess again?" Aunt Tess asked.

Slowly, Sabrina turned to face the three women. She leveled an accusing look at her aunt.

"Adam told her," Belladonna said, grasping her friend's arm.

"I know everything," Sabrina said, her gaze fixed on her aunt.

"Oh, Lord," Tess moaned.

"What did Adam tell her?" Courtney asked.

Ignoring her sister, Sabrina said coldly, "You should have told me, Aunt Tess, especially after Father died. I am very disappointed in you."

"I'm sorry, child," Aunt Tess said, taking a step forward. "I thought my silence was all for the best."

Whirling away, Sabrina rushed up the stairs and sought refuge in her own bedchamber. She locked the door and then sat in front of the hearth. Winston sat down in front of her and rested his head in her lap.

Sabrina sighed heavily.

Winston gave her an answering sigh and then wagged his tail.

Sabrina patted the top of his head. Now that her anger had passed, she felt depleted of energy. Remorse for the horrible things she'd said coiled itself around her heart. Never had she spoken so cruelly to anyone. Why had she chosen to vent her anger upon the marquess? He had been the soul of kindness to her and Courtney. And she had repaid his kindness with hurtful words. Oh, yes, he had been hurt. She'd seen the fleeting expression of pain that crossed his features.

It wasn't as if the thought of marriage to him repulsed her. With his dark good looks, he attracted her as no other man had before.

Sabrina leaned back in the chair and closed her eyes to summon the marquess's image in her mind. Adam was handsome, titled, and wealthy, and he was wanted by almost every female who saw him. So why did he wish to marry an adopted bastard, albeit a countess? What was in it for him?

Besides, Adam had lied to her. Failing to tell the whole truth *was* a lie.

Sabrina couldn't shake his brief expression of pain. Strangely, she hadn't felt any remorse when she'd rejected Edgar. Was that because she harbored a fondness for the marquess?

Sabrina knew she harbored more than a fondness for him. She was beginning to love the man who called himself her husband.

Husband. That word echoed within her mind.

Sabrina decided that she needed to speak to the marquess the first thing the next morning. After that, she would let him court her and see where their relationship went.

Rising from the chair, Sabrina crossed the bedchamber to the highboy. She took the winter rose betrothal ring out of the drawer and stared at it for a moment. Then she slipped it on the third finger of her left hand.

With that settled, Sabrina began pacing back and forth across the bedchamber. What words could she use to erase the pain she'd caused? Would Adam accept her apology? Would he even agree to see her?

She knew he would not come to Grosvenor Square if she summoned him. The man was too proud to do that. She would go to his town house on Park Lane.

And then an idea popped into her head and brought a smile to her lips. She would make the marquess his favorite sweets, nougat and Turkish delight.

"Come, Winston." Sabrina left the chamber with the wolfhound and hurried down the corridor to the stairs. When she reached the foyer, she called to the majordomo without breaking stride, "I need sugar, honey, eggs, almonds, pistachios, cornstarch, lemon and rose flavorings."

"Yes, my lady." Forbes started after her.

Baxter grabbed his arm and asked, "What is the countess baking this time?"

Forbes grinned at the other man's ignorance. "Nougat and Turkish delight, of course."

"Forbes, where are you?"

"Coming, my lady . . ."

At noon the following day, Sabrina stood in front of the marquess's town house on Park Lane. She carried a covered silver tray and reached out with her free hand to bang the knocker. Almost immediately, a tall and dignified-looking servant opened the door.

The majordomo looked down at her and asked in a haughty voice, "How may I help you?"

Uncertain in the face of his superiority, Sabrina hesitated, but then pictured the man staring cross-eyed at her. "I wish to speak with the Marquess of Stonehurst," she announced in a strong voice.

"Who should I say is calling?"

His wife, Sabrina thought. "Lady Abingdon," she said.

"Sabrina, is that you?" she heard Uncle Charles call from inside the foyer. Then, "Let the lady inside."

The majordomo stepped aside to allow her entrance to the foyer. Sabrina smiled as the duke rushed forward to greet her. "What are you doing here?" he asked. "Is something wrong?"

"I must speak with Adam," Sabrina said, dropping her gaze. "I suppose you already know the reason."

"Adam left for Stonehurst last night," Uncle Charles told her. "Stonehurst is his private retreat, a small, renovated castle built on its own island. Come to the study, and we'll speak privately."

Sabrina let the duke usher her down the first-floor corridor to the study. Wherever she looked, she felt Adam's presence.

"Sit here near the hearth," Uncle Charles said. "Would you care for refreshment?"

Sabrina shook her head and sat down. "Is it true, then?"

"As children, Adam and you were wed," the duke verified, sitting in the chair opposite her. "He never meant to withhold the truth, only to give you an option if you didn't care for him."

"Why did you and my father marry us off as children?" Sabrina asked. "I thought that barbaric custom ended centuries ago."

"Even today, the wealthy arrange marriages for their children," the duke said.

"A world of difference lies between arranging marriages and actually having children joined in wedlock," Sabrina countered.

The duke sighed. "The three of us thought Adam and you would make a good match."

"The three of us?" Sabrina echoed, confused by his words.

"Henry, I, and your natural father," he explained.

Sabrina stared in surprise at him. "You know who my natural father is? I asked you before—"

"Many years ago, I swore to keep the secret," the duke said. "I will tell you only if you agree never to reveal his identity."

Sabrina inclined her head. She would have agreed to anything he asked. What she had yearned for her whole life was about to be hers, the knowledge of where she came from.

"Your natural father is Prince Adolphus," he said.

"Prince Adolphus?" Sabrina exclaimed. "Are you saying that King George is my grandfather and the Regent is my uncle?"

Uncle Charles nodded. "You will never be acknowledged."

"And Courtney?"

"Prince Adolphus sired both of you. On different women, of course."

Sabrina stared into the hearth's flames. Which was more urgent, speaking to Adam or to Prince Adolphus?

"Who was my mother?" she asked.

"I don't know, but I do have some suspicions," he answered.

"Well, whom do you suspect?"

"I would never name any woman unless I knew the facts."

"Prince Adolphus will tell me," Sabrina said, and dropped her gaze to her hands folded in her lap. Though the knowledge she'd always yearned for was hers, the happy satisfaction she should have felt was missing. Now she felt disloyal to her father and aunt for wanting to know her true identity. Any parent who refused to acknowledge a child was actually no parent at all. Henry Savage had taken her into his home and loved her as though she were his. He was her true father, not the man who sired her.

"Sabrina?"

She returned her attention to the duke. "Thank you for telling me all this. When do you think Adam will return? I want to speak to him."

"Who can say?" Uncle Charles shrugged. "Why don't you go to Stonehurst?"

"How far is it?"

"Two hundred miles as the eagle flies."

Sabrina was unable to keep the disappointment off her face. Traveling two hundred miles was out of the question. The journey would take nearly a week, and a chaperon would be required. Neither Aunt Tess nor Belladonna would encourage such a venture. No, she would need to wait for his return.

"Traveling by ship will take less than a day," Uncle Charles said as if he knew her thoughts. "Stonehurst is built on an island off Cornwall. Adam does love his privacy."

"I have no ship and no chaperon," Sabrina replied. "What would people say about my staying at his residence?"

"Child, you are his wife and need no chaperon."

Sabrina wet her lips. If she went to Stonehurst, her future would be sealed. No annulment could be possible. On the other hand, did she really want to go through life without him?

"Several of my nephew's ships are moored in the Thames," Uncle Charles told her. "I am acquainted with his captains and will send them a message that the Marchioness of Stonehurst wishes to go home to her husband.''

Sabrina smiled. "When can I leave?''

"With tonight's tide,'' Uncle Charles answered. "Return to Grosvenor Square and pack your belongings. I assume that wolfhound will be accompanying you.''

"Winston goes wherever I go,'' Sabrina said, rising from the couch.

"I'll send you a message about the time,'' Uncle Charles said, escorting her to the foyer. "I personally will escort you to the docks.''

"Thank you, Uncle Charles.'' Sabrina leaned close and kissed the duke's cheek.

Fifteen minutes later Sabrina rushed into the foyer of the town house at Grosvenor Square. Still carrying the tray of sweets, she started up the stairs and called over her shoulder, "Send a couple of maids to my chamber to help me pack.''

"Pack, my lady?'' Forbes echoed.

"Yes, where is my aunt?''

"She's in the drawing room with the others.''

Sabrina burst into the drawing room and stopped short at the sight that greeted her. Edgar Briggs sat in one of the chairs and conversed with the two older women, her sister, and Dudley Egremont.

Briggs stood when he spied her. Smiling, he started across the chamber to greet her, but she held up her hand in a gesture for him to stop.

"I cannot visit with you today because I have another headache,'' Sabrina lied. ''Aunt Tess, may I speak with you upstairs?''

Lord Briggs closed the distance between them and said, ''I knew I should never have allowed you to come to London.''

''Allowed?'' Sabrina echoed in disbelief.

''I know I've lost you,'' Edgar said, dropping his voice so only she could hear him.

''I was never yours to lose,'' Sabrina told him, ''but we will always be the dearest of friends.''

''The marquess despises me,'' he replied.

As does Winston, Sabrina thought. ''Can we speak of this at a later time?'' she asked with a twinge of guilt. ''I am in a hurry.''

''You said you had a headache,'' Briggs said, unable to keep his suspicion out of his voice.

''I am in a hurry to go upstairs.'' Sabrina looked at her aunt and asked, ''Will you come with me? Where is Winston?''

Both Aunt Tess and Lady DeFaye rose from their chairs and crossed the chamber to where she stood with Edgar.

''We left Winston in your chamber so he wouldn't frighten any callers,'' Aunt Tess told her.

''Edgar, be a dear and run along,'' Belladonna said. ''Do visit us again.'' Belladonna put her arm around Sabrina and ushered her out of the drawing room, saying, ''Come, darling. I know just the thing for your headache.''

''What mischief are you up to?'' Aunt Tess asked as soon as the three of them reached the bedchamber.

"Winston and I are going to Stonehurst," Sabrina said. "Uncle Charles is making the arrangements."

"Thank God you've come to your senses," Belladonna said with relief. "Is there anything you would like to know about bedding your husband?"

"Bedding?" A high blush stained Sabrina's cheeks. "I only want to speak to Adam and cannot wait for his return."

"Adam will assume you want to be his wife if you go to Stonehurst," Belladonna told her.

"That's correct," Aunt Tess agreed. "You'll never go wrong if you follow one simple rule: Trust your husband in all matters."

Lady DeFaye nodded. "Adam will show you how it's done."

"How it's done?" Sabrina echoed, her face draining of color.

"There's nothing to fear," Aunt Tess assured her, patting her shoulder. "Would the world be so populated if there wasn't pleasure in the act?"

"Absolutely not! The world would be deserted," Belladonna answered her aunt's rhetorical question. Then she added mischievously, "To my knowledge, darling, there's only been one immaculate conception, and that occurred almost two thousand years ago. So, you see, millions of women have enjoyed bedding down with men."

Sabrina hadn't thought in those terms, but supposed Belladonna was correct. For better or for worse, she was going to Adam. . . .

By six o'clock that evening, Sabrina and Winston were ensconced in Adam's quarters on board *The Voy-*

ager. She'd never traveled by water before and hoped she wouldn't get sick.

Doubts began to swirl around in her mind. Her future would be sealed once she arrived at Stonehurst; she would be Adam's wife until death parted them. Was this what she wanted? More importantly, what did Adam want now? Would he welcome her after the terrible words she'd said? Even worse, would he make her his wife in fact and then exact revenge for what she'd said? No, that was too absurd even to consider. Adam St. Aubyn was a man of integrity.

Her confidence in him made her smile. After watching the wolfhound eat supper with his usual gusto, Sabrina let the ship's rocking motion lull her to sleep.

Sabrina was already dressed and waiting the next morning when someone knocked on her door. "Come in," she called.

The door opened, and Captain Tibbets walked into the cabin. A boy followed him, set a tray on the table, and left.

"I thought you would like a light breakfast while we drop anchor and prepare to disembark."

"We've arrived?" Sabrina said.

The captain nodded. "I have duties on deck and will return in a few minutes."

Alone again, Sabrina knew she would be unable to swallow a bite until after she'd faced her husband. She set the tray on the floor for Winston, who immediately began to eat both of their breakfasts.

Her husband.

Sabrina smiled to herself. Those two words warmed

her heart. The only frightening thing was the possibility that he would send her away.

A knock on the door drew her attention away from Adam, and she heard the captain call out, "My lady, are you ready to leave?"

"Yes, Captain."

Captain Tibbetts walked in and was followed by the two seaman who would carry her belongings on deck. Sabrina let the captain escort her down the narrow passageway to the stairs that led on deck.

No fog, Sabrina thought, stepping out into the bright sunlight. She breathed deeply of the crisp, salty air. Overhead, the sky was a healthy shade of blue, so different from London's yellow gloom.

"There's Stonehurst," Captain Tibbets said, pointing at an island in the bay.

The breathtaking beauty of her husband's rocky fortress caught Sabrina by surprise. Crowned by a jewel of a castle, the small island rose toward the heavens. The whole panorama seemed too perfect to be real, an idealized image conceived in an artist's mind.

"What are those buildings near the beach?" Sabrina asked.

"Those are the homes of his lordship's servants," the captain told her. "One can only reach the island by boat, though the trip across the bay is short. Come, my lady. The longboat awaits us."

Sabrina saw that the longboat had already been lowered into the water. Several men, including the first mate, sat in it. Only then did she realize that she would need to climb down the rope ladder to the boat.

"How will Winston get down?" she asked.

"Don't worry about the dog," the captain said. "We'll use the pulley reserved for the sick or injured."

He gestured to where his men were harnessing a struggling Winston into a slinglike contraption attached to a pulley. Taking the silver container of sweets out of her hand, Captain Tibbets said, "You go down first, and I'll see to the dog."

The captain helped her over the side of the boat, and Sabrina started to climb down. The first mate's hands were there to help her the final few rungs. Then Winston was lowered into the boat, and the captain climbed down after the dog was settled.

Within ten minutes the men were pulling the longboat onto the sandy beach near the stone houses of the little village. Several of the island's inhabitants had gathered to watch.

Captain Tibbets helped her out of the boat and handed her the box of sweets. Winston needed no assistance. He leaped out of the boat and began running around on the sand.

"Come, my lady," Captain Tibbets said, offering her his hand. "We must walk up that pathway."

Sabrina looked up at the castle. It seemed higher from the beach than it had from the ship.

"The walk is two hundred and thirty feet up," the captain said.

"*Captain Tibbets.*"

Sabrina turned toward the voice and saw Abdul making his way past the curious spectators. He stopped in front of her and bowed from the waist.

"Welcome, my princess," Abdul greeted her.

Sabrina was shocked by his gesture and words. How did this servant know Adam's pet name for her?

"Will you accompany us?" Abdul asked the captain.

"I'll leave the lady in your capable hands," Captain Tibbets refused. "I have a full cargo, and my men are anxious to set sail."

Abdul nodded and then turned to Sabrina, saying, "Please, come with me."

"Thank you, sir," she called to the captain. "Come, Winston."

Sabrina walked up the long pathway to the castle set on top of the mount. In silence, Abdul walked beside her while Winston raced to and fro and inhaled myriad new scents.

Abdul escorted Sabrina into the castle's great hall with its magnificently timbered ceiling. The walls had been painted a stark white, which emphasized the portraits, banners, and sconces adorning it. The furniture was oak, as was the floor. The white marble hearth blended with the walls.

"Sit, Winston," Sabrina ordered, standing near the hearth.

A small, rotund man rushed forward and spoke in a foreign language that she failed to recognize. When Abdul answered in the same language, the little man turned to her and bowed from the waist. Then he hurried out of the hall.

"Razi has gone to find his lordship," Abdul told her. He bowed again and then left the hall.

Alone now, Sabrina felt the insecurities and doubts

creeping back into her mind. She felt like an unwanted guest, an intruder. She didn't belong here.

And then Adam walked into the hall. Ignoring the wolfhound's enthusiastic greeting, he paused inside the archway and stared at her.

Sabrina had never seen him dressed so casually. In his black breeches and black shirt opened at the neck, he appeared even more handsome than she remembered.

"What are you doing here?" Adam asked, walking across the hall toward her.

Oh, Lord, he's keeping his expression placid, Sabrina thought. *No help there.*

"I stopped by to apologize for my bad behavior," Sabrina said, and gave him a tentative smile.

Adam cocked a dark brow at her. "You happened to be in the vicinity of my island and decided to stop by?"

"Yes, my lord," Sabrina replied, trying to hide her smile and dropping her gaze. When he said nothing, she ventured a peek at him and saw his gaze fixed on the betrothal ring she wore on her left hand.

"I've brought you a peace offering," she said, holding up the silver box.

"And what would that be?" he asked, lifting his gaze to hers.

"French sunshine and exotic locales."

Adam smiled then and crossed the remaining distance between them. He accepted her gift and set it on a table. Then he lifted her left hand to his lips and said, "I forgive you, Princess."

"And I forgive you for lying to me," Sabrina replied. Then she amended herself by saying, "As long as you never lie to me again."

"No more lies," Adam agreed.

"No half-truths or omissions either."

Adam inclined his head and smiled at her.

And Sabrina knew that his devastating smile would always remind her of French sunshine.

Adam took her hands in his and drew her toward him. He looked down at her through those blue eyes and said in a quiet voice, "I would have given you an annulment if you had met another gentleman you could have loved."

Sabrina smiled and placed the palm of her hand against his cheek. "I know you are a man of integrity," she said.

"I want to kiss you into a daze and then show you our home," Adam said, "but you look fatigued by your journey from London. I'll show you to your chamber." Before escorting her out of the hall, Adam called to the little man, "Razi, please bring a tray of baked eggs, bacon, rolls, and tea for my lady."

"Yes, master," Razi said.

"Why does he call you *master*?" Sabrina asked, walking with him out of the hall.

"Some of my men keep the old ways," Adam answered.

"What do you mean by the 'old ways'?" she asked.

"Razi hails from the East where employees call their employers *master* instead of *my lord*."

Adam guided her up the stairs to the third floor. When they reached the first closed door, Sabrina walked toward it.

"That is not your chamber," Adam told her. "Come this way."

"Oh, is it your chamber?" she asked.

"That door leads to the east wing, which remains unused," he told her. "Never venture inside, as it could prove dangerous before I finish my renovations."

Adam led her into an enormous bedchamber. The luxurious room had been decorated in pale blue and ivory.

Sabrina crossed the room to look outside at the picturesque mainland village of Marazion. Turning around to face him, she asked, "Where does that door lead?"

"My chamber," Adam said with his devastating smile.

Sabrina blushed, but a knock on the door saved her further embarrassment. Razi walked in with the tray of food and set it down on the desk.

In an instant, Winston was at the desk and trying to reach the food.

"Sit, Winston," Adam ordered, and the dog obeyed. "Eat while the food is hot. I will take poor Winston downstairs and give him something suitable for a dog."

Sabrina sat down at the desk. She reached for the fork but froze in surprise when Adam crossed the chamber to unbutton the back of her gown.

"When you have finished your meal, you will find a robe lying on the bed," Adam told her, leaning close to whisper against her ear.

Sabrina couldn't move or speak. His breath against her cheek made her feel hot and cold at the same time.

"Come, Winston."

Sabrina watched him go into the dressing room and

return with a robe. He set it on the bed and, after smiling at her, walked toward the door.

"My lord?" she called out before he left the chamber.

Adam turned around and focused his penetrating gaze on her, making her almost forget what she was going to say.

"No more lies?" Sabrina verified.

"I give you my word," Adam promised. "My lying days have ended."

Chapter 12

No more lies. That thought popped into her head as soon as she opened her eyes a few hours later.

Sabrina yawned and stretched and then lifted her left hand up to look at her winter rose betrothal ring. How different her life was than it had been only a few weeks earlier. Now she was the Countess of Abingdon, the Marchioness of Stonehurst, and the unacknowledged granddaughter of King George III.

No matter how exalted her new position in life was, Sabrina decided, she still had obligations to fulfill. The most important task would be proving her father had not committed suicide.

Sitting up, Sabrina saw the single rose lying on the pillow beside her. She smiled at her husband's gesture, but the thought of him watching her sleep embarrassed her and made her feel vulnerable.

A note lay on the pillow beside the rose. She picked

it up and read: *The garments in the dressing room are yours.*

Rising from the bed, Sabrina crossed the chamber to look out the window. She studied the shadows being cast on the mainland village across the bay and knew that the hour was late in the afternoon. She must have been more tired than she'd thought.

Sabrina turned away from the window and crossed the chamber to the dressing room. Gowns and shawls and cloaks and robes and every other piece of lady's apparel filled the small chamber.

Instantly suspicious, Sabrina wondered who owned the clothing. She couldn't believe that her husband would give her gowns that had belonged to another woman.

Trust is what a happy marriage is based on, she told herself. She needed to trust her husband.

Accepting the note's invitation, Sabrina selected a pale blue gown fashioned from the softest merino wool. A shawl and blue slippers complemented the gown.

Sabrina inspected herself in the full-length mirror on the far side of the chamber. Satisfied with what she saw, she left the chamber and walked down the corridor the same way she'd come earlier.

Passing the door to the east wing, Sabrina heard voices emanating from behind the closed door and stopped short to listen. One voice belonged to her husband, but he was speaking an unfamiliar foreign language.

Suddenly, the door opened and Sabrina leaped back a pace. Razi stepped outside the east wing and stared in surprise at her. She felt like an eavesdropper. Then he called something in that foreign language.

Adam appeared and closed the door behind him. "So, you have finally awakened," he said, giving her a warm smile of greeting.

"I suppose I was more tired than I'd thought," Sabrina answered. "I hope you don't think I was eavesdropping. I was merely passing by and heard your voice."

"Come, Princess," Adam said, offering his hand. "I want to take you on a tour of our home."

Our home, Sabrina thought, unable to keep the smile off her face. Those two words sounded wonderful to her.

"To whom does this lovely gown belong?" Sabrina asked as they descended to the second floor.

"I had them made for you, Princess," Adam told her.

"You were that certain I'd agree to be your wife?" she asked, giving him a sidelong look of disapproval.

"No, Princess, I was *hoping* you would agree to be my wife," he said, surprising her with his sentiment.

The drawing room, library, and his office were located on the second floor. Sabrina scanned his office filled with heavy oak furniture and then crossed the chamber to look out the window. It faced the south. A huge glass house had been built on the grounds outside.

"What is that?" Sabrina asked.

"My hothouse," Adam answered. "I raise delicate flowers there all year long. Like the rose I placed on your pillow."

Sabrina felt the warmth of his body close behind her, and her legs suddenly went weak. She didn't know what to do. She had almost no experience with men.

"Are you ready to see the rest of your home?" he asked.

Sabrina turned around and smiled at him. As they crossed the room toward the door, she spied a strange sword hanging above the hearth's mantel. Its handle was a lion's head carved from ivory, and the blade curved up at the end.

"I've never seen anything like that," Sabrina said.

"The sword is a scimitar and used in the East," Adam told her.

"It looks like it belonged to some barbarian chieftain," she said. "Where did you get it?"

"My fleet trades in the East," he said. Then added preventing further questions, "I would like to show you the grounds before the sun sets."

In silence, Adam and Sabrina walked one flight down to the great hall. Winston lay in front of the hearth, lifting his head when he spied them and wagging his tail.

"Come, Winston," Sabrina called.

The wolfhound wagged his tail again and then rested his head on his forelegs.

"He enjoyed a rather big meal at lunch," Adam told her.

Adam escorted her to the kitchens next. His staff was busy with dinner preparations, but each of them stopped his task when he spied his lord.

"This is your new lady, the Marchioness of Stonehurst," Adam announced, his pride evident in his voice. "My wife enjoys cooking and baking as a hobby. Please help her in any way needed when she comes to the kitchen."

Sabrina smiled at the servants, and then realized they were waiting for her to speak. "I am pleased to be here finally," she said in a soft voice, "and I appreciate your loyalty to my husband."

She looked at Adam for approval or disapproval. Relief surged through her when he smiled and nodded.

The north side of the castle faced the mainland village of Marazion in Cornwall. Walking clockwise around the mansion, the east faced Lizard Point across the water and beyond that lay the English Channel. The south faced the Atlantic Ocean.

Holding her hand in his, Adam gently drew her into the hothouse. The humid warmth inside the glass structure surprised her. The air seemed saturated with moisture. And the incredible sight of all of those flowers growing in winter delighted her.

"How do you manage to keep this house so warm?" Sabrina asked.

"My men learned many remarkable secrets when they traveled through the East," Adam told her.

Leaving the hothouse, Adam and Sabrina walked around to the western side of the castle. The sun was dying in an orange blaze of glory, and by unspoken agreement, they paused to watch the day's ending.

"Tomorrow I'll let you help me tend my flowers," Adam said.

"And I'll let you help me make Turkish delight," Sabrina replied.

"You have a bargain," Adam said with a smile.

"Let's go inside now. I have ordered dinner to be served earlier than usual."

Taking her hand in his, Adam led Sabrina to the private dining room on the first floor. He helped her into her seat to the right of his at the head of the table and then poured two glasses of Madeira. Winston sat at attention between them and drooled.

"This dog is not dining with us tonight," Adam said.

"Oh, but Winston—"

Abdul walked into the dining room and held the door open for Razi, who carried a tray. Unaccountably, Winston lifted his long nose into the air and left them to greet Abdul. The big man scratched behind the wolf-hound's ears, and Winston whined.

"Come, dog," Abdul said.

Followed by the wolfhound, the retainer walked out of the dining room. Behind them walked Razi.

"I've never seen him do that before," Sabrina said in surprise.

Adam winked at her. "Abdul carries a piece of meat in his pocket."

Sabrina laughed and then looked over the evening's fare. She'd never seen any of the dishes that had been set before them.

"What is all of this?" she asked.

"This is rice with chicken, saffron, and nuts," Adam answered, pointing to each dish in turn. "That is fried, minced lamb roll, and the vegetable is stewed leeks. For dessert we'll have cheese fingers in syrup with clotted cream."

Sabrina tasted a small piece of the lamb roll and

smiled. "I never realized French cuisine was so delicious," she said. "I thought the French used rich sauces."

"This particular recipe comes from the Mediterranean," he told her.

"Oh, the south of France."

"I'm glad you are wearing the ring and the brooch," Adam said in a husky voice, his gaze warm on her. "It bodes well for our future."

Sabrina blushed. How could she reply to that? She was still trying to become accustomed to being with her husband on his island fortress. Somehow, the whole situation seemed pleasantly unreal.

"If I kiss you, will you turn into a handsome prince?" she asked.

Adam smiled, his gaze on her warm. "Kiss me and find out."

Sabrina leaned closer, closed her eyes, and planted a chaste kiss on his lips. Opening her eyes again, she stared at him for a long moment while a smile flirted with her lips. "Nope, you are still a frog," she said finally.

"And you are an incorrigible imp," Adam told her.

"I've learned the identity of my natural father," Sabrina said, changing the subject. "However, I promised not to divulge it."

"Is that so?" Adam replied, cocking a dark brow at her, seemingly unaffected by her announcement.

Sabrina stared at him and wondered why he seemed uninterested. And then it struck her. "You already knew," she said in an accusing voice.

"Guilty on that charge," he said. "You must forgive me because I also promised never to tell."

"I absolve you of any wrongdoing," she replied. She stared off into space and added, "I have so many questions for Prince Adolphus and would love to know who my mother was. Uncle Charles doesn't know."

"That I cannot tell you."

"Can't or won't?"

"Princess, if I knew her identity, I would surely thank her for bringing you into the world," Adam said.

Sabrina blushed again. God shield her, but she could easily become accustomed to his flattery.

"Tell me about your childhood in Abingdon," he said.

"There's not much to tell," she answered. "I was blissfully happy until I learned that I had been adopted. At odd moments after that, I would wonder about my real parents and why they gave me away."

"The flaw lies with them, Princess."

When supper ended, Adam took her hand in his and stared into her eyes. "You came to Stonehurst of your own free will, so I assume you want to become my wife in fact."

Sabrina felt her cheeks heat. She dropped her gaze to her hands folded in her lap and nodded.

With one finger beneath her chin, Adam lifted her head and, leaning close, planted a sweet kiss on her lips. Surprisingly, he rose from his chair and crossed to the sideboard. He returned with a footed box in his hand and set it down in front of her.

"For you," he told her.

"What is it?" she asked, looking up at him.

"Your bride's box."

The footed box had been created in gold. Joined hands were engraved on one side of it, as well as the allegorical figures of trust, hope, prudence, love, and tenderness.

"Open it," he said.

Sabrina lifted the lid off the box and peered inside. She blinked twice in surprise when she saw what it contained. Gold coins filled it almost to the brim.

"It is a tradition in my father's land," Adam told her.

Hearing the pride in his voice, Sabrina looked up at him and said, "Thank you, but I have no gift for you."

"Oh, but you do, Princess," he said, and gave her one of his devastating smiles.

Sabrina stared at him blankly. She had no idea what he meant.

Adam stood then and offered her his hand, saying, "Let us retire now."

Sabrina suffered a momentary panic and said, "The hour is still early."

Adam captured her gaze with his own. "Trust me, Princess."

Sabrina inclined her head and stood. She placed her hand in his as if she were accepting a dance. Hand in hand, they left the dining room and climbed the stairs to the third floor.

"I have ordered a bath for you," Adam told her. "When you are ready to begin your new life with me, simply walk through the connecting door."

Sabrina walked into her bedchamber. Sure enough, steam rose from a bath set up in front of the hearth. She started to unbutton her gown, but a movement on the far side of the chamber caught her attention. And then a figure stepped out of the shadows.

"What are you doing here?" Sabrina demanded.

"I will help you undress and bathe," Razi answered. "The master—"

His words shocked her. "Leave this room at once," she ordered.

"Princess, you do not understand," the little man said with an ingratiating smile. "I am not like other men."

"Adam!"

Razi started walking toward her again.

"Adam!"

The door jerked open, and Adam walked into the bedchamber. Wearing a puzzled expression, he looked from her to his man and then back again.

"Tell this man to—"

"She won't let me do my job," Razi whined, cutting her words off. The little man began babbling in a foreign language.

Adam held his hand up in a gesture for silence. Using the same foreign language, he spoke to his man, who threw her a hurt look and then quit the chamber.

"I apologize for this misunderstanding," Adam said. "You may bathe at your leisure."

"That didn't sound like French to me," Sabrina said.

"It wasn't French," Adam replied. "Razi comes from Istanbul." The connecting door clicked shut.

Sabrina stared at the door for a long moment. She suffered the uncanny feeling that circumstances at

Stonehurst weren't what they appeared to be. Something was amiss, but she didn't know what.

Adam couldn't possibly be withholding information about himself, she decided. He had promised to be totally honest with her in all matters. Omission was a form of lying.

Without honesty, there could be no trust; without trust, there could be no happiness in marriage. Her husband had given her his word and would never risk their future by keeping something from her.

Sabrina disrobed and climbed into the tub. She sighed as she relaxed in the hot water. A bar of rose-scented soap floated on the water's surface, and, before washing, she lifted it to her nose and sniffed the intoxicating fragrance.

Stepping out of the tub, Sabrina toweled herself dry and then reached for the nightshift left on the bed for her. The silky material was nearly transparent and revealed more than it hid.

Sabrina looked down at herself, and felt the blush already beginning to rise on her cheeks. She'd never worn so little in her life and wasn't sure she had the courage to go through with this. How embarrassing to parade half naked in front of a man, albeit her husband. Holy hemlock, she'd known him for less than two months.

Summoning her courage, Sabrina opened the connecting door and stepped inside her husband's chamber. Quietly, she closed the door behind her lest she try escape.

Wearing a sapphire-blue bedrobe, Adam stood in

front of the hearth. He turned around slowly as if he felt her gaze on him.

Adam nearly laughed out loud at his bride's anxious expression. She had the look of a woman on her way to the gallows.

Dropping his gaze to her body, Adam felt his manhood stirring with anticipation, and his breath caught raggedly in his throat. She was too beautiful to be real, even more beautiful than he had imagined.

Adam admired her shapely legs, the alluring curves of her hips, and her pink-tipped nipples that played a teasing game of peekaboo through the gown's transparent material. All that he saw belonged to him. In a few short minutes, he would bury himself deep within her and possess her body.

She is uninitiated, he told himself when he lifted his gaze to her face. *Go slowly with her or you will regret it for the rest of your life.*

"Come, Princess," Adam said in a husky voice, holding his hand out in invitation.

Slowly, Sabrina crossed the chamber to stand in front of him. He held her gaze for one long moment and then lifted her hands to his lips.

Adam slipped the winter rose betrothal ring off her left hand and placed it on the third finger of her right hand. He smiled at her confused expression, reached into his pocket, and produced a golden wedding band.

"With this ring I thee wed," Adam whispered, slipping the scrolled band onto the third finger of her left hand while reciting its inscription, *"Pour amor say douc . . .* for love so sweet."

Sabrina smiled at him then, and it reminded him of the French sunshine he loved so much.

"Sit here on the chaise," he said. "We'll share a glass of champagne and talk."

"You only want to talk?" she exclaimed.

Adam couldn't tell if she was relieved or disappointed. He took her hand in his and walked the short distance to the chaise. "Sit beside me," he said.

For one awful moment, Adam thought she was going to refuse, but then she sat down. But she was stiffer than the oak desk in his office.

"Princess, look at me," he said. When she did, he asked, "Are you afraid?"

"I am not afraid of anything," she answered. "I am merely . . . worried."

"I promise there is nothing to worry about," Adam told her. "Making love feels better than French sunshine or making gingerbread."

That made her smile.

Adam felt encouraged. What he needed was to get the damned thing over with so she wouldn't be afraid. No, he needed to seduce her slowly. What he really needed was more experience with virgins.

"Will you lie on the bed with me?" Adam asked.

Sabrina looked at him through enormous emerald eyes that mirrored her worry. And then she nodded.

Adam stood and, without giving her time to protest, scooped her up. Sabrina entwined her arms around his neck, and he carried her across the chamber to place her gently on the bed.

Without removing his robe, Adam lay down beside

her and gathered her into his embrace. His lips sought hers in a slow kiss that seemed to last forever.

Sabrina returned his kiss tentatively, but her ardor grew to match his. She returned his kiss in kind.

"No other woman has ever visited my island," Adam told her. "I've been saving this place for you. Only you."

Sabrina smiled and then surprised him by asking, "Shouldn't we take our clothing off?"

"Is that what you want?"

"Yes."

Adam planted another kiss on her lips and then rose from the bed. He removed the nightshift from her body, and staring down at her, suffered the powerful urge to suckle upon her pink-tipped peaks. He unfastened the robe and shrugged out of it, letting it fall to the floor to mingle with her nightshift, even as they were about to mingle with their bodies.

Lying down beside her, Adam pulled her against his unyielding body to let her experience the incredible sensation of her female softness touching his masculine hardness. He kissed her thoroughly and felt her body arching against him; he heard the soft moan that escaped her lips. His hands caressed her breasts and then his lips moved down the column of her throat and beyond.

"So sweet," Adam whispered, and captured one of her nipples in his mouth. He felt her breathing turn ragged and suckled her nipple into aroused hardness before doing the same to its mate.

"Spread your legs for me," Adam ordered, his lips

returning to hers. He kissed her again and inserted one long finger inside her.

Sabrina tried to escape his probing finger, but Adam kept her from moving. He held her immobile to insert a second finger inside her and felt the muscles inside her gripping and sucking his fingers. God, but she was a passionate little creature.

"You were made for this," Adam said, gazing down at her. "The muscles inside you are holding me. You need to be filled."

He dipped his head and suckled her aroused nipples. His fingers began to move rhythmically, seductively inside her.

In response, she began moving her hips, enticing his fingers deeper and deeper inside her writhing body.

And then his fingers were gone. She moaned to protest their desertion, but he rose up between her thighs and rubbed his manhood against her.

"Tell me you want me," Adam said thickly.

"I want you," Sabrina whispered, dazed and delirious with desire.

With one powerful thrust, Adam pushed himself inside her and broke through her virgin's barrier. She cried out in surprised pain, but he lay still for several moments and let her become accustomed to the feel of him inside her.

Adam began to move his hips seductively and enticed her to move with him. Caught in the midst of passion, Sabrina wrapped her legs around his waist and moved with him. She met each of his powerful thrusts with her own.

Suddenly, Sabrina cried out as waves of molten sensation carried her to fulfillment. Only then did Adam lose control, groaning and shuddering and pouring his seed deep inside her.

They lay still, cradled in each other's arms, for several long moments. Finally, Adam rolled to one side and pulled her with him.

He planted a kiss on her cheek and drew her down on his body. "Are you all right?"

Sabrina nodded. "Are you?"

"I've never felt better in my life," he answered, a smile lurking in his voice. "Sleep now."

Sabrina nestled into him. When her breathing evened, he knew she slept.

Adam cursed himself for being ten thousand times a fool. He had done the unthinkable. He had given his heart to a woman. *And he had lied to her again.*

Chapter 13

Something wet tickled her face.

Swimming up from the depths of unconsciousness, Sabrina awakened and stared into dark eyes.

Slurp! Winston kissed her again.

"Good morning," Sabrina greeted the dog, and reached out to pat him.

Holding the coverlet up to cover her nakedness, Sabrina sat up and looked around. From the dimness in the chamber, she knew the hour was early, just before dawn.

She was alone. The bed beside her was empty, but the sheet was still warm where her husband had lain. The chamber was deserted, and the door had been left slightly ajar.

Sabrina slid from the bed and slipped her nightshift over her head. Then she padded on bare feet across the chamber to the door.

Stepping into the corridor, Sabrina saw her husband entering the east wing. He closed the door behind him.

What was Adam doing at such an early hour in the east wing? Should she follow him or not? Was he keeping something from her after he'd promised never to lie to her?

Sabrina lifted her hands. She looked first at her scrolled wedding band inscribed with the words *Pour amor say douc. For love so sweet.*

Then she shifted her gaze to the winter rose betrothal ring. The ruby rose, pearl snowdrops, and diamond ice glittered even in the corridor's semidarkness.

"Lovely, delicate, hardy in the face of adverse conditions . . . brave little blossom." Those were the words her husband had used to describe her.

Adam believed in her, Sabrina thought, turning away from the sight of the east wing's door. He deserved the benefit of doubt. No, her husband deserved her trust. He had promised never to lie to her again, and she needed the faith to believe in him.

Sabrina returned to the bedchamber and saw the wolfhound stretched out on the rug in front of the hearth. She walked to the window and looked out at the sky. The eastern horizon glowed with orange, enough to tell her that dawn had arrived. The rising sun promised another fair day.

What am I doing here with a man I barely trust? Sabrina wondered. She didn't belong here or in London. Longing for her home in Abingdon welled up within her breast. How she yearned to turn back the hands of the clock and return to a happier, safer time in her life when her father was alive.

Suddenly, Sabrina sensed a presence behind her and knew her husband had returned. She felt him lift her coppery mane aside and then brush his lips against the nape of her neck.

Without shame or modesty, Sabrina leaned back against the hard, muscular planes of his body. Every fiber of her being greeted him with warmth and tenderness. His strong arms encircled her and cupped the perfect globes of her breasts through the nightshift's thin material. His thumbs flicked seductively across her sensitive nipples, and her breath caught in her throat.

"Why are you awake so early?" Adam asked.

"Winston roused me with one of his kisses," Sabrina answered.

Adam turned her within the circle of his embrace and flicked the nightshift's straps off her shoulders. It fell to the floor in a pool of silk.

In answer, Sabrina unfastened the sash of his bedrobe and pushed it off his shoulders, letting it fall to the floor where her nightshift lay. She entwined her arms around his neck and pressed her nakedness against his.

"Now my kisses will rouse you," Adam said, scooping her into his arms. He carried her across the chamber to the bed.

Ever so gently, Adam placed her on the bed and lay down beside her. He captured her lips and kissed her slowly, lingeringly. She entwined her arms around his neck and returned his kiss with equal ardor.

Sabrina felt the feathery light touch of his hands caressing her cheek, her throat, her breasts. He glided his hand lower to trace the curve of her hip and then crossed her body to her inner thigh to tease the jewel of her womanhood.

Though his touch was light, Sabrina burned and longed to touch him as he was touching her. Tentatively at first and then bolder, Sabrina ran her hand down his neck to the mat of black hair covering his chest. Lower and lower, she slid her hand until she reached his manhood. Caressing it with silken fingers, she felt it stir and stretch and harden.

"Look at me," Adam said, slipping his finger deep inside her.

Sabrina opened her eyes and stared at him in a daze of desire.

"Tell me that you want me," he whispered in a husky voice.

"I want you," she breathed.

Adam reared up and positioned himself between her thighs. He caressed her for a moment with his stiffened manhood and then thrust forward, impaling her.

At first Adam rode her slowly, grinding himself deep within her, enticing her to follow his lead. Wrapping her legs around him, Sabrina met him thrust for thrust in their tender duel. They moved fast and faster, becoming one maddened bucking creature. Their cries of pleasure mingled even as they mingled their bodies.

Adam fell to one side and pulled her with him. "I never would have thought a prim miss from Abingdon could be so passionate."

"I had no doubts about you once the London gossip reached my ears," Sabrina said.

Adam burst out laughing. Then he asked, "What would you like to do today?"

Sabrina gazed meaningfully into his eyes.

"Princess, we've just done that," Adam said with a smile. "I want to show you all of my hothouse flowers. I even grow a few herbs there in the winter."

"Afterward, you may watch me cook lunch," Sabrina said. "We'll eat in the kitchen like ordinary people do."

"You want to be one of the ordinary?"

Sabrina nodded. "Ordinary people have always seemed so much happier to me."

Across the chamber Winston lifted his head and growled low in his throat, drawing their attention. Then they heard the noises on the other side of the connecting door.

"Who is in my chamber?" Sabrina asked.

"I ordered you a bath," Adam told her. "Razi will knock when it's ready."

"What did Razi mean when he said he wasn't like other men?" Sabrina asked.

"He meant that he is very, very short."

Sabrina narrowed her gaze on him.

Adam hesitated, but then added, "Razi is trained to see without really seeing."

"I don't understand," she said.

"Today you do not understand my words, but someday you will," Adam said, confusing her even more. "Trust me, Princess."

Sabrina inclined her head. At least he wasn't lying to her again.

An hour later Sabrina had bathed and dressed in a simple white muslin morning gown. She brushed her hair back and wove it into a knot at the nape of her neck. Picking up a cashmere shawl, she left the bed-chamber and started down the corridor. At the end of the hallway stood the door to the east wing.

Staring hard at the door, Sabrina closed the distance between it and her. Why would Adam have been inside the unused wing two days in a row? What business would he have in there before dawn?

Sabrina stopped walking when she reached the door. If she peeked inside, did that mean she didn't trust him? What would happen if she went inside and some-one caught her there?

Slowly, Sabrina raised her hand and reached for the doorknob, but pulled it back before touching it. She worried her bottom lip with her teeth and stood in inde-cision.

Sabrina reached out again, this time turning the knob.

Locked.

''Sabrina?'' She heard her husband calling her name as he climbed the stairs to find her.

''I'm on my way,'' she answered, pasting a smile onto her face.

Adam and Sabrina met on the second-floor landing. He pulled her into his arms and kissed her with pas-sion. Drawing back, he studied her face and then said, ''You look a little pale.''

''I feel fine,'' she assured him.

''Perhaps you are already with child,'' he teased, escorting her down the stairs.

Sabrina snapped her head around to look at him in surprised panic. Only a blind man would have missed her expression.

"You aren't looking forward to being a mother?" Adam asked, his expression disappointed.

"Of course I want children," Sabrina answered. "I hadn't thought much about it before and certainly wouldn't think that after one day of married . . ." Her voice drifted off. She blushed, unused to speaking intimately with a man.

"I understand," Adam said, putting his arm around her. "You must remember that a man and a woman need only join their bodies once to create new life."

They walked into the hothouse a few minutes later. The glass structure was rectangular, one of the longer sides directly facing south. The air was humid and perfumed with the mingling scents of flowers.

"I have placed the flowers that need the direct sun in the row facing south," Adam told her. "The ones needing less direct light are positioned to the east and the west. In the rear, I grow herbs for winter use. The shrubs, of course, remain outside and dormant during this time of the year."

"These are your winter roses?" Sabrina asked, pointing to several gigantic crates containing rose bushes.

"Yes, but they do grow wild in Abingdon," Adam said with a smile.

She felt momentarily confused, but then blushed as she understood what he meant. He was flattering her again.

"Roses are the oldest flowers known to man," he told her. "Every culture—Persia, Kashmir, Rome, or Greece—adores the flower of love."

Sabrina smiled and reached out to touch a rose petal. "I had no idea that roses were cultivated everywhere."

"You English think you invented everything, but your fondness for the rose has come relatively late," Adam said. He picked a rose and handed it to her. "One of my favorite legends concerns a nightingale and a rose. One night the songbird whispered words of love to a white rose. When she blushed, pink roses bloomed all over the world. At the nightingale's urging, the white rose opened her petals, and the songbird stole her virginity. The rose turned red with shame, and red roses bloomed all over the world. Every evening after that, the nightingale serenaded the rose with songs of love, but the rose kept her petals closed."

"How lovely and sad," Sabrina said, enchanted by the tale and the man. How could she not trust him?

"I know another tale about a wallflower," he said.

"Is it sad?"

"Yes."

"Then I don't want to hear it today," she said.

"You have a soft heart," Adam whispered, leaning close to kiss her.

"Have I told you yet how delicious you taste?" she asked when their kiss ended.

"Mint freshens the breath," Adam told her. He drew her down one of the rows of herbs and picked a tiny sprig, then offered it to her.

Sabrina popped it into her mouth and said, "Now I taste like you." Recognizing the parsley growing in the pot beside the mint, she picked a few pieces to garnish their lunch.

"Come, Princess," Adam said, taking her hand in his. "I want to show you everything."

He escorted her up and down the rows of hothouse flowers. Here were nodding violet bellflowers, dangling bleeding hearts, blue bachelor's buttons, blue Cupid's dart, and many others.

Sabrina admired his flowers and the man. Her husband had an interesting tale of how each flower got its name.

"Are you hungry?" he asked finally.

Sabrina reached up and drew his head down to hers. She planted a kiss on his lips and said, "I want no locked doors between us."

"Never," he promised, and raised her hands to his lips.

Sabrina smiled. He seemed so sincere, yet the east wing's door stood between them. Unless what lay behind it was truly unimportant . . . She would never know the answer to that unless she got through the door. And that brought her back to faith and trust again.

"Come on, husband," she said. "I will make you lunch, we'll eat at the kitchen table."

"And we will pretend to be ordinary people?"

"You can be the duke's gardener," she told him. "I will be his cook."

"Which duke would that be?"

Sabrina gave him a jaunty smile. "The Duke of Kingston, of course."

Adam laughed. Taking her hand in his, he said, "Oh, I am definitely looking forward to the next forty or fifty years with you."

Winston had waited outside the hothouse, and wagged his tail in greeting when he saw them. Followed by the dog, Adam and Sabrina returned to the mansion. Their unexpected arrival startled the servants in the kitchen.

"Everyone take the next two hours off," Adam ordered. "My wife and I want the kitchen to ourselves."

Nobody moved, just stared at him in surprise.

"That means get out," Adam said.

The servants sprang to life. They tripped over each other in their haste to leave the kitchen.

"Well done, my lord," Sabrina said.

"I'm the gardener," Adam corrected her. "Remember? Winston, sit down."

The wolfhound obeyed instantly.

"How do you do that?" Sabrina asked.

Adam smiled. "Winston knows that I am the top dog in this family."

"Are you implying that I'm a b—?"

"No."

"Shall I make you some French sunshine first?" Sabrina asked. "It doesn't take long."

"I'm still working on what you brought from London," Adam refused, patting his stomach.

"Would you like a piece of the sweet while I am making lunch?" she asked.

"I left it upstairs."

Sabrina hadn't seen the box anywhere in his chamber. "Tell me where it is, and I'll get it."

"Only a heartless wife makes her husband wait to eat," Adam said.

"I'll make a new batch of sunshine tomorrow," she promised. "What would you like to eat now?"

"Something light."

"How about eggs?"

Adam inclined his head.

"Scrambled eggs with mushrooms and truffle oil and a cup of tomato soup," she said.

Like an ordinary wife, Sabrina gathered the necessary ingredients for the egg dish along with bread and butter and then put the soup on to simmer. Like an ordinary husband, Adam sat at the kitchen table and watched her work.

"I really like James and Lily Armstrong," Sabrina said over her shoulder.

"We can visit them in Scotland next autumn if you like," Adam told her.

Sabrina turned around. "James has a home there?"

Adam nodded. "All of the Quality go grouse hunting from mid-August until late autumn."

"I don't like hunting," she said.

"I don't either."

Sabrina put the mushrooms and butter into a small pan and fried them for a few minutes. Then she added some parsley and truffle oil. "Prince Adolphus doesn't know that I know he's my father," she said. "How should I behave when I meet him again?"

"Be your wonderful self."

Sabrina walked over to the table and kissed him, saying, "Thank you for the compliment." Then she hurried back to the stove and added beaten eggs, cream, salt, and pepper to the mixture and began scrambling the eggs. "I feel guilty about not telling

Courtney," she said. "Do you think she'll forgive me?"

"How could she not?" Adam replied.

Sabrina scooped the scrambled eggs onto hot buttered toast and added the mushrooms on top of that. Then she garnished the eggs with parsley and set the dishes on the table before returning to the stove for the soup.

"It looks delicious," Adam said when she joined him at the table. He raised a forkful of egg to his mouth and then said, "And it tastes as good as it looks."

Sabrina set a dish of eggs and a bowl of soup on the floor for Winston, who instantly began gobbling it up. "I won't be completely happy until my father rests in hallowed ground."

"I'll go to work on that as soon as we return to London," Adam promised. "Tell me what you know about that day."

Sabrina shrugged. "I've told you everything I can remember."

"Will you be upset if I ask you a few questions?" he said.

"No."

"What did your father use?"

Sabrina stared at him blankly. "I don't understand."

"Did he use a rope, a belt, or something else to hang himself?" Adam asked.

"My father did not hang himself," Sabrina insisted. "My father died by hanging."

Adam grinned at her. "Princess, you would make an excellent barrister. Now, answer my question."

"A rope."

"Did he usually keep a rope in his study?" Adam asked.

"No, is that important?"

"It could be," he answered. "Either he brought the rope into the study that day or—"

"—someone else did," she finished for him.

"Was his neck broken?"

"No."

"What shape was the bruise on his neck?" Adam asked. "Was it a straight line or an inverted V bruise?"

Sabrina closed her eyes and tried to conjure the horrifying scene in her father's study. Again she saw Forbes and Edgar kneeling beside her father. Closer and closer she stepped to gaze down at his lifeless body.

"The bruise was a V," Sabrina said, opening her eyes. "Is that important?"

"I won't lie to you," Adam said. "A V bruise usually indicates suicide and a straight line indicates murder."

Sabrina knew her father could never take his own life. He would never wish to leave her and Courtney to fend for themselves. Tears welled up in her eyes, and she insisted on a choked sob, "My father did not commit suicide."

"Do you believe he was murdered?"

"I didn't say that," Sabrina answered, wringing her hands folded in her lap.

"Your father's death was no accident," Adam told her, reaching out to take her hands in his. "Suicide and murder are the only options."

"You just said a *V*-shaped bruise indicates suicide," Sabrina reminded him.

"If an assailant knocked him out and then hanged him, the bruise would appear to be a suicide's," Adam said.

"My father had no enemies," she replied.

"Princess, think hard," Adam said. "Was anything out of place or unusual about the study?"

"No, I didn't notice anything amiss," Sabrina said, looking him straight in the eye. She realized that nothing being out of place pointed to suicide.

"We will solve this puzzle with logic," Adam said. "Do you agree that your father's death was no accident?"

Sabrina nodded.

"Princess, our choices are murder or suicide," Adam told her. "No one knows your father better than you and Courtney. If given a choice of the two, which is the most likely to have happened?"

"Murder."

"Now, forget about the problem of how the villain could have entered a locked room, murdered your father, and then escaped without leaving any trace of evidence," Adam said, and then gave her an encouraging smile. "The man or woman who murdered your father had a grudge against him or something to gain by the earl's death. Do you know of anyone harboring a grudge against him?"

Sabrina shook her head. "My father was a wonderful man who treated everyone with respect."

"Then the person who murdered your father is someone who would gain by his death," Adam said.

Sabrina sat back against the chair. Suddenly she felt weak, as if she were going to faint. For some strange reason, the thought of Edgar's disappointment at being refused her hand in marriage popped into her mind, but she quickly banished such an absurd notion. Edgar Briggs had been a family friend for as long as she could remember. He would never do anything to hurt her or her family. She couldn't accuse him without any evidence.

"I will discover who that person is," Adam told her. "I promise you."

"I believe you will do it," Sabrina said, managing a smile for him. "That villain is no match for you."

"Thank you for the praise, Princess." Finished with his eggs and soup, Adam lifted the parsley garnish. "I always eat the parsley, though I know most people do not."

"That was laughing parsley," Sabrina told him. "Legend says you will die of laughing if you eat it."

"I will take my chances," Adam said, and popped the parsley into his mouth. Then he chuckled at her feigned look of horror.

"You see, the parsley is already working," she told him.

Adam threw back his head and shouted with laughter. "You must eat some too and die with me."

"Feed it to Winston," Sabrina said. "I never saw a dog laugh."

Adam picked up the sprig of parsley and tried to put it into her mouth. When he reached out with his free hand and tickled her, Sabrina laughed, and he popped the parsley inside.

"I have need of you upstairs, wife," he announced, rising from his chair to scoop her into his arms. "The servants will clear this mess."

Leaving Winston in the great hall with Razi, Adam carried Sabrina up the stairs to the third floor. She fixed a troubled gaze on the door to the east wing as they passed it.

"I'll have you for dessert," Adam said, tossing her onto his bed and falling gently on top of her. He gazed down at her and then dipped his head to claim her lips in a tender kiss. "Princess, you are sweeter than French sunshine. . . ."

Chapter 14

Four days, Sabrina thought. *Four glorious days of wedded bliss.*

Dressed only in her chemise, Sabrina stood in her bedchamber and gazed out the window. Sheets of rain slashed the window, making the village across the bay invisible.

This was the first stormy day since her arrival. God shield her, but she hoped the storm did not herald a bad omen for her marriage.

For the first time in her life, Sabrina was sublimely happy and knew she loved her husband. She refused to say those words to him until he said them to her, but her husband didn't seem to think that she longed to hear him profess his love.

Only the uncertainty of what lay behind the east wing's door had marred the almost perfect four days of her married life. Three times each day—morning, afternoon, evening—her husband disappeared into the east wing. Several times she'd tried to get inside, only to find the door locked.

"How about this gown?" asked a voice behind her.

Sabrina turned around to look at her newest acquisition, a lady's maid. Tilly was a seventeen-year-old from the village, whom her husband had hired to play lady's maid to her. After all, he couldn't let his valet help her dress and undress.

Tilly yearned to leave the dull life of Marazion and knew being lady's maid to the Marchioness of Stonehurst would be exciting. At least, that's what she'd said.

Sabrina shifted her gaze from the girl to the high-waisted forest-green gown with crossover bodice. "That will do."

Tilly helped her into the gown and then fastened the row of tiny buttons in the back. Then she handed Sabrina a matching cashmere shawl.

"I'll take the other gown downstairs and try to get the wine stain out of it," Tilly said, grabbing the soiled garment and heading for the door.

Sabrina stood motionless for several moments and wondered what she could bring to her husband's study to keep herself busy while he worked on his ledgers. Finally, she decided to take a book and her needlework.

After gathering those items, Sabrina left the bedchamber and walked down the deserted corridor to the stairs. She paused at the east wing's door and turned the knob. Locked, of course.

Sabrina continued down the stairs until she reached the study. She knocked on the door and heard her husband calling, "Enter." He didn't sound especially happy.

Opening the door, Sabrina stepped inside and closed the door behind herself quietly so she wouldn't disturb him. She smiled as her husband rose to his feet at her entrance.

"Is something wrong?" she asked.

"No, I am experiencing a minor difficulty with this column of numbers," Adam said, gesturing to the ledger book on the desk in front of him.

"Would you like me to try my hand at them?" Sabrina asked.

Adam grinned and shook his head, seemingly amused by her offer. This didn't sit well with Sabrina, but she remained silent.

"Make yourself comfortable," Adam said, gesturing to the study.

Sabrina crossed the chamber and planted a kiss on his cheek. "I'll sit over there near the hearth and keep busy."

"I should have these accounts finished soon enough," Adam told her. "Then we can move on to more pleasurable pursuits."

Sabrina crossed the study to the hearth, and Adam resumed his work. Placing the book and the needlework on the floor, she struggled to turn one of the chairs around to face the desk.

"What are you doing?"

Sabrina looked up from her task. "I want to sit this way so I can see your face whenever I want."

Adam smiled at her sentiment. He rose and crossed the study to her. After turning the chair easily, he gave her derriere an affectionate pat and returned to his work.

Sabrina made herself comfortable in the chair and then asked, "Where is Winston hiding?"

Adam shrugged. "He's probably sleeping off lunch in the great hall."

"That way he can smell the aroma of supper being cooked," she replied.

Adam lifted his quill and gave his attention to his ledgers.

Sabrina looked at the carpet where her book and needlework lay. Read or sew?

Deciding on the lesser of two evils, Sabrina picked up the book, *Pride and Prejudice* by Jane Austen. She read the first chapter and then peeked at her husband so engrossed in his ledgers.

Sabrina couldn't figure out what she loved most about him. What is it his penetrating blue eyes and midnight-black hair? Was it his devastating smile? Or could it be his intelligence and nobility? A smile touched her lips as she tried to picture him as a young boy.

"What are you doing?" Adam asked, looking up at her as if he'd felt her intense stare.

"Watching you," she answered with a shy smile.

"Princess, tallying a large column of numbers while you watch me is distracting," Adam said. "Why don't you try your needlework?"

"I'm sorry."

Sabrina set the book down on the carpet and lifted her needlework off the floor. Sewing crooked stitches easily frustrated her, and then the damned thread knotted. She yanked on the needle so hard, she pricked her finger and cried, "Ouch!"

Adam snapped his head up.

"I pricked my finger," she said by way of an apology for disturbing him again.

"I can see I will accomplish no work with you in my study," Adam said, setting his quill down on the desk.

"Do you want me to leave?" Sabrina asked, sending him a hurt look.

Adam shook his head and smiled. "How about an interesting game of chess?"

"I never knew that chess could be interesting," Sabrina remarked.

"Ah, but you've never played with me." Adam stood and held out his hand in invitation, saying, "Come, Princess."

Leaving her book and needlework, Sabrina rose from the chair and crossed the study to place her hand in his. "Where are we going?" she asked.

"Upstairs." When they reached the foyer, Adam called for Razi, who materialized out of nowhere. "Bring the chess set to my chamber."

"Yes, master."

Hand in hand, Adam and Sabrina walked upstairs to his third-floor bedchamber. Adam stoked the fire in the hearth while they waited for Razi. Within minutes, the little man delivered the chess set and then left the room.

Adam bolted the door behind his man and then turned around to give her his devastating smile. "Have you ever played chess, Princess?"

"Once or twice," she answered.

Adam dragged the small table close to the hearth and turned two chairs to face it. Then he began placing the chessmen on the table, saying, "Come, Princess."

Sabrina sat opposite him and asked, "How will you make this interesting?"

"Each player who loses a chessman must remove an article of clothing, and the loser must finish undressing if not already naked," Adam said, the hint of a smile flirting with his lips. "Do you still want to play?"

Sabrina felt the heated blush staining her cheeks, but inclined her head in agreement.

"Take your shoes off and make yourself comfortable," Adam said.

"You want me to wear fewer clothes so I'll lose faster," Sabrina accused with a smile.

"How can you even suggest I would try to do such an evil thing?" Adam asked, his expression innocent. "I'll take my own shoes off." At that, he yanked his shoes off to reveal bare feet.

"That makes me feel so much better," Sabrina drawled, making him smile. She looked closely at the chess pieces and asked, "Are these Saxons and Normans?"

"We are going to replay the Battle of Hastings," he told her. "Do you prefer being white William or black Harold?"

"I'll take the white."

Together, they set up the chessboard, and then Sabrina asked, "Who will move first?"

"Why tamper with history?" Adam said. "You make the first move."

Sabrina stared at their battlefield for a long moment and then began the game by moving her king's pawn two squares forward. This left her queen and one of her bishops open for action.

"Nice opening, Princess." Adam began by bringing out his queen's knight, which leaped over the pawns and was ready for further action. "How many times have you played before?"

"Do not distract me," Sabrina said, smiling at him. "Or is that part of your strategy?"

Adam caught her gaze and held it captive. "I do not need to cause any distractions in order to win a game of chess with you," he said. Then in a husky voice, he added, "I love it when you are distracted by desire."

The sensitive spot between her thighs throbbed with his words, but Sabrina willed herself to remain cool. She advanced her queen's pawn two squares. This gave her queen more scope and unblocked her other bishop. Both of her bishops were now free to move.

"I love that soft moaning sound you make in your throat when passion rules your senses," Adam said, moving his king's pawn two squares. Both his knight and his pawn were positioned to attack her queen's pawn.

Ignoring his words, Sabrina stared hard at the battlefield and then advanced her queen's pawn one square forward. This move threatened his black knight with capture.

"You didn't think I'd let a measly pawn dispatch my knight?" Adam asked, moving his knight away, out of harm's way.

"My lord, I never have any idea what you will do," Sabrina said primly.

Adam grinned. "I'll take that as a compliment."

Sabrina moved her king-bishop's pawn two squares forward. This pawn was poised to attack the black pawn.

Adam moved his queen's pawn one square. This defended his king's pawn under attack by the white.

Sabrina studied the board. If she captured his king's pawn, the pawn he'd just moved would capture hers. Instead, she brought her king-knight into play. Its new position threatened his pawn and his bishop.

"Have I told you how much I love it when you suck upon my nipples?" she asked in an effort to distract him.

Adam adjusted himself in his chair. Ignoring her words, he raised his brows and said, "Good move, Princess."

Sabrina dropped her gaze to his groin and said in a breathless whisper, "Thank you, my lord."

"Unfortunately, your move isn't good enough," he added.

Sabrina watched him move his bishop and pin down her white knight. Now if she moved it, his bishop would capture her all-powerful queen.

Mobilizing her forces, Sabrina brought her other knight into play. Adam countered by moving his knight to attack her king-bishop's pawn.

Instead of guarding her pawn, Sabrina made a counterattack and threatened to capture his bishop by moving her king-rook's pawn one square forward. Adam captured her knight with his pawn.

"Take something off, sweet, preferably the gown," Adam said, looking at her with a wicked smile.

"Very well, but you'll need to unfasten the buttons," Sabrina said.

"Be certain to stand very carefully," Adam said, rising from his chair. "I do not want this board overturned."

"Would I do that?" Sabrina asked, her expression innocent as she rose from the chair.

Adam stepped closer when she showed him her back. He unfastened the gown's buttons with the practiced ease of a man who'd undressed dozens of women. Lifting her heavy copper mane off her neck, he planted a kiss there and then reached up with both hands to slip the gown off her shoulders. It dropped to the floor.

"Turn around," he whispered close to her ear.

When she did as told, he looked her up and down. She stood only in chemise, stockings, and garters. "You could tempt a priest to sin."

"I'll take that as a compliment," she said pertly, echoing his words.

Resuming her seat, Sabrina moved her bishop to a square on which it threatened his king. "Check," she called, knowing he needed to get his king out of check before attacking her queen.

Adam inclined his head. He advanced his queen-bishop's pawn one square, interposing it between his king and the checking bishop.

Sabrina captured his black pawn with her queen's pawn. She knew he would think her daft because now he could attack her queen. She wanted to win the war, not the battle.

"Take something off, my lord," she ordered.

"The shirt or the trousers?" he asked wickedly.

"The shirt."

Adam pulled his shirt over his head and tossed it onto the floor. Then he fell neatly into her trap by capturing her powerful queen with his bishop.

"Remove your chemise," Adam said with a smile.

"I think not."

Holding her leg out tantalizingly, Sabrina removed one silk stocking. She left the garter in place on her thigh.

"Garters and stockings come in pairs," Adam said. "Remove the other stocking."

Without a word, Sabrina stood and rested her foot on his chair. Slowly, she rolled the other stocking off her leg and then resumed her seat.

"Your move," Adam said in a choked voice.

Sabrina captured his queen-knight's pawn with her pawn, leaving her bishop open to attack his king. "Check," she called out. "First, remove those trousers."

"With pleasure, my lady." Adam unfastened his trousers and pulled them down. Then he tossed the trousers over his head and got his king out of check by moving him away from her bishop's diagonal attack.

Sabrina smiled sweetly at him and then moved her knight, checking the king.

In a forced move, Adam moved his king one square forward to get out of check.

Sabrina moved her king-bishop's pawn one square forward and announced, "Checkmate." There was no square his king could move to in order to escape her men.

"You are a better player than I thought," Adam said, looking at her in surprise.

"Thank you, my lord." Sabrina sat back in her chair. "Now, stand up."

Barechested and barefoot, Adam winked at her and rose from his chair. He reached to remove his black silk underdrawers, intending to remove them.

"Stop," Sabrina ordered, rising from the chair. "I want to admire you first."

Adam inclined his head.

Sabrina walked around him slowly. She ran a finger down the flesh on his spine and then, standing on tiptoes, planted a kiss on his upper back. "I love the supple strength in those muscles," she whispered.

Sabrina walked in front of him and stepped closer. With both hands, she reached up and drew his head down to hers and kissed him thoroughly. She slid her lips lower, down the column of his throat, while her fingers flicked teasingly across his nipples.

Hearing his sharp intake of breath, Sabrina slid her hand lower. She pushed the black silk underdrawers down.

"Christ, but you've become knowledgeable in less than a week," Adam said thickly.

"I've tasted the forbidden fruit," Sabrina murmured, and flicked her tongue across his nipples.

Adam moved to yank her into his arms, but she pushed his hands away and reminded him, "I won the game, my lord."

Sabrina dropped to her knees in front of him and

wrapped her arms around his body, cupping his buttocks in her hands. She pressed her face against his groin, and taking his manhood in her mouth, sucked until it grew too big. Licking the long length of it, she flicked her tongue this way and that.

Suddenly, Adam drew her to her feet. He kissed her slowly, wetly, lingeringly as he reached up and slipped the straps of her chemise off her shoulders.

Then he stepped back and inspected her from the top of her head to the tips of her toes. All she wore was her glorious mane of copper hair and a garter on each thigh. The desire in his intense gaze was as tangible as the carpet beneath her feet.

"Touch me," Sabrina breathed, closing the short distance between them.

Adam caressed every inch of her silken flesh and then dipped his head to suckle upon her aroused nipples. He dropped to his knees in front of her and, using his tongue, teased the sensitive jewel of her womanhood, making her moan low in her throat. Without mercy, he slashed his tongue up and down her female crevice.

Surrendering to the exquisite feeling, Sabrina melted against his tongue. She cried out and clung to him as wave after wave of throbbing pleasure surged through her.

Adam stood and scooped her into his arms. He carried her across the chamber and gently laid her on his bed.

And then he gave her what she craved.

Adam plunged deep inside her and sheathed himself to the hilt. He withdrew slowly and then slid forward,

piercing her softness, teasing her until she trembled
with rekindled need.

With mingling cries, Adam and Sabrina exploded
together and then lay still as they floated to earth from
their shared paradise. He moved to one side, pulled her
with him, and cradled her in his arms until both fell
into a sated sleep.

Sabrina swam up from the depths of a deep, dreamless
sleep. What had awakened her? Turning her head, she
saw that the bed beside her was empty. She sat up and
looked around. The bedchamber was deserted.

The dimness within the chamber announced the supper hour was at hand. Sabrina rose from the bed and
slipped the chemise over her head. Then she grabbed
her husband's shirt and put that on over the chemise.

Sabrina hurried across the chamber to the door and
stepped outside. Noiselessly, she glided down the corridor to the east wing. The door had been left slightly
ajar. By accident or design? Should she enter or not?

Pushing the door open, Sabrina stepped inside. Holy
hemlock and henbane! She'd stepped into another
world.

The opulence of the chamber shocked her. Lavishly
tiled and luxuriously carpeted, the chamber featured an
enormous bronze brazier and opaque glazes on the
walls.

On her right was a narrow staircase leading to the
second floor. Sabrina started down the stairs. When she
reached the second floor, she looked around. The room,
as opulent as the one above, was deserted, but an al-

cove across the chamber caught her attention. She sensed a presence there. On silent feet she crossed the chamber, but then stopped short at the startling sight that greeted her.

Facing the east, Adam knelt on the carpet. His forehead touched the floor, and his lips moved in a silent prayer.

Shock made her momentarily speechless. Then she found her voice, asking in a frightened voice, "What are you doing?"

Adam whirled around. His expression mirrored his surprise.

"What are you doing here?" he demanded in an angry voice. "I told you never to enter the east wing."

"Who are you?" Sabrina asked, backing away from his angry tone.

"I am your husband," Adam said, almost wearily, standing to face her.

"You deceived me. You are not who you said," she accused him. She looked around at the exotically decorated chamber, adding, "You are someone else."

"I am Adam St. Aubyn, the Marquess of Stonehurst, heir to the Duke of Kingston," he said.

"No more lies," Sabrina said, meeting his gaze unwaveringly. "I want the whole truth now."

"Let us sit on the pillows over there," Adam said, inclining his head. He offered her his hand, but she refused to take it.

Instead, Sabrina turned her back, crossed the chamber to sit on the pillow beside a small table, and folded her hands on top of it. If she didn't hold on to herself tightly, he would see her hands trembling.

"What would you like to know?" Adam asked, sitting down across the table from her.

"The truth would be nice for once."

"Sarcasm does not become you," Adam said. "My real name is Karim Osmanli. I am a Moslem prince of the Ottoman Empire."

"A heathen?" she exclaimed.

"In my land, you are heathen," he said.

"You made me your wife under false pretenses," Sabrina accused him. "You lied when you promised never to lie to me again."

"Forgive me, Princess. Lying to you was wrong," Adam said with anguish in his voice and his eyes. He reached across the table to place his hand on top of hers, but she dropped her hands to her lap.

"Your apology means nothing, merely empty words," Sabrina said, steeling herself against the unmasked pain in his gaze.

"Will you listen to my explanation?" he asked.

She answered with a nod. No matter what he said, though, she would never forgive him for this. If she absolved him of these lies, tomorrow there would be more.

"First of all, Princess, I feared that you would never accept me as your husband, and I didn't want to lose you," Adam began. "You British are not generally known for your tolerance of other cultures."

"You are British," she countered. "Or are you?"

"Yes, but my Britishness is tempered by the fact that I also have ingrained in me the beliefs of another culture," he replied. "I follow the practices of both Islam and Christianity. I worship in my Islamic religion whenever I enjoy the privacy of Stonehurst, but I follow the Church of England because I am an English aristocrat and expected to adhere to that religion.''

"I wouldn't have cared if you were druid if only you had refrained from lying about it,'' Sabrina said coldly, insulted that he didn't trust her.

"Princess, I apologize for not trusting you to accept this aspect of me,'' Adam said. "However, I had other factors to consider. If my real identity became common knowledge, my life would be endangered.''

"Before you tell me what that means,'' Sabrina said, holding her hand up in a gesture for him to stop speaking, "I need to know if my father knew your real identity.''

"Yes, Princess, both your adoptive father and your natural father knew about my origins,'' he answered.

That piece of information surprised her. She would never have thought that her wonderful father could give her in marriage to a stranger from a strange land. What had possessed him to do it?

Sabrina stared him straight in the eye and asked, "Does Aunt Tess know who you are?''

"As I said a moment ago, my life could be forfeit if my identity became known,'' he answered. "Your aunt knows me only as the Marquess of Stonehurst.''

"You may continue with your explanations,'' she said.

"My mother is Charles St. Aubyn's sister—''

"*Is* or *was*?''

"*Is* . . . My mother was the second wife of the Grand Turk himself, who happens to be my late father,'' Adam told her. "Twenty-seven years ago, my mother became betrothed to an aristocrat from the south of France. On her ocean voyage to his home in order to be married, she was abducted by pirates and ultimately given as a gift to Sultan Abdul Hamid, my father. Upon his passing, my older brother became sultan. My mother sent me to England, and I assumed a new identity because the custom in my country placed me in danger.''

''What custom?''

''When a new sultan begins his reign, he locks his brothers up in the Golden Cage,'' Adam explained.

Horrified, Sabrina could only stare at him.

''It is not actually a cage,'' he added. ''It is simply house arrest, which is kind when compared with what they used to do. The new sultan's brothers, potential political rivals, were executed.''

''One brother kills another brother?'' Sabrina exclaimed in horror.

''We Ottomans believe there can be only one sultan,'' Adam told her. ''To ascend to the sultanate without restraining the other male heirs can only lead to civil war. Look at your own country, for example. Many wars have been fought and lives lost because one prince coveted another prince's right to wear the crown.''

''I see,'' Sabrina said. Now she understood the reasons for so many lies, but she wasn't certain those reasons made a difference in how she felt.

He had lied too many times, Sabrina thought. How could she ever trust him again? She should have had the right to know in advance the identity of the man she was supposed to marry. This whole situation was almost too much for her to endure. She didn't give a fig where he came from, but if she forgave him this lie, two months from now she would catch him in another.

"I am leaving in the morning for London," Sabrina said, steeling herself against the pain in his blue eyes. "I need time alone to think."

"You cannot leave," Adam told her.

"Am I your prisoner?"

"Don't be ridiculous."

"Then I am leaving you in the morning," she said.

"You are my wife, my princess," Adam told her, his gaze holding hers captive. "There can be no annulment, and there will be no divorce. You made the choice when you came here. Our fates are sealed together."

"The devil fiddle your fate," Sabrina cried, rising from the pillow. "Either I leave in the morning, or you will need to lock me in that chamber for the rest of my life."

Adam stood and stared at her for a long time. Finally, he inclined his head and said, "I will make the necessary arrangements."

"I wish to travel by land this time to delay seeing my relatives," Sabrina said, uncertain if she felt relieved or disappointed. "I will leave you to . . . whatever you were doing." At that, she turned away and marched across the chamber toward the stairs.

"Sabrina?"

She turned around. "Yes?"

"Where are you going now?" he asked.

"To the kitchens."

A ghost of his devastating smile appeared on his lips. "I thought so," he said.

Without bothering to reply, Sabrina turned away and climbed the stairs. She suffered the heart-wrenching feeling that the "French sunshine" in her life had been blocked by the clouds of distrust.

Chapter 15

"Winston, we're home." Sabrina reached out to pat the wolfhound, asleep on the seat opposite her.

For the past six days, Sabrina had ridden alone in the coach on their journey to London because Tilly preferred Abdul's company to Winston's. She couldn't imagine why the silly girl feared so gentle a creature as Winston, but in the end she'd been glad the girl preferred riding up above. The heaviness in her heart precluded polite conversation. Winston, on the other hand, seemed indifferent to the long, pregnant silences and the deep, heartfelt sighs.

For the hundredth time, Sabrina wondered if she'd taken the right action in leaving Adam. She loved him with all of her heart, but how could she live with a man who'd lied to her at every turn. That he was a foreigner with a different religion and customs didn't trouble her in the least. What mattered was his constant lack of honesty. Annulment and divorce were out of the question. If they separated for a time, perhaps Adam would—

The coach door swung open. "Princess, we have arrived," Abdul informed her.

Sabrina nodded. "You must remember to call me *my lady*."

"Yes, Princess." Abdul helped her down from the coach.

"Come, Winston," Sabrina called.

The wolfhound leaped out of the coach and bounded up the stairs to the Grosvenor Square town house. Tilly followed behind them.

"Welcome home, my lady," Baxter greeted her.

"Thank you, Baxter," Sabrina said, walking into the foyer. "Forbes, this is Tilly, my maid. Please show her to my chamber so she can settle in and unpack my belongings."

Both majordomos hesitated. Sabrina was unable to read the look that passed between them.

"We'll take care of everything," Forbes assured her.

"The other ladies are in the drawing room," Baxter added.

"Come, Winston," Sabrina called, and started up the stairs to the second-floor drawing room. Barging into the room, she startled them by announcing in a loud voice, "I've separated from my husband."

"Darling, I'm so sorry to hear that," Belladonna drawled. "Sit here and let us commiserate with you."

Sabrina crossed the drawing room toward them. They didn't seem the least surprised that she'd abandoned her husband. Now, why was that? she wondered, beginning to become suspicious.

"Courtney, go upstairs to your chamber," Aunt Tess ordered, turning to her sister. "Belladonna and I want to advise your sister."

A mulish expression appeared on Courtney's face. "I am old enough to—"

"You are an innocent maiden," Aunt Tess interrupted in a voice that brooked no disobedience.

Courtney rose from her chair. She left the drawing room, mumbling to herself, "I always have to leave the room at the most interesting times."

"Now, darling, what is the problem with your husband?" Belladonna asked.

"Adam lied to me about our betrothal and our marriage," Sabrina said. "No sooner had he promised never to lie again when I caught him in a lie about his—" She stopped speaking, unwilling to betray her husband's secret in front of her aunt.

"Darling, don't worry about Tess," Belladonna said with a smile. "I had to whisper the truth about your husband in her ear, but she's vowed to take his secret to the grave. Now then, Adam is who he said he is."

"He conveniently omitted to tell me the whole truth," Sabrina replied. "Omission is a silent lie."

The two older women looked at each other and smiled. Sabrina had no idea what they found amusing. Separating from one's husband was not a laughing matter.

"How delightfully naive she is," Belladonna said.

Tess nodded in agreement and then asked her niece,

"Would you have trusted the marquess with your life before you came to know him better?"

Sabrina shrugged. "What about afterward?" she argued. "He could have told me when I was at Stonehurst."

"Darling, sometimes men behave like boys," Belladonna told her. "Once my nephew had promised never to lie to you, he probably feared telling you the truth. Confessing a sin to his wife puts a man at a disadvantage, and my nephew always insists on having the upper hand."

"The problem is, you allowed the marquess to gain the upper hand with you in the first place," Aunt Tess told her.

"I remember the first argument my late beloved Francis and I had," Belladonna said. "On our wedding night Francis threw his trousers at me and ordered, 'Put these on.'

" 'I can't wear them,' I protested. 'They're too big.'

"Francis looked me straight in the eyes and warned, 'Remember, wife. I wear the pants in this family.' "

"What did you do?" Sabrina asked.

Belladonna gave her a feline smile. "I tossed my underdrawers at him and said, 'Put these on.'

"Francis held them up, saying, 'I can't get into these.'

"I warned, 'Remember, husband. If you don't adjust your attitude, you won't get into them.' "

Aunt Tess burst out laughing. Even Sabrina managed a smile.

"And what did your Francis do?" she asked.

"What else could he do?" Belladonna replied. "He adjusted his attitude and apologized."

"If you forgive the marquess," Aunt Tess told her, "you will never catch him in another lie."

"My nephew will have adjusted his attitude," Belladonna said.

Sabrina gave them a mulish look. "I cannot forgive him."

"Your marriage has been consummated," Belladonna said. "Your place is with your husband."

"And if I choose not to return to him?" Sabrina countered.

"That would be very foolish," Aunt Tess said.

"Darling, guilt is such a lucrative emotion in a man," Belladonna told her. "A wise woman would forgive and reap the rewards of her forgiveness. If you make him wait, he'll make you pay for hurting his feelings."

"I think not," Sabrina said. "My husband cannot expect me to ride all the way to Stonehurst when I've just arrived in London. I'll send him a note and take a few weeks to think the situation through."

The two older women looked at each other and smiled.

"She's so innocent," Belladonna drawled.

"Innocence can be a powerful aphrodisiac," Tess reminded her.

Belladonna nodded. "Quite true."

"What are you talking about?" Sabrina asked.

"Your husband returned to London several days ago," Tess informed her.

"What did you say?"

"You heard correctly, darling," Belladonna said with a feline smile. "While you took a week to travel overland, your husband sailed home on one of his ships. Adam moved all of your belongings to Park Lane."

"He's stolen my property?" Sabrina cried, bolting out of the chair. Whirling away, she marched toward the door, muttering to herself, "He can't get away with this. I'll have him arrested."

Ignoring the older women's laughter, Sabrina hurried down the corridor to the stairs. Excited, Winston ran ahead of her. She retrieved her cloak when she reached the foyer below and yanked the door open.

"Vicar Dingle, what are you doing here?" Sabrina cried. She stepped back to allow the man entrance.

"I must speak privately with you," the vicar said. "Would that be possible?"

"Yes, of course." Leaving the wolfhound in the foyer, Sabrina led the vicar down the first-floor corridor to the enormous dining room. She closed the double doors behind them and sat at one end of the table. The vicar sat beside her.

"I apologize for not taking you to the drawing room," Sabrina said. "Aunt Tess and Lady DeFaye are there."

"The dining room will suit." Vicar Dingle glanced at her forest-green gown and said, "You've broken your mourning."

Sabrina narrowed her gaze on him. "Have you ridden from Abingdon to scold me?"

"No, Lord Briggs requested my presence in London,'' the vicar told her. ''He feels that your aunt is incapable of controlling your baser tendencies.''

''My what?'' Sabrina exclaimed.

Vicar Dingle gestured that he wasn't finished. ''Lord Briggs believes that your trust in the St. Aubyns is misplaced,'' the vicar said. ''I agree with him. Your best course of action would be to marry the baron. He would make you an excellent husband.''

So that was it, Sabrina thought. Edgar believed the vicar could change her mind about marrying him.

''I appreciate your concern for me,'' Sabrina said. ''However, I am already married to the Marquess of Stonehurst. Unless you are promoting bigamy?''

''I had no idea,'' Vicar Dingle said, unable to keep the shock off his face. ''I am sorry for intruding. Apparently, Briggs has no knowledge of this.''

''My father and his uncle married us together when we were children,'' Sabrina told him. ''That is the reason my father vetoed Edgar's proposal.''

''Are you certain this marriage is legal?''

''Prince Adolphus confirmed it.''

''Then it must be so,'' the vicar said. ''I wish you and your husband all the best. Will you be living at Abingdon?''

''I'm uncertain,'' Sabrina said. ''Vicar Dingle, would you please reconsider burying my father in hallowed ground?''

''Since the Church officially declared him a suicide, I cannot change their ruling,'' he replied. ''I'm sorry I ever listened to Lord Briggs.''

His remark puzzled her. ''What do you mean?''

''I wanted to record your father's death as accidental,'' Vicar Dingle told her. "The baron insisted the earl committed suicide.''

"I had no idea Edgar persuaded you to declare my father's death a suicide," Sabrina said, surprised. Apparently, Edgar carried a grudge against her father for refusing his marriage offer. Could Edgar actually have murdered her father? Why would he do such an evil thing? No man was so much in love that he'd murder to gain a wife.

The land, Sabrina realized suddenly. Edgar had always wanted to join their estates. How could she ever prove his guilt?

"Lady Sabrina?"

She focused on the vicar. "Again, I thank you for your concern," she said. "You've only done what you think best."

Vicar Dingle smiled at her in obvious surprise, as if he'd been expecting an argument.

"I'll walk you to the door," Sabrina said.

Sabrina raced up the stairs to the third floor as soon as Vicar Dingle left. She knocked once on her sister's bedchamber door and then burst into the room without being invited. Courtney sat on the chaise in front of the hearth, and Sabrina hurried across to plop down beside her.

"I have several startling things to tell you," Sabrina said. "You must promise not to swoon, scream, weep, or tell another soul."

Courtney looked puzzled. "I promise."

"Prince Adolphus is our father," Sabrina said without preamble.

"What?" Courtney cried. "How do you know?"

Sabrina gave her a warning look. "You promised."

Courtney nodded and took several deep, calming breaths. "How do you know?" she whispered.

"Uncle Charles told me before I went to Stonehurst," Sabrina answered. "That is the reason Father married me off to Adam St. Aubyn, and that is the reason Adolphus has taken an interest in our social success."

"Why didn't they marry me off to anyone?" Courtney asked.

Sabrina shrugged. Her sister had a good point, but she could not explain that Adam was an exiled prince from an Eastern country. If there had been two princes, their father probably would have married her sister off to the other one.

"I'm glad they didn't marry me off," Courtney gushed. "Oh, Sister, I am so in love with Dudley Egremont. He has asked Uncle Charles for my hand in marriage. We were waiting for Adam and you to return to London before we made the announcement. Don't you think Dudley is the handsomest man you've ever seen?"

Sabrina rolled her eyes. "I have even more startling news for you."

"What could be more startling than being an unacknowledged princess?" Courtney asked.

"I have reason to believe that Edgar Briggs murdered Father," Sabrina said as she grabbed her sister's mouth, effectively muffling the scream. Leaning close, she whispered against her sister's ear, "If I take my hand away, will you promise not to scream?"

Courtney nodded.

Sabrina removed her hand slowly. Satisfied that her sister would not scream, she dropped her hand to her lap.

"How do you know?" Courtney asked. "What will we do about it?"

"Vicar Dingle just told me—"

"Vicar Dingle told you that Edgar murdered Father?"

"No, Edgar sent Vicar Dingle here to talk me into marriage," Sabrina explained. "The vicar told me that he had planned to call Father's death accidental, but Edgar persuaded him to name Father a suicide."

"That villain," Courtney exclaimed. "But why would Edgar want Father dead?"

"Edgar said it himself," Sabrina answered. "He wants the Savage land, but Father had refused his marriage offer. Edgar assumed he could then purchase the land at auction because a suicide's assets are forfeit to the Crown. He hadn't counted on the St. Aubyns. Of course, I cannot prove this in a court of law so we must find a way to get a confession out of him."

"What will the marquess do to get a confession out of Edgar?" Courtney asked.

"Since we are not in accord, my husband will remain ignorant of this. Sister, Henry Savage was *our* father. We must be the ones to restore his good name," Sabrina said. "By the way, how could you let the marquess steal my belongings?"

"How could I stop him?" her sister countered.

Sabrina nodded in understanding. "Are you willing to help me ferret the murderer out?"

"You know I will."

Sabrina cocked a copper brow at her sister. "Even if I must use you as the bait?"

"What do you have in mind?" Courtney asked.

"Let me think about it," Sabrina answered. "I need a way to entice Edgar, lead him to believe he still has a chance to gain our land. Do not mention this to Dudley Egremont."

Courtney made a gesture as if buttoning her lips together.

"Has Uncle Charles taken up residence here?" Sabrina asked, rising from the chaise.

"Yes, I believe he retired to his study," her sister told her.

"First I must speak with Uncle Charles," Sabrina said. "Then I am going to Park Lane. I'll see you tomorrow morning."

Courtney smiled, saying, "Good luck, Sister."

Sabrina hurried down the corridor to the stairs. Reaching the foyer, she saw Abdul, Tilly, and the two majordomos waiting for her. They looked at her expectantly, but she held up a hand.

"I must speak with His Grace," Sabrina told them without breaking stride. "Then I'll be leaving for Park Lane. Abdul, bring the coach around front again."

Sabrina knocked on the study door and opened it when she heard the duke call out to enter. Stepping inside, she closed the door behind her and beamed warmly at the duke, who was smiling as he rose from the chair behind his desk.

"Come in, child," Uncle Charles said. "Please, sit down."

Sabrina sat in the chair in front of his desk. The duke sat when she sat.

"So, is the married life agreeing with you?" he asked.

"I believe you already know the answer to that," Sabrina answered. "I haven't come here to speak to you about that. I need a favor from you."

Uncle Charles inclined his head. "Ask away, child."

"I must speak with Prince Adolphus as soon as possible," she told him. "Would you be willing to persuade the prince to meet with me here tomorrow morning?"

"Consider it done," he answered. "Shall we say eleven o'clock?"

Sabrina nodded. "Thank you, Uncle Charles." She started to rise from the chair, but the duke stopped her.

"Please, linger a few minutes," Uncle Charles said. "I want to speak to you about Adam."

Sabrina felt as if her heart were sinking to her stomach. She didn't have the strength for this conversation and then a confrontation with her husband. But what else could she do? The duke had just granted her a favor.

"What did you want to discuss?" she asked.

"You must reconcile with Adam. My nephew loves you very much."

Sabrina managed a faint smile. "I find that hard to believe."

"Oh, but he does," the duke assured her. "I doubt that Adam will tell you because, as you may have noticed, he is a proud man."

"I noticed that about my husband," Sabrina said dryly.

"Do you realize that you just referred to Adam as your husband?" Uncle Charles said, giving her a broad grin. "I want to explain a few things about his background."

"I am aware of his background," Sabrina told him.

"You know only the facts," Uncle Charles insisted. "You know nothing of his emotional upheaval and suffering."

"My husband suffered?" Sabrina echoed in surprise, leaning forward in the chair, alert and interested.

"Because he'd been overshadowed by his older brother, the heir apparent, Adam arrived in England a shy ten-year-old. He was badly frightened, too. His mother had sent him into exile—for his own good, of course—to a strange land with strange customs. He was old enough to know the reason he'd been sent away, but too immature to appreciate his mother's sacrifice. I'm positive he always felt abandoned by her. Not only that, he was forced to hide his true identity." Uncle Charles stopped talking and stared into Sabrina's eyes, now filled with unshed tears. "Until he met Jamie Armstrong, Adam didn't fit in at Eton. The other boys considered him a despicable Frenchman at a time when Napoleon was doing his worst. One young man— Cedric Appleby, the Earl of Stockton—was especially cruel to Adam. He even persuaded his chums to ambush and assault him."

"Oh, Lord," Sabrina whispered, her heart breaking at the thought of what her husband had endured. She suddenly felt sick to her stomach, but needed to know the rest of the story. "What happened?" she asked.

"Those ten cowards caught him alone and nearly killed him with their beating," Uncle Charles said, his own complexion a shade paler than when she had walked into the study. "Ten against one, I still can't believe it. Jamie Armstrong found him near the rugby field. From that day on, Jamie never let Adam walk the grounds of Eton alone."

"What happened to the other boys?" Sabrina asked.

"Appleby was thrown out of school, and his accomplices were suspended for a time," Uncle Charles answered. He smiled at her then and added, "Later on, Adam exacted his own special brand of revenge."

"Which is?"

"Three years ago Adam seized the opportunity to ruin Appleby financially by making several business deals," the duke said. "Unfortunately, my nephew's hardened exterior hides a sensitive heart. When he heard that Appleby had children he couldn't support, Adam made another several business deals to ensure that Appleby recovered his money."

Sabrina felt the hot tears brimming over her eyes and rolling down her cheeks. A lump of raw emotion caught in her throat.

Her husband appeared to be an arrogant, autocratic aristocrat. But he was actually kindhearted.

Adam had rung her father's death knell.

She had repaid that kindness by abandoning him.

And yet she couldn't move past those lies. Understanding the reason behind them, though, did ease her troubled spirit.

"Thank you for telling me that," Sabrina said, rising from the chair.

"Please don't tell Adam we had this talk," Uncle Charles said. "I promise Adolphus will be here in the morning."

Fifteen minutes later Sabrina alighted from the coach in front of her husband's Park Lane town house. Adam would not appreciate her pity or sympathy for him, and so she vowed never to show him in any way that she knew how miserable his childhood had been. Steeling herself, she marched up the front stairs like an invading general. Behind her followed the foot soldiers—Winston, Tilly, and Abdul.

Sabrina lifted the door knocker and slammed it down hard. Almost instantly, the door opened an inch, slammed shut, and then opened an inch again. The door seemed to be struggling with itself. And Sabrina heard two voices raised in argument.

"I'll get it."

"No, I will."

"I am His Lordship's majordomo."

At that, someone yanked the door open. Sabrina recognized Higgins and Razi.

"Good afternoon, my lady," Higgins greeted her. "We've been expecting you."

Razi bowed from the waist. "Welcome, my pr— lady."

Sabrina walked into the foyer and ordered, "Tilly and Winston, sit down." She looked at Higgins and asked, "Where is His Lordship?"

"I believe he is in his study," the majordomo answered. "I will be happy to announce you."

"No, I will," Razi snapped at the man.

"I prefer announcing myself," Sabrina told them, and marched down the long corridor. She hesitated a moment outside the last door on the right, but then burst into the room without knocking.

Adam shot to his feet. With him was Jamie Armstrong, who also stood at her abrupt entrance.

Harnessing her fury the way nature gathers its forces, Sabrina fixed her gaze on her husband and asked, "By what right do you steal my property?"

"Princess, we have company," Adam said, ignoring her anger with an infuriating smile, fanning the flames.

"I want my belongings returned to me," Sabrina demanded, ignoring their guest. "I am taking up residence with my aunt."

Without a word to her, Adam turned to his friend and said, "Will you excuse us?"

Jamie Armstrong smiled first at Adam and then at Sabrina. He left the study, but Sabrina heard the sound of his laughter as he walked down the corridor to the foyer.

Adam caught her gaze and said in a deceptively quiet voice, "Never behave so rudely in front of a guest again. Do you understand?"

Holy hemlock, he's angry, Sabrina thought absurdly. She'd never seen him like this and hoped she would never be treated to a repeat performance. The forbidding look on his face urged her to step back a pace or five.

"Sit down," Adam said.

Sabrina lifted her nose into the air. "I prefer to stand."

Instead of arguing, Adam surprised her by walking around the desk and lifting her into his arms. He sat down in one of the chairs positioned in front of his desk and, despite her squirming to free herself, managed to keep her prisoner there. Realizing that he had the superior strength, Sabrina demonstrated her rebellion by turning her head and refusing to look at him.

"Listen carefully, Princess," Adam said, gently but firmly turning her head to face him. "I will say this one time only."

"I'm listening," she told his chest.

"A divorce is as impossible as an annulment," Adam informed her. "Therefore, you will live with me and bear my heirs. Other than that, we will live separate lives if that is what you prefer."

Sabrina suffered the urge to scream that having separate lives was not what she preferred. She wanted a loving husband who told her the truth.

"Furthermore, the day you stoop to play the wanton will be your last day on this earth," he added.

"What are you talking about?" she asked, shifting her gaze to his.

"I mean that you will be sorry if you even consider taking a lover," Adam warned.

"Take a lover?" Sabrina cried, leaping off his lap. She rounded on him and demanded, "What kind of woman do you think I am? Consorting with London harlots has jaded your thinking!"

Sabrina glared at him. He appeared to be struggling against a smile. Was he laughing at her now?

Adam ignored her outburst. "Higgins will show you

to your chamber," he told her. "Dinner is served promptly at seven. Good afternoon."

Good afternoon? Sabrina thought. The man was incorrigible and issued orders like a prince. Well, she had news for him. He wasn't a prince to her, he was merely a marquess.

"You're not a prince," she said in a scathing voice. "You, my lord, are a toad."

And then he had the audacity to smile at her. "You have recalled the story incorrectly, Princess. The woman kissed a *frog* that turned into a prince."

"There's no bloody damned difference between a toad and a frog!" That remark brought an infuriating grin to his face. Without another word, Sabrina stormed out of the study. The only thing she felt certain about at the moment was that he would never let her live with her aunt, which was what she'd expected before she walked through the door.

When she reached the foyer, Higgins was nowhere in sight but Razi was there. She felt tired from her journey and her warring emotions.

"Razi, please escort me to my chamber," Sabrina said. "Then order the staff to prepare a bath for me. Tilly, go to the kitchen and eat. Afterward, bring me something. I want to have a bath first."

Sabrina sat in the chair in front of the hearth in her chamber while Razi directed the footmen who arrived to set up her bath. She noticed the door across the chamber right away and knew it had to be her husband's chamber. Having her live in his house wouldn't be any fun if he couldn't torment her with his presence.

"Your bath is ready, my princess," Razi said.

Sabrina looked over her shoulder. The footmen had left, leaving her alone with the little man. She hoped he wasn't going to try to assist her again.

"You may leave, Razi," Sabrina said, rising wearily from the chair.

"As you wish, my princess." The little man stood rooted to the floor.

"What is it?" she asked.

"You should have more respect for your husband," Razi scolded her. "Your husband is your master, and you have upset him deeply. Shame on you."

Sabrina arched a copper brow at him. "Am I truly your princess?"

"Yes."

"Then I order you to begone."

Without another word, Razi bowed from the waist. He crossed the chamber to the door, but paused to bow again and then left.

Sabrina bathed herself and then found her bedrobe in her dressing room. She lay down on the bed and slept, refusing to awaken even when Tilly brought her a meal.

At precisely seven o'clock, Sabrina left her bedchamber. She dressed in one of her favorite gowns, a green and gold brocade. She'd taken special pains with her appearance, having decided that she and her husband needed to make peace. Now she understood the reasons for his lies and, in time, would recover from the pain she'd felt. Perhaps Adam could think of some way to get Edgar to tip his hand. More important, she'd missed him.

Higgins met her in the foyer and escorted her to the

enormous dining room. It was deserted except for servants. He helped her into her chair at the head of the table, and she looked at him in confusion. She opened her mouth to speak but he turned away and said to the servants, "Everyone out. I will serve her ladyship."

When all the servants had gone, Higgins turned to her and said, "His Lordship has already left for the evening and won't return until late."

"Thank you, Higgins." Sabrina felt humiliated and dejected. Her first night in her husband's London town house and he'd left her alone. She folded her hands in her lap and tried to put a brave face on the situation.

Higgins served her roasted chicken with potatoes, braised leeks, a variety of cheeses, and wine. Sabrina ate very little. Swallowing with that lump of raw emotion in her throat proved too much for her.

Finally, Sabrina turned to Higgins, who stood near the sideboard, and asked, "Do you have any aprons in the kitchen?"

"Why, I believe so," the man answered.

"Good." Sabrina rose from the dining room table and said, "I will need flour, butter, sugar, currants, eggs, lemons, apples, raisins, and any kind of nuts you may have in the cupboard."

"Whatever for, my lady?"

"I am going to bake cookies and pie."

Higgins looked positively shocked. "Cookies and pie?" he echoed.

"Yes, Higgins," Sabrina said, turning to leave the dining room. "Lemon cookies and humble pie."

Chapter 16

🌱 *She loved her husband and wanted him back in her arms.*

Sabrina knew that as surely as she knew she'd used every ounce of flour in her husband's cupboard.

Except for his constant lies, Adam St. Aubyn was all that she'd ever dreamed about in a man. Adam was handsome and wealthy and titled, but he was also romantic, kind, and honorable. *And she loved him.*

How could she possibly initiate a reconciliation? Sabrina wondered, sitting on the chaise in front of the hearth in her bedchamber. She couldn't very well go down to breakfast and say to him, "By the way, I'm sorry for abandoning you. Let's begin again."

Or could she? Perhaps a bit of subtlety was required.

That was it, Sabrina decided, rising from the chaise. She would go down to breakfast and send him longing, flirtatious looks. Then she would strike up a casual conversation, and from there, intimacy would grow.

She would tell him about her conversation with Vicar Dingle, and together they could hatch a scheme to trap a murderer.

With Winston in tow, Sabrina left her bedchamber and marched like a woman with a purpose down the corridor. She and the wolfhound walked down the stairs to the first floor, where the dining room was located.

When she stepped into the dining room, Sabrina felt her heart sink to her stomach but managed to maintain a placid expression. The room was deserted except for Higgins, who rushed forward to assist her into the chair.

"I'll have a pot of tea," Sabrina said. "Nothing to eat."

"My lady, you ate nothing last night," Higgins replied. "Let me serve you a hot roll with butter."

"Very well," Sabrina agreed, and then gazed down the long length of the table to her husband's empty chair. "His Lordship hasn't come downstairs yet?"

"I haven't seen him this morning," Higgins replied, without meeting her gaze. "I must tell you how appreciative the staff is of your gift of lemon cookies. Several maids were eating them for breakfast."

"Thank you, Higgins," Sabrina said with a smile. "It's nice to be appreciated."

One of her husband's footmen walked into the dining room and handed her a parchment with the Duke of Kingston's seal. She opened it and read the message. Turning to the majordomo, she asked, "Would someone deliver a message to the Duchess of Kinross after breakfast?"

"One of the footmen will do it," Higgins answered.

Sabrina glanced down the length of the table just in time to see the footman set a newspaper in front of Adam's place. "What is that?" she called.

"*The Times,* my lady."

"Give it to me, please."

The footman brought her the newspaper and then left the dining room.

Sipping her tea, Sabrina set the paper down on the table to thumb through it. She reached the third page and froze in agonized despair as she read the column. The article concerned Lady Meade's ball the previous evening. Surprising everyone, the Marquess of Stonehurst had left his bride at home and escorted the Countess of Rothbury to the gala. The writer hoped the marquess's marriage to the lovely Countess of Abingdon was not doomed to failure.

Sabrina stared through tear-blurred eyes at the account of the party. She felt like she'd been kicked in the stomach, the pain and the humiliation of her husband's defection almost too much to endure.

Hot teardrops rolled down her cheeks and dropped onto the newspaper. While she'd been suffering the humiliation of dining alone, her husband had been flaunting his mistress around town.

So much for happy reconciliations, she thought bitterly.

And then Higgins was standing beside her. "My lady, what will make you feel better?" the majordomo asked solicitously.

The man's kindness was her undoing. "Wa-wa-walnut creams," she sobbed.

"Walnut creams?" he echoed in obvious surprise. "I'm not sure we have any in—"

"I want to make them, not eat them," Sabrina interrupted.

"Dry your tears, my lady," Higgins said, brightening. "Tell me what you'll need."

Sabrina wiped her tears away with the napkin. "I'll need sugar, eggs, rose extract, walnut halves, and shredded coconut."

"I can manage to get those," he assured her.

"Could you gather the ingredients by this afternoon?" she asked.

"Yes, my lady."

"And will a footman deliver my message to the Duchess of Kinross?"

"Of course, my lady."

Sabrina rose from the chair and turned to leave, but stopped short when she spied her husband entering the dining room. Still dressed in evening attire, Adam barely spared her a glance as he passed her chair to take his seat at the head of the table.

"Black coffee," he ordered.

"Your exploits reached Park Lane before you did," Sabrina said in a voice filled with contempt.

Adam looked at her but said nothing.

"You could have dined with me on my first night here," she said.

"I didn't think you cared," he replied, seemingly unaffected by her words.

"You humiliated me in front of the household staff," Sabrina told him.

"I am very tired this morning," Adam said. "Would it be possible to discuss this later?"

"Drop dead twice and go to hell." Sabrina whirled away and marched toward the door.

"Higgins, what did you spill on my paper?" she heard her husband ask.

"Her Ladyship's tears," the majordomo answered, his voice filled with disapproval.

"Sabrina, stop," Adam ordered.

She paused and turned around.

"Why have you been weeping on my newspaper?" he asked.

Sabrina met his gaze unwaveringly. Without bothering to reply, she turned and walked away.

"Damn it, Sabrina. Where are you going?"

"To visit my sister," she called over her shoulder.

Fifteen minutes later, Sabrina walked into the town house in Grosvenor Square. Forbes helped her with her cloak, and Baxter informed her, "His Grace and His Royal Highness have retreated to the study. Shall I announce you?"

Sabrina shook her head. "I know the way."

"Lady Sabrina?" Forbes said.

She turned around to meet the majordomo's gaze.

"I knew it. You've been crying," Forbes said. "What did the marquess do to you?"

Sabrina reached out and touched his forearm, saying, "I appreciate your concern but I am fine."

Forbes gave her a skeptical look.

"No one ever died from injured pride," she assured him.

Reaching the study at the end of the corridor on the

first floor, Sabrina paused for a moment to collect herself and organize what she wanted to say to the prince. Finally, she took a deep breath and knocked on the door.

"Come in." The voice belonged to Uncle Charles.

Pasting a bright smile onto her face, Sabrina opened the door and stepped inside. Both men rose from their chairs when she entered.

Sabrina curtsied to the prince before crossing the study. Uncle Charles met her halfway.

"Child, you look lovely," Uncle Charles said, kissing her hand. "Marriage to my nephew must agree with you."

"Marriage to Adam certainly has had an effect upon me," she agreed.

"I know you wish to speak privately with the prince," Uncle Charles said. He turned to Adolphus and said, "I'll be waiting in the foyer."

Smiling at the prince, Sabrina crossed the chamber to the desk and sat in one of the chairs perched in front of it.

"So good to see you again, my dear," Prince Adolphus greeted her. "Good . . . good . . . good. I understand from Charles that you have several things you would like to discuss with me."

"Yes, Your Royal Highness," Sabrina said, meeting his gaze. "I know that you are my natural father."

Prince Adolphus didn't look surprised at all. "So Charles told you, heh? I suppose it was time . . ."

"I have several questions concerning that," she said.

"Ask away."

"Why did you marry me off as an infant to the Marquess of Stonehurst?"

"Child, I am familiar with Adam St. Aubyn's history," the prince told her. "You were an unacknowledged princess and he was a prince in disguise from one of the world's greatest dynasties. I felt the union would be beneficial to both of you. His St. Aubyn bloodline promised intelligence and integrity. Both of you were of equal rank, in a manner of speaking. Not only that, but marriage to the Marquess of Stonehurst ensured you a respectable place in society. All of us agreed that the match was excellent. Yes, we did . . . did . . . did."

"What about Courtney?" Sabrina asked. "Why didn't you arrange a marriage for her?"

Adolphus smiled. "Why, child, I'd run out of available princes. Princes don't grow on trees, you know. If another had been available, I certainly would have arranged a match for her."

Sabrina inclined her head, accepting his answer. "I want to know my mother's identity," she said.

Prince Adolphus grimaced and looked away, as if struggling with himself about what to tell her. Finally, he looked at her and said, "You possess your mother's beauty and temperament."

"Her name?" Sabrina pressed him.

"Madame Esmeralda."

Shocked, Sabrina sagged in the chair. She'd been speaking with her natural mother at the coming-out ball and hadn't known it.

"Does she know—?" Sabrina broke off, unsure if she really wanted to hear the answer to that.

Prince Adolphus nodded. "That is the reason Esmeralda agreed to sing at the ball. It was her gift to you."

Sabrina stared at her hands folded in her lap and tried to summon the courage to ask her next question. "Did you love her?" she asked without looking up.

"Very much."

"Why didn't you marry her?" she asked, raising her emerald gaze to his.

"The marriage would have been illegal," the prince told her. "By law, I am required to marry a German princess only."

"How could she have given me away?" Sabrina asked in an aching voice.

"Esmeralda gave you away because she loved you," Adolphus said, reaching out to cover her hand in consolation. "She wanted you to grow into womanhood as a lady accepted by society, not illegitimate issue."

"I see," Sabrina said, though she didn't see at all. What she'd needed all those years was the security of knowing her natural parents had loved her, not given her away because she was somehow flawed. "I suppose I should visit her."

"You will need to wait to do that," the prince told her. "Esmeralda left a few days ago on a tour of Europe. France was her first scheduled stop. Ah, Paris . . . Paris . . . Paris."

Brushing off her anguish, Sabrina took a deep, calming breath and became all business. "Sir, I need a favor."

Adolphus stared at her expectantly, awaiting her request.

"I want control of the Savage estates returned to me immediately," Sabrina told him.

"You don't trust your husband?" he asked.

"Yes, I trust Adam," she answered. "However, we are not in accord at the moment. You see, I am convinced that Edgar Briggs murdered my father."

"What did you say?" the prince exclaimed.

"You heard correctly," Sabrina said. "The only way to ferret him out is if I regain control of my assets."

"I can arrange that for you," Adolphus said. "Tell me why you believe the baron is the culprit."

"My father disappointed Edgar when he refused his marriage offer," Sabrina told him. "More than anything else, Edgar wants to join the Savage lands with his. I don't know how he managed the deed with the study door locked, but Edgar is no magician so I'm positive there is a logical explanation. Besides that, Vicar Dingle recently told me that Edgar persuaded him to rule my father's death a suicide. Don't you see? Edgar thought he could purchase the land at auction, but he hadn't foreseen the St. Aubyns' arrival."

"Does your husband know about this?" Adolphus asked.

Sabrina looked him straight in the eye and said, "Nobody knows, which is how I want it kept."

"What a little schemer you are," Adolphus said, and then chuckled. "You must have inherited that from my family."

Sabrina smiled at the prince but remained silent. The Hanovers were not considered university material.

Undoubtedly her intelligence had come from her mother's family.

"Is there anything else?" Adolphus asked.

"Papa told Courtney and me that we had the same sire but different mothers," Sabrina said. "I want you to tell my sister who her mother was."

"Very well, I'll tell her right now if she's at home," the prince replied.

"I'll have someone get her," Sabrina said, rising from the chair. She walked across the study and opened the door, calling, "Forbes, tell Courtney that His Royal Highness wants to speak with her."

Sabrina returned to her seat and a few minutes later heard a light rap on the door. "Come in," she called.

Courtney walked into the study and dropped Prince Adolphus a curtsey. Then she crossed the room to the desk.

"Please, Your Royal Highness, you needn't give me your chair," Courtney said.

"I don't *need* to do anything," the prince replied, leaning against the duke's desk. "I want you to sit there so that I can admire my two beautiful princesses."

Courtney smiled and sat down.

"My sister and I realize that we can never be acknowledged," Sabrina spoke up. "The knowledge of who our natural parents were is enough."

Prince Adolphus inclined his head and then looked at Courtney. "I've just told your sister that Madame Esmeralda is her natural mother and that your mother is a different story. Are you certain you wish to hear this?"

"Was she evil?" Courtney asked, becoming frightened.

"Nothing like that," the prince assured her. "However, your mother passed away many years ago."

Courtney relaxed. "I want to hear about her."

"Surrendering Sabrina to Henry Savage and his wife caused Esmeralda unimaginable anguish," Prince Adolphus began. "Oh, the pain . . . pain . . . pain. In an effort to relieve her emotional suffering, she decided to tour Europe and share her voice with the Continent. She even sang for Napoleon, you know."

"What about Courtney's mother?" Sabrina prodded him.

"Oh, the impatience of youth," the prince said with a smile, making her blush. "I became lonely while Esmeralda was away. One night at the ballet, I spied an angel dancing in the chorus—your mother, Courtney. Her name was Eugenia Darlington, and, oh, what a darling she was. No sooner had Eugenia gone on tour with her ballet company, than Esmeralda returned from Europe. Eugenia must have learned from newspaper articles that I had resumed my friendship with Esmeralda. I didn't see her again until she was seven months heavy with you. Eugenia had run out of money and had nowhere to go, so she decided to ask Esmeralda for shelter. Confident of my affections, Esmeralda took the girl into her home and provided for her. When Eugenia died in childbirth, Esmeralda suggested that I send you to Henry Savage. After all, Sabrina and you were half sisters."

With tears in her eyes, Sabrina reached out and

grasped her sister's hand, saying, "We will always be grateful to Esmeralda for bringing us together."

Courtney nodded, but was too overcome with emotion to speak for several minutes. "Can you tell me where she is buried?" she asked the prince.

"Your mother lies in St. Paul's churchyard," Adolphus told her.

"I would like to visit her," Courtney said.

"And now I must be leaving." Prince Adolphus looked at Sabrina and promised, "I will take care of that other matter immediately."

"Thank you, Sir."

After seeing Prince Adolphus and Uncle Charles off to their ride in Hyde Park, Sabrina turned to Baxter and asked "Has the Duchess of Kinross arrived?"

"Her Grace is in the drawing room," the major-domo answered.

"Please send her to us in the study." Sabrina and Courtney retraced their steps down the corridor. This time Sabrina sat behind the desk in an unspoken gesture of being in command. She only hoped that Lily would help her unmask the murderer.

The door swung open. The duchess burst into the study.

"Sit down," Sabrina said. "I have a plan to ferret out my father's murderer, but I'll need help from you."

Cautious, the Duchess of Kinross gazed at her friend for a long moment and then said, "You may speak freely. I won't betray you. However, whether I'll help or not depends upon the plan."

"That is fair enough," Sabrina agreed. She looked at her sister and said, "Courtney, you are the bait."

"Edgar won't try to murder me, will he?" Courtney asked.

Sabrina shook her head. "Being the bait will have the opposite effect on him."

"What is your plan?" Lily asked.

"Prince Adolphus has agreed to revert control of the Savage assets to me, which means I can do anything I want without my husband's permission," Sabrina told them. "Lily, I want you to send a piece of gossip to that society writer for *The Times*. Tell him that the Marchioness of Stonehurst is relinquishing her Savage title and the family assets to her younger sister."

"Sabrina, are you mad?" Courtney cried, clearly appalled by her sister's intention.

"I am the Marchioness of Stonehurst, and my husband is one of the wealthiest men in England," Sabrina reminded her. "I don't need the Savage assets. Consider it a wedding gift from me."

"Are you certain you want to do this?" Lily asked.

"I will do anything to clear my father's name of suicide," Sabrina answered. "The only way to accomplish that is to get a confession out of the murderer."

"How will giving your assets to Courtney help?" Lily asked.

"Don't you see? Edgar killed my father because he'd refused the marriage proposal," Sabrina said. "Briggs assumed he could purchase the land at auction, but never counted on the St. Aubyns showing up. If Briggs shifts his attention to Courtney once the gossip spreads that she is the Countess of Abingdon and in control of the Savage estates, then that proves he is the murderer. Of course, we'll need to find a way to make him confess, but I can only think one step at a time. I will come to Grosvenor Square each day to await Edgar's next move, and I daresay he won't wait too long with Dudley Egremont courting my sister. So, what do you say?''

"What will Dudley think?'' Courtney asked uncertainly.

"Your Dudley will be none the wiser,'' Sabrina assured her. "If he should find out, well—''

"A man in love will excuse anything,'' Lily finished.

Courtney nodded. "Very well, I'll do it for Father.''

"I'll send that note as soon as I get home,'' Lily said.

Without warning, the duchess hiked the skirt of her gown up to her knee. Attached to a garter strapped on her leg was a small black leather sheath. Lily unfastened the garter, held it up, and removed a dagger from inside the sheath. The blade appeared to be about four inches long.

"It's my weapon of last resort,'' Lily said, smiling at their surprised expressions. "Wearing it is an old habit from my days of clandestine activities back in America.'' She passed it to Sabrina, saying, "I want you to wear it whenever you come here.'' She slid her gaze to Courtney and added, "I'd offer it to you for protection, but I believe you'd swoon dead away rather than use it on the baron.''

Much to her sister's obvious dismay, Sabrina flipped the bottom edge of her gown up and strapped the garter to her leg. "I'm going to wear it home,'' she said.

"You won't use it on the marquess?" Courtney asked.

Sabrina smiled and shook her head. The three of them stood and walked toward the door.

"You will return in the morning?" Courtney asked, unable to keep the panic out of her voice.

"Don't worry, Sister," Sabrina said, putting her arm around her. "I will return as soon as I can. Do not go out alone after today, though. A man who is capable of murder is capable of anything."

"You're frightening me," Courtney moaned.

"There's no need to be afraid," Sabrina assured her. "You trust me, don't you?"

"Yes, I trust you."

Staring out the coach window on the short ride to Park Lane, Sabrina hoped that her plan would work. If Edgar Briggs was as greedy as she suspected, there was little chance of its failure. She would need to guard her sister carefully, though. If anything happened to Courtney, she would never forgive herself. Too bad there was no other way to ferret the villain out.

The closer she got to Park Lane, the more she thought of Adam. Would he be angry when he discovered what she had done? What if he refused to let her leave the town house?

There was little chance of that happening, Sabrina decided with a heavy heart. Her husband seemed quite content to ignore her and squire his harlot around town. She would think about that later, though. For now, her thoughts needed to remain focused on her sister and their father's murderer.

At five o'clock that afternoon, Sabrina dressed in a tea gown of white lawn material with short, scalloped sleeves edged in ruffled lace. Then she tied a pink ribbon around the wolfhound's neck and left her bedchamber.

While making walnut creams that afternoon, Sabrina had decided to behave as if her marital life was normal. She refused to give her husband or his staff the satisfaction of knowing she'd been hurt by his defection.

Walking into the drawing room, Sabrina stopped short when she spied Adam standing near the hearth. Then she realized the hour was still too early for his wicked activities. Only the dead of night could hide disreputable pursuits like adultery.

Adam turned around and stared at her with a little smile on his face that she didn't like one bit. "I'm staying home this evening," he told her, reaching down to unfasten the pink ribbon around the wolfhound's neck.

"Whatever for?" she asked indifferently, though her heartbeat quickened.

"Because, Princess, I generally prefer my morning paper without tears," Adam said.

"I assure you that will never happen again," Sabrina replied, sitting down on the couch. She offered Winston a cucumber sandwich, and the dog gobbled it up in one bite. Then she offered him another.

"You are encouraging his bad behavior by doing that," Adam told her, sitting close beside her on the couch, when she passed the dog a third sandwich.

Sabrina made no reply. Instead, she passed the wolf-hound a fourth sandwich and gave her husband a rebellious glare.

"Did you enjoy your visit with Courtney?" he asked with forced politeness.

Sabrina knew he was dying to scold her for feeding the dog. So she offered Winston another sandwich and answered, "Prince Adolphus was visiting Uncle Charles. He told me my mother is Madame Esmeralda."

"I suspected that," Adam said.

"You did?"

He nodded. "You resemble her so much that I feared someone at your coming-out ball would comment on it. I've had news from Istanbul. My mother knows of no plot or assassins sent to kill me."

Sabrina turned her head to look at him. "Edgar Briggs tried to murder you just as he did my father."

Adam cocked a dark brow at her. "How can you be so certain?"

"Woman's intuition."

He smiled at her answer. "So why didn't your woman's intuition tell you this before?"

"Your unexpected presence in my life confounded it," Sabrina answered. "I have recovered sufficiently," she added with a smile.

"Why would Edgar Briggs want to kill me?" Adam asked.

"You ruined his scheme to gain control of the Savage lands and other assets," Sabrina answered.

Adam snapped his brows together and ordered, "Tell me more of your theory."

"Edgar killed my father because his marriage offer had been rejected," Sabrina told him. "Vicar Dingle paid me a visit and admitted that Edgar persuaded him to rule my father's death a suicide. Edgar knew that a suicide's estates are sold at auction, but he hadn't planned on your appearance or our marriage."

"Do you have any proof?" Adam asked.

Sabrina shook her head.

"Theories do not send men to the gallows," Adam said. Then he leaned close and asked, "Why were you cooking this afternoon?"

"Sometimes I cook for my own pleasure," she answered, trying hard not to leap away from him. Letting him know how nervous she felt wouldn't do at all.

"Princess, you are absolutely the worst liar I've ever met," Adam said with a smile.

"And you of all people should know what a good liar is," Sabrina shot back. "Why I do anything is none of your business."

"I am your husband," he reminded her. "I hold the receivership rights to your assets."

Not for long, Sabrina thought. Arching a copper brow at him, she asked, "Are you baiting me?"

"Would I do that?"

"There isn't much you wouldn't do to upset me."

"Did I mention I'll be staying home for dinner?" Adam asked, changing the subject.

Sabrina stared straight ahead and mumbled, "Yes, and only old people repeat themselves."

"How about an interesting game of chess with an old man?" he whispered close to her ear.

Sabrina turned her head to look at him. In spite of herself, her lips twitched with the urge to laugh.

"Is that a smile you are struggling against?" he asked.

Sabrina burst out laughing.

"I knew I could make you smile," Adam said, putting his arm around her shoulder, his hand beginning a slow caress. "What else did you do today?"

"Lily Armstrong met me at Grosvenor Square, and the three of us visited," Sabrina told him.

Adam nibbled on her earlobe, sending delicious shivers dancing down her spine. "What did you ladies talk about all morning long?"

"Oh, this and that," she hedged.

Adam gently turned her face toward him. After gazing for a long moment into her emerald eyes, he captured her lips in a wet, devastating kiss. Their kiss lingered and melted into another. And then another.

Sabrina felt herself falling under his powerful spell and wondered at the magic in his touch. When his hand caressed her breast over her gown, she leaned into his touch and yearned to feel his naked skin caressing hers.

Wrapping her arms around his neck, Sabrina returned his kiss in kind and pressed her young body against his. And then somehow her gown was unbuttoned, and his hands were cupping her breasts. He flicked his fingers across her aroused nipples, igniting a throbbing heat between her thighs.

They could fight later, Sabrina decided when Adam rose and walked across the room to close the door.

Offering her his hand, Adam helped her onto the rug near the hearth and then undressed her. His own clothing followed hers, and he lay down half on top of her. His mouth swooped down to capture hers in another kiss, and then his tongue licked its way down the column of her throat and beyond. After suckling upon her breasts, he moved lower to the crevice between her thighs and sweetly tormented the dewy pearl of her womanhood until she was delirious with passion, crying out for him to take her.

Adam rose up between her thighs. He entered her slowly and then withdrew, repeating this movement over and over and over again, rekindling her desire.

"Love me," she pleaded in a breathless whisper.

And Adam gave her what she wanted. He rode her hard, and they exploded together.

Adam fell to one side and pulled her with him. The only sound in the drawing room was their labored breathing.

And the crunch of someone eating cookies?

Adam and Sabrina snapped their gazes toward the coffee table. Taking advantage of their inattention, Winston had already devoured the cucumber sandwiches and was just finishing the last of the lemon cookies. When the wolfhound completed his meal by slurping the tea left in their cups, Adam and Sabrina howled with laughter.

"My princess," Adam said, smiling down into her face.

"My prince," Sabrina said on a sigh. Entwining her arms around his neck, she drew his handsome face toward hers, ordering, "Kiss me again . . ."

Chapter 17

"My princess . . ."

Awakening with a smile, Sabrina recalled her husband's whispered words of endearment. The glow from the previous night's lovemaking remained with her still and warmed her all over.

Sabrina rolled over in her husband's bed and found his place empty. One perfect rose lay across his pillow, a gift of love for his wife. She hadn't yet forgiven him for lying to her, or for escorting Alexis to the ball the other night but she'd learned that the value of arguing was making up.

Too bad he'd already risen, Sabrina thought, leaning close to his pillow to inhale his clean masculine scent. She would have loved to feel his nakedness pressing her down in the bed.

Reliving each precious moment would be the next best thing. Sabrina snapped her eyes shut and conjured her husband's image in her mind's eye.

Again Sabrina saw his devastating smile inching closer to her face.

Again she felt the hard planes of his body caressing her softness.

Again she heard his voice—

"Sabrina!"

Startled, Sabrina bolted up in the bed. Clutching the coverlet to shield her naked breasts, she looked around in drowsy confusion. The voice belonged to her husband, but where—?

The bedchamber door flew open. Adam marched into the room with a whining Winston following in his wake.

Sabrina dropped her gaze to his hands. Her husband was holding a copy of *The Times* in a white-knuckled death grip.

"What is the meaning of this?" he demanded, tossing the paper onto the bed.

Sabrina assumed he'd read the column with the piece of gossip Lily had so kindly given to the writer. But she hadn't counted on this reaction from Adam. She decided to bluff him.

"What are you talking about?" Sabrina asked, feigning innocence, her enormous emerald eyes feigning the confusion she did not possess.

Adam held her gaze captive with his piercing blue eyes, eyes that she'd loved until this moment. Those damned eyes of his seemed to see to the depths of her soul.

"Do not lie," Adam said. "I want you to tell me what this is about."

"Let me read it." Sabrina scanned the offending

column, which stated that the Marchioness of Stonehurst was intending to give the Savage title and estate to her younger sister.

"Oh, that," she said without looking up.

"Oh, that?" Adam echoed, incredulous. "Then it's true?"

Sabrina smiled brightly. "Quite generous of me to give everything to Courtney, wouldn't you say?"

"You do not have the power to give anything away to anybody," Adam informed her, his tone implying she was a simpleton. "I hold the receivership rights to your assets. Remember?"

"You did hold those rights until yesterday," Sabrina informed him, taking perverse pleasure in the surprised look that appeared on his face. "Prince Adolphus promised to revert them to me."

"Why?"

"The prince trusts my judgment."

"Damn it, Sabrina. That's not what I meant," Adam snapped. "Why do you want to control the Savage assets? Don't you trust me?"

"I needed control so I could sign them over to Courtney," Sabrina said matter-of-factly, as if that explained everything. Though she really didn't think he'd accept her answer. "What does it matter to you? You are rich beyond belief."

"I don't give a damn about your piddling inheritance, but I don't want to see it thrown away either," Adam replied, the muscle in his right cheek beginning to twitch.

Lord, but her husband looked like he wanted to throttle her. Sabrina wondered for a moment if she should tell him the truth, but then decided to keep her own counsel. If by some slim chance she was wrong about Edgar's involvement in her father's death, her husband's presence in her scheme would make the situation worse than it was. Edgar might even challenge Adam to a duel. If she kept her plan from Adam, and it proved wrong, no one would be the wiser. If her suspicions proved true, there would be time enough to tell her husband.

"Don't you realize what you've done?" Adam asked. "We were negotiating Courtney's betrothal agreement with Dudley Egremont. Now, every fortune hunter in London will be camped out on her doorstep. A few may even try to snatch her in order to assure themselves of her riches."

That is exactly what I want, Sabrina thought, staring up at him. Briggs should be showing up on her sister's doorstep that very day.

"What is it you're not telling me?" Adam said.

Sabrina dropped her gaze to the bed. "I have nothing more to say."

"Now I'll need to speak with the prince," Adam muttered, turning to march back across the chamber to the door. "Winston, come," he called over his shoulder.

The wolfhound looked from Adam to Sabrina, who patted the bed beside her in invitation.

"Do you want to eat?" Adam asked.

Winston bounded after Adam, the master's invitation too appealing to give up.

"Traitor," Sabrina grumbled. Dogs were supposed

to be loyal, weren't they? This one had a lopsided view of the world; he followed whoever offered him food.

After the door clicked shut behind her husband, Sabrina leaped out of the bed. The morning was growing old, and she wanted to get to Grosvenor Square before noon.

Returning to her own chamber, Sabrina washed hurriedly, brushed her hair back and secured it with a ribbon, and then dressed in a midnight-blue serge riding habit. She pulled on her black leather boots and grabbed a matching midnight-blue hooded cloak. She paused a moment and then retrieved Lily's weapon of last resort from her reticule. After fastening the garter with the sheath and dagger to her leg, she dropped her skirt into place.

Sabrina knew she could never use it, but wearing it meant she needn't lie to Lily when questioned about it.

Wrapping the cloak around herself, Sabrina left her chamber and walked down two flights of stairs. Higgins and Razi stood at attention in the foyer.

"Good morning," Sabrina called to them, walking across the foyer to the door.

"Good morning, my lady," Higgins greeted her with a smile.

Razi bowed from the waist as if she were a queen. "Good morning, my pr—lady."

"Are you going out, my lady?" Higgins asked. "Shall I have the carriage brought around?"

Damn, Sabrina cursed her own stupidity. She'd been so concerned with escaping from Adam without her intentions being detected that she'd forgotten to order the carriage brought around.

Sabrina didn't want to wait for the carriage. By the time the horses were harnessed and brought around, she could already be at Grosvenor Square. The walk was a short one.

"No, I believe I'd rather walk," Sabrina told her husband's servants. "His Grace's town house is practically around the next corner. If my husband asks for me, tell him I've gone to flush a weasel out of his hole."

Upon leaving the town house, Sabrina pulled the hood of her cloak up to cover her head and started walking at a brisk pace down Park Lane. Edgar might not show up today, she told herself. If he failed to tip his hand today, she would return to Uncle Charles's town house every day for the next month as a precaution.

Sabrina turned left when she reached Upper Brook Street. From there, Grosvenor Square was only two blocks away. Within minutes, she'd reached her destination and started up the front stairs. Thankfully, she hadn't seen anyone who knew her.

"Good morning, Baxter," Sabrina greeted the duke's majordomo. "Good morning, Forbes."

"Good morning, my lady," the two majordomos chimed together, making her smile.

"Is His Grace at home this morning?" Sabrina asked.

"His Grace and Prince Adolphus have gone riding in Hyde Park," Baxter informed her.

"What about my aunt and Lady DeFaye?"

"Both ladies have gone out for the morning," Forbes told her.

Sabrina smiled. "I hope I haven't come to visit an empty house," she said.

"Lady Courtney is in the drawing room," Baxter told her.

Sabrina headed for the stairs but stopped short when Forbes added, "Lord Briggs is with her."

Edgar had wasted no time, Sabrina thought with a certain amount of satisfaction. Though it would prove nothing in a court of law, his timely arrival to visit her sister indicated his involvement in her father's murder.

Sabrina started up the stairs slowly. She hadn't reached the first landing when it occurred to her that in spite of the servants' presence in the house, Courtney and she might be in danger. After all, a man who murdered was capable of anything. She did have that ridiculously small dagger strapped to her leg but didn't think she had the courage to use it.

Whirling around, Sabrina called, "Forbes, I need someone to run to Park Lane and tell my husband that I need him here immediately. Tell him it's urgent."

"I'll do it myself," Forbes told her, and left the town house on the run.

Sabrina started up the stairs again. The last place she wanted to go was into that drawing room. Only the disturbing thought of her sister's being alone with a murderer gave her the courage to put one foot in front of the other. . . .

While his wife was walking up the front stairs to his uncle's town house, Adam sat in his study with Viscount Dorchester. Winston lay curled up in front of the hearth.

"So the farmer persuaded the duke that even his

cock laid eggs,'' Adam finished telling his guest the joke.

Dudley Egremont burst out laughing, and Adam joined in his merriment. The two men waited patiently for the solicitor to prepare a tentative betrothal agreement.

Things were progressing nicely, Adam thought. Nothing unplanned had happened, probably because Sabrina hadn't popped into the study. He hoped she wasn't baking. On the other hand, baking was better than shopping. What if she shopped every time something upset her?

Though he knew Egremont was smitten with Courtney, Adam wasn't going to let the younger man leave until an agreement had been signed. Those were his orders from Prince Adolphus and Uncle Charles. Too many unforeseen events could happen unless an agreement was signed, especially since the bride-to-be was adopted.

"My lord, whatever was that gossip in *The Times* about?" Dudley asked him. "I never thought that paper would print such outrageous lies."

"The article was fact, not rumor," Adam said, relaxing back in his chair. "My wife is giving her inheritance to her sister. Courtney and you are welcome to it. Your estate is only two miles from Abingdon. Too bad Lord Briggs's land separates your estate from the Savage's."

"Marrying Courtney is reward enough for me," Dudley said.

"Spoken like a man in love," Adam replied.

The solicitor returned with the tentative agreement.

First, Dudley Egremont signed and then Adam in his uncle's absence.

"Thank you, Mr. Wembly," Adam said in dismissal.

"You are welcome, my lord." Before leaving, the solicitor turned to Egremont and said, "May I offer you my sincere congratulations?"

Dudley Egremont grinned. "Thank you, sir," he said, shaking the man's hand.

Adam poured two drams of whiskey and passed one to his guest. Raising his glass in salute, he toasted, "May your marriage be blessed with harmonious days, satisfying nights, and several strong sons."

Before the younger man could reply, the door flew open. Higgins and Razi raced each other into the study.

"My lord—" Razi began.

"Mister Forbes is here with an urgent message from your wife," Higgins finished.

"Send him in," Adam said, puzzled.

"Come on inside," Razi shouted.

"Good day, my lord," Forbes said, walking into the study. "Lady Sabrina needs you at His Grace's town house. She said the matter is urgent."

Adam glanced at Dudley Egremont and smiled, saying, "You'll learn soon enough that when it comes to the ladies getting what they want, everything is urgent."

"I believe it has something to do with Lord Briggs visiting Courtney," Forbes added.

"What?" Adam shouted.

Before Forbes could repeat himself, Higgins said,

"Her Ladyship told us she was going to catch a weasel."

"You should have told me this earlier," Adam snapped at his retainers as he bolted out of his chair. "Come with me, Egremont. I'm certain our ladies are in trouble. Razi, tell Abdul and Sagi that I'll need them immediately." Then he turned to the viscount and explained, "My foolish wife set out to prove that Lord Briggs murdered her father. The gossip in *The Times* was intentionally dropped in order to entice Briggs to seek out Courtney."

"*My* Courtney?" Dudley cried, bolting out of his chair.

At that, Adam opened a drawer in his desk and withdrew a pistol. After verifying that it was loaded, he headed for the door. Viscount Dorchester walked behind him, and Winston followed them out. Forbes hurried after them.

Sabrina walked down the second-floor corridor like a woman on her way to the gallows. Her feet moved slowly as if she wore leaden shoes, but her heartbeat quickened with each step forward.

Her father's murderer was sitting in the drawing room, pretending that he was civilized, Sabrina thought. How could she trick him into confessing? Her husband would know what to do. She was certain of that.

And then Sabrina reached the drawing room. Oh, Lord, the door was closed. She pressed her ear to the door and listened to the voices inside.

"You cannot love me," Courtney cried. "Why are you doing this?"

"For the land, of course," Briggs answered. "Now, remove your underdrawers, hike your gown up, and lie down on the sofa. Once the deed is done, no man but me will want you in marriage."

"And if I refuse?" Courtney challenged him.

"Refusing me would be very unhealthy," Briggs threatened. "If you try to alert the servants, I'll shoot them."

Sabrina knew what she had to do. She lifted the bottom edge of her skirt up and removed the tiny dagger from its sheath. With a badly shaking hand, she held the dagger tightly, as if her life depended on not dropping it.

That last moment in the corridor nearly felled Sabrina. She felt her heart pounding frantically, and the blood rushing through her made her feel faint.

Taking a deep breath, Sabrina squared her shoulders in dogged determination and reached for the doorknob. Her only chance was the element of surprise. Almost noiselessly, she turned the knob and slowly opened the door. Stepping inside, she saw that Edgar stood with his back facing the door. She started forward silently.

"I said to lie on the sofa," Edgar growled at her sister. "Remove those underdrawers first."

"I will never let you violate me," Courtney insisted. "I don't believe you even carry a pistol."

Sabrina stood just behind Edgar. Lifting her hand, she touched the back of his neck with the dagger's sharp point.

"Every pot has a lid, but you won't be covering my

sister,'' Sabrina said. ''I do believe I've flushed a weasel out of his hole.'' Then she ordered, ''Courtney, step away from him.''

When her sister was out of harm's way, Sabrina said, ''Turn around, Edgar, and—''

Edgar whirled around quickly and grabbed her wrist. Caught by surprise, Sabrina dropped the dagger, and he kicked it across the chamber.

Releasing her wrist, Edgar pulled a pistol from inside his waistcoat and pointed it at Sabrina and Courtney. ''You realize that both of you must die now.''

''The game is up,'' Sabrina told him. ''Surrender yourself to the authorities before my husband gets his hands on you.''

Edgar laughed without humor. ''Dearest Sabrina, we could have been so happy together. I would have—''

''Spare me your distorted vision of what might have been,'' Sabrina sneered with contempt. ''You never measured up, Edgar. I wouldn't have married you even if you were the last—''

Silencing her, Edgar struck out, and the force of his blow sent her crashing to the floor. Courtney screamed and screamed and screamed.

''Shut up,'' Edgar snapped at her, pointing the pistol at Sabrina. ''I'll shoot her if you don't stop screaming.''

In an instant, Courtney stifled her screams, but her body shook visibly with the effort to keep her horror contained.

''As long as you are going to murder me,'' Sabrina said, ''I want to know how you managed to murder my father in spite of the fact that the study door was locked.''

Edgar remained silent for one long moment, and Sabrina stared unwaveringly into his eyes, eyes that held no more emotion than a fish's. Strangely, she had never noticed that until this moment.

"I sneaked into the study through the unlocked floor-to-ceiling window," Edgar said finally. "I knocked him out and then locked the study door from the inside. After hanging him, I slipped out the window again and hid in the woodland. An hour later I returned to ask for your hand in marriage."

"But the window was locked," Sabrina said in confusion. "Forbes saw you break the pane of glass."

"I only pretended the window was locked," Edgar admitted.

"And what about the attempt on my husband's life?" Sabrina asked. "Were you behind that too?"

Edgar smiled and shrugged. "Unfortunately, luck was running against me when it came to your husband, but my plan to murder your father worked rather nicely."

"How very clever of you to overpower a man who was nearly twice your age," said a voice from the doorway.

Sabrina shifted her gaze and smiled at her husband. With pistols in their hands, Adam and Dudley Egremont stood there. And then from somewhere behind her rescuers, she heard her dog's distinctive growl.

"Give it up, Briggs," Adam said, his voice deceptively quiet. "There are three of us, not counting Winston, and you can only get one shot off. My retainers will be here any moment, and Forbes has gone to get the authorities.''

In one swift movement, Edgar reached down with one hand and yanked Sabrina to her feet. Then he pointed the barrel of the pistol at her head.

''I'll shoot her if you don't drop your weapons,'' he threatened.

Unexpectedly, Winston dashed forward into the drawing room. Edgar shifted the pistol away from Sabrina and aimed for the wolfhound.

''Don't shoot my dog,'' Sabrina shrieked, whirling around to stay the baron's hand.

At the same moment, Winston leaped into the air and tackled Edgar to the floor. The pistol flew out of his hand and landed across the room; the force of its hitting the floor discharged a bullet, startling everyone.

''Get him off me,'' Edgar shouted.

When Adam stood over Edgar and leveled his gun on him, Sabrina pulled Winston away. Across the chamber, Dudley Egremont retrieved the baron's pistol.

Abdul and Sagi raced into the drawing room. At a gesture from Adam, the two men dragged Edgar to his feet.

Sabrina flew into her husband's waiting arms. She hid her face against his chest and began weeping uncontrollably.

''Don't ever pull a stunt like this again,'' Adam said, tightening his hold on her. ''I died a thousand times when he pointed that pistol at you.''

''I-I w-won't,'' Sabrina sobbed. ''I never thought you would g-get here.''

Uncle Charles and Prince Adolphus chose that moment to return from their ride. Both looked shocked, even more so when a troop of Bow Street Runners brushed past them into the drawing room.

"What is happening in my home?" Uncle Charles demanded, staring at their weapons.

"My wife has managed to squeeze a confession out of the baron," Adam told him. "Edgar Briggs murdered Henry Savage, and he nearly killed my wife and her sister today."

"I'll see him hanged for Henry's murder," Prince Adolphus promised as the authorities led Edgar out of the room.

Adam kissed the top of his wife's head and then called to the wolfhound, "How many times do I need to explain the difference between a weasel and a wolf?"

Everyone in the drawing room laughed. Sabrina stopped her weeping and smiled up at him.

"From now on, Winston is allowed to eat as many cucumber sandwiches as he wants," Adam told her. "Even better, we'll set a place for him at the table."

"I'll never keep anything from you again," Sabrina promised.

"Nothing?"

Sabrina shook her head.

"I love you, Princess," Adam whispered just before his lips claimed hers. "I'll always be truthful with you."

Sabrina giggled against his lips, and when he drew back to look at her, she said, "Oh, so now that all your secrets are revealed, you'll promise to be truthful?"

Adam gave her his devastating smile.

Turning in the circle of his arms, Sabrina saw Dudley kissing her sister and asked, "Is that permissible before the wedding?"

"Quite permissible," Adam answered, his love for her shining in his intense blue gaze. He lowered his head and claimed her lips, pouring all of his love into that single, stirring kiss.

"I love you, Princess," Adam whispered. "I plan to spend the rest of my life making you happy."

"And I love you, my prince," Sabrina vowed, gazing up at him through gleaming green eyes. "I'm so happy. I may never bake again."

Epilogue

London, 1817

"Happy fifteenth wedding anniversary," Adam said in a loud whisper, walking into his chamber at the Park Lane town house. He crossed the distance to the bed.

"That was yesterday," Sabrina told him.

"You were busy yesterday," Adam said, dropping his gaze to his one-day-old daughter. Gingerly, he sat on the edge of the bed and, with one finger, caressed his daughter's cheek. "Baby St. Aubyn feels softer than silk . . . like her mother."

Sabrina smiled. "Baby St. Aubyn?"

"Well, what should I call her?" Adam asked. "We haven't named her yet."

"What do you think of Farrah?" Sabrina asked. "Farrah means beautiful one, and Farrah St. Aubyn sounds pleasant."

"I don't think so," Adam answered, giving her a boyishly charming grin. "In my land, Farrah means wild donkey."

Sabrina laughed, but then grew serious. "What is your mother's name?"

An expression of sadness crossed her husband's face, but he quickly banished it. "Her name is Regina."

"Regina St. Aubyn," Sabrina repeated. "I like the sound of it. We'll call her Regina."

Adam lifted her free hand to his lips and said in an aching voice, "Thank you, my love."

"I only wish my father were here to see his first grandchild," Sabrina said, a wistful note to her voice. "At least he now lies in hallowed ground."

"And the villain who did him in will never have the chance to hurt anyone else," Adam said.

"Let's never mention Edgar or his execution in front of Regina," Sabrina said. "I don't want her marred or sullied by even hearing the villain's name. I want Regina to hear nothing but laughter and words of love."

Both Adam and Sabrina shifted their gazes to the door when they heard someone knock. "Enter," Adam called.

The door flew open. Higgins and Razi rushed into the bedchamber.

"I'll do the announcing," Razi said.

"No, I will," Higgins insisted.

Having been relegated to the corridor for one whole day, Winston scooted around the bickering retainers and made straight for the bed. The wolfhound rested his head on Adam's knee and stared at the baby. His nose twitched as he caught the new scent. Then he walked away and curled up in front of the hearth.

"My lord—" Razi began.

"Prince Adolphus and Madame Esmeralda have arrived," Higgins announced, earning a glare from his rival.

"Are you ready for this?" Adam asked Sabrina. When she nodded, he instructed his man, "Send them in."

Higgins nodded and started for the door. Razi had apparently had enough of the English majordomo.

Cupping his mouth with his hands, the little man called, "Your Royal Highness, you may enter the room now."

Adam laughed, and Sabrina dissolved into giggles. Horrified, Higgins turned around and slowly walked back to Razi. He cuffed the side of the little man's head and sneered, "You blinking idiot."

Wearing an amused smile, Prince Adolphus escorted Madame Esmeralda past the two bickering men on their way out the door. The prince and his longtime mistress crossed the chamber to stand beside the bed and peer down at the sleeping infant.

"Esmeralda, we have a granddaughter," Prince Adolphus said, a catch of emotion in his throat.

"I have a daughter and a granddaughter," the diva said with tears streaming down her cheeks.

The woman's tears brought the same to Sabrina's eyes. One tear brimmed over and slid slowly down her cheek. Adam reached out and brushed it away with his fingertips.

"I want you to know that I never meant for you to feel abandoned," Esmeralda said to Sabrina, the prince's arm around her shoulder lending emotional support. "I—we wanted only what was best for you, a respectable place in society."

Sabrina nodded, the lump of raw emotion stealing her voice for a moment. Finally she said, "What is done is past. I know you wanted what was best for me, but why have you stayed in Europe so long? I have been expecting this conversation for the longest time."

"I was afraid that you would reject me," Esmeralda admitted. "I was wondering . . ." The diva hesitated as if afraid to continue.

"Would you care to come to tea one afternoon?" Sabrina invited her. "I'm sure you would like to see Regina."

"I would like to see *you*," Esmeralda said. "I hoped we could be friends."

Sabrina smiled. "I would like that very much."

"So, you've named the babe Regina," Prince Adolphus said.

"Yes, we named her for Adam's mother," Sabrina told him.

"I've just finished arranging for the exhumation of Courtney's mother's remains. They will be delivered to her in Dorchester," Prince Adolphus said. "Dudley and Courtney want Eugenia buried on their estate."

"I'm glad for my sister," Sabrina said. "You know, Your Royal Highness, that Courtney is expecting her first child. You'll be a grandfather again before the end of the year."

"This certainly is the year for babies," Adam said. "Lily Armstrong delivered a son the day before yesterday."

"Why didn't you tell me?" Sabrina asked.

"Darling, Regina kept you busy yesterday," he answered.

Prince Adolphus and Esmeralda smiled. "We must be leaving," the prince told them. Then he asked Sabrina, "Will you be well enough to travel to Abingdon next month for your father's memorial service?"

"Nothing could keep me away," Sabrina answered. She looked at the opera singer and suggested, "If you are in London at that time, perhaps you would consider attending my father's memorial service. You could plan on visiting with us at Abingdon Manor for a week or two."

Tears gleamed in the older woman's eyes, and she reached out to touch her daughter's arm. "God bless you," Esmeralda said. "I don't deserve this."

"Yes, you do," Sabrina replied, covering the woman's hand with her own.

"I will always be grateful to you for bringing Sabrina into the world," Adam spoke up.

"And I'm glad that everyone is thrilled with everyone else," Prince Adolphus said, clearly uncomfortable with the raw emotion in the chamber. "We'll see both of you again . . . again . . . again." With those parting words, the prince and his mistress left the bedchamber.

"That was very kind of you," Adam said. "Giving you to Henry Savage could not have been easy for her. I know that I do not possess that much inner strength."

"Oh, Adam, how could I do otherwise?" Sabrina said. "I am so happy."

"Does this mean you won't be making Turkish delights and nougats?" he asked.

"I would do anything for you," she answered. "I'll even make those disgustingly sweet candies."

Adam leaned close. Being careful not to disturb Regina, he planted a kiss on her lips. Then he stood and sat down beside her, leaning against the headboard. Together, the new parents watched the exciting sight of their baby at sleep.

"Adam, there is something I've wanted to ask you for a long, long time," Sabrina said, glancing sidelong at him. On the night of Lady Meade's ball last year, did you and Alexis Carstairs—?" She broke off, unable to finish.

"I did not," he answered, knowing what she was asking.

Sabrina gave him a doubtful look. "No decent gentleman would lie to his wife."

Adam cast her an appropriately offended look. In an insulted voice, he asked, "Have I ever lied to you?"

Sabrina burst out laughing, a sweetly melodious sound that reminded him of the night he met her. "Then where did you spend the night?"

"I slept in your room at my uncle's town house," Adam told her. "In the morning I slipped out the back by way of the servants' stairs because I refused to suffer the embarrassment of having our families know I was afraid to go home."

"Afraid?"

"I feared your rejection."

"I wanted you," Sabrina said, tears welling up in her eyes.

"I know that now," Adam said, lifting her free hand to his lips. "You cannot imagine the torment I suffered that night in your chamber. Everywhere I looked, I saw you. When I tried to sleep, I swear your rose scent on the pillow kept me awake.''

''I love you,'' Sabrina told him.

''And I love you,'' he promised.

Adam covered her mouth with his lips in an endless kiss that seemed to linger for an eternity. Their kiss melted into another. And then another . . .

Her loving kiss had transformed the frog into a charming prince, and the prince had made her his princess.